CLOTI'S SONG

DANI FINN

DRAGONHEART PRESS

CONTENT WARNINGS

This book is intended for **adult audiences** and contains drinking, drug use, wartime violence, and numerous explicit, consensual sex scenes, many of them involving multiple partners and including light bondage and sex toys.

AUTHOR'S NOTE

The events in the Time Before trio take place several millennia before the Maer Cycle and the Weirdwater Confluence. The three series are vaguely linked but independent and can be read in any order.

Cloti's Song is a sequel of sorts to *Wings so Soft* and contains references to events in *The Delve* but can be read as a standalone. I promise. The book has this background woven in, but for those desiring the information upfront, a brief summary of relevant details from the other two books is included below, with as few spoilers as can be managed.

In *The Delve*, the Maer and the humans were on the brink of war. A Maer knight named Yglind Torl led a team to investigate why the Deepfold mine, the most important source of the brightstone the Maer relied on for their magical and military devices, had gone dark. They discovered that humans had attacked the mine, and the Maer defeated them in a long, bloody campaign. They captured one of the humans, a spy named Feddar, and brought him back to Kuppham, where he surely faced a grim fate at the hands of his Maer inquisitors.

In *Wings so Soft*, set several years later, an owl handler named Mara and an artificer named Uffrin fell in love in Kuppham under the cloud of looming war. Their time together was brief but passionate before duty flung them apart to surveillance on distant fronts. The Maer armies were routed, and Mara and Uffrin pushed themselves to the limit to find each other again in a secret mountain lake far from the ravages of war. Of special note: we met the protagonists of *Cloti's Song*, Cloti, Aefin, and Ludo, in *Wings so Soft*, as Uffrin's parents. Cloti developed a special bond with Mara through her meditation practice and helped her disabled sister escape the city before the humans arrived.

Cloti's Song takes place in the now human-occupied Maer capital of Kuppham.

1

— • —

Cloti touched herself softly as she watched Ludo and Aefin kissing in the lonely light of a single candle. Ludo's posture was stiff at first; he held Aefin loosely, hesitant hands framing her shoulders. Cloti could taste his distraction like the re-steeped darkroot tea they'd been subsisting on since Kuppham had fallen. He'd been so busy negotiating the withdrawal terms that everyone but him knew were just a formality. The humans weren't going anywhere. The city they'd known for all their lives was gone. All they had left was each other.

She pushed out a spark through their connection, which had grown ever closer since they'd been quarantined for months on end. She smiled as Ludo's body relaxed, and his hands slid down Aefin's back, gripping her hips and pulling her closer to him. Aefin braided her fingers through his hair, deepening their kiss. Cloti felt their tongues swipe across each other's, lips moving with sudden urgency. She'd allowed herself a sip of Earth Milk this evening, and she felt their every touch, every frisson of pleasure.

She traced delicate lines with her fingers, coaxing herself gently open, then removed her hand and let her mind take over with the help of the Milk. Ludo and Aefin's kiss filled her mouth, and her body warmed with the movement of their hands, urgently gripping, kneading, stroking. Ludo's desire rose quickly, and Cloti swelled along with him, heat flowing through her core, filling her with bright notes of joy. Ludo's fingers glided between Aefin's legs, and Cloti's breath caught as they twiddled and teased. She matched Aefin's moan with her own, and Ludo moved with more certainty now, fingers slipping inside her, beckoning her pleasure as he caressed her with firm but gentle strokes.

Cloti's hand felt the warmth of Ludo's stiffness as if she were gripping it herself, pumping him slowly as his fingers moved in and out in rhythm with her strokes. Her fingertips traced across the fine hair on her thighs, edging between her legs, but she stopped them as Ludo's grip tightened inside Aefin and his other hand cupped her backside, almost lifting her off the ground. Cloti throbbed with the pressure, her mind flooding with their sensations, Ludo's driving need, Aefin's melting resolve, her own pleasure swirling together with theirs. As Aefin pulled Ludo back onto the bed and he kissed his way down her body, Cloti slumped in her chair, hands clutching her thighs, letting herself bleed further into Aefin.

Ludo's hot breath filled her, his nuzzling lips and curious tongue sending shockwaves through her. She lost herself in their play as Ludo drove Aefin hard and fast, then slowed down when she approached the edge. Aefin gripped his hair, pulling him into her, pushing up to envelop him, their bodies molding together as Aefin spiraled toward climax.

Cloti pushed out another spark, and as Aefin ground against him, Cloti's legs tensed, and her hips rose off the chair, lifted by the fire of their passion. Aefin's voice rose from a low moan to a plaintive, almost musical note, filling Cloti's mind with a rainbow of ecstasy. Her body followed, flooding with wave after wave of joyous release. She shared her pleasure, Aefin's pleasure, with Ludo, whose lips froze in place as Aefin pulsed against him. As his body let go, gushing like a bottle of over-fermented ale, stars of a thousand colors streaked through his mind, slowly diminishing, leaving him empty of everything except blind contentment.

Cloti slid off the chair and joined them on the bed, slipping between them as Ludo rolled onto his back. She kissed him, savoring Aefin's taste on his lips, then rolled over to kiss her, caressing her gently, resting her hand on Aefin's hip.

"Remember we have that party tonight." Ludo's cheery pronouncement swept away the magic of the moment in an instant. Cloti groaned, nuzzling into Aefin's beard.

"Do we have to? Wouldn't it be nicer just to lay in bed all day?" She wiggled her behind against Ludo, who leaned into it and kissed her on the ear.

"There's always after," he murmured.

"It's not until quarter-dusk." Aefin rolled to face Cloti, her eyes twinkling as her hand moved over Cloti's hip and squeezed her behind. "And you didn't get to play." Aefin's eyes closed as they kissed, and Ludo scooted in closer behind Cloti, reaching his long arm over her and pressing them together. Cloti writhed between them as their limbs and lips tangled, fingers clutching, breath mingling. She poured her heart out through her body, giving to one as she received from the other, bathing in their communal pleasure until their voices rose in unison once again, echoing off the stone walls.

Afterward, they lay draped over one another, breathing in their shared warmth, sighing little hums of contentment into each other's bodies. Though she hardly recognized the occupied city outside their doors, they'd managed to keep this space intact.

Aefin and Ludo's breath soon leveled with sleep, but Cloti's mind flitted restlessly about like a caged bird. Their time together during the occupation had brought them closer, but when the pleasure ebbed, it left a residue like silt in its wake. The city was filled with a hundred thousand vibrant hearts, and she longed to move among them, catch the whiff of a beautiful spirit from the crowd, find a dark place, and swirl her energy together with theirs. Without this renewal, she felt herself being emptied day by day, with less and less to give to her spouses. There were only so many bodies and souls in the Cliffside neighborhood, and even fewer of them to her taste.

She'd even found herself entertaining fantasies of pulling one of the human guards off the streets and having her way with them. Before the war, she'd often fantasized about humans, almost as a point of pride; she still believed that they were no different than Maer, except for the lack of body hair. If she pushed hard enough with her mind, she could find that erotic—the naked frailty, the veins and muscles visible beneath a thin layer of skin. But after seeing the savagery the humans were capable of, these fantasies had largely vanished, and she had agreed not to speak about her theory that humans and Maer were the same people. She still believed it deep down; Maer had done the same or worse to each other and the humans over the centuries. It was just harder to imagine sharing hearts and bodies with someone who had done to her people what the humans had done.

Now, as she lay between her lightly snoring spouses, she imagined luring one of the human soldiers into her home, his eyes alight with the promise of forbidden pleasures. *Turn around*, she would say, and he would comply. She would unbuckle his armor from behind, then bend him over a table and yank his pants down, pushing his head into the wood as she hissed into his ear. *Is this what you want?* He would gasp as her spit-slicked fingers slid him open, her palm flattening his cheek against the table. *Is this why you crossed the mountains?* As she roughly forced his pleasure, he would cry out, *Yes, yes, oh, gods, please. Oh, gods!* She would finish him with a flurry of ruthless strokes, then walk away, leaving him a gasping, sprawling mess.

Their human escorts waited politely in the street outside their yard, weapons sheathed and visors raised as they greeted them in awkward bits of Maer. Cloti almost pitied them, tools of a regime that cared so little for the life of humans or Maer. Each of them had family and loved ones hundreds of miles away, and Kuppham was a dangerous place for a human soldier, with the Shoza leading nightly raids on their makeshift barracks. The Maer hated the humans and quietly cheered on the raids, though they were careful never to speak their approval out loud lest they be overheard by the omnipresent human spyballs.

The Torls were hosting a communal dinner with the human leadership this week, which must have been especially galling since they'd lost a son to the war. Two if she counted Yglind, who'd been whisked off to hibernation only weeks before the city fell. A group of human scholars was in town, and everyone was expected to make nice and pretend like this was just a simple cultural exchange. Iudan was holding court in the foyer, resplendent in a gown of flowing orange silk.

"Ambassador, so good to see you." Iudan bowed to Ludo, then Cloti and Aefin in turn. "Cloti, Aefin, thank you both for coming!"

"We wouldn't have missed it." Aefin took Iudan's hands, and they shared a brief glance of silent understanding, the standard greeting when humans were around. Though their families had never been the closest, their bonds had tightened during the tense days of the occupation. "Say, I don't think I've seen that tapestry before. Is it new?"

Cloti touched Aefin gently on the back, then slipped away toward the bar, waiting behind two humans in officers' uniforms who laughed and spoke in rapid-fire Islish as they watched the bartender pour their drinks. Cloti didn't catch a word of what they'd said, and she exchanged a glance with the bartender, who looked down quickly, nervous agitation on her face.

"Mushroom wine, if you have any."

"Make it two," said an oddly familiar voice in barely accented Maer. She turned and saw the unmistakable green eyes and mottled face of Feddar, the Chief Administrator of Kuppham. He was considered handsome for a human, despite the scars suffered during his imprisonment, but Cloti struggled to see it. What she did see, beyond the striking color of his irises, was his frank demeanor and the complete absence of fear or disgust in his aura. She could always sense it beneath the surface in those humans who managed to keep it off their faces. At any rate, he was the administrator in charge of the so-called de-occupation of the city, and she had promised Ludo to make nice if she met him. She plucked a glass from the bartender's hand and offered it to Feddar.

"Most humans can't stomach it."

"Most humans are barbarians," he said quietly, his eyes twinkling as he took a sip. "Though, to be honest, I'm more of a fan of silver spore."

Cloti winced as she tasted the wine, made from honeycomb fungus, aged for far too short a time. The fact that Feddar could tell the difference was impressive.

"I suppose in such times, we should be happy with what we can get."

They clinked glasses, and Cloti felt his eyes not straying to her cleavage, his body not closing the space between them, but his attraction was no less plain. It stirred something in her, though she felt more than a little conflicted about it.

She'd never seriously considered putting her fantasies to the test—in truth, she did find the skin off-putting, but there was something different about Feddar. He seemed to see her for who she was, not as Other. It didn't hurt that he was built like a Shoza, and now that she had a chance to study him, she had to admit that his facial structure was pleasing, freakish lack of hair notwithstanding. He was considerably younger than she, though it was hard to tell with humans, but he carried himself like someone closer to her own age. It was perhaps to be expected, given all he'd been through. He'd been caught and tried as a spy and saboteur, and he'd paid a heavy price for his crimes, as evidenced by the burn marks on his face. Ludo had proclaimed him a fair and honorable man, though he was predisposed to think that about everyone.

"You speak Maer better than any human I've met." She touched his elbow, guiding him through an open space in the crowd into a sitting room whose walls were adorned with antique armaments that had not been polished since the last time she was here.

"I had an excellent teacher." He spoke in a melancholy tone as his eyes surveyed the artifacts on the walls. A lover, she thought. One who had passed on or gone out of his life. Though liaisons between humans and Maer were not unheard of during the occupation, this would have been before his imprisonment if she read his aura right. Perhaps one of those who had accompanied Yglind on his fabled Delve when Feddar was captured. Feddar's eyes lingered on a large, green book on the table, whose pages were sprayed copper to match the copper inlays on the cover. She realized it was a copy of the official chronicle of the Delve of Yglind Torl, Iudan's son, who'd been sent off to hibernation shortly before the humans had arrived. She'd have to do her homework, as she'd forgotten most of the details.

"Indeed. Humans are thought not to be very skilled with their tongues." Cloti's cheeks burned as she spoke, and the quirk of a smile on Feddar's lips showed she'd hit her mark.

"We might surprise you. You should meet our linguists—Damias, over there talking with your husband, speaks it like a native, I'm told. Knows several of the Free Maer dialects as well and can read the language of the Time Before."

Cloti took a large sip of her wine, trying to process the fact that Feddar knew who she was, wondering whether that would be a problem. She also wondered why a group of linguists would be visiting if the humans were planning on de-occupying before the next winter came, as they claimed.

"It's a shame all this linguistic knowledge didn't stop things from getting to this point." She regretted it as soon as the words were out of her mouth, but she sensed something in Feddar, almost a kinship, as though he liked the Maer more than the humans, despite what they'd done to him.

"What has happened is a tragedy." He set down his empty wineglass and clutched his hands to his chest. "I have done things I will regret to the end of my days, and I have paid a heavy price, but it is not enough. It will never be enough." He picked up his empty glass, then set it back down. There was nothing in his voice or his aura that suggested subterfuge, but she reminded herself that he was a trained spy, so she remained on her guard.

"You speak with such frankness." Cloti glanced around her for prying ears, but everyone seemed to be giving the Administrator a wide berth. "Few dare speak their minds openly in these times."

"It's why they picked me for the job no one wanted, I suppose. Come, let's see if the second glass goes down better than the first."

He fetched them more wine, and they migrated with their glasses out into the back garden, where paper lanterns marked the footpaths running throughout Iudan's prized hedges. The soft tones of a goat harp played from across the garden, where humans and Maer drifted in twos and threes, talking and laughing quietly. It felt for a moment like the war had never happened, like this was just another dinner party, until the brash voices of a group of human officers broke the spell, calling out what sounded like curses in Islish.

Feddar stuck two fingers in his mouth and let out a sharp whistle. The calls ceased in an instant. Laughter tinkled from across the courtyard, and the officers hurried back inside, bowing slightly toward Feddar.

"Barbarians, as I said." He turned to Cloti with an embarrassed shrug. "But somewhat trainable."

"Anyone is, with the right master." Cloti turned away, smiling at the hedges, at her boldness.

"To serve the right master is the honor of a lifetime." His eyes burned into hers when she turned back to him. She covered her mouth as his words sparked a twinge of desire. It would be a rich irony indeed to bend the Administrator to her will, and as she felt his need radiating off him, she let her hand graze across his. His skin was so soft under her fingertips, his warmth so immediate; she wanted to touch him all over, feel his heat sizzling just beneath the surface. It had been so long since she'd been with someone truly new, and his response was intoxicating, but this had gone too far. She removed her hand, and Feddar gave a little gasp.

"Excuse me, Cloti, I..." He touched his chest, looking down as if trying to regain his breath. She had inadvertently lowered her barriers and let her desire bleed into him. It must have been the wine. He looked at her with eyes full of confusion, kindling her fire anew, but she kept it inside.

"Are you feeling all right?" She touched him on the sleeve this time, and he shook his head and smiled.

"This wine's stronger than I thought. I'm going to get a glass of water and freshen up." He half-turned, then stopped, looking back over his shoulder with hesitant eyes. "I was hoping..."

"Yes?" Butterflies circled her stomach as he turned back around.

"Well, it's just, I know a little of your practice from one of the guards when I was in the Tower. He showed me a few things, and it...it helped me get through some difficult times. I know with the rules against large gatherings, you haven't been able to lead your cycles as you're used to, but I was hoping we could change that."

"What do you mean?" She clasped her hands together, not daring to believe what she was hearing.

"I've found a loophole in the charter, allowing exemptions for religious observances, and since you used to hold practice in the temple, I thought..."

"Our practice isn't religious, Administrator."

"Please, call me Feddar. And it doesn't matter—we would just call it that, *I* would call it that, to the Regional Administration."

Cloti looked away from Feddar's eyes, which glowed too brightly in the lanternlight.

"Our practice is all about truth. You can't spread the truth through lies."

"Even if it means you could hold daily practice in the temple with up to a hundred participants?"

Cloti closed her eyes, picturing the serene faces of the acolytes, a hundred pairs of hands pressed together at a hundred chests, the energy they could summon. If the city was to hold together, they needed communal rituals. If the humans chose to see it as religion, wasn't that their problem?

"I will meditate on this. I appreciate your offer, and I will give you my answer tomorrow if that suits you."

"Only if you deliver it in person." He handed her a silver medallion with the seal of the Islish administration imprinted on it, a star within a circle. Such a medallion granted access to anywhere in the city without an escort. Even Ludo did not have such privileges.

She slipped the medallion into the pocket of her robe and took his soft, hairless hands in hers, pushing out a wave of warmth, which flowed back to her threefold. Feddar smiled as his fingers slipped from hers.

"Tomorrow, then." He bowed, then turned and disappeared into the maze of the hedges.

"You were awfully friendly with the Administrator this evening." Aefin ran a fine pick through Cloti's beard, stopping periodically to retie a loose braid.

"He's an interesting fellow."

"He's also a spy, and a murderer, and a snitch." Aefin touched up Cloti's beard once more, then set the pick down. "And I want to go on the record as saying, though I know you will do what you will do, I think it's a terrible idea. He can't be trusted." Her gray and brown filigreed eyes were furrowed with concern.

"I never said I was."

"You didn't have to. I knew from the moment you handed him his drink."

"Well, I'm seeing him tomorrow, as it happens." She fended off Aefin's phony slap with a giggle. "Not like that. He made me an offer. I promised I'd give him my answer tomorrow."

Aefin perked up, a glimmer of hope sparking in her eyes. Cloti didn't need to read her to see that, not that she would have; her shield slid up unconsciously whenever Aefin entered the room.

"Well, go on!" Aefin poked her gently in the stomach, then sat cross-legged on the bed next to her. "Spill!" Her almost childish energy was just what Cloti needed to break the tension that had been swirling inside her since the party.

Cloti kissed her, grabbing Aefin's surprised face and pressing it to hers. It took Aefin a moment to kiss her back, and they lingered in the moment, never delving too deeply, though their hands did begin to roam a bit. Aefin stopped and took Cloti by the shoulders, her face suddenly serious though her voice was soft.

"Tell me."

"He's offered to let us use the temple again. To hold practice, every day, for up to a hundred Maer."

Aefin covered her mouth with her hand as she huffed a noisy breath in.

"Just like that?"

"I read his aura. It was no lie."

"Ludo's going to love this. Any chance to get cozy with the administration." She rolled her eyes, but her face did not say no.

"But Aefin, just think of it. Practicing in public again? I thought those days were gone forever."

"And with the Stream definitively dead, it's really the only way to connect." She shook her head, eyebrows raised. "You really think you can trust him?"

"Aefin, I looked into his eyes. There was no deception at all."

"I bet you spent a good bit of time looking at those eyes. So green you can see them from across the room."

"I won't pretend I didn't notice. But it's what's behind those eyes that interests me."

"Skundir's balls, Cloti! You're a goner already, and you've just met the man!" Aefin pushed her shoulders away, a serious half-pout on her face. Cloti took her hands and locked eyes with her, and Aefin's expression softened. They'd been through too many cycles like this for her to hide anything from Aefin.

"Aef, it's not like that. Not yet, anyway."

"I fucking knew it." Aefin looked away, trying to pull her hands away, but Cloti held them tight.

"Aefin. Look at me." Cloti sighed. Aefin wasn't going to like this, but they'd made a pact never to refuse each other a lover without a frank discussion first. "I can't predict how this is going to go, but if you object, I'll respect your wishes. You and Ludo always come first. You know that."

Aefin looked down, but not before Cloti saw her eyes filling with tears. She cried easily these days, and Cloti's eyes began leaking as well.

"Cloti, I would never want to rein in your heart." She looked up, wiping her eyes on her sleeve and laughing as she sniffed away her tears. "And honestly, I can't exactly blame you. He is built like a godsdamned Shoza, but he seems...oddly gentle. Even if he is a..." She snorted as if holding in a laugh. "A skinfucker." She giggled, breaking the tension like a rock through a window, and a cackle rose in Cloti's throat. Soon they were swaying with laughter, holding onto each other to avoid falling over sideways onto the bed.

"I know, and you're right," Cloti said, wiping her eyes as the laughter subsided. "It really would be stupid of me."

She sighed as Aefin's hands slid up around her neck. Their foreheads touched, their breath mingling as their beards tangled.

"Promise me something," Aefin whispered.

"Anything, love."

"Remember who he is. Remember who we are. Don't lose yourself."

Cloti's heart swelled even as it felt like it was being bound by iron straps. Their lips met, and she poured everything she had into the kiss. She pressed Aefin back onto the bed, pinning her arms above her head, smothering her with her lips, her body, trying to shatter the bonds keeping her heart at bay. The world outside might be unrecognizable, but in this bed, this moment with Aefin, she could keep herself from falling apart.

2

— · —

Cloti slipped out of the covers when she woke at middlemorn, padding through the dark house by feel. She walked softly out of long habit in case any of Uffrin's little bronze cogs were lurking in the carpet. It had been decades, but her feet still remembered the pain. She wondered where he was now, if he'd found a community at Eagle Lake. She knew he and Mara had made it there; she'd seen it in the Thousand Worlds with the help of the Earth Milk. She'd checked at Winter Solstice and seen that they'd survived the war and made it there together. She hadn't dared look again for fear of news her heart wouldn't be strong enough to take.

The garden was quiet, the fountain still and mossy since the water towers had been destroyed. The smell of algae filled the courtyard, whose stones glowed pale between the shadows cast by a reluctant moon. She removed the key from her neck and unlocked the greenhouse door, taking a deep, calming breath before she opened it and stepped into its rank, humid confines.

The purple light from the hotsilver shone through the tinted flameglass globe, which was supposed to reduce the risk, but she never felt entirely comfortable around it. She pulled on her visor, apron, and gloves, feeling a bit like a knight heading out on a Delve. She tapped the visor's light into life and shone it on the ooze, which looked to have almost fully recovered from the last division. She'd taken a portion of it on that long, strange trip to the Isle of a Thousand Worlds, to save for the Time to Come.

She opened the dome, picked up the long spoon, and tested the surface of the ooze, which responded just as it should have, yielding without sticking to the bronze. She dipped the spoon into the salt and mineral fertilizer and sprinkled it on top of the ooze, which quickly absorbed it into its pearlescent surface. The effects of the ooze fumes flowed through her mind, transporting her instantly to the sea cave on the island. She'd hoped to meet the Maer of the Time to Come, but it was humans she'd encountered instead.

"We are human, but I don't know when we are," one of them had said.

The younger woman, Gilea, had been a practitioner; Cloti could feel it in the way she navigated the Thousand Worlds, the smoothness of her mindspeech. It was reassuring to know her practice had found its way into human society. She liked to think she'd helped them become less warlike over the centuries. But what of the Maer? The humans had known about them, so she knew they hadn't died out. Did they still practice? She wished she'd been able to ask the humans, but their control was nebulous, and she'd had to hurry out before the fumes from the ooze overwhelmed her.

She shook her head and returned the spoon to the table, then carefully closed the dome, waiting for the hiss indicating it had sealed before removing her protective gear. She could handle the fumes from the ooze, but hotiron emissions were not to be messed with. Her heart warmed to see the ooze thriving while everything else had gone to hell. She hoped she could keep it all secret from the humans, but even if they found it, they wouldn't know what to do with it, and it would die without her care. At least now she knew there was a second source, though it would be centuries before anyone could puzzle out the clues she'd left spread across a dozen texts in the Archive. She closed the door, locked it tight, and took a seat by the fountain, her mind floating from the effects of the ooze. Her fingers curled into rings at her sides. She had only to blink, and the glassy water of the fountain expanded into an infinity of glittering darkness.

Thoughts from the day flitted by like comets, burning out one by one as she felt herself dispersing into the emptiness. When she had shooed the thoughts away, the Thousand Worlds were as silent as an abandoned temple. The humans had confiscated and destroyed every cradle and circlet they could find, along with most of the Earth Milk, which they seemed to be able to find with their magic. She'd only managed to conceal the ooze during their inspections by using its power to redirect their mages. Without the Milk, the cradles, and the circlets, only a very few had the skill to access the Thousand Worlds, so Cloti's travels were solo affairs these days. Though lights twinkled in the distance of time and space, the familiar pull of friends near and far was gone, as if they'd never existed, and she floated like a single leaf on a still pond. It took her a moment to embrace the weightless silence and open her mind further.

Movement invites chaos, which must be balanced with stillness.

The words whispered out of her memory, but the stillness could not hold her for long. Without the familiar lights of the larger community, she was adrift, though she moved slowly. Practice required solitude, but solitude lost its meaning without communion with others. The interdiction on public gatherings meant no temple practice, which had thrown her out of balance, and she struggled to keep her center. There was a hollow place inside her that she never could seem to fill, no matter how much time she spent in meditation or wrapped in her spouses' arms. There was always something missing, like a sunny winter's day, whose brief warmth and light fooled one into thinking the colder days were over.

She imagined that the disappearance of the Stream had a similar effect on those who used it, which was practically everyone. And as much as she hated it, Aefin's use of the Stream had helped spread their practice to those who couldn't make it out to her public cycles. Aefin had shown her views from all over the Stream with Maer practicing, together or in groups, teaching each other, studying, and passing on the good word. Without that connection, what would become of their practice?

She had no choice but to accept Feddar's offer. Even if the humans surveilled their every meeting, the communion of hearts and minds they forged together would help keep the practice alive. In a time when most Maer were shut up in their homes or penned in together in the Riverside camps, they needed something to grasp onto, no matter how small. There would be many details to sort out, but her choice was clear. In the morning, she would meet with Feddar and strike a deal. She would let her heart decide if anything more than that came of their meeting.

Her mind twitched at a faint pulse coming in from somewhere in the infinity of the Thousand Worlds. She didn't recognize the signature, which was fragmented and unstable. There were few experienced enough to access the Thousand Worlds on their own, and possession of the Earth Milk was punishable by death. If this wasn't just an echo of some random point in time and space, it could be someone who didn't know what they were doing. She struggled to center herself enough to follow the signal, but it faded before she could get a lock on it.

The courtyard lit up in warm yellow as the sun peeked over the wall. She would check again tomorrow at dawn. She hoped whoever sent the signal would try again. It was a message she desperately needed to hear.

The guards in front of Feddar's house opened the doors for her before she could even pull out her medallion. It had been the mayoral residence, but the mayor had been killed in the fighting, and his family had moved in with relatives. Cloti had spent too many evenings attending formal functions there with Ludo before the occupation, and it was just as she had remembered. Either Feddar liked the décor, or he was too lazy or busy to change it. The same gilded throw pillows were tucked in the corners of gaudy divans and settees, and the plants in the big brass pots looked well-watered and tended. Two Maer with ledgers entered through the garden door, arguing in hushed tones. They stopped and bowed when they saw Cloti, and she heard their whispered conversation pick back up as they walked through the foyer and out into the street.

"Come on back to the garden," Feddar's voice called out in Maer.

Cloti had always loved the mayor's garden, overflowing with dark vines and exotic flowers in pots and barrels and pockets of earth set in low, curved walls of cream-colored tile. It had been a refuge at the official events Ludo was required to attend, and when it was her turn to accompany him, she'd always gravitate outside unless it was raining hard enough to pierce the foliage. Fountains burbled, and little streams crisscrossed the garden, with stone footbridges along the paths leading to the main patio. Feddar stood from his chair behind a desk covered with scrolls, ledgers, and loose papers, bowing deeply as she approached. Too deeply, which was an easy mistake for outsiders to make; Kuppham was a lot less formal than the cities to the north.

"I trust you have had time to meditate on my proposal?" Feddar moved around the desk with a spry step, stopping and clutching his hands together at his waist. She studied his face, smooth reddish-tan skin marred by the bright red splash mark of an acid burn across his left cheek, which she gathered he'd suffered during his captivity and torture at the hands of the Maer. His expression was pleasant but impassive, and she had decided not to actively read him, but the only vibe he gave off was hope.

"I believe I can trust you." She took a step closer to him, studying his green eyes, which smiled just a little more than his mouth.

"You absolutely can, Cloti. Like I said, I learned some of your practice in the Tower, and I hope to learn more."

"You would join us in our cycles in the temple?"

"If you allow it." His eyes dropped for a moment, then he looked up at her, his head still lowered.

"What is inside me is open to you." She pressed her hands together at her chest and blinked slowly.

"And me to you." He repeated her gesture, then turned to the desk and picked up a neat stack of paper. "I got up early to finish the paperwork this morning, and I'll deliver it to the attaché at our lunch meeting."

"And you believe they will accept your proposal?"

"Yes, absolutely." He closed the distance between them, lowering his voice a little. "They chose me to keep the peace during de-occupation, and we've had enough of lockdowns. It's time to start opening up a little. Get this city up and moving again."

"Like it was before the invasion."

Feddar sagged against his desk, and Cloti immediately regretted her words, but once a thought was in her head, it seldom stayed there.

"I hate what they did. What we did. And I know I can't make it right, but I'm hoping I can make it a little less wrong."

Cloti nodded. If anyone could make things better, it would be him. Most humans hated the Maer, and the sentiment was more than reciprocated. If anyone else were in charge, things would surely be a lot worse. She did wonder if he really believed in the de-occupation rhetoric, but if he could get her what she wanted, perhaps it didn't matter.

"How long before we can hold our first cycle?"

"Well, we have to inspect the building to make sure it's safe, and then if the attaché agrees, I suppose we could get a response via falcon in two or three days."

"Can I go take a look this morning? I'd like to see how much work will be required to make it ready."

"Only with an escort." He pulled a neat leather bag from a hook and shouldered it. "If I may presume?" He gestured toward the house, his eyes twinkling with confidence.

"You may presume whatever you like, so long as you are prepared to be surprised."

Feddar's face seemed to redden, and his eyes slid down her body for a moment, then flickered away.

"If you want to fill your water bottle, this fountain is potable, and the water is cool and fresh." He turned toward the fountain, bending as he unscrewed the cap and held the bottle under the thin stream. His behind was tight but rounded, his legs steady and strong. She briefly imagined stepping up behind him and sliding her hand between his thighs to grip and control him, his surprised gasp, his guttural whine.

"I'll fill yours for you if you like." He turned halfway around, leaving his backside on full display, and she wondered if he didn't know exactly what he was doing. She watched as his body curved toward the fountain, the muscles in his back and shoulders tight against his shirt. He handed her the bottle, then turned and drank from the fountain, angling his head sideways to catch the stream in his mouth. He wiped the water from his face, flinging a few drops into the foliage and wiping the rest on his pants.

"Shall we?" He led the way along the winding path through the courtyard garden. Cloti followed, feeling a smile creep across her face. The Chief Administrator of Kuppham had just cleared his schedule to walk down to inspect the temple with her. In a week's time, she would be leading a meditation cycle with a hundred acolytes, sharing their energy, boosting each other, and re-forming their bonds. It might take time to build, but this could be the spark the movement needed to grow strong enough to face what was to come.

The temple was musty and disheveled, with evidence of the humans having searched, though gods knew what they expected to find. There was no real damage, only things tossed about, emptied, and moved aside. Nothing that couldn't be sorted out in a day. The morning sun reflecting in through the high circular windows cast the space in a hopeful golden light. Feddar stood staring at the windows, at the patterns of light scattered across the walls.

"What kind of temple is this, anyway?"

"It's a temple to the old gods, the ones no one believes in anymore. It's mostly used for weddings, funerals, festivals, and the like. And practice, of course. The architecture has a certain...resonance."

"Our scholars are going to go nuts for this. A temple from the Time Before. And these engravings?" He pointed to the script carved in the dome, the flowery calligraphy of the Elder Scribes.

"Even our scholars argue about what it says. The shape of the letters is thought to be as important as the words themselves." She'd cribbed certain flourishes from the script for her mystography, thickening and simplifying the shapes so they flowed like seaweed. The only recipes for the Earth Milk were written in this unique script, which only a handful of Maer could read. She doubted if even the most knowledgeable human scholars could crack it.

"And you would sit...here?" Feddar hopped up on the circular dais, turning in a slow circle as he surveyed the space.

"That's right. We'll have to air out these mats." She swatted one of the thick reed prayer mats, and dust billowed into the air.

"I can get you chips for a dozen helpers if that's enough, so you can make the place ready." He stepped down from the dais, gazing up at the ceiling again, then turning his wonderstruck eyes back toward Cloti. "This really is the most amazing space!"

She bit back a tear as she pictured the cycle from the last Solstice before the invasion, acolytes crowded in every corner of the temple and spilling out into the street, the smell of flowers and candles and sweat, hundreds of souls summoning the sacred voice at the same time, filling the marble walls with their reverberations.

"I'm sorry, I...I got carried away." Feddar's voice was soft as he moved toward Cloti, stopping just out of reach. "It makes you sad, doesn't it? Because of what you've lost."

"Nothing is lost if it remains in the hearts of Maer." Cloti blinked away an errant tear threatening to spill. She smiled up at him, and he grimaced and closed his eyes for a moment. "Get me the chips, and I'll round up my crew and bring them tomorrow."

As they left the temple, a Maer with a cart of smoked fish was crouched near the entrance, fixing one of the wheels on his cart.

"I'm glad you've decided to trust me on this." Feddar's hands were tense as he spoke, and he glanced around as if worried he might be overheard. "I know you don't believe it, but I think this de-occupation thing is going to happen. Nothing's been said officially, but I don't see the kind of build-up I would expect for an extended occupation. Once the king is convinced the Maer pose no threat, I hope he'll decide—"

Cloti's focus narrowed in an instant as a single desire pierced her awareness: *Kill*. She whirled to see the fishmonger darting toward Feddar from behind, knife in hand.

"No," she said in a calm voice, holding her palm toward the Maer. He stopped, his eyes suddenly blank, and his knife clattered to the ground. Feddar spun around, his fist flashing toward the Maer's face, which caved as he made contact. The Maer's legs buckled, and he collapsed to the ground, coughing blood. Two humans in light armor materialized, blocking out Cloti and Feddar and cuffing the Maer in a matter of seconds. Cloti watched in horror as they jerked the Maer to his feet, one of them holding him while the other elbowed him repeatedly in the face until his body went limp.

"Stop!" Cloti yelled, and the humans staggered back, dazed, letting the Maer slump to the ground. "Make them stop," she said to Feddar's chest. His arms wrapped protectively around her, and he held out his hand to the men, who had recovered and were glaring at Cloti with murder in their eyes. Feddar spoke to them in Islish, and they did not relax their posture at first. When he released Cloti and stood up straight, they took a step back and lowered their heads. He spoke firm words to them, his voice booming across the space. They nodded, picked up the half-conscious Maer, and trundled him off in the direction of the Tower. Four heavily armed humans came running up, and Feddar stopped them with a flurry of Islish words. Two of them joined those with the prisoner, and the other two fell into step behind Feddar as he kept one arm around Cloti's waist and began walking back through the city.

"My guards would have stopped him, you know."

"They would have been too late." Cloti's heart hammered in her chest. She had never used her power that way, and she felt dirty, as if she'd been up all night drinking and hitting the tarpipe. But it hadn't even been a choice. Feddar had been in danger, and her body had reacted.

"Well, in that case, I suppose I owe you my life. Let me know what I can do in return."

"Just keep your promise." She stopped, pulling away from Feddar's arm, though she still felt dizzy from the haze of violence following her like a cloud of angry bees.

Feddar fixed her with an intense gaze, his face still and serious.

"I won't let them spin this against us. Prepare to hold your first cycle in a week."

He might have been deluded, but his aura was clear. He believed what he said. Cloti chose to believe it, too, for now.

3

— · —

"Gods, Cloti, are you okay?" Ludo stood from the bed, gripped her shoulders, then pulled her in for a crushing hug.

"I'm fine. I don't think I was in any danger." She pushed back enough to look into his worried eyes. "I'm just a little shook up, that's all."

"Of course you are. I would have absolutely died of fright. But they say you—that is, what I heard was..." He lifted his eyebrows in question, and Cloti blinked slowly.

"I just saw him rushing in, and I said 'No,' and he stopped cold and dropped his knife. Feddar knocked him down with one punch, and the guards were on him before I'd taken my next breath." She felt queasy, and she melted into Ludo's arms, pressing against his chest, tears trickling through the hair on her face. "They just kept hitting him, and I told them to stop, and they did, but the way they looked at me..."

"You used your...powers?"

Cloti nodded, her heart wrenched with guilt.

"You did the right thing." Ludo's hand cupped her head, massaging her neck. She pulled away after a moment to sit on the bed, holding her face in her hands.

"They'll torture him, won't they?"

Ludo put his hand on her knee, answering with a long moment of silence.

"It's not your fault. If he'd succeeded, things would be much worse."

"I know." She sniffed, wiping her eyes and pushing against her knees to sit up straight. "Feddar said he won't let it stop us from starting the cycles in a week."

"You've made quite an impression on him, it would seem." A hint of amusement—and perhaps something else—crept into his tone. "That's a very good thing."

"I suppose." She pictured the soft depths of Feddar's eyes and felt his desire to please her. Now that she had saved his life, he would submit to anything she asked. She pictured him leaning over the fountain filling the water bottles, and she bit her lip as desire rose within her. She shook her head.

"But don't you think it's risky being associated with him?"

Ludo sighed. "We are a subjugated people, confined to our houses and squalid camps. You said it yourself—if there's anyone who can improve our lot, it's him. Imagine if he had been killed, the chaos that would have ensued."

"I know. I know." She leaned into his shoulder, her hand finding his thigh and squeezing. "He said...he hinted that the humans weren't planning on staying here indefinitely. That he thinks the de-occupation is real. His aura was clear, Ludo. He believes it."

Ludo nodded, his eyes full of hope muted by long years of bureaucratic experience.

"And I...do...too." He kissed her forehead between each word. "As long as the damned Shoza don't ruin everything."

Cloti's breath caught at the vehemency of his statement. She'd long hated the Shoza as tools of an oppressive regime, doing its dirty business in deniable secrecy. As resistance fighters against the human occupation, she found she had a bit more sympathy for them. But Ludo was right. Every time they attacked, the humans used it as an excuse to tighten restrictions. And every time restrictions were lifted, they attacked again. The cycle was doomed to perpetuate violence until one side or the other was destroyed.

"We can always hope."

"Nothing is too much to hope as long as we have each other." His hand lifted to her cheek, and he kissed her softly, breaking the spell of her distraction. She let her hand slide between his legs, feeling him stir as she sucked his upper lip into hers and started milking it. The world outside was so uncertain, but Ludo's touch made it all dissolve. She half-stood, pushing him back onto the bed, still kissing him, still gripping his growing hardness. She released his lips, smiling down on him as she straddled him, sliding both hands up to peel apart his robe to reveal the silky hair on his chest and his stiff, hungry nipples.

"Do you want me to..." She pushed out a pulse through her fingertips, and he arched beneath her, gasping.

"Yes," he whispered. She lowered down, hovering just above his straining body, and poured out a burst of desire. Without the Earth Milk, she couldn't feel everything he felt, but their connection was strong enough that she could still project into him. His eyes burned hot and desperate, and she curved down to kiss him, sending out a hundred tiny pulses through her fingertips as she sank down onto him. He let out the tiniest whine as his lips fumbled for hers, his hands finding her hips and holding her gently. His pleasure trickled into her, mingling with thoughts of Aefin, of Feddar, the four of them tangled together. As his whine morphed into something more animalistic, she tried to slow down, to make it last, but her pleasure surged through her, spilling over, and she released it into him in gushing waves. His whine rose to a shout, then a wordless gasp, and she ground into him as they came, soaking each other in a burst of hot, wet ecstasy.

"This will do." Cloti leaned against a pillar and surveyed the freshly tidied and swept temple, which looked exactly as it had before the occupation. She'd brought a dozen acolytes from the Cliffside circle, who still managed to meet with some regularity, as their chips allowed them to circulate in their immediate neighborhood without escorts. Two human guards stood outside the open door, facing the street, as Feddar had negotiated. Their presence was like a tiny splinter in her mind, not truly painful but irritating enough to prevent her from feeling quite at home here. She would need some help. She walked over to the dais, slipping off her sandals before stepping up onto the worn, buttery marble. She looked to her acolytes, making eye contact with each one, then lowered down to sit cross-legged in the center of the dais, facing away from the open doorway. They all picked up mats and formed a semi-circle behind her so none of them had to see the human interlopers. Though she could not see them, their bond was immediate, enhanced by the harmonics of the temple.

She laid her hands to her side, then slowly curled her arms upward, two sturdy baskets ready to support the weight of the universe. Power surged through her as the acolytes repeated her gesture, tightening their connection and channeling their power into one. She closed her eyes, and her mind painted a picture of a forest lake, dark skeletons of trees reflecting on the still surface. She floated, a single leaf in the watery mirror, weightless, inert. The trees grew, looming toward her, intertwining to form a protective shell of branches. A haven.

She floated out of time, out of space, out of mind. The universe was in her, and she in it. Coppery filaments flowed from her, interlacing with the shell and streaming out into the teeming void. They linked and intertwined with a thousand other threads, and she dispersed into them, her mind coursing with the echoes of countless minds and worlds. She emptied herself, and the universe filled her, erasing her and drawing her anew. She melted into it again, spreading through its every dark corner until she was the universe. The water and the leaf, the forest and the lake.

The world was still.

Cloti lowered her arms and relaxed her mind, which buzzed with the reverberations of her first temple cycle in months. She turned around to face her acolytes, squinting against the glare of sunlight through the front door, the silhouettes of the soldiers dark against the sunshine's warmth.

"As it was before, so shall it be again."

She pressed her hands together at heart's center, and a wave of tears welled up in her to see her acolytes' smiles as they repeated her gesture and honored her with a bow. She returned the honor, then relaxed her face and shook out her arms.

"I don't know about you all, but I'm famished. And with this little medallion, I can get us into the human food hall."

Their faces lit up with excitement and curiosity. She hoped they wouldn't be too disappointed by the bland food the humans seemed to prefer.

Feddar leaned back in his chair, inspecting the meditation coin.

"So, this isn't currency?"

She shook her head, smiling. "No. You study the eye until you slip into the blankness at its center."

"And the shiny side?" He flipped the coin in his dexterous fingers to show the mirrored surface.

"Sometimes the thing you're looking for is already inside you."

He flipped the coin and stared into his reflection for a moment, then laid it on the table.

"May I keep this one?"

"Of course. And give one to someone else. Someone who needs it." She flipped another coin to him, and he plucked it out of the air without breaking eye contact.

"Thank you. And you say you have a hundred of them?"

"More than that, but I was planning to give out a hundred at the camps, and when they return, they can give them to someone else for the next day's cycle."

"It's genius." He raised both hands, then let them fall to his lap. "They'll have to go through medical control for Ulver's cough, though."

"Of course. No one wants the disease to spread through the cycles."

"The temple is big and airy. At a hundred souls, properly spaced, it should be safe enough." He picked up the coin from his desk and pointed it at her. "Make it so."

"So, you're giving me orders now?"

"Gods, no, I'm sorry, I just—"

"I'm kidding." She smiled at the color that rose in his cheeks. Humans wore their emotions on their skin. "I'll go down to the camps this afternoon. With your permission, of course."

"I could join you." He shifted in his seat, glancing at her hopefully. "I'm overdue for an inspection to make sure conditions are up to standards."

"I don't think that will serve the cause. It doesn't do either of us any favors to be seen together at this point."

"Of course, of course." His voice fell, and he stared down at the coin in his hand. "I had hoped..." He tapped the coin on the desk several times, then looked up sheepishly. "I had hoped for a chance to spend more time with you." His voice quavered slightly, and she could almost taste the nervous energy he emitted. She stepped around the desk, and he swiveled toward her, his eyes widening as she put her hands on the arm of the chair and leaned in close.

"You know the value I place on openness and honesty, Feddar."

He nodded, swallowing. "They're the most important things."

"In the spirit of openness, I want to spend more time with you too. But not in public. Not in front of prying eyes." She dropped her shields just a bit, letting a whiff of her desire float into him. "Would you like that?"

His eyes widened, and he licked his lips. "Y-yes," he stammered.

"I don't know what your customs are, but my marriage is an open one. My spouses know my feelings for you."

"Your what?" he whispered, bewilderment in his eyes.

"And I know of your feelings for me. It's more than mere curiosity on both our parts, I think, but how much more remains to be seen." She glanced at his plump lips, then back into his bright green eyes. "In the before times, if you were Maer, I'd have you pressed against the wall right now with my tongue down your throat and my hand down the back of your pants." She pulled her face closer to his, his breath warm in her beard, his longing radiating into her.

"You could do anything you want to me." She felt his whispered voice as much as heard it.

Her hand found his hairless cheek, which was smoothly shaven and shockingly soft. She ran her thumb across his mouth, pulling his lower lip down, then let her fingers trace down his neck, which was prickly with stubble. A trail of sparse hair teased at the collar of his shirt, and her mind spun, trying to imagine what he would look like without it, how much hair there would be, how much soft skin. Feddar's breath caught as she pulled her hand back and raised the shields she'd inadvertently let slip at the shock of his softness.

"Gods, Cloti, I—" Feddar's eyes were wide with disbelief. "I felt something, you—"

She smiled, hoping to avoid the conversation for the moment. It was always awkward when she let herself slip like that with a new lover.

"Can I call on you tomorrow night? I could give you a report of my distribution of the coins and the plan for rotation of acolytes at the cycles."

"Make it so." His mouth quirked into a grin, and she paused for a long moment, staring at his glossy lips, wondering what he would taste like. How he would feel. How quickly he would yield. How hard it would be for her to stop herself.

"Tomorrow, then." She bowed, and he returned the gesture with the correct amount of incline this time.

"Tomorrow."

Cloti hadn't visited the riverside camps, and it was a surprise to see Maer hanging up laundry, making tea over small fires, and chatting amiably while children played between neat rows of tents. There were no fences, only posts stuck in the ground with the tops painted red delineating the camp's borders. Armed human soldiers stood or wandered along the periphery, looking bored, some of their helmets sitting atop the posts. The guards at the entry tent tensed as she approached, then relaxed as she flashed her medallion.

"Good afternoon," said a man with a passable accent and a friendly-enough manner. He held a pencil and a clipboard, and he studied her medallion for a moment and made a note. "What is your name, please?"

"Cloti Looris."

"Ah, yes, the Administrator left a message." He flipped the pages on the clipboard, running his finger down a column of fine script, then stopping to read for a moment. "You are...giving out a hundred...coins?"

"Yes, I have them here." She held out the bag, which he took, tucking his clipboard under his arm. He pulled out one of the coins, studied it for a moment, then dropped it back in the bag.

"Very good. You may enter, but..." He glanced at the camp, shielding his eyes from the afternoon sun. "We've had ah...some new cases of Ulver's cough. Not as bad as in winter, but you might want to cover your face." He pulled up his scarf in demonstration.

Cloti adjusted her scarf, smiling with her eyes, and he let her pass.

The camp stretched along the riverside as far as she could see, square pods made up of evenly spaced rows of tents, with posts separating each pod from the next. There were said to be close to twenty thousand Maer in the camps, the population of the hightops the humans had taken to house their soldiers when the city had finally fallen. The area around Skundir's Bridge was clear, and a half-dozen guards stood around it. Pairs of human soldiers walked through the camps, steering clear of the Maer, who avoided them as well, growing silent as they approached. Something glistened in the periphery of Cloti's vision, and she saw a glass marble floating at eye level, one of the infamous spyballs the humans used for surveillance. She walked right toward it to see if she could read it, and as she grew close, she could feel its faint energy, a connection with someone nearby, most likely one of their mages in the white tents just outside the camp. The ball slowed as she approached, and she veered away, hoping it didn't follow her.

She could see what Feddar meant about the humans not staying for the duration. Between the soldiers, the mages, and the spies, they had to be spreading their resources pretty thin, so far from their home range. There were rumors of a rebellion brewing in human territory, possibly fomented by the Shoza, though she wasn't sure how they would manage such a thing. But then again, they'd almost succeeded in assassinating Feddar, and she was sure some of the Maer she walked among in the camp were Shoza as well.

"Cloti!" The familiar voice was one of her most faithful acolytes, whom she hadn't heard from since the occupation began.

"Juiya!" Cloti moved to embrace her, but Juiya stepped back, pulling up her scarf, and bowed.

"I haven't had any symptoms, but I want to keep you safe. Our pod lost two to the cough this winter, and several more were sent over the bridge to the nursing camps this spring. One of them has not come back."

Cloti nodded, tears welling in her eyes. If the tales were true, many of those who went to the nursing camps never returned. The Cliffside residents had been pretty well buffered from Ulver's cough, and there hadn't been any cases there since winter.

"I'm glad you are well. I've come bearing good news."

Juiya took half a step closer, her eyes bright and expectant.

"Fedd—er, the Administrator has agreed to let us hold cycles in the temple again. For up to a hundred Maer."

"I heard the rumors, but... After what happened?" She lowered her voice. "Is it true that you—"

"It's true." Cloti closed her eyes for a moment against the memory of violence flaring in her mind. "I acted on instinct. It was an ugly moment, and I try not to think about what the poor Sh—what the poor Maer is going through right now."

"I will keep him in my thoughts during our cycle tonight. We've been holding them in the amphitheater every day at dawn and dusk, but the thought of going to the temple again..."

Cloti reached into the bag and held out a coin. "Take this. It will allow you passage to the temple."

Juiya smiled, pulling a coin from her pocket. "I still have the one you gave me when we first met! It's the only thing I managed to bring with me, except for my clothes." She gestured down at her worn robe, which had been hemmed and repaired in several places.

"Perhaps you could distribute the coins, then? To those who most need a cycle? We'll be holding daily practices at midday, though we may want to push them earlier as summer approaches. After their cycle, they can keep it or pass the coin on to someone else for the following day."

Juiya accepted the bag, peering down into it, her brow knitted in thought. She smiled and nodded after a moment.

"We will figure out a system." She glanced around, tucking the bag into the pocket of her robe. Cloti followed her eyes, watching in silence as a spyball floated by.

"We begin on Fourthday." Cloti pressed her hands together at her chest, pushing out a wave of warmth to Juiya, whose eyes lit up with joy as she received it and returned it in kind.

4

— · —

Cloti let her orgasm flourish as Ludo thrust one final time. She collapsed atop Aefin, who kissed her with soft abandon, cradling Cloti's face with her hands. Ludo snuggled in beside them, running his hand along Cloti's backside, squeezing a few times, then moving gently up her back. They lay tangled in each other, the smell of sex and breath and candle wax filling the room. Ludo rolled over and pinched the candle out; they were down to only two boxes, and there was no telling when they'd be able to get more.

Aefin pulled out her tarpipe and took a careful hit, holding it for a long time. She offered it to Cloti, who waved it away.

"Remember, I've got my date with Feddar tonight. I want to be on top of my game."

"You'll be on top of something, that's for sure." Ludo smacked her behind, and she wiggled off Aefin and pressed it into him, feeling him stir beneath her touch, even so soon after their lovemaking. He reached around and took her nipple gently between his thumb and forefinger, and she breathed out slowly as she felt her desire rise yet again. Ever since her first encounter with Feddar, she'd been even more amorous than usual with her spouses. She shook him off and rolled over to face him.

"Not on the first date. I'm not that kind of girl." Ludo smiled into her kiss, but Cloti felt Aefin's disapproval like the chill of winter rain. She rolled back over to Aefin, who stared at the ceiling, her face pensive and blank. Cloti reached out to touch her cheek with the back of her hand, and Aefin moved her head ever so slightly away from her touch.

"Aefin, are you sure you're okay with me and Feddar? I know you don't think it's a good idea, but if you truly aren't comfortable with it, I won't go."

"That would be cruel. He's probably already stroked himself ten times thinking about you since you first met." Her frown turned into a smirk as she reached for Cloti's hand and moved it to her cheek. "I'm fine with you going. I'm happy for you, even. He's got amazing eyes and is built like a Shoza. And it's probably good for Ludo's negotiations. But I'm nowhere near ready to trust him."

"Understood." Cloti ran her knuckles along Aefin's cheek, trailing her fingers along her jaw and the soft down of her neck. "I'll report back with my findings, and if it turns into anything more, I'll let you know."

Aefin turned toward her, fixing her glassy eyes on Cloti.

"I love you." She kissed Cloti gently but did not linger. "Just promise me you'll be careful."

Cloti had to pull her scarf over her head and run the last few hundred yards to Feddar's house as the sky opened up and pelted her with fat drops of warm rain. The guards under the portico stepped aside at her approach, nodding as they opened the double doors into the foyer. Cloti shook the rain from her scarf and took a moment to compose herself, using the convenient little mirror someone had been wise enough to install. In the hollow light of a single hanging brightstone lamp, her face looked old, stripes of gray hairs singing out from the carpet of brown that had always been her face. But Feddar didn't desire her for her face, or her body, for that matter, though he did seem to appreciate her curves. She'd sensed it from the moment they'd talked at the party: he wanted to give himself to her. She had that effect on some people. It was a little like how things had started with Ludo when he was a geeky young scholar with the social graces of a tree rat.

Feddar, on the other hand, was mature, polished, and confident, but his shell of composure peeled aside when she poked it, revealing a delectably soft center she was more than a little curious to taste.

Cloti ran her fingers through her beard one more time, though, since human women didn't grow beards, there was probably nothing she could do to make it appealing. She crossed the open space of the sitting room toward the door to the garden, which glowed with a warm, golden light. Rain pattered down more irregularly now, and she followed a trail of little brightstone lamps leading to the gazebo, which was ablaze with the light of half a dozen candles. Feddar stood as she approached, setting down a full glass of wine and pressing his hands together at his chest.

"I think we can do better than that," she said, taking his hands in hers and leaning up to press her lips against his. He made a surprised little sound in his throat, which turned into a low hum as they kissed. She kept her shields fully up, but even so, she could feel him bleeding into her, his body warming in response to her touch. She pulled back, biting her lip and smiling at the starstruck expression that flashed across his eyes before he regained his composure.

"It is...good to see you, Cloti." He gestured toward the chair opposite him at the small table, which was laid out with an assortment of little bowls containing nuts, cheese, dried fruit, and some kind of shredded meat. He picked up a decanter of wine, raised his eyebrows, then poured her a glass when she nodded. "This is a silver spore, about ten years old if the cask is accurate. It was here when I arrived, and I've been nipping at it ever since."

Cloti clinked glasses with him and took a sip. It was mellow, pleasantly earthy, with a whiff of smoke.

"You really lucked out on that cask. We've been living on wines people brought to parties that we never got around to opening. But I suppose we should be grateful; the Maer living in the riverside camps aren't drinking any wine at all, I expect."

He winced, frowning into his glass. "From what I hear, they make their own out of some kind of berry that grows along the edge of the cliff. It's supposed to be pretty good." He looked up hopefully, and she decided not to belabor the point.

"Stainberry wine, just like in the Time Before."

"I'm sorry?"

"It's from one of the longstories about a couple who ran away from their pre-arranged marriages and eloped together into the wilderness, living on mushrooms, forest snails, and stainberry wine."

"It doesn't sound half-bad, actually. Fresh air, natural diet, plenty of exercise." He waved his glass around, took a sip, then gestured toward the bowls on the table. "I've got a few noshes here while we have a drink. This one here you might find of particular interest." He picked up a shred of the dried meat and held it out. Cloti didn't eat meat as a rule, but he had piqued her interest, so she leaned forward and let him put it in her mouth. It was tough and dry, but as she chewed, her mouth filled with a rich flavor reminiscent of field ox but milder, with less of a funk.

"Gods, that's amazing." She continued chewing, searching her memory, but she couldn't identify it. She snapped her fingers as it came to her. "Is this *beef*?" She used the Islish word for the legendary meat of the humans' fatty field oxen.

"It is. The regional governor sent me a barrel at my appointment. I take it you don't have *cows* here?"

She shook her head. "Just field ox, which do a good enough job pulling a plow or a wagon, but they're not much for eating. I mostly eat fish anyway."

"Well, I'm glad to hear it because I've got some spicy fish stew headed our way from a Maer stall in the food hall."

Cloti swallowed the *beef*, washing it down with a gulp of wine as an unexpected sadness rose within her. She pictured the lively Riverside food hall, the crowds of Maer jostling for position in overlapping lines, sitting on tall stools at narrow counters, laughing, chomping, slurping, cutting deals.

"It sounds delightful. To be honest, I'd worried you might serve me human fare, which does tend to lack in seasoning if you'll excuse my observation."

"You are not wrong, though the food back in Gheil is worlds above what our cooks here can muster."

Feddar spoke of his hometown with love and longing, his words painting a picture in her mind and melding with her childhood fantasies of visiting human lands. She had always imagined endless fields of grain drenched in sunlight, with sparkling rivers twisting between farms and little villages. He described a city of learning and culture, of music and food and honey wine, and she wondered what it would be like to visit there, though she doubted such a thing would ever be possible after all that had happened.

The soup arrived, carried by a soldier, who avoided eye contact with Cloti as he carefully set the delivery box on a side table, bowed, and hurried off. Feddar dished out two bowls from the steaming crock, then set down a communal bowl of crispy fried scraps. The soup was red with chili oil, with chunks of silver floating amid rafts of fresh herbs. As the smell hit her nose, she was certain she'd eaten it before, and she could even picture the dingy little stall and the curmudgeonly Maer who dished out soup with a frown day and night. She sprinkled a few fried scraps on the soup and dug in, closing her eyes as the spice penetrated her throat and nose. Aefin and Ludo were both pretty good cooks, but this was the work of an artist. It was good to know at least some things hadn't changed.

"So good, right?" Feddar was so enthusiastic, so desperate to please her, it made her want to forget all the rest and just be with him in this moment.

"It's been a while since I had something this spicy!"

"They sell out early every night, so I had them set aside a crock just to be sure."

They ate in near silence, punctuated by slurping and Feddar's exclamations about the spice, the quality of the fish, and the fresh herbs. His enthusiasm added an extra flavor to the soup, which warmed Cloti to her core, though the tingle in her mouth after she finished was a bittersweet reminder of what had been lost. There were a few Maer food stalls left, catering to the humans and to the few Maer cooperative enough to have access to the city at large. But what about the hundreds of restaurants, stalls, and food carts that had kept the city bustling before the occupation? Most of those cooks were likely living in the camps, along with the bartenders, waiters, and cleanup staff who made the culinary engine of Kuppham run. They were no doubt working miracles with the rations afforded by the humans, but it was hard to imagine the foodie scene ever returning to its glory days, even if the humans packed up and left tomorrow.

"Is something wrong?" Feddar rested his chin on the bridge of his hands, fixing her with a worried look.

She smiled, her glass hovering just beneath her lips.

"I was just thinking about the food hall, the way it used to be, so crowded, so lively, with Maer lining up every night for that soup, along with a hundred other delicacies. And the restaurants and food carts, and all the Maer who used to run them. How most of them are in the camps now." Feddar's eyes fell to his bowl, and when he looked back up, they were glassy, as if he was about to cry. She reached out and took his hand, squeezing it gently, pushing down her own tears. "I'm sorry, I didn't mean to ruin the mood, it's just...the soup really hit me where I live."

"Cloti, you haven't ruined anything. It's we who wrecked it all. Me, and my gods-damned companions, and the king and his bloodthirsty advisors, not to mention the entire fucking army. They were itching for this fight, looking for any excuse. Cloti, I'm so sorry. You didn't deserve this." He pulled his hand back, covering his face, and when he picked up his wine glass again, his cheeks were streaked with tears.

"Our leaders bear just as much responsibility, Feddar. They pushed and they pushed and they pushed, thinking they could get the upper hand, thinking they were invincible, and now..." She trailed off, wanting this whole conversation to be over, wishing she could kiss the tears from his cheeks and forgive him. He hadn't done this; or rather, whatever he'd done, he'd paid for, hadn't he? She glanced at the acid burn on his face, imagining him strapped to a table in the Tower while Shoza tortured him for months on end.

"If there's anything I can do, any action, however big or small, that you think will help, I am ready." He downed the rest of his wine, wiping his tears with his napkin, and slid his hand into hers again. It was warm, still damp from his tears, and soft, so soft. She raised it to her lips and kissed it, and Feddar's eyes sparked with surprise.

"You could start by bringing us some dessert."

He smiled, his eyes flashing green and bright.

"I have just the thing."

Cloti sucked the last of the honey from the spoon, humming at the sweet, buttery aftertaste of the cakes.

"And you made this yourself?"

Feddar beamed. "I did. My mother sent me the honey and the flour, as crazy as that sounds, when she heard I was alive. She says wheat from the Eastern Plains makes all the difference, and the honey comes from my uncle's orchard."

"Well, thank you for sharing. It was delightful. I don't suppose she sent any of that honey wine, did she?"

"I kind of already drank that as soon as I got it. Sorry! There's some hotstone in the cabinet if that's of any interest."

"I wouldn't say no."

She watched as he weaved along the path through the garden, his step light and playful. She closed her eyes and lost herself in the burble of the fountains and the occasional patter of raindrops on the foliage. His footsteps sounded again, slower now, and she opened her eyes to see him carrying a leathered brass tray with a half-full bottle of hotstone and two tumblers. He poured them each a splash and raised his in a gesture she had seen the other humans do.

"To what shall we drink?" His voice and eyes danced with joy and wine.

"To a delightful evening, with the promise of much more to come."

His face flushed as they clinked, and the spicy burn of the hotstone spread through her, warming her chest and fanning her tamped-down desire. Feddar's eyes were soft in the candlelight, which showed his stubble in a thousand tiny points of shadow across his cheek. Cloti took another sip, and the warmth spread through her loins as his hand found hers across the table. The soft pads of his fingertips traced delicate lines across her palm.

She downed the rest of her glass, wincing against the fiery liquor, and Feddar drained his as well, breathing out through his nose in a satisfied way. She took his hand in hers, leaning forward to slide her fingers up the soft, hairless underside of his wrist.

"I like your skin," she said, pressing her fingers to feel his pulse running hot and strong just beneath the surface. "I want to see more of it."

Feddar's eyes dipped to her cleavage, then back up to her face. "I am yours in any way you would have me."

"I would have you in a more private location if such can be found."

"There…are some papers I need you to sign in my office before the first temple cycle, as it happens."

They carried glasses of hotstone into the office, which was much neater than when the Mayor had occupied it; the burnished darkwood of the desk was actually visible, with only a few neat stacks of papers and writing implements decorating it. The black leather sofa was likewise unencumbered, and Cloti lounged on it as Feddar sat ramrod straight in the chair and maneuvered several sheets of paper into the center of the desk.

"You really are an Administrator at heart," she said over the rim of her hotstone.

"I have to admit, it beats the job I had before." He shot her a wry smile, uncapping an ink pen and setting it atop one of the sheets. "You can sign here whenever you like."

Cloti stood, maneuvering next to Feddar, leaning into him with her breast as she hunched over the desk to examine the documents. One was in Maer, the other in Islish, which she could barely read.

"They say the same thing. Your husband did the translation himself."

"I trust you." She picked up the pen, signing where he indicated with his finger on both documents.

"Very good."

Feddar filed the papers back in their stacks, then stood up awkwardly as Cloti was half-draped over him. He took a half-step back into a corner where the desk met the wall, and she shadowed him, running her fingers lightly across his chest.

"Very good," she whispered, closing the distance slowly, watching his eyes melt, his lips part, his breath heady with hotstone and desire. She kissed him quickly, just a taste, pressing her hands into his chest, feeling his solid muscles beneath the silk. She took it more slowly this time, working his soft lips with hers as she undid the buttons of his shirt one by one. His tongue responded to hers, lavishing her with welcome, drawing her ever deeper. Her fingers spread out across his chest, so smooth it was almost obscene, broken up by little tufts and clouds of hair, especially around his nipples. He moaned into the kiss as her fingertips teased and circled, and he squeaked when she pinched him and held on for a long moment.

She pulled back from the kiss, gazing into Feddar's hot green eyes, then down at his pebbled pink nipples. He was nearly a head taller than she, and while she had to crane upward to kiss him, his chest was in easy striking range. Feddar gasped as she peeled aside the meager hair around one nipple and plastered her mouth to it. She sucked in long, hard pulses, holding his back as he arched into her with a groan. She slid one hand between his legs, finding him stiff as a broomstick beneath his trousers. She moved to suck the other nipple, gripping him firmly in her hand and holding him tightly without movement. Before long, Feddar's groan rose to a whine she knew all too well. She sucked harder, battering his nipple with her tongue, and when Feddar's breath got that desperate staccato cadence to it, she let go with her mouth and hands all at once. Feddar's eyes shot wide, his mouth stuck in an oval of astonishment. Cloti closed his mouth with her lips, kissing him through his trembling orgasm.

She stayed with him until his breath settled and his body relaxed. Their lips stuck together when they finally pulled apart from the kiss. Not once had his hands strayed from his sides. He looked down sheepishly at the wet spot on the front of his pants, and Cloti flashed him what she hoped was a reassuring smile.

"Maybe next time we can try that with your pants off."

Feddar flashed puppy-dog eyes when she refused his offer to stay the night, but he needed to be alone with his desire, and she needed her spouses and her bed. She planned to meditate at dawn, hoping to catch the mysterious pulse she'd felt that morning. She gave him a long, lingering goodnight kiss, smiling as she felt his hardness press against her through the clean pants he'd changed into. She leaned into it, cupping his face in her hands.

"I need you to do something for me."

"Anything."

If she'd asked him to drop to his knees and pleasure her with his tongue, he wouldn't have hesitated for a second, but as tempting as that thought was, she decided it would be better to make him wait to taste her.

"I don't mind if you touch yourself and think about me." She paused, kissing him once more. "In fact, I hope you will." Her hand slid down between his legs, tracing his rigid outline through the fabric. "But you mustn't spill until I see you again." She grabbed him tightly, and he gasped, his eyes wild and hot. She kissed him again, hard and deep, then released him suddenly and stepped back, relishing his palpable desperation.

"Do you promise?"

"I promise," he whispered.

She accepted his offer of an armed escort through the city streets, though she felt less safe with two human soldiers than she would have on her own. A few Maer trundled carts and schlepped bags of provisions, and groups of humans clustered outside the few bars and restaurants that were still open, with a handful of Maer among them, mostly sex workers. Everyone else was sequestered in their homes or hunkered down in the camps, whose fires she glimpsed in the distance as she climbed the hill toward Cliffside. The guards bid her a stiff goodnight once she passed the checkpoint into her neighborhood, and she breathed a sigh of relief when she finally passed through the door of her home.

Cloti slipped into bed behind Aefin, who was spooning Ludo, as usual. Aefin snuggled into her with a sleepy, contented hum, and Cloti wrapped her arm tight around them both.

5

—·—

S he woke at half dawn as usual, though she was somewhat groggy from the alcohol of the night before. It took her a little longer than usual to settle into her routine, but eventually, she brought her breathing under control and peeled away the layers of distraction one at a time. She poured herself into the pristine mental space at the center of her consciousness, settling like water in an underground lake. Darkness surrounded her, comforting in its apparent emptiness, though, in reality, it was anything but. It moved in slow waves, undulating, spreading through her. But what force was moving it? Was it the competing pull of the various points in time, space, and realities that created the motion?

A faint coppery thread struggled its way toward her from the depths of the blackness, familiar in its movements. She sent out a tendril of her own, weaving through the swirling currents, feeling the aura of the thread like a word on the tip of her tongue, present but inaccessible. She stretched herself as far as she could go without the Milk, and for an instant, she felt it, the pulse from the morning before. She sent a wave of welcome, but the tendril broke apart, coppery flakes dissipating in the ether, and was gone.

She studied the moment she'd felt the pulse, turning it over and over in her mind, seeing it from all angles. It came from a disciplined mind, one with training, but it was coded differently, and she didn't have enough information to decipher it. Perhaps it was one of the Free Maer; several tribes were known to travel the Thousand Worlds. She'd communed with one of them before, though it had taken some time to match patterns for a full exchange. She supposed it could have been a human who'd gotten hold of the Earth Milk, but if they'd drunk the Milk without training, they most likely would have gone mad. In any case, they certainly wouldn't have had the wherewithal to send a coherent message. She was certain this was a message if she only had a strong enough connection to tease it out. Tomorrow at dawn, she would be back, with the power of the Milk to guide her to the source.

Cloti took Aefin with her to the temple to bring candles and incense in preparation for the first cycle two days hence. The two human guards recognized Cloti by now, and they propped open the doors at her approach.

"Good afternoon," she said, stopping to bow to them.

They looked at each other, and one of them started to bow back but was stopped by the scowl of his partner.

"Good afternoon, ma'am," said the scowler, not without a hint of kindness.

The temple was cool in the way only hefty stone buildings can be, a welcome respite from the precocious summery heat. They arranged the candles around the dais and set the incense stands on either side of where Cloti would be sitting. There wasn't much else to do, so they sat across from each other and did a cycle. Aefin had fallen off her practice a bit, preferring to hit her tarpipe and paint or draw, and Cloti didn't blame her for finding her solace where she could. They hadn't talked about last night; it hung like mist between them, but Aefin joined Cloti with renewed purpose, and the temple amplified their energy. Their connection was immediate. They brushed aside their surface troubles to the core of love and support that had sustained them through the dark days of the occupation. They re-formed their emotional bonds, which the arrival of Feddar in Cloti's life had frayed somewhat. The smile they shared when they closed out the cycle felt like coming home.

A deep boom reverberated around the temple walls, coming from somewhere far in the distance but powerful enough to charge the air with its vibrations. Aefin fixed frightened eyes on Cloti, who forced calm into herself, then pushed it out toward Aefin. The guards in the doorway looked west, and after a brief and heated discussion, one of them ran off after a group of soldiers clanking through the streets in their steel armor. Cloti approached the doorway, and the guard held out his hand for her to stop.

"Not safe." His eyes were fixed on some point in the distance, which Cloti assumed must be smoke from the explosion.

"Are you saying you won't let us leave?" Aefin appeared at Cloti's shoulder, her tone sharper than Cloti would have liked.

"Not. Safe." The guard turned to face them now, one hand sliding to the hilt of his sword.

"There's no need." Cloti gestured toward his sword hand, then sent peace into him. He relaxed, staring at her hand as his dropped away from the hilt. "There's no danger. We can go now."

"There's no danger," he repeated as if reciting a lesson. "You can go now." He cocked his head as if realizing something for the first time, then stepped aside. "Good afternoon," he chirped as they passed through the doorway and out into the street.

A plume of thick gray smoke billowed out over the skyline, widening as it spread into the sky.

"The artificers' compound," Aefin said, stopping to squint at the smoke. "Retaliation for the assassination attempt, I bet."

"I hope they didn't kill anyone." Cloti's heart wrenched at the thought. She felt somehow responsible for saving Feddar, though things surely would have been worse if the attempt had been successful.

"Come. We'd better get home." Aefin took her hand tightly and stepped up her pace. They took the roundabout way home, avoiding the area around the compound, and arrived in time to see Ludo chopping fresh herbs onto a meager egg salad.

"Thank gods you're safe!" He wrapped them both in an herb-encrusted hug, holding them tight for a moment.

"We were far from danger," Cloti assured him, adding a kiss for good measure, which seemed to calm him considerably. "What's for dinner?"

"There was no fish left when the vendor got here, and no flatbread either," he said over his shoulder as he seasoned the salad and tossed it a few times. "But I did get these little crackers, which is better than nothing."

"Did you hear it?" Aefin hugged Ludo from behind, and he nodded.

"It seems the humans found a Shoza lab, and the Shoza blew it up, along with themselves and a dozen human soldiers."

"Oh gods, that's awful." Cloti hugged Ludo from the front, gripping Aefin's shoulders.

"They'll spin it as a terrorist attack," Aefin said.

"Not if I can help it." Ludo extricated himself from the group hug, dishing out the egg salad onto three plates and placing three long crackers on each one. He licked his fingers, then picked up the plates and headed toward the dining room, turning in the doorway to say, "Grab the water?"

They ate their little meal, which was surely better than what those in the camps were eating, though Cloti hadn't noticed anyone looking like they were starving. Ludo had a way with simple dishes, and the tang of mushroom vinegar balanced the richness of the eggs delightfully. When they'd cleaned out the bowls with their fingers, and the last crumbs of the crackers were gone, Ludo stood with a sigh.

"I've got to prepare a brief for an emergency meeting tonight. I have to leave at quarter-dusk. I hope Feddar can keep the military hotheads in check. They're going to be out for blood after this one."

"We'll clean up." Cloti gave Ludo a peck on the lips and gathered the plates. Aefin followed her into the kitchen with the rest of the dishes, where they washed and wiped everything as best they could with the limited water supply. The humans had promised to repair the aqueducts before summer, but if they'd made any progress, she hadn't heard of it. For now, they were stuck with one barrel a week, which was hardly enough for dishes and bucket baths. She missed having a hot shower or going down to the baths in town. She supposed she could go with Feddar's medallion, but there was no question of sharing a bath with a group of unknown humans, and unless Aefin and Ludo could go, it wouldn't be fair.

Aefin's hands slipped over Cloti's shoulders, massaging them lightly.

"I'm going to go upstairs and try to finish my drawing, but afterward, I was hoping you could tell me more about your night with Feddar." The expected disapproval in her voice had been replaced by something between jealousy and curiosity. "You've hardly said a word about it all day."

Cloti turned around, putting her arms around Aefin's hips to test the waters. Aefin angled in for a soft kiss, then pulled back, her eyes soft and bright.

"I didn't want to bring up a sore topic, but it was...nice."

"Did you kiss him?"

Cloti's ears burned as she imagined the feel of Feddar's mouth opening to hers, the inviting sweeps of his tongue. She nodded, licking her lips. Aefin's eyes softened further, and she kissed Cloti again, with a little more heat this time. She was always more amorous when Cloti came back from a tryst, eager to taste the echoes of her lover's warmth.

"Did you do more?" Aefin breathed between kisses, her hands roaming over Cloti's backside, lifting her cheeks, pressing their bodies together.

"A little. I—" Cloti's breath caught as Aefin's hand rounded her thigh and slipped between her legs, pressing her against the counter and holding her with steady pressure.

"Did you fuck him?" Aefin squeezed harder, and Cloti pushed her hand down gently. Aefin's grip softened, sliding around to her hips, then up her body to her face, which she held tenderly as her kisses petered out.

"I'm sorry," Aefin said in a thick voice, touching foreheads with Cloti. "I have no right to be jealous, or mad, or anything. I just—"

"You have every right to feel whatever you feel." Cloti kissed Aefin's forehead, her nose, and her mouth, which was hot and wet and soft, and she suddenly wanted it all over her body. "But no, I didn't fuck him."

Aefin's mouth hitched into a half-smile. "What exactly did you do, then?"

"I could tell you, but wouldn't it be more fun if I showed you?" She touched her forehead, then Aefin's, in the unspoken symbol they had for the Earth Milk. Ludo would be off working late, and they'd have the whole night to themselves. They hadn't gotten to play like this in quite a while, and as stressful as their day had been, they deserved it.

"I'll see you upstairs in a little while then." Aefin kissed her once more with enough heat that Cloti wondered if she was going to skip the drawing and take her right there on the counter. Aefin finally broke from the kiss, breath heavy and eyes dancing, and spun out of the room.

Cloti felt Aefin's presence before she heard her. She continued transcribing one of her poems into her coded script, pretending not to notice. When the floor squeaked right behind her chair, Cloti set the pen in the inkwell and tented her fingers.

"Take three steps back," she said, and the squeaky floor announced Aefin's compliance. She rose from her chair and turned around to see Aefin standing with dark, glassy eyes, barefoot in her pink silk slip. Cloti let her eyes roam over Aefin's figure, which the slip enhanced to perfection, outlining her thick nipples and slinking down her hips. Cloti wanted to go to her, press her against the wall, and take her hot and fast as she had Feddar, but Aefin wanted something more.

Cloti uncorked the vial of Earth Milk, which was almost empty. She'd have to make more soon, but that would require firing up the alchemical stove, which she hadn't done since lockdown, as it might draw attention. Aefin sat on the bed and folded her hands in her lap, her lips poised to take the dram spoon Cloti held out. She'd filled it a little over halfway; Aefin didn't need much to form the connection, and Cloti would be the one doing the bulk of the sharing work. Aefin's eyes went glassy, and her posture took that sensual curve Cloti knew so well. Cloti took a full dram, and the foul taste of the Milk soon dissolved as Aefin's hot, desperate mouth found hers.

They drifted to the bed, wrapped in each other's arms like seaweed. Cloti pushed out the image of Feddar leaning over the fountain, of her kissing him in the courtyard, then in the study. Aefin's lips and tongue explored Cloti's mouth, her ears, and her neck, working her way down as Cloti shared what she'd done with Feddar. Aefin devoured her body, stripping her gown as she went, licking and sucking, fingers teasing their way through her wetness. Cloti gasped as Aefin straddled her, throwing her arms above her head and plundering her nipples with her mouth as her hand gripped Cloti tightly between the legs as she had Feddar. Her pleasure rose as Feddar's had, faster and harder than it ever should have with only the deep pressure of Aefin's hand and the relentless battering of her lips and tongue.

As she felt her pleasure cresting, Aefin's lips and hand released suddenly, just as Cloti had done to Feddar. A devilish grin spread on Aefin's face as Cloti's orgasm started to ebb.

"Please," Cloti whispered, gripping Aefin's wrist tightly.

Aefin's eyes darkened as she lowered between Cloti's legs, and soon the hard sweeps of her tongue flushed away Cloti's desperation, carrying her to new heights of pleasure. She locked Aefin in with her thighs and fingers threaded through her hair, not letting go until she'd exhausted her muscles and her voice with wave after wave of ecstasy. She shared her sensations with Aefin, whose muffled voice joined hers as their orgasms flowed together in a foamy tide of slowly receding bliss.

They lay entangled, slick and matted with sex and sweat, breath intermingling between soft kisses. The edges of their minds overlapped like waves crossing on the beach; hazy feelings, stray thoughts, sleepy contentment. Aefin's jealousy had turned to full-blown curiosity, but streaks of concern remained.

"Do you think Ludo is in a meeting with him right now?" Aefin asked in the dim candlelight. Cloti blew air through her lips and shook her head.

"Could be. Who even knows what he does? It must be weird, spending so much time in rooms full of humans."

"Not any weirder than sucking a human's nipples and making him spill in his pants."

Cloti's own snort-laugh surprised her, and Aefin's cackle echoed off the walls of their bedroom.

"Touché. But I guess that's why he trusts Feddar. He's seen him up close in those meetings. He's seen how he fights for us." Cloti rolled onto her side to face Aefin. "And the temple, Aefin. If he makes that happen after everything else, surely that must mean something?"

"It means he'll do anything it takes to get in your pants."

Cloti's anger rushed into her ears. "That's not why he's doing it, Aef. He offered before—"

"I know. I'm sorry." Aefin reached out a hand toward Cloti's cheek, but she turned away from it. "I just want you to consider the possibility—just the *possibility*—that the humans aren't planning on going anywhere. And shit, maybe Feddar truly believes they are! Maybe he's just as much of a fool as you and Ludo! Maybe you're all just deluded that this nightmare will ever come to an end." Her voice broke into muffled sobs as her hands covered her face. Cloti put a gentle arm over her shoulder.

Aefin rolled against her neck, face warm and damp with tears, arms clutched tight to her body. Cloti held her, nuzzling her forehead, sending soothing waves through their mindlink. Aefin's body relaxed a little, melting against Cloti, one arm wrapping around her hip. A brief thought of Ludo flitted through her mind, poring over his notebooks and papers as the humans shouted and argued. She banished the thought as Aefin gave a great shaking sigh and her breath steadied into its sleep rhythm. Cloti sank into her warmth and drifted off, clearing her mind of everything except for this moment, this Maer in her arms.

6

The greenhouse was still ripe with the heat from the day before, and Cloti worked quickly, touching the long spoon to the ooze gently so the tiniest smear stuck to the bronze. When she had closed the containment vessel and removed her protective gear, she licked the spoon clean, fighting off the wave of nausea that swept over her whenever she tasted it. She exited the greenhouse, locking it behind her as her mind swam with the first flush of the ooze, so much purer than the bottled Earth Milk. She made it into position on her mat, and the Thousand Worlds came rushing in, and she into them. She felt the faraway pulse like a spider sensing a fly in its web, and she shot across the worlds toward it. She surrounded it and cradled it within her until its shape and frequency took on voice. The words were strange, familiar but inverted somehow, but when she turned them inside out, she could hear the repeated message clearly:

On Solstice dawn, the walls come down, and the path to freedom is open.

She formed words with her mind, then inverted them, and sent her response:

We will make ready.

Whoever it was must have received her words, for the message stopped for a time before repeating itself several times, then went silent.

Cloti floated in the Thousand Worlds, pondering who had sent the message and what she had agreed to make ready for. She had a month to figure it out, but in the meantime, she had her first temple cycle since before the invasion to prepare for. She cleared her mind and let the Worlds flow through her like laundry billowing in a summer breeze.

Aefin padded in while Cloti was making tea, her hair disheveled and her sleep-wrinkled slip draping appealingly over her body. She pressed into Cloti, wrapping her arms around her belly, and hummed into the nape of her neck.

"Good morning, love. Cup of tea?"

"Mmm." Aefin clung to her as she poured two cups, and she smiled as she focused on not spilling a drop of the weak, re-steeped tea. Aefin's hands slipped away to take the cup, and she sat sideways on her chair, her bleary morning eyes gazing into Cloti's.

"I love you, Cloti."

Cloti's heart trilled in her chest, and she took Aefin's warm hand in hers.

"I love you too." They didn't say it often enough.

"Ludo still not back?"

Aefin sipped her tea, giving her head a little shake. "I guess they pulled an all-nighter."

"Gods, how dreadful! He's going to be a mess today."

"I'll make sure of that." Aefin's eyes sparkled behind her teacup.

"Well, look at you, all raring and ready to go. I love to see it."

"You got me good last night." Aefin set down her cup, staring down into the steam. "I still have some hesitations, but…" Her eyes were hungry when she looked back up. "I trust you. So if you trust him, and Ludo trusts him, maybe—" She stopped as voices sounded from outside. The door opened, and Ludo's voice rang out.

"It's not a palace, but it more than suits our needs. Come, I smell tea. Fancy a cup?"

"I can think of nothing I'd fancy more, in fact. I—"

Ludo entered the room, and Feddar stood in the doorway, his half-open mouth stretching into a smile as his eyes fell upon Cloti, warming her to her core.

"Cloti you know, of course, and I believe you and Aefin have met?"

"Briefly." Feddar bowed, and Cloti rose to bow back. Aefin's shock reached her in a sudden burst. "It's a pleasure to see you, Aefin. Cloti." He nodded to them in turn. "I'm sorry to burst in on you while you're still having your morning tea."

"Not at all." Cloti brushed Aefin on the shoulders as she went to pour Feddar a cup, feeling Aefin's annoyance in that brief moment of touch. "I'll have to make some more for you, Ludo. Feddar, do you take honey?"

"I'm from Gheil. It runs through my veins!" His smile faltered as if he'd realized how it had come out, but he recovered quickly. "Thank you." His hand touched Cloti's as he took the cup, sending a little electric charge through her.

"I'll make nutbread," Aefin said, rising from her chair. Cloti noticed Feddar's eyes flitting to Aefin's figure for a moment, then darting away. "But first, I'm going to put on something less wrinkled."

"I'm sure Feddar doesn't mind." Cloti pushed out a tendril of warmth to Aefin, but it bounced back as she hurried out of the room. Ludo threw himself onto a chair, laying his head on the table. Cloti put more water on to boil, observing Feddar out of the corner of her eye as he watched her work.

"I trust everything went well?" she said as cheerily as she could manage.

Ludo sat up with a gruff laugh. "If by that you mean it ended without further recriminations, then yes. But things are on a knife's edge at the moment. Thank gods we've got Feddar on our side."

"The temple cycles will go forward." Feddar sat down heavily, sipping his tea and smacking his lips. A flood of relief washed over Cloti as she poured a cup of tea for Ludo. "The General insisted on a military presence inside the temple, but as it happens, I still have my rank from my days with the service, so he agreed to let me play the role." He looked at Cloti with apologetic but hopeful eyes. "If that is acceptable?"

"Our practice is open to all those who wish to partake." She knew some would not be comfortable with a human in their midst, but better that than no practice, and better Feddar than some unknown soldier. "But may I ask why a military presence is required at a meditation cycle?"

"The Shoza, love." Aefin sat down in front of her tea, dressed in a purple robe that cinched tight around the waist. A whiff of muskwood reached Cloti's nose, and she smiled into her cup. "They think the Shoza will use the cycles as a way to organize."

Feddar closed his eyes and nodded. "I tried to convince him it wasn't necessary since the cycles are generally silent, are they not?" Cloti nodded. Feddar didn't know that communication was possible without words in the temple. "But that was his sticking point, and I had no real leverage to resist, so here we are."

"I assure you his worries are misplaced, but thank you. I appreciate your efforts on our behalf."

"Cloti tells me you practice?" Aefin's tone was polite, but there was something beneath it Cloti couldn't quite grasp.

Feddar shook his head. "A little. One of the guards in the Tower taught me. I feel like we could all use it right now, though, with all that's going on."

An idea sparked in Cloti's mind. "Would you join us in a short cycle, Feddar? It might help clear your mind from your night's endeavors."

"Absolutely, though I'm not sure if I really know what I'm doing."

"As long as you don't talk, you'll be fine." Ludo winked at Cloti.

"You should join us too, love." Ludo rarely practiced, but he couldn't well refuse a cycle with the Administrator. Cloti hoped it would help bring them all a little closer together, which might bode well for her eventual plan of bringing Feddar into their bed.

"Sure. Why not? I could use something to keep all this diplomatic language at bay for a while." He set down his cup and lowered his hands to his sides.

Cloti glanced at Aefin, who blinked and gave a small nod, then lowered her hands as well.

"So...right here at the table?" Feddar's voice trailed off as he finished.

Cloti nodded, pushing out a gentle wave of comfort. Feddar glanced around at the others, then let his hands fall to his sides.

"Floor cycles are more traditional, but I like to mix in practice with the little domestic moments as well." She lowered her arms and closed her eyes slowly enough to see that Feddar did the same. She searched for an appropriate verse to begin, and a line appeared in her mind from a poem she'd transcribed the day before.

"There is order to Chaos, though we see it not."

She gathered her energy in the tips of her fingers and sent out little tendrils to each of them. Aefin linked to hers right away, and Feddar joined her with a whiff of surprise. It took a little longer for Ludo to make the connection, as he seldom practiced, but Cloti wove their energies together, teasing Aefin's slowly toward Feddar. Ludo and Feddar's bond was strong, and she briefly wondered if their evening might have included something beyond diplomacy. Cloti smiled as Aefin's energy cozied up to Feddar, who was positively humming with enthusiasm at the experience.

She gave the bonds a moment to cement themselves, then moved her arms slowly upwards, feeling the group moving with her, though they were a little out of sync at first. They clicked about halfway up, and by the time their hands were pressed together above their heads, their energies commingled as comfortably as if they'd been practicing together for years. Feddar's strength drew Ludo in, which had always been a struggle, and Aefin seemed to have shed her mistrust of Feddar, at least for the moment. Cloti imagined the chaos of the Thousand Worlds, the infinity of swirling blackness, the points of light scattered throughout, and she shared with the others. Their bond stretched and tightened as they drifted together, spinning slowly like four spokes on a wheel. She let them spin as they floated, without direction, through the space between worlds.

She felt Ludo's energy flagging, and she pulled her hands apart and began the slow descent. She let their bond dissipate little by little, so by the time their hands fell to their sides, only a faint warmth remained between them. She kept them in that warmth for a long moment, then opened her eyes.

Feddar's wide-eyed smile sent a spark to Cloti's heart.

"Thank you so much for including me." He took Cloti's hand, then Ludo took his. Aefin hesitated, then reached across the table to wrap her hand around his and Cloti's.

"I'm glad you joined us, and I'm glad you'll be joining us tomorrow at the first temple cycle." She pulled her hand back, and Ludo and Aefin did the same.

"I wouldn't miss it." Feddar looked at each of them, his face tense as if he had something he wanted to ask.

"What is it?" Cloti asked.

Feddar covered a little laugh with his hand. "Well, I was thinking, if it's not too bold, I'd like to invite the three of you over for dinner tomorrow night. I'm told the reds are running in the lake right now, and I make a mean grilled red."

Every hair on Cloti's body tingled at the invitation, and she felt Aefin's yes even before she spoke.

"That would be lovely, Feddar," Aefin said smoothly. "We'll bring salad and goldeneye roots from our garden."

"And I've squirreled away a bottle of thirty-year-old hotstone I've been keeping for a special occasion."

"Ludo!" Aefin whacked his arm. "We made a vow to be honest with each other *at all times.*"

"You would have drunk it all!"

"Isn't that what thirty-year-old hotstone is for?"

"That all sounds delightful." Feddar yawned, then blinked a few times and pushed himself to stand. "But if you will excuse me, I've got to go meet with the camp chief now, then go home and collapse. See you tomorrow at the temple, then?"

Cloti stood, wishing she could go to him and kiss him, but she didn't want to push anything. She bowed to him, and Aefin and Ludo followed suit, then Ludo shook his hand, human-style.

When Feddar was gone, the three of them sat quietly sipping their now-cold tea, each lost in their own thoughts, but Cloti detected a hint of a smile on both their faces.

7

Cloti used a dab of ooze to find the pulse the next morning, which was easy now that she was familiar with the signature. She detected the same message:

On Solstice dawn, the walls come down, and the path to freedom is open.

She'd turned the pulse over and over in her head in odd moments, and she'd come to the conclusion that it must have been one of the Shoza who'd been out with the army when it had been routed. Some had been killed, and others had returned to blend in with the population, but many were thought to have vanished into the hills to find a way to fight the occupation from the outside. Solstice was twenty-one days away, which was not much time for whatever they had in mind. She'd long avoided having any contact with the Shoza, and though Ludo would probably have connections, she didn't want to endanger him with this.

Who should I tell?

There was a long pause, then a response came:

We are among you. Look, and you shall find.

The connection dissipated, and she tucked away her annoyance and let herself stretch out, thoughtless, into the Thousand Worlds. She imagined herself in the temple, surrounded by a hundred acolytes, their collective energy filling the high dome and encompassing them all. Feddar was there, Aefin, and even Ludo, faces among the many, stars in the galaxy. They were all one. Everything was one. And then they were gone, and only the swirling blackness remained, surrounding her like a cocoon. She rested in this support and enjoyed a long moment of peace.

Aefin walked with Cloti to the temple after breakfast, shadowed by several humans who reminded her of Shoza in their dress and how they carried themselves. Ludo stayed behind to do some paperwork, promising to meet them there. There were eight guards outside the temple this time, including the two regulars, who greeted them and opened the doors while the other six stood watching the street.

"I hate seeing them out there," Aefin said under her breath as they crossed the airy space. "It feels like they're defiling the temple."

"There's nothing to defile, love. It's just a place, and the Maer inside it are all that matter." She touched Aefin's face, and Aefin kissed her palm.

Cloti went through a standing cycle while Aefin hung flowers from their garden on the pillars, goldeneyes and cupflowers and wild sage adding color and fragrance to the temple's stillness. One of the guards leaned into the doorway and gestured, and Cloti joined Aefin at the door.

A group of armored soldiers led a parade of acolytes through the streets, each carrying one of Cloti's coins. Many had wildflowers in their hair and beards, and as the soldiers parted, Juiya pressed her hands to her forehead, smiling at Cloti with eyes near tears. Cloti repeated her gesture, bowing to each of the acolytes as they entered, a seemingly endless line of Maer filling the space with positive energy that was almost palpable. Some she recognized from her public practices, and other faces were new to her, but with each new soul entering the temple, her heart expanded until she feared her chest could no longer contain it. Feddar entered last, pressing hands to his forehead as the others had done, and Cloti showed him no different treatment than any of the others. She knew some would be watching, and she needed them to accept him as just another one of them.

The acolytes sat on the mats, which Aefin had spaced around the temple so no one was sitting too close to one another to minimize the risk of spreading Ulver's cough. Feddar had told her all those leaving the camps would be scanned for fever, but that was not a guarantee. Juiya sat directly in front of Cloti, a serene smile on her face, and the closest circle was filled with the other acolytes she knew best. Aefin lit the incense, small cones to add ambiance without overwhelming the senses, then took her seat a few rows back. Ludo arrived shortly thereafter, lowering himself awkwardly and beaming at Cloti. He had only come to a temple cycle once, on Aefin's insistence, but his face glowed with rejuvenated energy. Feddar sat on the mat nearest the door, eyes closed and arms at his sides.

The temple was silent once the rustle of cloaks and mats had died down. Cloti stood on the dais, pressing her hands to her chest and turning in a slow circle to look upon every face for a moment. She lowered herself to sit cross-legged, facing the sunlit rectangle of the open doors, which offered a convenient focal point for her mind. She closed her eyes and felt a hundred pairs of lids flutter shut. She sat in silence, letting the stillness of the temple and the whiffs of incense and flowers envelop her, then spoke.

"The world is in us, and we in it."

She kept her hands pressed together, letting the energy build within her until it suffused her body. She lowered her arms, her fingers brushing the cool marble floor, and let her mind drift like the smoke from the incense toward those closest to her. Juiya and the others in the innermost circle were the first to connect, their energies commingling and bonding in a taut ring. They pushed out together to the next circle and the next until a hundred hearts and minds were linked in stillness and concentration, boosted by the temple's harmonic architecture. Cloti lifted her fingers from the stone and began the slow upward curve, letting her mind flow and pool in each individual consciousness like water trickling down over leaves. Each received her in their own way, some with peace, others with joy, and her arms felt strong as the collective energy lifted them toward the ceiling with calm purpose.

One mind gave her pause, presenting an unyielding surface like a waxy leaf she could not penetrate. Though no one was required to share anything they did not wish, this resistance suggested a level of discipline beyond what most were capable of. She shrugged it off, letting the group's momentum bring her hands together above her head. The pressure that built in this shared gesture opened a communal space, and she painted the image that had dominated her meditations of late: the leaf on the lake, the trees on the water, the sky between the trees. Every mind went flat like the lake's mirrored surface, and she floated on that effortless tension, free from gravity, movement, and thought. In time, she inverted her mind to become the lake, with each acolyte a single leaf balanced on her glassy surface. She became the sky and the trees, the reflections on the water, the cool, crisp air. The moment stretched on beyond time, space, or consciousness. All was one.

She let her fingertips peel apart one at a time, then her palms, feeling the group's collective exhale as she began the slow descent of her arms, the gradual loosening of bonds. A slight ping caught her attention, one mind distinct from the others, somehow familiar, and she captured its outline in her memory so she would recognize it if she felt it again. By the time her knuckles touched the smooth stone once again, she realized what had drawn her attention to that signature. It was almost the same as the pulse she'd been feeling at dawn. A Shoza, one with training, though the features of their discipline were tighter and more controlled than the rest of her acolytes. She opened her eyes and felt their presence behind her. She did not dare turn around to identify the face, but she was sure if she were close to them, she could recognize them in an instant.

"Thank you all for joining me in this common journey." She pressed her hands together at her forehead, and the room filled with the sound of a hundred cloaks rustling as all repeated her gesture.

"We will practice here every midday, gods willing. You may keep your coin and return tomorrow or pass it on to another in need of a cycle. In time, I hope to re-forge the bonds between everyone in this great city so we can once again know unity and peace. Spread the word and go with stillness in your hearts."

Cloti circulated through the temple as the acolytes stood, talking quietly amongst themselves. She greeted those she knew and many she didn't until she felt the mind she'd sensed during practice. Cloti turned and bowed to the Maer, whose robe could not hide her muscled physique. The Maer bowed in response, her eyes showing she had noticed Cloti's attentions.

"Thank you for joining our cycle."

"It is an honor. Your practice has helped me through many challenging times."

"Your mental discipline is an inspiration. Perhaps you could lead a cycle someday."

"I believe my path lies elsewhere, but I am humbled by the suggestion."

"We must all follow where our heart leads us." Cloti studied the Maer's sharp eyes, the tight braid of her hair, and her trim beard. There was no doubt she was Shoza. "What is your name?"

"Gielle." She blinked as she said it, glancing toward Feddar, who stood just inside the door talking with Ludo. She continued in a voice just above a whisper. "I am in sector seventeen, Riverside, in case you ever need anything."

"I will not forget, and I hope to see you again soon."

"Either I or one like me will join you in every cycle." Gielle fixed her with serious eyes that made Cloti a little uncomfortable. "From now until Solstice dawn." The hair on Cloti's neck bristled at the phrase, but she kept her surface calm.

"Go in peace." They exchanged bows, then Gielle joined the others, who were filing out the doors, where two lines of human soldiers stood on either side, forming a funnel of shining steel. When the last of the acolytes had left the temple, Feddar glanced at Aefin and Ludo, then at Cloti. He hovered in the doorway for a moment, and she moved close enough to speak.

"Thank you, Administrator, for joining our practice. You are welcome any time."

"I shall return, for I have much to learn from you." His face quirked into a smile as he bowed, then turned and followed the procession out into the bright sunlight, back toward the camps.

"That seemed to go well." Ludo approached cautiously, knowing she liked her space after a cycle. She reached out her hand and took his, and he pulled her in for a gentle embrace. She sank into him, suddenly exhausted, and his hand clasped around her neck.

"It did," she said into his beard, tears flowing through the hair on her face. She felt Aefin's breath on her ear and Ludo's arms wrapped around them both as they stood in the empty temple with whiffs of incense and flowers filling the air.

Cloti watched Aefin put on her earrings, the dangly ones with little stars hanging inside crescent moons, then dab a little muskwood on her chest and underarms. She wore a curve-hugging dress that showed off her tight behind to great effect. Cloti sidled up close to her, sliding her hands from Aefin's hips down to her backside and squeezing gently.

"You look good enough to eat." She nuzzled Aefin's neck, the scent of soap and muskwood bringing up a tingle of desire. "You smell good too. I wonder if anyone will get close enough to notice?"

"That's your job tonight." She turned around with the bottle of muskwood, pressing her finger to the bottle and turning it upside down. She smiled as she touched her finger to Cloti's face, her neck, and her chest, then tipped the bottle again. She raised Cloti's robe and ran her finger up her inner thighs, slipped it inside her underwear, then tapped her gently between the legs. Cloti grabbed Aefin's hips and thrust against her, pushing her against the vanity as she pressed in for a kiss. Aefin greeted her with open lips and an eager tongue, and they made out like teenagers, hands roaming over each other's bodies. They did not stop when Ludo's footsteps sounded in the hall and stopped in the doorway; if anything, Aefin kissed her more ferociously, gripping her behind with both hands and pulling her in even tighter. Cloti pulled back and looked over her shoulder at Ludo, who was leaning against the doorframe, hands in his pockets, a sly smile on his face.

"Don't stop on my account."

"You should probably save some for later," Aefin said, her gaze intense, and she moved in to kiss Cloti once more, then let her hands slide off her.

"As should you." Ludo's eyes were fixed on Aefin, who covered her mouth with her hand in pretend modesty. "It's been a while since I had you all to myself."

"It's been a while since I strapped you to the bed and made you cry out my name, too."

Cloti smirked, and Feddar's eyebrows raised toward the thick mop of curls he'd grown since the grooming salons had closed down.

"Ooh, maybe I should stay home after all. This sounds like fun."

"I think you need to do some further investigation into Feddar's qualities." Aefin tucked a stray lock of hair behind Cloti's ear and kept her hand pressed against her cheek. "There's only so much you can tell about a person without sleeping with them."

Cloti blinked a silent thanks, clutching Aefin's wrist for a moment.

"I've got the goldeneye roots washed and scrubbed, and I see the salad's all chopped and ready to go." Ludo's voice was chipper; he was clearly as excited as anyone about the invitation.

"What about that bottle of hotstone you so conveniently forgot to tell me we had?" Aefin shot Ludo a faux angry look.

"The perfect party gift for a personal dinner with the most important public figure in the city."

Cloti covered her face with her hand; Ludo's obsession with transactional diplomacy often bordered on the maddening.

"Ludo, you're standing in front of the most important public figure in the city." Aefin put her hands on Cloti's shoulders and turned her to face Ludo directly. His face fell with regret, and he crossed the room to kneel before Cloti in a gesture of surprising genuineness.

"You are...so right." He glanced at Aefin and blinked, then took Cloti's hand and looked up into her eyes. "What you did today, what you started, I could *feel* the temple buzzing with energy, like the air after a lightning strike. What you're doing is incredible. *You're* incredible."

Cloti bit her lip to push back her tears, but surrounded by such an abundance of love and support, there was no reason not to let them flow. She lifted Ludo's hands, and he stood, bumping his forehead against hers, clutching her fingers in his. Aefin's hand slipped between them, and she draped herself over Cloti's shoulder. The familiar smell of their bodies was a bond as strong as any they'd shared in practice; the tang of Ludo's breath, the muskwood, the taste of Aefin's lips lingering on hers. No one spoke as they stood, still as statues. Breathing together. Being together.

8

— · —

The smell of wood smoke greeted them as they walked onto the patio. Feddar stood tending the grill, a glass of wine in his hand, wearing a bright yellow shirt and black pants. Tinkly music played from a little box on a bench beside the grill, and Feddar's head bobbed in time with the music. He turned around as they made their way through the curving path, raising his glass in their direction.

"Thank you so much for coming!" He set his glass down and bowed with hands pressed at his chest. The movement was so smooth and practiced he would have seemed like a Maer if it weren't for the skin on his face and the wide V revealed by his half-unbuttoned shirt, showing dangerous wisps of curly black hair. Cloti returned his gesture, then closed the distance and gave him a quick peck on the lips. He held her eyes, his expression surprised and joyous, then picked up a bottle and poured three glasses.

"I trust a little wine wouldn't be unwelcome?"

They clinked and drank, exchanging pleasantries as Feddar stirred the coals. He and Ludo got into a serious discussion about how best to roast the goldeneye roots, and Cloti nudged Aefin as she noticed Ludo repeatedly touching Feddar on the arm.

"It seems I'm not the only one with a case of skin fever."

Aefin giggled, slipping her hand around Cloti's waist as she sipped her wine.

"I'm going to have to drag him away."

"You can be very persuasive."

They drank their wine and admired the garden until Feddar and Ludo had seasoned and oiled the roots and put them on the edge of the grill, which hissed and flared up. They danced around with their tongs, scooching the roots farther to the edge, then shook their hands and laughed.

"You boys need any help?"

"No, I think we've got it under control," Feddar said, wiping his sweaty forehead with the back of his hand. "The fire's a little hotter than I thought. We'll have to wait a bit before we put the fish on, or it'll burn." He gestured toward a tray on which four foot-long reds lay prepped and stuffed with herbs and chunks of garlic.

"A perfect opportunity to break open that bottle of hotstone." Aefin picked up the bottle and pried off the cork, which came loose with a deep *whump*. She poured them each two fingers in the glass tumblers Feddar had set out, and Feddar raised his human style, and they all did the same.

"To friendship."

"And more," Cloti added.

Feddar's eyes sparkled as he clinked with each of them, and they drank.

"Oh, gods, thank you so much for holding onto this, Ludo." Aefin leaned into him, sneaking in a kiss between sips.

"I was just waiting for the right occasion, and I can't think of a better one than this." He raised his glass, and they took another sip. The hotstone was smooth and smoky, with a spicy aftertaste and almost no sweetness at all.

"This…is…spectacular." Feddar held the tumbler beneath his nose and closed his eyes, then took another tiny sip. "Human whiskey can't hold a candle to this."

"It's the mountain limestone." Ludo held his glass up to the brightstone light above the grill. He started holding forth about the whiskey, and Cloti made a game of trying to distract Feddar, who was nodding and smiling at Ludo while sneaking glances at her.

"Did you want to turn those goldeneyes?" Aefin commented drily, smirking as Feddar picked up his tongs and moved the partially blackened roots onto another part of the fire.

"Sorry, I've never cooked these before. They smell amazing."

"We pulled them this morning." Aefin set down her empty tumbler and poured another finger in, winking at Ludo. She held out the bottle, but no one else had finished theirs yet. Cloti's heart warmed as she noticed Aefin standing closer to Feddar, laughing at his little jokes and even touching him on the shoulder as she switched from whiskey to wine. Feddar played the host well, bouncing the conversation off each of them even as he spread out the coals and put the fish on the grill. By the time they sat down to eat, they were all talking loudly and laughing like a group of old friends, spurred on by the alcohol and the cozy, leafy environs.

"Feddar, these are cooked to perfection." Cloti closed her eyes as the rich, succulent flesh melted in her mouth. "And is that purslane I detect?"

"Yes! And mint. It's how we cook silvers back home." His face fell for a moment, and Cloti could feel his regret.

They ate every scrap of the fish, along with the goldeneyes, which were a bit crispy but still tasty, and the salad with its tangy stainberry vinaigrette. They finished the bottle of wine, and the hotstone came back out, though Cloti took only the tiniest bit, and she noticed Feddar holding back as well. His eyes were bright, and his face filled with smiles as he talked with Ludo and Aefin, but his glances at Cloti had a softer tone. She could feel his want, taste it almost, and she longed to put her hands on his soft skin and make him tremble for her.

Feddar served them more of the honey cakes for dessert, and Ludo yawned as he licked the last bit of honey from his spoon.

"Don't you poop out on me," Aefin said, pushing his shoulder. "You've got to walk me home and keep me company tonight." Her eyes flickered to Cloti, her mouth twisting into a half-smile. "And we don't want to keep these two apart any longer."

Feddar's face flushed, his eyes bright with bewilderment and booze. Cloti let her hand slide atop his, which was hot to the touch. The warmth flowed from her fingers throughout her body, which tingled with anticipation. She could hardly concentrate as Ludo and Aefin made their excuses, exchanging human-style hugs with Feddar. Cloti kissed them both, feeling Ludo's approval, the teasing almost-jealousy in Aefin's eyes.

And then they were gone. Feddar and Cloti stood in the sitting room, the house suddenly quiet, the weight of their aloneness taking a moment to sink in.

"Your spouses are lovely." Feddar leaned against the back of a couch, his eyes distant, his brow slightly furrowed.

"I've wondered if you'd find our arrangement...peculiar. I don't know if humans..."

"Not as a rule, no. Which is a shame, really, because what you have is so..." His hands seemed to search for the words in the air, then fell against his thighs as his eyes returned to hers. "So beautiful."

Cloti's heartbeat slowed in that instant, and a smile spread unbidden across her face.

"It doesn't bother you, then?"

"No no no, not at all! I love it!"

She stepped toward him, walking slowly so her hips swiveled with each step.

"You seem to find them both attractive."

Feddar swallowed, nodding vigorously. "Yes, I mean, of course, I—" He stopped talking as her fingers trailed up his arms and she moved in slowly for a kiss, stopping just short, feeling his breath on her face, his heat radiating into her.

"If things go the way I hope, maybe someday I'll bring you home to join them." She closed her eyes and kissed him, feeling his arousal and confusion and a little twinge of shame. "But tonight, you're all mine." She kissed him again, more deeply this time, but still slowly, savoring his tender lips, his agile tongue, his strong hands on her waist. She slipped her fingers inside his shirt, running them across his chest, shocking smooth skin over lean muscle, nipples pebbling beneath her fingertips.

"I want to be all yours," he whispered between kisses.

Feddar stood before her in the bedroom, clothes pooled at his feet, eyes soft and deep green in the candlelight. She stepped close to him, letting her fingers brush against his hardness, which leapt at her touch. She ran her fingertips up his stomach, tracing the thick pink scar that ran neatly across his body, then slid her hands up to heft his smooth pectorals. She massaged his chest, feeling him poke against her stomach, smiling at the liquid desperation in his eyes. She put her hands around his throat, rough with stubble closer to his face, and angled in for a kiss that was as soft as it was brief. She kept one hand around his throat and let the other roam down across his body, her fingers feathering across his nipples, then following the trail of thickening hair leading below his waist. She grabbed him firmly and held tight, kissing away his gasp, devouring his lips, and sucking his tongue into her mouth as she tightened her grip. A whine rose in his throat, and she stopped the kiss, loosening her hold on his neck, cradling him gently as he throbbed against her hand.

"Did you think about me when you touched yourself last night?" she whispered into his mouth.

"I did." His lips found hers, and she let him kiss her for a moment before pulling back.

"Did you keep your promise? Not to spill?"

He nodded, his eyes soft and pained, and she let him kiss her again, just for a moment.

"Good boy." She let go and took a step back, and Feddar gasped, hands clenched at his sides. "I want you to undress me now."

Feddar licked his lips as he looked her up and down, then stepped toward her. His fingers found the buttons on the front of her dress and undid them deftly. A fire rose within her as he pulled the dress open and slid it off her shoulders.

"You can touch me if you like."

Feddar's eyes bored into hers as his hands ran up her arms and over her shoulders, squeezing gently, then slid down her chest, running the backs of his knuckles over her stiff nipples. His hands moved to her hips, then down her thighs, rubbing her hair the wrong way as he moved them back up, then smoothing it on the way down. She put two fingers under his chin and pulled him in for a kiss, gently milking his lips as his hands settled on her hips. He hadn't touched her between the legs, and his forbearance stoked her fire all the hotter. She deepened the kiss but kept their bodies barely apart until Feddar's whine began again, and his hands tightened around her hips.

"Since you've kept your promise, I know you'll need to spill before you'll be of any use to me. Do I have permission to make you come?"

Feddar's face melted, and he nodded, eyes full of confusion and want.

"We'll just take care of you quickly, then we can get down to the reason we're here together."

She grabbed him tight and tiptoed to move him between her legs, pressing her weight down against his sturdy erection as she squeezed her thighs together, trapping him tight. Feddar's eyes were positively feral, and she thumbed his lower lip as she bore down harder, feeling him hot and pulsing beneath her. She half-closed her eyes and angled in to kiss him. His lips were soft, his mouth hungry, his breath hot and strained. She lowered down further, putting more of her weight on him, and he groaned into her, his hands clutching her backside, sending a little shiver through her.

She stopped the kiss and looked him dead in the eyes.

"Come for me."

She squeezed tighter with her thighs, and Feddar took in a long, harsh breath, then groaned it out as he spilled.

"Shh," she whispered in his ear, clutching him to her chest as the moment drained out of him. She kissed him once more, then released with her thighs and stepped delicately off him.

"All better now?"

"Much." Feddar's voice was thick with relief but also with desire. Release was not what he was after. Which was good because she was going to make him earn his next one.

"Towel?"

Feddar pointed toward a basket with several towels rolled up inside it. She took one and wiped them both up, then tossed the towel, turning to see Feddar watching her with hunger in his eyes. She turned back toward him, touching his cheek, feeling the roughness of his stubble beneath her fingertips.

"Have you thought about how you'd like to pleasure me tonight?"

Feddar's eyes sparked as his gaze traveled down her body, a wave of tingles following in its wake. He sank to his knees, his eyes fixed between her legs, and he took her thighs in his warm hands. He nuzzled through her hair, his hot breath stirring her, his hands gripping her tighter, then looked up with earnest, probing eyes.

"May I taste you?"

Cloti stirred at his words, and she shifted her legs wider apart and cupped her hands around his ears.

"You may."

He spread her with his fingers, then moved in slowly, his stubble dragging across the hair on her thighs, the heat of his breath filling her. She gripped his ears tighter as he painted her with deft strokes of his tongue, like an artist hurrying to capture an approaching storm. Everything built so fast, and soon the lightning and thunder shook her. She angled into him, singing out with pleasure as he brought her spilling over the edge. Lights flashed in her mind, the Thousand Worlds emblazoned on an infinity of swirling blackness. She soared through them untethered, careening through the chaos. Her body shook, but Feddar held tight, and another wave of ecstasy rolled over her, breaking her control and sending her staggering back, bending down to clutch her knees as she struggled to catch her breath.

Feddar looked up at her, his face wet and smiling, his arousal impossible to miss.

"How else can I please you?"

Cloti grinned and gestured toward the bed, and Feddar threw the neatly tucked cover aside and stood next to it, awaiting her instructions. She wasn't ready for the next round quite yet, but by the time she was done teasing Feddar to within an inch of his life, she would be. She moved next to him, letting her greedy fingers run all over the soft skin of his chest and arms, then up to his face. She brushed her thumb across his lips, then pushed it into his mouth, and he clamped down and sucked on it. His tongue flicked against the pad of her thumb, and she felt her desire mounting once again. She removed her thumb and her hand down his neck, closing her fingers around his windpipe gently.

"I bet Aefin and Feddar are doing the exact same thing right now, thinking of us."

She kissed his lips, still steeped with her taste, and he pulled her in with little nips and swipes of his tongue. She pressed her thigh between his legs, pressing against his hot stiffness, and wrapped her arms around his back, tight muscles bunched beneath tender skin. Her hands slid down to his sculpted buttocks, squeezing over and over, pressing him harder against her. She broke from the kiss and lightened the pressure of her thigh as a low whine rose in his throat.

"Are you thinking of them?"

"I'm thinking of you," he whispered.

Her heart tightened, then flooded her chest, and she let go of him and pushed him back onto the bed. He landed with a gasp, and she crawled over his legs on all fours, then stopped, sitting back on his thighs, surveying the rippled landscape of his body. His eyes devoured her, and she gripped him with both hands, holding him stiff, and stared at him without moving. She had decided not to lower her shields for tonight, to have the purely physical experience of making love to him, the joy of watching his desperation grow. She held tight with one hand, letting the fingers of her other hand thread through the hair leading up to his stomach.

"I want you inside me," she whispered, squeezing him tighter, and his eyes widened with joy and confusion. "But not yet. Not until I'm convinced you want it more than I do."

"I've never wanted anything more in my life," he croaked.

She grinned, lowering down and giving him a single lick, then sat back again.

"Let's see what we can do about that."

She toyed with him for a long time, making use of a bottle of oil with a copper pour spout that sat conveniently on the bedside table. She watched his eyes melt as she took him through cycles of arousal and torment, stopping periodically to stretch her body over his and ply him with deep, soft kisses. Watching his eyes and the trembling of his body wound her up, and she lay down beside him, letting go of him for a moment while she splashed a bit of oil between her legs.

"I want you to bring me with your hands." She gripped him again, moaning softly as his fingers caressed her, exploring every fold, then finally slipping inside her. He touched her with strength and grace, expertly massaging all the right spots, and she squeezed him tightly as her breath grew short.

"Don't stop," she huffed, "and whatever you do, don't spill."

She closed her eyes as her pleasure rose, her hips rising into his touch, and she gripped his wrist, guiding him to the pace and force she needed. He learned her rhythm quickly, and soon she was writhing against him, holding his hand in place as she quivered around his fingers. She released his wrist, and he withdrew, resting his hand on her thigh as he leaned in to kiss her ear. They lay breathing for a while, and she rolled over to face him, her hand finding him still hard, and she smiled into his lips.

"You're so patient." She cradled him with her hand as she kissed his pliant lips. He lay still as they kissed, pulsing against her fingers. She worked him with gentle strokes until he was just exactly as she wanted him, helpless against her touch, accepting what he had no power to resist.

"I'm going to ask something of you," she said, moving to all fours and lowering her mouth toward him as she squeezed him tight and shiny.

"I will do anything you ask," he groaned. "Anything. *Please*."

"I want you to wait for my command." He nodded, his eyes watery with want. She breathed on him, then took him in her mouth, lavishing him with her lips and tongue, pausing whenever she felt him start to tense. Over and over, she brought him to the edge, and each time she left him gasping.

"You're almost ready," she said, giving him one last lick. She rose above him, gripped him firmly, and lowered herself onto him as slowly as her aching muscles would allow. Feddar sucked in a shaky breath, gritting his teeth as he tried so desperately to hold it for her. She pressed both hands into his chest and brought her face close to his, staring into his liquid eyes as she increased the pressure from within her. His breath came in shallow gasps, and she gripped the hair on his chest as she ground slowly against him, aching with the pressure. In time, the ache blossomed into pleasure, and she held in place, letting it build slowly, coaxing it with her mind until she felt it welling up inside her. Her hands found Feddar's throat, clasping gently, safely, and her arms shook as she braced herself above him, squeezing against his girth.

Feddar's legs began to tremble, and he let out a pained whine. Cloti inched back against him, and something snapped inside her, flooding her with a wave of sudden ecstasy that snatched the breath from her lungs. Feddar's eyes bulged, his mouth open and breathless, and she whispered into it:

"*Now.*"

Feddar's groan vibrated through her, and his hands clutched her behind as he bucked into her. His body went rigid as he came, barking desperate moans that rose as his back arched, then collapsed. She ground against him once more, then sank down onto his chest, both of them breathing hot and hard into each other's faces, their lips pressing together awkwardly between breaths. His grip on her softened, then his hands slid up to her hips.

She melted against him, laying tiny kisses across his lips until their breath settled. She rolled off him, her arms flopping to the side as her back hit the bead. Her fingers fell against his, and his pinky wrapped around hers as they lay breathing together in the warm candlelight.

9

— · —

"Was it everything you hoped for?" Aefin gave Cloti a peck on the lips and poured her a cup of tea.

"It really was." Cloti sat down at the table, staring at the steam rising off her tea, thinking of Feddar's skin, his muscles, and most of all, his eyes, full of the purest want she had ever witnessed.

"I bet he's thinking about you too." Aefin sat across from her, dusting her hands on her apron. The smell of baking nutbread hit Cloti like a summer breeze.

"I surely gave him plenty to think about."

Aefin giggled, and Cloti smiled at the complete lack of subtext in Aefin's laugh. "But tell me, did you enjoy your alone time with Ludo?"

"He was a soldier." Aefin smiled into her cup, and her face softened. "It was nice. He's been so busy lately."

"And by lately, you mean always? If he didn't have us, he'd do nothing but work."

"Well, we're lucky we have someone in the house who still can. I don't see anyone buying my paintings any time soon unless I want to start selling to the humans."

"You should have thought of that when the scholars were in town. They would have eaten it up."

Aefin shook her head, a wave of sadness floating across the table. Cloti stretched out her hand, and Aefin slid hers just far enough to touch her fingertips.

"I'm sorry, I just..." Aefin's face crumpled, and she pulled her hands up to cover it. Cloti bit her lip against the contagious tears, but there was no stopping them. "Even if the humans left tomorrow, would the city really be able to recover? So much death and destruction, not to mention that damned cough they brought with them. Did you hear the Torls have it? The Huelins too, and a few others. Their pod is on lockdown for at least half a cycle until it passes."

"Are they okay?" Ms. Torl's health had always been a bit fragile, and her mother was pushing eighty.

"They've gotten some medicine, so they should be fine, but you never know. I'm a bit surprised we didn't catch it at that party. One of the humans must have had it. I hear they don't usually show symptoms."

Cloti paused, thinking of all she'd shared with Feddar. It was a risk she probably shouldn't have taken, but her heart had left her little choice.

"Well, enough of the bad news. I think the pipberries are starting to ripen in the back garden. I was thinking of making some jam..." She sighed as she realized there was no sugar to be had, or honey for that matter. "I guess I could mix it with some stainberries and cook it down until it sweetens up."

"No sugar, no honey, no proper tea...it's just like the Time Before." Aefin's fingers found hers on the table, the pads of their fingertips touching, warmth flowing between them. They had been together so long Cloti didn't even have to concentrate to feel her.

"None of that matters, love." Cloti's heart warmed as she said the words, and she started to believe them. "We could live off mushrooms and forest snails, drink water from the mountain streams, and go to sleep curled against each other on a bed of pine needles every night. As long as we have each other, time has no meaning."

"You should put that in one of your poems."

Cloti laughed. "I probably have. I lose track. There are so many of them, and the last batch was off to the printer when..." She shook her head to clear it. "Actually, I should see if it's still there. I think Feddar could get me in."

"Feddar is a convenient friend to have." Aefin's voice was measured, and a hint of hesitation crept in.

"Aefin." Cloti squeezed her fingers tighter and stared Aefin's eyes back up to meet hers. "Feddar is not a convenience. He is a good...person, and he is trying to help us any way we can. I trust him, and so should you."

"But can you trust your feelings not to get in the way?" Aefin's voice softened.

"I follow my feelings to happiness. You know that. And Feddar makes me happy."

"Do you love him?"

Cloti cocked her head as a tingle bloomed in her chest, spreading out to warm her head and limbs. How could it be true when she'd known him for so short a time? She took in a long breath, then let it out slowly.

"Yes, I think I do. And I think you could, too, in time. But that's up to your heart to decide."

"He is very charming." Aefin picked at her fingernails, a smile creeping across her lips. "And he does have a nice...build."

"You noticed, huh? He's got eyes for you, too, in case you missed the memo."

Aefin's smile bloomed on her face. "I thought I might have gotten a vibe. He's got it bad for Ludo, too, if my eyes weren't deceiving me."

Cloti hummed as she pictured Feddar and Ludo kissing, their hands on each other's hips.

"I would love to see them together."

"Love to see who together?" Ludo stood in the doorway, and Cloti got the impression he'd been there for a bit.

"You and Feddar. Don't tell me you haven't thought about it."

"It had occurred to me to wonder if that was something I might discover in the near future."

"No one's stopping you, love," Cloti teased.

"I know, I just...well, it seems like you and he are really having a nice time. I want you to enjoy it for a while and only share if that's what you think he wants."

"Oh, he wants. But there's no hurry, right? Speaking of Feddar, I was going to go to the library today and see if I can read about the Delve where he was captured. Either of you want to come?"

"The library," Ludo said dreamily, then sighed. "I'm swamped in paperwork, sadly. The farming allotments are coming in, and they need all the translators they can get their hands on."

"I'm going to do a bit of gardening and paint. Help me pick the berries, and I'll get the jam started while you're gone." Aefin pulled the bread out of the oven, golden brown and dotted with too few bits of nuts. "We'll let this cool while we're picking."

"That sounds lovely. Ludo, don't work too hard now." Cloti gave him a peck on the lips, which he turned into a proper kiss, grabbing her around the waist and pulling her to him.

"I've told them I have to make dinner tonight, and if they don't like it, they can get someone else to translate."

"We have a few carrots left over from the last allotment," Aefin said. "The next one is due today, so hopefully, there'll be something to go with that."

"Well, whatever it is, I'm sure it will be fine." Ludo's cheerful tone was a balm to Cloti's soul. "We can always eat beans if not. We do have beans left, right?"

"Some." Aefin's voice fell. They'd been eating smaller meals, so if an allotment was late or short, they wouldn't go hungry, but the result was that they were hungry most of the time. Cloti had lost a little weight, which she didn't hate, but the uncertainty was a constant drain on her attention.

Aefin handed her a basket and pointed to the garden door with her thumb.

"See you for dinner then."

Cloti kissed Ludo on the cheek and followed Aefin out into the garden.

The human guards made Cloti wait outside the library while one of them took her medallion inside, and she felt naked without it. Any Maer found in public without one was taken to a holding camp. It could take days before they came back home, and they had been known to disappear and never be heard from again. The guard returned her medallion without a word and opened the door, and she entered the dimly lit foyer. Only two brightstones remained in the elaborate chandelier that had so entranced her as a child. The rest would have been used for the war effort or stockpiled by the Shoza along with the city's reserves of hotiron and oil in the last days of the siege. A human sat behind the desk, broad-shouldered and bespectacled, looking more like a wrestler than a librarian.

"You may carry the Administrator's medallion, but access to the stacks is limited to library personnel." His Maer was crisp, if a little stilted like he'd learned it mostly from books. Cloti looked around to see if there were any library personnel nearby, but the building was silent and still.

"I'll get you what you need if it's not classified." He clicked his pen and looked up at her, hand poised over a ledger.

"I'm looking for the official chronicle of the Delve of Yglind Torl."

The human frowned as he wrote in neat letters in his ledger. "Recent Delve chronicles require administrative approval." He tapped a bell, and footsteps sounded from somewhere off in the library. "I'll need your name and address, please." He opened another ledger filled with perforated slips with lines and words in Islish and began writing.

A human just entering adulthood hurried down the steps, stopping to stare at Cloti for a moment before bowing to the librarian. When he had finished writing, the librarian blotted and tore out a slip from the ledger. He spoke weary words to his assistant, who bowed and hurried out the door with an awkward sideways glance at Cloti.

"With any luck, the district administrator will sign off, but we might have to go to the Administrator himself. Is there anything else I can get for you in the meantime?" His voice was low and steady but not unkind.

Cloti smiled. "May I look through the catalog?"

"Be my guest." He gestured toward the long tables with massive tomes arranged neatly along their length. "Just write the title and author down and bring the slip to me." He tore a slip from a third ledger and handed it to her, along with a stubby pencil.

Cloti searched through the catalog and selected a collection of longstories from the Time Before, which could be dry and repetitive, but they often gave her inspiration for her own writing. She handed the slip to the librarian, who stood with a groan, eyeing her mistrustfully.

"Don't touch anything while I'm gone. I'll know."

He brought back the book, along with a smaller one that looked very familiar. He handed the heavy book to her, and as he tucked the other one under his arm, she recognized the cover.

"You've got my treatise on the Thousand Worlds."

"It's not every day I get to be in the presence of an author, especially one of your renown. You would think, being a librarian, I would have more opportunities, but you are my first."

"My renown? I'm sorry, you must be mistaken."

"Oh no. You have quite a cult following in Wells. I've only read it in translation, but I'm keen to read it in the original."

"So, you're a librarian back in…"

"Wells. It's the capital of the Isle. Just to the north of the continent."

"I've heard it has the biggest market in all the human lands."

"It does, and there are a few who deal in Maer books, but they're unbelievably expensive, and I've never seen a copy of it until now. I hope you don't mind…" His grumpy demeanor had melted, and a humble, excited man now stood before her.

"I hope you find something that speaks to you."

He nodded, his face eager and a little contrite. He turned and hurried off to his desk, where he lowered the brightstone lamp and delicately opened the cover.

Cloti retreated to a desk near a window so she could read by natural light. It took her eyes a few minutes to adjust to the antiquated language, but soon she was crossing snowy mountain passes with King Igibor, hot on the trail of the bandits who had kidnapped his son. She'd read several versions of the story; this one went a little deep into the depictions of the snow and the wind, and she soon lost patience and closed it. She glanced over at the librarian, who was poring over the book, running his finger across the page as he moved his lips. The thought that a human would know her work, let alone be able to read it in Maer, was not something that would ever have occurred to her. How could a culture that produced a man like this librarian or like Feddar also be capable of the destruction and malice they'd shown during the war?

The young man returned, red-faced and out of breath, with a slip, which he slapped down on the librarian's desk, then leaned on his knees and heaved.

"The Administrator himself signed this, eh?"

The assistant half-stood, nodding.

"He said Cloti can check the book out if she wants."

The librarian studied the slip, eyebrows raised, then pushed himself up to standing.

"It would seem you have friends in high places." He moved quickly for a man his size, and in no time, he was up the stairs, moving with purpose. The younger man had mostly recovered his breath, and he snuck not-so-subtle glances at Cloti. She wondered if he knew her work too. The librarian descended the stairs moments later carrying a large format book bound in green ox hide with copper lettering and page edges, the same edition as she'd seen on the Torl's sitting room table.

"This is some exquisite binding." He examined the lettering, running his fingers over the cover, then seemed to remember why it was in his hands and held it out toward Cloti. "Let me just get you to sign the slip. It's most unusual, I must say. This will be the first book to leave the collection since I've been here."

Cloti took the book, which was even heavier than the longstory collection, with copper-sprayed edges and a small, engraved brass placard indicating it was number twenty-seven out of a hundred copies made.

"I promise to bring it back in perfect condition." She tried to put it in her bag, but it was too tall to fit, so she tucked it under her arm instead. She took the quill and signed where he had put an X; the letters on the slip were all in Islish, and she couldn't make out a word.

"See that you do. We know where you live." He pointed toward his ledger with what he probably thought was a charming smile, but it chilled Cloti to think of it.

"Thank you for going to all the trouble." She glanced over at the book of longstories, which she'd left on the table by the window.

"I'll take care of it. If you don't mind, when you come back, I'd like to ask you a few questions about your book. There are some passages I've always wondered about."

"I look forward to it. Thank you again." She half-raised the book, then turned and pushed open the door.

The streets were subdued, the heat slowing the pace of the human soldiers, who had little to do but watch the Maer schlepping carts and guiding ox-drawn wagons full of supplies through the city. She noticed two humans shadowing her as she crossed the street, and she tried to ignore them, but it was upsetting to be followed around like that. She hurried toward home, but as she neared the River Market, she heard a din from up the street, followed by several shrill whistles, and groups of soldiers went running toward the sound. Cloti stopped and looked, but she couldn't see much. Two pairs of strong hands gripped her biceps, and before she knew what was happening, she was being marched toward the park in the direction of the camps.

"Let go of me! I have a medallion from the Administrator. Just let me show you!"

The humans did not respond, remaining grim-faced as they squeezed her arms so hard, she almost cried out in pain. They hurried her along, and soon she was being herded with a number of other Maer through the camp entrance and corralled into a fenced-off area between the humans' pavilions and the endless rows of tents of the encampment. Several dozen Maer stood around looking bewildered and frightened, none of them talking for the moment as they watched the newcomers arrive. Cloti pulled up her scarf as the pen got crowded. Soon, a soldier with a clipboard appeared at the edge of the pen and shouted in broken Maer:

"If you live in the camps, form a line by this gate. If not, stay where you are."

The bulk of the Maer in the corral moved toward the gate, where four human soldiers awaited them. The one with the clipboard took their names and let them through one by one, and the other soldiers led them toward a large, closed tent, one of several in the guard compound. The Maer emerged from the tent one at a time a few minutes later, looking dazed and fearful, and were allowed to drift off into the camps.

Cloti pulled out her coin and stared into the eye, trying to will calm into her mind, which kept spinning with the possibilities. Had there been another attack? The Shoza launched periodic raids on human soldiers and barracks with varying degrees of success, and they mostly avoided getting caught. She wondered how many Shoza were left in the city and how many were at large in the mountains. The presence she'd felt in the Thousand Worlds had said the walls would fall at Midsummer and the doors to freedom would be opened. Were they working in tandem with the Shoza inside the city walls? It would be difficult, but not impossible; farmers and other tradesmaer from the outlying areas periodically brought in food and goods, and they could have found a way to pass on messages through them somehow. But the fact that they'd reached out through the Thousand Worlds suggested they needed help communicating. She wanted to help, but was it worth the risk?

"State your name and address." The human with the clipboard stood outside the corral near Cloti, pencil in hand, a dull agitation in his voice. It took her a moment to realize he was talking to her, and she gave him her information, though it worried her to have it in a record like this. Would this mark her as a troublemaker?

"I have a medallion from the Administrator. I was in the library, getting this. The librarian can vouch for me!" She held up the book, which the soldier took, glancing at the cover, then passed it to a colleague, who shuttled it off to one of the tents. He inspected her medallion and made a note on his clipboard. Cloti's heart sank as she saw it disappear into his pocket.

"Did I do something wrong?"

"Your medallion and records will be checked against the registry. Stay here until someone summons you." He ignored her pleading gesture and turned to the next Maer, who she thought she recognized from one of Ludo's official functions. A historian, if she recalled correctly. She turned away, tears in her eyes, as she pulled the coin back out and tried to focus, but it was no use. Without the medallion, she suddenly felt naked. To the human soldiers, she was just another furry prisoner and potential suspect. She was not an author, or the leader of a meditation temple, or a wife, or a lover. She was a beast that needed sorting, like livestock. She felt dirty and exposed, and her tears flowed all the more when she realized that's what the Maer in the camps must feel like all the time. How could they keep their spirits up in these conditions?

She took several deep breaths and forced herself to stare at the coin again. In time she was able to circle past the outer rim into the iris, which pulled her in slowly to the center, and she rested in its calm, the eye of the storm. She was not in any imminent danger. Her medallion was legitimate, her errand sanctioned by the Administrator himself. Feddar. Her heart warmed as his face appeared in her mind, laughing at one of her quips, sipping his wine, nibbling on food, his eyes never leaving hers. He never stopped wanting her. She could feel it in his every breath, and her heart strained with the need to see him again. Feddar could make this right. Feddar *would* make this right. She was sure of it.

"Here's your medallion and your book."

The soldier handed them to her, and she bowed.

"Thank you. Did something happen? Why am I here?"

He stared off toward the tents, his mouth drawn in a tight line.

"You'll have to stay in the camp overnight, under orders from the General. There are free tents in..." He flipped through the pages of his clipboard, turning it sideways, and tapped on a grid of squares. "Sector thirty-four. That way." He pointed toward the sea of tents stretching all along the riverside. "The Head of Sector will help you get settled. Report back here at noon tomorrow."

Cloti nodded, looking down as the soldier opened the gate and stood back. She walked out into the open area between the human compound and the first group of tents and breathed deeply. The air was heady with spring flowers, coal smoke, and roasting fish. Children played with a wooden hoop in a patch of trampled-down grass. Pairs of human soldiers crisscrossed the field, going to and from the compound and the camp. A spyball floated past her, and she resisted the temptation to try and read the essence of its controller. She thought she'd be able to do it, but the risk of getting caught was not worth it, so she kept her head down as she entered the main path leading through the camp.

10

— • —

It was like a miniature city, equal parts chaotic and ordered. The tents were laid out in blocks of sixteen, separated by wide paths like side streets off the main avenue. Maer served food from various grills and pots, all using coal fire canisters like the army carried. Cloti was sure they still had a few at the house from their past camping trips to Eagle Lake. She clutched her chest, thinking of Uffrin, wondering if he was still alive. The Shoza who'd delivered Mara's sister Kaela had managed to get a message back that she'd made it all right and that Mara and Uffrin were okay. Cloti's vision had confirmed it; she'd seen a vision of Uffrin and Mara side by side, staring out at the lake at dusk. It had been a great comfort, but how would Uffrin have survived the winter? He could barely feed himself in the city, let alone out in the mountains.

The Shoza had said the camp was next to a Free Maer settlement, so hopefully, they'd managed to find a way to integrate, but it couldn't have been easy. And assuming they had made it through the winter, there was a chance Mara could be pregnant by now. She wouldn't have had access to contraception unless she'd brought some with her, though the Free Maer surely had methods of their own. It was hard to imagine bringing a child up in such circumstances, but with the love the two of them had for each other, they might just have managed to believe in a future worthy of the fruit of their union. Which might make her a grandmother. She touched her chest, which stirred at the idea. She'd always longed to hold a little furball of her own again, nuzzle into its hair and bask in its innocence. Her heart clutched at the thought she might never have a chance to see her family's future.

Based on the handful of pregnant Maer she saw, the future was ready to be born, heedless of circumstances, and the Maer in the camps had not given up all hope. She saw several large tents that were set up as classrooms, complete with chalkboards. A makeshift market occupied a muddy space between sectors, which were delineated by wooden posts with numbers painted on them. She had just passed sectors one and two, and the path cut between three and four. She wove her way through the crowds, dodging children and hand carts and the occasional stray dog, lean and attentive as they slunk about on careful paws. As she passed into the teens, she sensed someone watching her, and she stopped to adjust her sandals, glancing back as she stood up again. A Maer with serious eyes shied away from her glance a little too quickly, looking down at something in their pocket, but she knew. She continued, stopping to examine woven reed bracelets at one of the markets, and saw the Maer keeping pace behind her, looking down at a small rolled-up paper.

They were still behind her when she passed thirty and thirty-one. She was hot, tired, and thirsty, and she had no patience for games. If this Maer was coming to kill her, let them do it in front of everyone. She turned and marched directly toward them, and the Maer stood rooted in place, feigning surprise, as she stopped and spoke.

"I couldn't help noticing you following me, and I wonder if there's anything I can do for you."

"I'm here to keep you safe." They bowed, scanning the crowd with worried eyes. "My name is Senefal."

"Well, I suppose you already know my name, but I'm Cloti. Nice to meet you." She bowed and gestured down the camp road. "Can you help me find sector thirty-four?"

"Of course. I'll help you get set up, then there's someone who'd like to speak with you."

Her tent was a simple affair of canvas on a wooden platform, with several piles of straw for sleeping. Senefal brought her water and a dry, saltless cracker with amaranth seeds, then stood facing the camp while she ate. Senefal had the taut muscles of a Shoza without an ounce of fat showing anywhere. Shoza were known to be lean, but conditions at the camp had taken their toll. Senefal led her through a side path to the latrine pits, which she could smell long before she reached them. She pitied the souls whose tents were set up nearby. Afterward, they led her through the narrow paths between tents to one whose flaps were all pulled down, despite the heat. Senefal clucked with their tongue several times, and one of the flaps opened to let her in.

Gielle sat cross-legged on the straw, with an array of sticks and pebbles on a clear patch of floor in front of her. She pressed her hands together at her chest and bowed, and Cloti did the same as she lowered herself onto the straw facing Gielle. Gielle spoke, but it took Cloti a moment to realize what she was saying. It was Ormaer, an ancient dialect, one of the languages of the Time Before, which she had studied in school years ago. She was accustomed to reading it, but she hadn't heard it spoken in decades.

"Do you understand me?"

Cloti nodded. "If you speak slowly."

"I apologize for the precautions. There are some humans who speak Maer, but I doubt if any of them speak Ormaer. I assumed you would, given your education."

"It's been a long time, but I still read it occasionally." The language came back to Cloti with surprising ease; she wondered if her use of the tincture had boosted her linguistic powers.

"Good. Let me be quick, as your presence here will not have gone unnoticed. You have heard from our counterparts outside the city."

"I have. They spoke of Midsummer, the walls falling, the path to freedom opening. What does it mean?"

"Plans are underway, but we will need your help. The humans have confiscated the cradles and the circlets, so we cannot access the Thousand Worlds to coordinate. Only one such as yourself can."

"Gielle, I want to help, but this is not my path. I am no Shoza, and if I am seen helping you, everything I am trying to build will be lost."

Gielle stared at her, eyes burning with dark intensity.

"We are all Shoza, now. We have lost so much already. If we do not act, we lose everything."

Cloti's mind filled with visions of the city teaming with humans, crowding in the food halls, breezing in and out of the library, while Maer carried loads and served them tea. It was happening already, but it could be so much worse. She forced a smile and nodded.

"What do you need me to do?"

Cloti slept fitfully, imagining the scene that had caused her to be sent to the camp. Word had spread quickly of a Shoza attack on a human officers' barracks. Eight humans had been killed and several more wounded, and one Shoza had been killed. The others seemed to have escaped, though some rumors said one had been captured and taken to the Tower, just as the Shoza would have done to anyone suspected of such an attack against the government in the time before the humans had arrived. Just as they'd done to Feddar.

Cloti had always feared the Shoza as heartless killers, tools of the same military that had brought them all to the point of ruin. If she chose to work with them, she would be responsible for the deaths they caused. How would she sleep knowing that her practice had been used in the service of violence? But if she shied away from their cause, how many Maer would suffer and die or live in perpetual misery and servitude? It was a perfectly impossible choice, and it fragmented her sleep into a thousand shards that left her more exhausted than when she'd lain down.

Senefal was waiting with a bowl of water and a cloth when Cloti awoke. When she had washed up and visited the latrines, Senefal brought her a bowl of porridge. As she ate, Cloti noticed a handful of Maer seated cross-legged in a semi-circle on the ground in a little clearing not far from her tent.

"I'm glad to see Maer practicing even in the camps." Not long ago, she would never have dared to mention practice to a Shoza, but she was coming to realize the Shoza had their own version of practice.

"They're hoping you'll join them."

Cloti regretted not having any tea, but she drained her cup and walked out of the tent toward the clearing. Juiya, who was leading the practice, smiled and bowed to her, then moved to the side. Cloti recognized only a few of the acolytes, but it was clear they all knew her. She smiled as she pressed her hands together, lowering herself to sit on the raggedy mat Juiya had left. Senefa stood to the side, watching the surroundings like a guard dog on high alert.

Cloti felt the warmth of the assembled souls like the morning sunshine peeking through the clouds, and she closed her eyes and searched for words she could share with them.

"No night is so dark or so long it can stop the sun from rising."

As she took them through a cycle, their connections grew fast and thick like vines intertwining on a fence. Several of them showed strong training; Juiya and two others, one of whom had the disciplined energy she'd felt from Gielle and the voice in the Thousand Worlds. Though their practices differed, they had more in common than not, and she sent a pulse of approval to the Shoza, a broad-shouldered Maer with calm, gentle eyes.

She wished she could commune with them the way she could with Juiya or Aefin, but it took time in practice together to develop that kind of bond. As she closed out the cycle, the group's energy suggested another, and the collective support lifted the weariness from her heart. When her hands pressed together above her head, she pushed out a word—*Midsummer*—and felt two pulses in response from Juiya and the Shoza. When they had finished the cycle, she opened her eyes to see scores more Maer standing at a respectful distance, watching with hands pressed together at their hearts. Her heart swelled to see the Maer in the camp so united in practice.

"There will be no temple cycle today, but I want you all to go lead a cycle at noon wherever you can, no matter your experience. Gather a few Maer who will join you and find a common purpose together. The Time to Come is in your hands." She bowed several times, facing the onlookers in all directions, then stepped off the mat, and the crowd slowly dispersed. She summoned Juiya with her eyes and motioned her back toward her tent.

"What happened?" Juiya asked quietly as they sat facing each other on the straw. Cloti leaned forward, and Juiya pressed foreheads with her. Their connection was immediate.

I had just left the library when the attack took place. Human soldiers herded every Maer in the streets down to the camps. Like cattle.

I am glad you were not harmed.

I am fine, and I now see that you are aware of the Shoza's plans.

Only a little. Gielle approached me as she did you. I did not know what to say, what to do. It goes against all your teachings.

I am still learning. I need you to find out more and report back to me at the next temple cycle. Whenever that is.

I will.

And if you can, form a group of the strongest practitioners and practice together right at dawn every day. If you combine your focus, you may be able to reach me.

I don't see how, but I will try.

If you can get to the Thousand Worlds together, I will find you.

Juiya pulled away, her eyes suddenly tired, her face drawn. Even Cloti felt a little out of sorts. Mind to mind could be intense if one didn't do it very often.

"I'm glad to see you're keeping up the practice in the camps. That means a lot." Cloti put her hand on Juiya's knee, and her eyes brightened.

"I think we can make a real difference. Living here is very stressful, and practice helps us get by until something changes for the better." Her eyes seemed to search Cloti's for an answer to her unspoken question.

"It will. We just have to decide what we want our role in that to be."

Feddar was waiting at the gate when she arrived just before noon. His eyes flashed for a moment, and he gave a curt nod. She looked away, hiding her smile behind her hand, until she saw the soldier with the clipboard.

"Cloti Looris, you have been cleared to go. The Administrator himself has agreed to accompany you back to your home." His eyes shot to Feddar, then back to Cloti, and he shook his head. "Sign here." He handed her a pen, and she signed, though she could not read the Islish words on the paper she was signing. He gestured her toward the gate without a word, and she walked past a dozen human soldiers dressed in full armor with swords at their sides before she made it outside the gate, where Feddar stood wringing his hands. She wanted to go to him, fling herself around his neck and cover him with kisses, but his aloof stance told her she could not, for appearance's sake.

"I am so sorry you had to go through this. Believe me, if there had been anything I could have done...Are you okay? You look..." He gestured her up and down, a smile growing on his face. "You look great."

"I'm fine, thank you, and I don't blame you. It was good to get a better look at the camps. I was prepared for worse, honestly. You hear all sorts of things, you know?"

"I tour them personally at least once a week. I know it's not a permanent solution, but it could be worse." He gestured toward the road, and they walked together. "I see you still have the book. Have you read it yet? I'm curious to see what it says about me."

"I've been too preoccupied to read, but I'll be sure and give you a full report when I see you next."

"I hope you read fast."

His fingers brushed against hers and stayed close as they walked, neither of them daring to intertwine them in public, but the occasional touch of their knuckles brought little sparks of joy to Cloti's heart. He told her of the attack: ten humans killed, and two Maer. The rest vanished without a trace.

"They're going to be increasing security all over and looking for Shoza hiding in the camps. I'll try to keep things under control, but it's not going to be pretty." He shook his head, and she could feel his regret, even without trying, as if they were partially linked. She felt that way with Aefin and Ludo and a few of her stronger acolytes, but she'd never felt it with any of her lovers.

"What about the cycles in the temple?"

"You'll have to wait three days minimum, and that's the General's order. He outranks me, so it's out of my hands."

"Can I send a message to one of my acolytes?"

"I'll make sure they are informed." His hand grazed her back for a moment, and she wanted to sink into him, bystanders be damned.

As they walked up the hill toward her house and approached the cliffside checkpoint, Feddar put a little more distance between them. She'd noticed the soldier's reaction at the camp when Feddar was there to meet her. She imagined the rumors were already out there, but appearances had to be kept up. She knew that much from Ludo's work in diplomacy. Her heart beat faster as they passed the soldiers, who nodded and stepped aside to let them pass. As they passed the final checkpoint into their pod, the anxiety she'd been suppressing for the past day suddenly flooded through her body, and she had to force her shaking legs forward with each step.

When they finally got into her front garden, behind the cover of some bushes, she stopped and threw herself on Feddar, sobbing into his chest as she clutched him tight. He just held her, saying nothing, his lips kissing her hair until her tears were spent. She pulled back, dabbed her eyes with a nervous giggle, and smoothed out the hair on her face. She looked up into his eyes, which shone brightly against the dark green foliage behind him, and tiptoed up for a soft kiss. His hands rested gently on her hips, and she wanted them all over her body, wanted him to lay her down among the flowers and roughly bring forth her pleasure. She kissed him more deeply, and his hands tightened around her waist for a moment, then slid up her back as he pulled away.

"I imagine Aefin and Ludo are worried sick about you."

She let her head fall against his chest for a moment, then pushed back with a shuddering sigh. She took a deep breath, turned, and walked toward the door, which opened before her hand touched the doorknob.

Aefin's eyes were bright with tears, and her lips were hot on Cloti's, murmuring "Thank gods" between kisses as she held Cloti's face in her warm hands. Ludo appeared in the doorway, watching them wistfully. Cloti released Aefin and went to him, collapsing against his chest and squeezing him with all her strength. Her tears flowed anew, and the built-up tension vibrated her body. She kissed Ludo roughly, then turned toward Feddar, who stood a bit back, eyes cast down.

"Thank you, my friend." Ludo let Cloti go and stepped to Feddar, who seemed surprised when Ludo wrapped him in a strong hug. When Ludo let him go, they locked eyes for a moment, then Ludo stepped back as Aefin swooped in, embracing Feddar with enough force that he staggered back a little. His uncertain hands fell on her back, and when she pulled away from the hug, Aefin's hands remained on Ludo's shoulders for a moment, and it almost looked like she was going to kiss him.

"Thank you so much, Feddar. We heard about the attack, and we had no idea what had happened to Cloti."

"I'm sorry I couldn't bring her here sooner, but the General's orders supersede my authority."

"Do you think the lockdown will be lifted after three days?" Ludo asked, putting a hand on Cloti's waist and pulling her toward him.

Feddar sighed, but he nodded. "I do. Assuming there are no more attacks." His eyes flitted to Cloti for a moment, then back to Ludo. "They will probably round up some Shoza or Maer they claim are Shoza, and..." His eyes dropped, and his fingers twisted together.

"I should think at least twenty, if not more." Ludo spoke with a heavy voice. "If I've read the General's communiqué correctly."

"I will do what I can, but that may not be much."

Aefin moved next to Cloti, wrapping one arm around her waist so she now stood sandwiched between her and Ludo, which helped keep her from collapsing from the stress of recent events.

"When the lockdown is over, would you consider joining us for dinner?" Aefin's voice quavered just a bit as she spoke. "So we can thank you properly for saving Cloti."

"I didn't save her. I just walked her home. But I would be..." He looked down, then back up, his green eyes shining. "It would be my absolute pleasure." He half-turned as if to leave, making eye contact with Cloti, who held out a hand to stop him, and he paused.

"Thank you again, Feddar. You remember your promise?" He nodded, a slight grin creeping across his lips. "You don't have to keep it now. Unless you want."

"I will take that under advisement. And now I'll leave you to your domestic bliss. I have...four more meetings today, I think." He shook his head, bowed to them, then turned and left.

11

—·—

The shivo tea was sickly sweet as always, but it did its job, releasing Cloti from the constant connections to everyone she was in a room with. She could normally suppress them with little effort, but the cumulative effect of recent events had made her boundaries leaky. Since her experience at the camps, her heart felt like it wasn't seated quite right. She needed rest, and she needed release, but first, she needed her mind to be at peace for a moment. She was so often in charge, and she needed to let someone else take the reins for a while.

Aefin padded into the room with the kit, laying the black and silver case at the foot of the bed. She pulled out the cuffs and set one on each corner of the bed, her fingers trailing along Cloti's body as she moved, stirring her like the first breeze before a storm. She hovered over Cloti, her eyes soft and searching, her hand across Cloti's chest, fingers kneading lightly.

"Are you ready to be restrained?"

"I am."

"And if you want us to stop?"

"Frasti."

The leather padding on the cuffs was buttery soft; Aefin took pride in maintaining her equipment. Aefin tightened each strap with care, checking with Cloti before moving on to the next until she was securely bound to the four brass loops on the bed, which supported her with their symmetry. Aefin crawled onto the bed above her, looking down again with those tender eyes so full of compassion. They fluttered closed as Aefin lowered for a kiss, letting her body rest lightly atop Cloti's, touching but without pressure. Cloti gave herself up to Aefin's hungry lips and exploring tongue, which fanned her desire, and she strained against the restraints for a moment just to make sure they would keep her secure.

A shadow fell across her, and Ludo loomed, a dark shape against the orange light of the single candle. Cloti made eye contact with him as she kissed Aefin, and his hands moved down to touch himself, though he was already visibly aroused. Cloti lost herself in Aefin's kiss, in the gentle pressure of her body, her taste, her scent. She wanted all of her, and having only this part, this kiss, was sweet torture.

The bed creaked as Ludo kneeled in behind Aefin, who rose into him, keeping her lips locked on Cloti as her hips cocked up. Cloti wanted to reach out to her, touch her body as Ludo moved in, first with his fingers, then his tongue. Aefin's breath grew irregular, her kisses sloppy and stuttering, and she clutched Cloti's shoulders tightly when Ludo moved up again and eased into her. Cloti took up the slack in the kiss, drawing Aefin's attention back to her as Ludo began moving, rocking against her with slow, steady strokes. Aefin's kiss faltered again when Ludo picked up the pace, and her lips froze, locked against Cloti's as she came, gasping hot breaths into Cloti's mouth. Ludo drove into her two more times, then held tight against her, breathing heavily through his nose. Their bodies relaxed at the same time, and Aefin collapsed onto Cloti, shifting off to the side, breathing into her ear as her hand moved lazily across Cloti's stomach. Ludo lay down on the opposite side, and they crossed their arms over her body, nuzzling against her, their breath still fast and warm. Her body thrummed with desire, but her heart warmed with the closeness. She could wait. Just a little.

After a time, their hands started moving, exploring Cloti's body, lingering when she tensed beneath their touch but always moving on. Ludo kissed her now as Aefin's fingers, slick with oil Cloti hadn't even noticed her applying, slid up and down her thighs and between her legs. Aefin knew Cloti like the palm of her own hand, and she worked her with soft swirls and strokes for so long Cloti thought her heart would burst from her chest. Ludo's kisses remained gentle, his silky tongue teasing her lips but never going deeper. Cloti was stretched to the limit between the twin sensations, and a groan escaped from her throat as Aefin's fingers pulled away, leaving her aching at the loss of touch. Ludo's lips left hers, and she pleaded with her eyes, panting.

Ludo smiled, putting his hands gently around her neck, then running them down her body, his fingers feathering over her nipples, tracing down her belly as his lips followed, kissing and licking. His breath warmed her as he nuzzled between her legs, his hands gripping her thighs. Aefin leaned her face in close, looking from Cloti's eyes down to Ludo, whose tongue washed over her, bringing her steadily up to the brink.

"Take it slow, Ludo," Aefin said, shushing Cloti's whine of complaint with an indulgent smile. "She's not ready yet. Are you, my love?"

Cloti closed her eyes and shook her head, her hands clenching as Ludo buried himself in her, moving just a little too slowly to bring her. Her mind began to float amid the pleasure flooding her body. There was nothing she could do to hurry Ludo and nothing she could do to stop him from pushing her over the edge any time Aefin gave the word.

The word was a long time coming.

Ludo and Aefin took turns with fingers and mouths, sometimes kissing her as the other worked, other times just looking down into her eyes, watching her come apart. She had long since stopped fighting the restraints. Her hands hung limp, clenching into fists when one of them brought her a little closer, then relaxing as they backed away. After what seemed like hours, Aefin pulled up from between her legs, looking at Ludo, who blinked. Aefin moved next to Cloti, resting her head on her outstretched arm, draping her leg over Cloti's thigh. Ludo did the same, and Cloti's body coursed with desire, squeezed between them, exposed but cradled in their warmth.

"Are you ready now?" Aefin breathed into her ear.

Cloti took a deep breath, then let it out with a shaky sigh. She blinked yes to Aefin, who squeezed her hand tight, and Ludo did the same from the other side. Aefin's other hand slid over the bump of her hip and down between her legs. She touched Cloti with the tip of her index finger in just the right spot, and pressure built in her slowly as Aefin's fingertip bore down. Ludo's free hand cupped her gently, and as they held her tight, Cloti's blood rushed wild and reckless through her body. No movement was required; a white-hot blaze grew beneath Aefin's finger, summoning a pulse from deep within her, and her mind flashed with stars streaking out of the blackness. Her pleasure distended, stretching into infinite space at speeds neither her body nor mind could keep up with, and she sang out, wails of delicate agony echoing off the bedroom walls. Her body tensed, then trembled as she came like a swimmer tumbled against the shore by a violent sea, trapped in the undertow as wave after wave crashed over her, leaving her soaked and breathless. Aefin's voice echoed in from far away, cooing, calming, becoming words as the pressure of her finger lessened.

"Everything about you is beautiful," Aefin whispered, pressing her lips against Cloti's as Ludo began undoing the straps. "I could travel the Thousand Worlds for a million years and never find your equal."

"We love you," Ludo said, laying down behind her as Cloti curled into Aefin's warmth now that her limbs were finally free to wrap around her. "And we'll always be here for you, no matter what happens in the world outside these walls."

Cloti let out a rumbling sigh of contentment as she wiggled against him, and he pressed in close, his breath hot on her neck. Their warmth enwrapped her, and she sank into their comfort and took shelter in the dark place inside her where stray thoughts and ill dreams could never reach.

Cloti slept past dawn, and she hoped the Shoza out in the mountains would not take her absence amiss. She would reconnect tomorrow once she'd had time to process what had happened and figure out what to do next. She was still shaken by her captivity, but her session with Ludo and Aefin had helped her find her center again, and by late morning she was ready to dive into the book.

The binding was beautiful, though it felt obscene that so much money and Maerpower had been devoted to celebrating such a violent, archaic ritual. Delves were a relic of the Time Before, and there hadn't been any meaningful ones in centuries. But this one, the Delve of Yglind Torl, would be studied long into the future—if the future for the Maer included the preservation of books and history, which was not at all a certainty. At the very least, there was a copy of the text in the Archive, though the elaborate illustrations that adorned the book would not have made it into the cylinder scrolls. She scanned the pages, relishing the artwork, especially of the dragon, a waadrech, which the artist had rendered terrifying and gruesome, gore dripping from its jagged teeth in every illustration. There were several drawings of Feddar as well, though the simpering weakling depicted did not match the reality of the man himself. One showed him being interrogated by Laanda, the queen of the Timon, who leaned over his cowering figure, her hard face and chiseled muscles making her determination clear. The second showed him crouched over a pool of what looked like vomit, with a severed foot still in its boot lying in a puddle of blood. Cloti turned the page quickly as her stomach roiled. She'd never had any taste for the violence of longstories, and the narrative of this book spared no detail.

She read with great interest the passages involving Feddar, trying to imagine them from his point of view. He had frozen the Maer with some kind of magic item and stolen their weapons and gear, but he hadn't killed them, which he repeated during his interrogations by the Timon. Aene, the Maer mage, had questioned him as well, and the tone of their interview suggested she was sympathetic toward his cause. Cloti wondered if Aene had been drawn in by his soft eyes, just as she had. She hummed as she remembered Feddar speaking of a Maer lover, and she realized it could only have been her. The last illustration showed him being delivered to the guards at the Tower, looking back at Aene, whose face was shown in profile. The artist had added what might have been a tear in the corner of her eye, and Cloti wondered if they had known.

What was less clear, and there were many pages of testimony of his secret trial on the subject, was whether he had killed any Timon or had been directly responsible for any deaths. The human knight and mage were shown as bloodthirsty beasts, both in words and in gruesome illustrations of them cleaving and blasting Timon into pieces. But Feddar's case was more complicated; the Timon had found him innocent of the early killings, but by his own admission, he had opened the gates of the Timon keep, allowing them to enter and slaughter scores of Timon. The High Council had found him guilty of espionage and complicity to murder and sentenced him to death, but they had never carried out his execution. Rumors told of his extensive torture in the Tower, and the scars on his face suggested there was truth to the rumors. Presumably, they had kept him as potential leverage in negotiations with the humans, and in the end, the Council had absolved him of his crimes under pressure from the human occupiers.

It was hard to imagine the Feddar she knew, the man he had become, being a part of such wanton destruction. He would have been like a Shoza, sent on a mission by his government to undermine the Maer's brightstone operations, just the sort of mission the Shoza did against the humans. In his testimony, he claimed to be a pawn of forces beyond his reckoning, and he repeatedly expressed regret for the many deaths that resulted from his actions. Perhaps it was this regret that drove him to submit to Cloti so fully, as if by bringing forth her pleasure at the expense of his own, he could atone for his sins. She smiled as she pictured the soft gleam in his eye, and she wondered if he had decided to keep his promise. When he finally came over for dinner, two days hence, she would have her answer.

Ludo came back late from his meetings with a sheepish look that immediately got Cloti's attention.

"Long day again?"

"The longest." He kissed her briefly and sat down at the table, taking a long sip of the wine she poured him. "You'd never believe how much administrivia there is to a lockdown. Food still has to be made and delivered, and the produce from the outlying farms can't sit in the heat for three days until it's over. Honestly, it's probably more trouble for them than it's worth."

"Did you hear anything about their hunt for the Shoza?"

Ludo sighed. "They've rounded up two dozen from the camps, and they've found one of the hardened bunkers, though, from the sound of it, they're having a hell of a time getting in, even with their exploding spyballs. I heard the number twenty bandied about."

"They're going to execute twenty Maer?" Cloti was sickened at the thought.

Ludo nodded into his glass, then downed half of it. "It would have been thirty without Feddar's intervention. Excess retribution is what they call it. They lose ten, they take twenty or thirty. Doesn't matter if they're really Shoza or not. It's all about making a point."

The air hung heavy between them, and neither of them said anything until Ludo had finished his wine. He glanced at the bottle wistfully, then pushed his glass away. They only had a few dozen bottles left, and they had to make it last, as there was no telling when they'd be able to get more.

Ludo stood up slowly, hovering for a moment, and the sheepish little smile crept back across his face.

Cloti stood with him and rounded the table to take his hands. "There's something good you're not telling me."

He raised his eyes to hers, and she felt it almost before he spoke.

"I kissed Feddar," he said in a small voice, wincing and smiling at the same time. Cloti grabbed his face and planted one on his lips, suddenly giddy with the thought.

"Ludo, that's fantastic! I mean, was it fantastic?"

Ludo's face softened with relief, and he grinned. "Why didn't you tell me he's such a good kisser?"

"Gods, he really is." Her lips tingled with the thought, and she pressed them to Ludo's again, kissing him with some heat this time, feeling his body respond. She wanted to share with him as she did with Aefin, feel Feddar's kiss through Ludo's memory, but Ludo was always a little more private with his thoughts, and he didn't have the training to share easily.

"Who kissed whom? Was it just kissing, or was there more? I need all the details!"

Ludo slipped from her grasp to pour another half-glass of wine, and she nodded when he gestured to pour one for her.

"We had just finished the fourth, no, fifth meeting of the day, and all the military types and interpreters had gone to get tea. I was sorting through some papers, and I noticed Feddar lingering by the door. He closed it and leaned against it, and he hit me with those piercing green eyes..." He took a sip of his wine, staring out the window into the darkness. "I took my nerves in my hand and went to him, and then his lips were on mine, his hands on my waist, pulling me in." He closed his eyes and hummed a little in his throat. "Gods, Cloti, if I hadn't been worried about a pack of humans bursting through the door any second, things might have gone much farther than they did. Skundir's balls, the body on that man!"

"Mmhmm." Cloti took a sip and set down her glass, then slid her arms around Ludo's waist, pressing against him. "You should see him naked." She kissed him again, and he grabbed her behind with his free hand, angling toward the table to set his glass down. They made out like teenagers, and Cloti summoned the image of Feddar's body, the hairless expanse of his chest, his muscular legs, and his thick erection. She pushed the thoughts toward Ludo, whose lips and tongue responded as she walked him toward the wall and pressed him hard against it. Ludo broke from the kiss for a moment, gasping, and fixed her with somber, serious eyes.

"When he comes over for dinner in two days..."

"We're going to have him for dessert."

12

— • —

Cloti visited the greenhouse before her pre-dawn cycle to tend to the ooze and put a dab on her tongue. Though she wouldn't need it to reach whoever was on the other end of the pulse, she thought it might help her strengthen their connection so they could communicate more fully. She slipped into the Thousand Worlds the moment she crossed her legs, and she could sense where the signal would come from even before it began.

On Solstice dawn, the walls come down, and the path to freedom is open.

She latched onto the message, flowing toward the source, nestling around it, whispering in its ear.

Gielle sends her regards.

Cloti slipped in closer as they paused, and when they responded, she could hear them almost as if they were speaking.

Can you put us in touch?

Cloti hesitated. If she could get Gielle some Earth Milk and Gielle could control it well enough, she could use it to find them in the Thousand Worlds. Cloti could easily make a batch and share it with her, but the risk of transporting it past the humans and into the camps was too great. They might be searched at a checkpoint, and their belongings could be confiscated at any time in the camps. But if she could get Gielle a vial, she could share it judiciously, and the Shoza could communicate amongst themselves with no possible human surveillance, as humans had never learned its secrets.

Can you put us in touch? The voice repeated, urgent.

Give me three days.

She felt a pulse, then the signal evaporated.

Cloti crawled around the garden with Aefin, pulling weeds and thinning seedlings. They'd doubled down on root vegetables since they could sustain a Maer more than most crops, but they'd kept a tidy little patch of salad greens. They didn't have much space, but every single plant helped. She clipped the outermost leaves carefully at the base, trimmed the browning bits, and layered them in her basket, shaking the dirt off as best she could, given their limited water supply. She clipped some peppery fernleaf to go with it and brought it inside for washing. As Cloti was dunking the leaves in a bin of water, Aefin breezed in and dropped four nice fat radishes on the counter, splaying dirt in a rough circle around them. Cloti sighed. Some battles just weren't worth fighting, and she had bigger things on her mind.

"Can I ask your advice?" She cocked her head at Aefin, who dusted her hands and put them on her hips.

"Of course, love. What's this about?"

Cloti held up an index finger, then moved to close the door to the patio and the rear windows. Aefin took a step closer, eyebrows raised.

"I need to talk to someone about this, and I'm not ready to share with Ludo yet." Cloti's fingers were trembling slightly.

"Anything."

Cloti took a deep breath. "I've been in communication with the Shoza, both those inside and outside the city. Through the Thousand Worlds."

Aefin's brows furrowed, and her eyes took on a pained look. She nodded for Cloti to continue.

"They're planning something. Something big. At Midsummer." Aefin took her hands, and Cloti gripped hers as she continued. "I think they're going to free the camps and anyone else who wants to flee the city. They said they're going to bring down the walls."

"You can't tell Ludo," Aefin murmured, looking over her shoulder, though they both knew Ludo was at work. "It would put him in danger to know."

Cloti nodded, her heart heavy with the weight of the secret she must keep from her spouse, to whom she'd sworn before her family and friends and entire social circle to always be fully open and honest, no matter the circumstance.

"I won't. I didn't want to tell you for the same reason. But I couldn't carry this alone." Cloti melted into Aefin's arms. Aefin held her tight, reassuring her, enclosing her with her arms. Keeping her safe.

"You're never alone. Unless you want to be."

"I don't." Cloti pulled back to look into Aefin's unflinching eyes. "I need you. Always." Cloti kissed her gently, and Aefin's fingers traced across her cheek.

"So, what are you going to do? About the Shoza."

Cloti touched her forehead to Aefin's, clasping her hands behind her neck. "I'm going to help them."

Aefin paused, and Cloti could hear her breathing through her nose. She never made that sound when she was happy. Her fingers settled around Cloti's shoulders, warm and gentle, and she pulled back with deep, serious eyes.

"Just let me know what you need, and I'm with you." Aefin kissed her once more, then pushed away, turning toward the radishes. "In the meantime, I'm going to clip these greens for soup while you finish washing the salad, then we'll swap places. Oof, I need to wipe down this counter. Sorry!"

Cloti smirked as she swished the leaves around in the bin.

"At least you noticed."

Cloti prepped her alchemical furnace that afternoon. It hadn't been used since before the invasion, and it needed a little extra attention, but she found everything where she'd left it and had it ready to go before night fell. She lit the grill, throwing on a few of the early potatoes stuffed with spices to mask the smell of her alchemy. The Earth Milk wasn't difficult to make, which was good since her alchemical skills had atrophied in recent years as she'd focused more on the meditative side. All she had to do was dilute the ooze to the proper proportions and stabilize it at room temperature. She'd made it scores of times, but nearly every vial that remained prior to the occupation had been found and confiscated. The human mages seemed to have a second sense for it, which Cloti had been able to divert when they'd searched her greenhouse so they'd seen nothing more than a few plants and some fungus.

The greenhouse was rank in the summer heat, but the ooze seemed perfectly content with the heat, its surface pearlescent and smooth.

"I'm sorry, but I'm going to have to take a small part of you to help my friends." Cloti wore her mask tightly affixed this time, as she needed all her wits to make the Milk. "Not the ones from the Time to Come. These friends are here and now, and they're going to try to set us free." The ooze showed no sign of comprehension or response, but Cloti liked to treat it the same way she would any living creature and assume it understood her. Did it feel pain when she harvested a segment? She'd tried to read it, but it gave off no more sentience than a mushroom. Given the powers it bestowed, it wasn't hard to imagine it was conscious on some level.

She used the spoon to slice off a portion the size of her thumb, dropping it in a lead-lined jar and sealing it tight. She brushed some of the shimmering liquid from the ooze's surface over the exposed gelatinous center, which she believed helped it heal, though she never really knew if it was necessary. She replaced the lid with care, then removed her gear and hurried out of the greenhouse. Aefin was tending the furnace, humming a snippet from *Stainberry Wine*. She took the jar from Cloti and set it on the table with the rest of the supplies: a splash of cooking oil, some distilled water, powdered sourfruit rind, and a bit of crusted honeycomb she'd salvaged from the bottom of a jar. Pure beeswax would have made a better emulsifier, but this wasn't going to be sitting long, and she was lucky to find the honeycomb.

"We should make something fun while we have the furnace out." Aefin touched up the coals, then shut the door and adjusted the vents. "Like that red oil we used to make?" Aefin's eyes twinkled with mischief, bringing forth Cloti's smile. Though she could increase sensitivity and prolong orgasms using her mind, the oil had been a lot of fun.

"We don't have the right oil, or any sky root chili for that matter. Let's just get this made, and we'll see if we can't find a way to have some fun the old-fashioned way."

Aefin kissed her, then stood aside, hands clasped in front of her, waiting for her orders. Cloti searched her mind for the recipe, which was simple enough, and set to work. Aefin handed her what she needed, stirred the coals, and adjusted the vents so Cloti could concentrate on proportions. She almost let the honeycomb congeal on the bottom of the bain-marie, but she stirred it up just in time, and before the potatoes were done cooking on the grill, she had four vials of Earth Milk prepared and sealed.

She wiped the sweat from her brow, sitting on the little stone bench as Aefin closed down the furnace and sorted the ingredients. Within minutes, there was nothing in the garden to show they had done anything other than roast potatoes. She hadn't heard any movement in the neighboring gardens, so she was pretty sure it was safe. She buried the vials inside a bag of sand in the shed and came out to see Aefin pulling the perfectly browned potatoes off the grill and onto a platter.

"You've still got it, my love!" Aefin sat down next to her, running her fingers lightly over Cloti's back.

"The instinct to do the exact thing that could get me in the most trouble? Yep, still got that."

"Where's the fun in playing by the rules?"

"I know, but this is serious business, Aefin. They're probably executing Shoza as we speak."

Aefin went quiet, and Cloti put her hand on her knee.

"Don't worry. I'll be safe. I've still got Ludo's medallion, and if there's any trouble, I'm sure he'll help sort it."

"I hope you're right about him."

Cloti took Aefin's hands and turned to face her. "He brought me home from the camps. He let us re-open the temple. And Ludo said he negotiated the number of Shoza to be killed down from thirty to twenty."

"Tell that to the families of those twenty." Aefin was facing straight ahead, and Cloti couldn't get her to look her in the eye.

Cloti let her head fall on Aefin's shoulder, and Aefin's posture relaxed. They sat like that for a while until Aefin shifted and Cloti sat up.

"Tomorrow night, when he comes over for dinner, do you think...?" Aefin's question hung in the air, her tone difficult to read, and Cloti squeezed her hands.

"I think it's up to us."

"You mean it's up to me." She turned to Cloti, her eyes bright, almost defiant. "I know where you stand, and since Ludo's sampled his apparently divine kisses, that leaves me to decide for all of us."

"Hey, it doesn't have to be anything but dinner. Ludo sees him often enough at work, and I..." Cloti sighed. It had been a while since Aefin had taken a lover, and they hadn't really talked about it enough. "You know how I feel. I'm going to be with him sometimes. But I'll be with you always and forever. Nothing's going to change that."

Aefin nodded, wiping a tear from her eye as she pitched a small laugh.

"I know, Cloti. I do. And the thing is, I *want* to bring him to our bed—I really do. What you shared with me the other day, the way he felt, that pure desire to please you...I want that. I want to pin him to the bed and do wicked things to him, with you, with Ludo. I've been fantasizing about it ever since the first night you went to his house."

Cloti kissed her, but Aefin turned aside after a moment. She wasn't done talking.

"But?" Cloti asked.

"But I don't want to lose what we have. Ever since the humans came, since we've been trapped in our house, just the three of us...in a weird way, it's been the best time of my life. I've come to love and appreciate you, both of you, to truly understand what you mean to me. What we have together. I just...I don't want anything to change."

"Everything changes, Aefin." Cloti kissed her again, and Aefin's eyes were deep and probing. "Everything evolves. Just like we evolved after the humans came. Change brings a chance at renewal, a chance to experience parts of ourselves we hadn't yet discovered. Another world in our mind to explore."

"Gods, I love it when you talk metaphysics." Aefin grinned, cupping Cloti's cheeks and kissing her with some heat. "I want this, for tomorrow at least. I want to see those green eyes burning into mine, feel the heat of his desire. I want to temper and shape it into something new and beautiful at your side."

"I love you," Cloti murmured as she lost herself in Aefin's lips.

13

C loti used the Milk for the next morning's cycle, and it worked to perfection. She informed the Shoza on the other end of the signal about the executions. After a pause, they responded:

"The few give up their lives for the freedom of the many."

Cloti had heard that phrase used to describe the Shoza from before, and it had always rankled her, given the role they served in limiting freedom before the invasion. But now it felt like an actual noble cause. Maybe the overthrow of their civilization had an upside.

The temple practice had been postponed for another day, so she and Aefin spent the morning cleaning and dusting, rearranging pillows, and filling vases with fresh flowers from the garden. Ludo had lined up several bottles of wine before leaving for work, one of which was twenty-four years old, no doubt pulled from the same secret stash the hotstone had come from. They prepared what they could in advance, and when the market wagon came rolling up, Cloti was delighted to see leatherback eels in the ice bin. She picked two, along with a limp seedbread, which would crisp up nicely in the oven. Aefin disappeared after lunch and returned with a fresh mind puzzle, which she laid out on the table with a pencil.

"For Feddar?"

Aefin smiled. "If he figures it out before his second glass of wine, I might show him some mercy later."

Cloti glanced down at the design, which was dense and elaborate, even by Aefin's standards.

"Poor Feddar." She touched Aefin's hand, then lifted it to her lips to kiss her knuckles. "Are you sure this is what you want?"

"Positive." Her hand twisted out of Cloti's grasp to touch her chin, pulling her gently closer. The kiss was brief, but heat lingered on Cloti's lips.

They prepped the eels, the salad, and the potatoes, then tidied up, and it was still only half dusk. Cloti sat on the couch, leafing through the Delve chronicle, but her attention drifted between thoughts of Feddar and the terrible events of the previous days. Was he putting himself at risk by coming here after accompanying her home from the camps? What rumors would fly if he were seen scurrying away from the house in the dead of night or, even worse, in the harsh light of morning? He served at the pleasure of the General, who was no doubt already irritated with his efforts on behalf of the Maer. Did the humans have a law against inter-species relations, or was it merely taboo, as it was among the Maer? Did they have songs and longstories about ill-fated lovers just as the Maer did? Perhaps the Maer of the Time to Come would sing the story of Feddar and his Maer lovers. But would it be a romance or a tragedy?

Ludo came home early, smelling of lavender as he gave Cloti a brief kiss.

"You've been to the baths?"

"I have," he said with a mix of joy and sheepishness, kicking off his dusty sandals and wiping his feet with a towel. "Feddar said I deserved it after all the hard work I've been doing, and I can't say I disagreed. You're all set to resume practice tomorrow, by the way." He handed her a paper written in Islish and Maer, signed by Feddar, laying out the terms for temple practice. It was nearly the same as they'd agreed on, a hundred acolytes, accompanied to and from for a cycle of no more than an hour. It even specified that the Administrator would be the sole human in the temple unless he chose a surrogate.

"Everything looks good. Surprisingly good."

"Feddar was bullish on the details. He even gave an impassioned little speech about the importance of letting us have our public cycles, though the General was noticeably unimpressed. What's for dinner? Did you get something good from the cart?" He padded into the kitchen, pouring a glass of water and downing it in one long gulp.

"We got some nice leatherbacks from the cart, potatoes, and salad."

"Delightful!" He kissed her again, then picked up the bottle of twenty-four-year-old wine. "We'll want to decant this." He pulled out the silvered glass decanter, which they hadn't used in over a year, and gave it a rinse, then set it in the rack to dry.

"Got anything stronger in that secret stash of yours?" Aefin stood in the doorway with eyes like daggers, but she couldn't keep a smile from bursting forth.

"Sadly, I really don't. Unless we want to get oozy." He fluttered his fingers in the air, laughing, and Cloti smiled through the jolt of panic and guilt that shot through her.

"Love, you can't handle your ooze, and you're unwilling to put in the work to train yourself."

"I would, except that there's this..." He searched for the words with his hands. "This occupation going on. You might have heard of it? It's put a damper on my free time."

"Well, I'm glad you got off work early tonight. You need a break from all that gloom and doom stuff." Cloti squeezed against him, wrapping her arms around his waist. She eyed Aefin, whose smile bloomed as she pressed against Ludo from the other side. Ludo put his arms around both their shoulders, and Cloti could hear his smile through his voice.

"This is going to be the most interesting night in a very long time."

Feddar arrived right at quarter-dusk, a bouquet of flowers in one hand and a bottle in the other. He bowed awkwardly, looking surprised when Cloti leaned up to kiss him.

"Well, it's lovely to see you as well, Cloti. And Aefin! I hope you won't mind my saying that your dress is gorgeous."

"I won't." Aefin's eyes sparkled, and Cloti stepped out of the way as Aefin moved in, took Feddar by the silk lapels, and kissed him full on the lips. Feddar blinked several times as Aefin pulled away, then he quickly regained his composure and offered the flowers to Aefin with a little bow.

"If we're greeting our guest with kisses, I wouldn't want to seem rude." Ludo stepped to Feddar, put a gentle hand on his chest, and angled in slowly for a kiss. Feddar's eyes closed, and their lips pressed together for a long moment before Ludo pulled back.

"You have all made me feel most welcome." Feddar ran a hand through his hair and smiled. "And I've brought something to replace the hotstone you were so generous as to bestow upon me."

Ludo took the offered bottle, and Aefin leaned around him to read the hand-written label, wrinkling her nose as she looked up at Ludo, who was mouthing the words with a smile.

"This is from Gheil, isn't it?"

Feddar nodded, covering his smile with his hand.

"Apple brandy! And the year is...sorry, it always takes me a moment to convert. This is twelve years old?"

"Sixteen. My uncle sent me a whole case."

"Well, come on in. Let's not wait sixteen years before we have a drink!" Ludo whirled around and marched into the kitchen. Feddar removed his sandals and wiped his feet, then followed them into the kitchen.

They sipped the fiery brandy as they made small talk in the garden. The potatoes were roasting, the eel was prepped, and the grill's smoky bouquet perfumed the air. Aefin chose the chair next to Feddar, and she hung on his every word, laughing and touching him on the arm when he said something funny, which was often. Feddar was in fine form, engaging with Aefin while keeping Ludo and Cloti in the loop. When Ludo stood to put the eel on the grill, Feddar started to rise, but Aefin pulled his sleeve, and he sat back down, putting his hand atop hers. Cloti excused herself to use the washroom, and when she looked back from the kitchen door, Aefin had pulled Feddar in by the chin and was kissing him. They sat with wet lips and mischievous smiles when she returned, and she gave them both a wink.

"Make room! Make room!"

Ludo held a platter of steaming eel and crispy roasted potatoes, and they hurriedly moved the glasses and bottle out of the way so he could set it down.

"Gods, Ludo, this smells divine!"

"Just a little dried liro pepper and some salt. With eel, you want to keep it simple."

The eel was as good as it smelled, and they ate it down to the bones. Feddar was even game to try one of the eyeballs, though he made an adorably pained face as he swallowed. They sat drinking wine once Ludo had cleared the table, and Aefin's hand was now permanently attached to Feddar's, her fingers moving over his bare skin. Something stirred in Cloti as she watched, and from the look on Feddar's face, he was not unmoved by Aefin's caresses.

"I'm sorry we don't have any dessert," Ludo said as he brought over the decanter. "We haven't been able to get any sugar for quite a while. But this wine has been waiting twenty-four years for this moment." They all went silent as he poured, and they raised their glasses high. "Here's to a future brighter than our past and another drink to make the present last."

The wine flowed golden down Cloti's throat, and she smiled at the warmth that had grown between them. They swapped stories, and everyone managed to steer clear of any mention of the current troubles. They told of their childhoods, the games they used to play, and what they liked to eat. Feddar asked Aefin about her paintings and Ludo about the dialects of the Time Before. He was good at asking follow-up questions, and he led the conversation without dominating it. When he poured the end of the wine into Aefin's glass, he held the decanter high until the last drop had fallen, then set it aside and raised his glass.

"Thank you all once again for having me. Though the circumstances of our meeting are indeed unfortunate, I am most honored to find myself in your company." His eyes were glassy from the wine and perhaps something else as well. His gaze stayed with Cloti's as they all tilted their glasses and drank. No one said anything for a long moment. They sat sipping their wine, their faces lit by the three-wick candle on the table, which Aefin had been saving for a special occasion. The night air was cool, and the faintest breeze tickled the hair on Cloti's cheek.

Aefin downed the last of her wine and set the glass down rather hard on the table.

"Paintings!" she exclaimed, looking at Feddar. She stood, pulling him up with her. "I must show you my paintings."

"Well, of course, I was wondering when I'd get a chance to see them, but I didn't want to be too forward."

"Well, if you're not going to be, I suppose I'll have to take the lead." She threw a suggestive glance over her shoulder at him as she pulled him along, and he shrugged at Cloti and Ludo as he followed her inside.

"This is going rather well," Ludo said after a moment. He raised his glass toward Cloti, who clinked and let the wine spill down her throat. She was warm and buzzing all over, and the thought of what Aefin and Feddar were doing sent tingles into her core.

"We should probably give them a moment." Cloti turned her chair and scooted it closer to Ludo, taking his hands in hers and looking into his smiling eyes.

"Yes, but not too long. We can't let her have all the fun."

"We can let her have a little." Cloti put her hands on Ludo's thighs and slid them up, leaning forward, lips parted. Ludo sighed into her kiss as her fingers crept between his legs and kneaded him through his pants. She kept the kiss light, despite Ludo's attempts to deepen it, as her fingers teased him stiff. Ludo's eyes flashed with hurt as she pulled away.

"Let's save some for upstairs."

They found Aefin and Feddar in the living room, legs touching as they sat on the couch. Feddar was pointing to one of her paintings on the wall, a close-up of a cluster of honeydew flowers. Aefin held a sprig of the flowers in her hand, collected from their garden that morning and added to the vases. Neither of them seemed to have noticed Cloti and Ludo in the doorway.

"We have those too," Feddar was saying. "On my uncle's orchard, they grow wild along the fences. We used to pull out the stamens and try to get a tiny drop of nectar."

"Like this?" Aefin delicately removed a stamen, and a tiny drop quivered on the end. She held it up to Feddar's mouth, and he closed his lips around it, humming in his throat.

"Gods, that takes me back. Let me try!" He took the flowers from her, pulling and discarding several stamens until he got one with a drop, which he touched to Aefin's lips. She sucked on the stamen, then grabbed Feddar's hand and pressed her lips to his fingers, then his palm, then the tender underside of his wrist, eliciting more humming from him as his other hand moved up and down her thigh. Ludo slid his arm around Cloti, pressing into her behind, his warm lips grazing her ear.

They watched as Aefin moved her hand to cup Feddar's cheek, then leaned over to kiss him. Feddar's hand rested delicately on her shoulder as their lips moved with obvious heat. Aefin slid one hand down and began unbuttoning Feddar's shirt, then pulled back for a moment, cocking her head, and turned toward the doorway with a wicked smirk.

"I hope you don't mind if we watch for a bit," Ludo said.

Aefin turned to Feddar, her hand moving inside his shirt, and he blinked at them rapidly, then nodded, a confused and excited look on his face. Aefin slid his shirt off his shoulders, her hands massaging his chest. She slung one leg over him and sat back, her fingers exploring his skin. Feddar's hands slid up her thighs, under her dress, and she let out a sigh Cloti recognized all too well. Her heart swelled to see Aefin taking to Feddar so completely, and she felt Ludo stiff against her backside as his hands slid up her body, cupping her breasts and thumbing her nipples through her dress. She pressed back into him, pushing him against the doorframe, and his hands roamed freely, unbuttoning her dress and gliding down between her legs.

Aefin had pushed Feddar down onto the couch by now and was kissing and sucking his chest, her hands running over his smooth shoulders. Feddar's eyes were wide, and his mouth stuck in a rictus of pleasure. Aefin surged forward and devoured his lips, hands tight around his neck as her body ground against his. She stopped suddenly, panting, and tore the dress over her head, taking the slip with it. Feddar's eyes were soft and adoring as he stared at her pert figure. Ludo slid Cloti's dress the rest of the way off, his fingers tracing down her belly and sliding between her legs, teasing her through her underwear. Aefin sat back on Feddar's lap, kneading his chest with her fingers. Cloti could almost feel the hot pressure of his hardness against Aene as she bore down on him. His hands cupped her behind, and she leaned down to kiss him again, pressing her body against his, running her hands through his hair. Ludo's fingers slipped inside Cloti's underwear and rubbed across her, squeezing, then spreading her. She gave a little moan as one finger slipped partway inside and began its slow, torturous path upward.

Aefin moved off the couch to remove her underwear and was back on Feddar in an instant, unbuckling his pants and yanking them down to his ankles. She ran her fingers up and down his length, then held him stiff, studying him like she would a precious work of art. Her back arched as she lowered her mouth onto him, and though Cloti could not see exactly what was happening, Feddar's deep moan left little to the imagination. Cloti gasped as Ludo's finger reached its destination, caressing her with the most delicate touch, sending jolts of pleasure through her core. She pushed back into him, grinding him against the doorframe, feeling him as hard as marble between her cheeks.

Aefin lifted her head, then kissed her way up Feddar's chest, lingering to suck on each nipple as his groan turned into a whimper. She let her breasts fall over his mouth, and Cloti saw his hand slide between her legs, tracing up and down her wet pink flesh, slipping one finger in, then another. Aefin gasped, lowering herself onto his fingers just as Ludo's slipped into Cloti, massaging and working their way into position. She pushed back hard against him as he found the spot and began moving his fingers in slow circles, starting the spiral upward toward ecstasy.

Aefin lifted herself off Feddar's hand and slid forward, propping one knee on either side of Feddar's head and lowering herself down onto him. Cloti could hear his tongue lapping against Aefin, mixed with Ludo's hot breath in her ear as she pushed backward in rhythm with the movement of his fingers. Aefin moved like a Maer possessed, her body arching and curving, moving faster and faster as Feddar's erection bobbed and flailed in the air with the movement of their bodies. Aefin's rising cries of pleasure shot through Cloti like hot lightning, and she pounded Ludo against the doorframe as his fingers gripped her tight, squeezing and sliding so fast and hard her moans rose to join Aefin's. Feddar and Ludo added their baritone to the symphony, which echoed off the walls.

Aefin ground against Feddar, shuddering. Her cries became more desperate, thinner, until at last, she froze. She let out a gasp as her body jerked wildly, then froze. Feddar's hands clamped tight around her waist as he flipped, throbbed, and spilled all over his stomach and chest. Cloti slammed against Ludo, whose fingers moved in a flurry of uncontrolled strokes, and she ground against him as she came. His hot wetness leached through the fabric, and she smiled, pressing into him for a moment longer until they were both a hot, sticky, breathless mess.

Aefin lifted herself from Feddar's face, then slumped down against the couch, leaning her head against his heaving chest. She blinked at Cloti, eyes still shining with pleasure. She had never looked more beautiful.

Feddar clasped his hands behind his head, looking up adoringly at Ludo, who wiped him clean with a wet towel, then leaned down to kiss him gently.

"I've got to change clothes," Ludo said, gesturing at the large wet spot on his pants. "I'll be upstairs in the bedroom if anyone needs me." His fingers trailed down Feddar's stomach and between his legs, and Feddar leaned into his touch. Ludo kissed him again, a bit harder this time, then pushed off his chest to stand.

"Me too." Cloti looked down at her dress, which was wet front and back. She took Ludo's hand and pulled him after her.

"I'll bring him up in a minute once I can walk again," Aefin called after them.

Cloti washed herself and Ludo, grinning up at him as he began to rise beneath her touch. He had always recovered quickly, but this was fast even for him. Feddar seemed to bring out the best in all of them. She wiped him dry, holding him with the towel as he stiffened further. She pulled him onto the bed and kneeled next to it, dropping the towel and cradling him with her hands.

"Gods, Cloti," he murmured as she gave him a long, slow lick, then let go, watching him bob and strain in front of her face. Low voices and soft footsteps sounded from the stairs, and she brushed her lips against him.

"Looks like it's their turn to watch."

Ludo let out a sharp cry as she took him into her mouth, one stiff inch at a time, gripping his tight behind in her hands. She heard a gasp of surprise from the doorway, and she pulled back, making eye contact with Feddar, who stood with his mouth agape. She angled to the side so she could maintain Feddar's gaze as she took Ludo all the way in. Feddar's hand reached down to the growing bulge in his pants, and his eyes took on a desperate softness, stirring her to her core.

She patted the bed next to her, and Feddar approached, with Aefin following. Aefin stopped him just before he reached the bed, reaching around him to undo his pants and pull them down. Cloti slid her mouth off Ludo and took Feddar's stiff length in her fingers, covering his tip in a dozen tiny kisses. She rose to meet his lips, kissing him softly, then pushed him down to where she had been kneeling. He stared hungrily at Ludo's erection, then glanced back up at Cloti as if waiting for permission.

"Make him whine, but don't let him spill," she said, her fingers grazing Feddar's smooth cheek.

Feddar kissed her hand, then gripped Ludo's thighs and opened his lips to take Ludo in. Cloti looked into Ludo's face, her heart stirring at the soft heat in his eyes. They had brought in lovers before, but never had she seen both of her spouses so utterly taken with anyone else. Aefin's arms wrapped around her, and Cloti took a step back into her, moving them sideways so she could kiss her while still watching Ludo and Feddar.

Feddar moved with languid strokes up and down Ludo's length, stopping to lick and admire him whenever Ludo whined, which was often. Aefin kissed Cloti with slow heat, eager hands roaming over her body, and Cloti could feel her wife's desire rising like steam from a hot spring, enveloping them both in a cloud of sensual delirium. She kept Aefin's hands in check but could not stop her from falling to her knees and nuzzling between her legs. Feddar stopped for a moment, his eyes dark with lust as he watched Aefin work, Ludo's tip hovering just in front of his lips. He turned and took Ludo in again, moving faster, and Ludo's whines rose suddenly to the point Cloti worried he would spill, but Feddar pulled back again, holding Ludo firm and covering him with soft kisses. Cloti hummed as Aefin stroked her gently with her tongue, repeating the same pattern over and over until Cloti was ready to boil over. She gripped Aefin's hair and pulled her back, and Aefin looked up at her, face wet and matted, eyes mischievous and curious.

"Feddar," Cloti said, her voice thick with desire, "give poor Ludo a break." She moved in front of Feddar as Ludo pulled back with a sigh, and Feddar looked up at her, his breath hot between her legs, his eyes bright and eager. "Kiss me for a while." She ran her fingers through his hair, pulling him in, and he picked up where Aefin had left off. She closed her eyes and bathed in the sensation of his tongue and lips exploring her, every inch, every fold. She fisted her hands in his hair, and he gripped her behind tightly, pulling her cheeks apart a bit as he delved into her with his nose. She briefly considered pushing her sensations into him, but he seemed to know what she was feeling already, putting pressure in all the right places at just the rhythm she liked. As she approached the edge, she yanked his head back, and he breathed hot and hard into her, his eyes questioning.

"Onto the bed with you." She gestured, and Feddar lay back, scooting up so he lay in the middle of their oversized bed, which was built for three but could easily accommodate four. She turned to see Aefin teasing Ludo with her lips and tongue, and Aefin stopped, a devilish smile growing on her face as she saw Feddar splayed out on the bed, thick and fully erect. His eyes searched theirs as if wondering which of them was going to ravish him next.

Cloti answered by circling the bed on all fours, then turning around and lowering herself over his eager mouth, pinning his arms down with her knees. She kept herself just out of easy reach, so he had to struggle to fully connect, and she felt his desperation grow. He was the most unselfish lover she'd ever had, as if he lived only for his partners' pleasure, with his own as an afterthought. She rewarded him by lowering herself down all the way and pressing back against him as she fondled his nipples, which stiffened beneath her touch. His little moans vibrated up into her through his expert tongue, and she had to lift herself partway off after a moment, as she was not ready for another climax just yet.

Ludo sidled in, throwing his leg over Feddar's and kissing him all over his chest. Cloti guided him to Feddar's nipples, pressing his head down on one, then the other, and Feddar's mouth froze for a moment each time Ludo's lips made contact. Aefin arrived on all fours, and Cloti raised up for a moment so Feddar could watch her. She hovered between Feddar's legs, fondling him gently with her fingers. Studying him.

"Wait for me," Aefin murmured before taking him in with glacial slowness. Feddar let out a long, desperate whine, which Cloti stifled by pressing down against him and holding him in place.

Aefin and Ludo took turns pleasuring him with their mouths, neither of them for long enough to make him spill, but Cloti could feel in the uneven movement of his lips and tongue that he was getting close. She rose off him, motioning Aefin and Ludo to do the same, and Feddar's eyes were hot and wild, begging for release as he looked from one of them to the other.

"Soon, my love," she murmured, then kissed him, his breath heady with her taste, his lips and tongue eager, so eager. "Do you want to watch first?"

"Yes, please. Gods, yes!"

"As you wish."

She leaned over his body and took Aefin's face in her hands, studying the dark gleam in her eyes as they closed in. Aefin kissed her recklessly, her arousal hot in Cloti's mouth. Aefin's hands moved over her body, gripping, almost painfully at times, as their lips crushed together. Cloti sneaked a look at Feddar, whose eyes bored into hers, hard and sharp with want, sending her heart spinning. She poured everything she had into that kiss, that embrace. Hands squeezed and fingers delved, and their breath grew fast together. Feddar's little gasps and whines sparked something deep inside, and Cloti had to feel his mouth on her again without delay. She pulled away from the kiss, eyeing Aefin toward his leaking erection as she angled back over Feddar and melted onto his face. Aefin grasped him tightly and held him upright, then sank down onto him, sending a shudder through Feddar's body.

Ludo stepped up close, and Aefin grabbed him and stroked him carelessly, her face transforming as her body rocked atop Feddar. Cloti planted her hands on Feddar's chest as she moved against him, slipping back and forth over his chin while his tongue lapped her mercilessly. She looked up at Ludo, who watched her with eyes whose warmth rivaled their heat. As Cloti's body exploded with pleasure, her walls disintegrated, and the words *I love you* flooded out of her mind. Aefin's piercing cry as she crested seemed to answer her, and Cloti saw tears in Ludo's eyes as he spilled. Feddar's tongue continued with gently decreasing strokes until, at last, he stopped, and she collapsed to the side, her arm flopping onto his chest. Ludo grabbed a towel and took care of the mess while Aefin rolled onto her side, her fingers tracing across Cloti's shoulder. Soon Ludo joined on the other side, and they all crowded around Feddar, who lay spent, silent, and smiling like a baby. His hands moved to touch each of them, his voice thick with emotion as he spoke.

"This means so much to me. I've never been this close to anyone in my entire life as I am to each of you right now. I know it sounds dramatic, but it's just the way I feel, and I thought I should say it."

They kissed away his tears, murmuring sweet nothings to him as they snuggled in and drifted together into a warm, cozy sleep.

14

— · —

Cloti eased out of bed at quarter dawn, creeping across the room on soft feet, watching as Feddar stirred. He rolled toward Aefin, and she snuggled into his chest, her arm sliding over his hip with a hitching yawn. Ludo lay sprawled in the space Cloti had freed, finally able to take up half the bed as usual. She smiled, put on her slip, then padded out of the room and down the stairs. She took a furtive sip of the Earth Milk and washed it down with a glass of stale water from the cask before taking her place on her mat in the garden. The air was heavy, and the sky was gray; rain was sure to come by noon.

Her head was thick from last night's wine, but the power of the Milk and the cozy thoughts of the warmth of the shared bed soon eased her mind, and her arms curved slowly upward with strength and ease. The Thousand Worlds felt different, empty now that the cradles were all inactive, and if anyone else was accessing them using the Earth Milk or the power of their minds, they weren't doing it at the same time as she. She quickly found the signal and created a space around it without thinking.

Our temple cycles begin again today, she mindspoke almost conversationally.

And the Earth Milk?

I will deliver it tomorrow. Look for them the day after. I will make them ready.

You risk much for the cause, Cloti.

Hearing her name almost tore her from her trance, but she clung to the signal and soon settled back in.

The few give up their lives for the freedom of the many. It felt strange saying it, even to a disembodied voice in the Thousand Worlds, but she felt it was true. She had glimpsed the Time to Come and a few moments in between, and while she did not know what her own fate would hold, she knew the Maer would persevere. Though it was humans who would discover the ooze she'd left on the Isle of a Thousand Worlds, they knew of the Maer, proof that they had endured.

Our success depends on you. Risk only what you must and let the Shoza take the heat.

Cloti thought of the twenty, Shoza or not, who would soon be dead if the humans hadn't executed them already. Sadness swelled within her; she pushed out her sympathy and felt gentle thanks in return. Something shifted in her mind, and her awareness returned to her body. She opened her eyes and saw Feddar sitting across the garden, eyes closed, arms slowly lifting upwards.

Two days, she mindspoke, then let go, slipping out of the Thousand Worlds and fully occupying her body once again. She matched her arms with Feddar's and moved with him, though he went too fast to fully center himself. She pushed out a wave toward him, and his eyes popped open for a moment, and when they closed again, his movement slowed. She led him through the cycle, amazed at their connection, despite his limited practice. When their hands reached the ground again, she stood and walked across the garden toward him.

"Good morning, beautiful." He touched her hips tentatively, and she closed the distance, pressing a gentle kiss into his waiting lips as his hands cradled her body.

"Did you sleep well?"

"I can't remember when I've slept better." His eyes half closed as he angled in for another kiss. When they opened again, their warm intensity melted Cloti's heart.

"It wasn't all too much?" she asked, her fingers sliding up the back of his neck.

"It was…" He bit his lip as if trying to hold back tears. "I don't want to make a fool of myself, but it was…the most beautiful night of my life."

She kissed him again, heat rising inside her as she pressed into him, feeling the restrained strength of his hands on her body, wishing she could unleash that strength and make him claim her.

"We could make it beautiful again." She gripped his behind, clutching him closer, feeling his arousal as she deepened the kiss.

He pulled back with a stuttering sigh, his grip lightening, his hands sliding up her back.

"Gods, Cloti, I wish I could stay, but I'm already going to be late for my first meeting."

She let her forehead fall against his, clutching the back of his neck for a moment before relaxing her grip.

"I'll see you at the temple, yes?"

Feddar cocked his head, then blinked rapidly, smiling. "Yes, yes, at noon. I'll be there."

"And maybe later?"

He grimaced, baring his teeth. "I have a dinner tonight with a delegation from the Realm. They're here to oversee our progress with the de-occupation. I'm just glad they weren't here when..." He shook his head. "I hope nothing else happens while they're here. I'm doing all I can, but the General is a bloodthirsty bastard. If there's another attack, I fear the reprisals will be much worse. If there's anything you can do..." He searched her eyes, and she looked down, wondering if he somehow knew of her connections to the Shoza. She wasn't sure if she held any sway, and she feared they would redouble their efforts after the reprisal.

"I'll see you at noon." She kissed him once more before he released her and turned slowly away toward the house.

Some of the acolytes were tense as they entered the temple, and Cloti did her best to ease their minds, pushing out peaceful, reassuring vibes to each of them as she bowed to them. It was tiring, and by the time she moved to the dais, she worried she wouldn't have the strength to complete the cycle. She discretely sipped from her water bottle, to which she'd added a dose of the Milk. By the time she'd settled into her cross-legged position, the harmonic lines of the temple ceiling flowed into her, boosting her further. As she looked into each pair of eyes, she saw them, felt their focus, their fears, their joy. She saved Feddar for last, and in the instant their eyes met, she saw such naked admiration it made her lose her center.

She pressed her hands together to refocus, and every pair of hands in the temple did the same in crisp unison. She spread her arms wide, letting the backs of her hands rest against the cool marble. The power of the temple flowed through her and out into every one of the hundred acolytes present.

"If you travel far enough into the future, it becomes the past."

Her words echoed in the quiet temple as her hands left the marble and began their slow ascent. She made an hourglass pattern this time, and by the second hump, the group's energy was as strong as any cycle she'd ever felt. Juiya was here again, as well as Gielle and two other Shoza, but even among the other acolytes, she sensed strong training. They had lost nothing during the occupation; if anything, they were stronger, though their thoughts had a different structure, perhaps influenced by the Shoza's disciplined approach.

When her hands reached the top of the cycle and pressed together above her head, she summoned the leaf on the lake, but this time she showed it from underneath the surface of the water. The leaf's dark mass nearly blotted out the sun, but a few stray rays made it through around the edges, refracting through the crystalline surface of the lake. The dark skeletons of trees jutted out all around, but the leaf floated in the space in between, wreathed in sunlight the darkness couldn't block out entirely.

She left them with that image while she sank farther below, circling around to find Gielle, whose guarded aura was easy to spot. She flowed around Gielle, begging communion, but it took her a while to open up.

I have the Earth Milk. I will bring it to the camp tomorrow.

But how? They're searching everyone who comes in and out.

I will find a way. When you receive it, make ready, for you need to go find them in the Thousand Worlds at dawn the next day.

There was a pause. *We can't be seen together. Not now. Deliver it to Fiola, the sector nurse. She's one of us. She'll make sure it gets to me.*

We need things to be peaceful between now and then; if we're in lockdown again, I won't be able to come at all.

Understood.

Cloti pulled away, returning her focus to the leaf on the lake. The chill of the deeper water near her toes beckoned her, but she floated just out of its reach where the sun still held some sway, and the leaf rested weightless on the glassy surface. A hundred minds joined in this shared vision, and their combined energy flowed through Cloti like so many points of light in the Thousand Worlds. A few of them twinkled in unison, and Cloti felt little murmurs of conversation sparking between them. Most remained focused on the leaf, but in time they might come out of their shells a bit. If they could learn to do this on their own, with the help of the Earth Milk, they could communicate in real time over distance without any chance for the humans to intercept their messages. It would change the game entirely.

She let the leaf fade, and the minds began the slow process of re-individuation as their arms lowered and Cloti gradually loosened the common bond. When her knuckles hit the marble, she let them go entirely, but she still felt echoes of them in the air around her, as if their connection were not entirely gone.

She stood, bowed to the acolytes, and took Aefin's offered arm. She was suddenly exhausted, and the effort of bidding the acolytes goodbye was almost more than she could bear. Feddar paused in the doorway, gave a gentle blink, then pulled his hood over his face and followed the acolytes and soldiers out into the suddenly pouring rain.

Aefin was especially eager that night, teasing Ludo for almost an hour with a dizzying combination of patience and frenzy. She held him firm as she strapped him into the harness, heedless of his whines, keeping him rigid and jutting toward the ceiling. She left him trussed and desperate and took her time pleasuring Cloti with her mouth, fingers, and strap-on while Feddar watched, his erection helpless and immobile in the harness. His eyes took on an almost pained look as Cloti huffed in his face while Aefin thrust and rubbed her to a shuddering climax above him. Cloti collapsed onto the bed and could only watch, spent and amazed, as Aefin lifted Ludo's legs, teased him open with one, then two fingers, then slid the strap-on into him, eliciting shouts that mixed pain and ecstasy. Aefin pulled out when Ludo's shouts grew too loud, teasing him with her fingertips, then plunging in again, repeating the cycle until Ludo's eyes were wide and glassy, his mouth held in a fragile circle of acceptance. A growl rose in Aefin's throat, and her thrusts grew more persistent. Cloti crawled closer to Ludo, studying his face as it broke. His groans of pleasure filled the room and echoed out into the garden as he spilled all over the harness and his stomach.

Aefin pulled out, hastily unbuckled the strap-on, and climbed over Cloti, her eyes hot and desperate. Cloti nodded, taking Aefin's hips in her hands and guiding her down onto her face. Cloti barely had time to get into a rhythm with her lips and tongue before Aefin was grinding into her, hands gripping Cloti's hair roughly as she came with an almost pained groan, flooding Cloti's senses and soaking her face and the bed beneath her. Aefin flopped over onto her side, her eyes full of gratitude. Cloti turned to her, kissing her forehead, her eyes, her nose, and her lips. Ludo tossed the soiled harness onto the floor, wiped himself, then rolled over to press against Cloti, his arm draping over both of them. Though no one spoke his name, Cloti was sure that Feddar floated in and out of their thoughts as they drifted off together into a deep sleep.

15

Cloti visited the Thousand Worlds in her morning cycle for just long enough to inform the Shoza of her progress. She spent the rest of the cycle exploring the farther reaches of the infinite space. The words she'd spoken at the temple the day before echoed in her mind, and she longed to explore the worlds at her leisure again as she'd done before the invasion, dipping into one time or another, slipping between worlds and realities. She hadn't been in the right headspace for such exploration since the occupation, but she found her strength growing again, her center more stable than it had ever been. The temple practice had given her a boost, but it was also the renewed bonds with her spouses and the fiery spark Feddar brought into their bed. So much closeness, such tight connections with others, had created a strength within herself she never could have achieved on her own. And now that she had a ready supply of the Earth Milk, there was no limit to what she could discover. But she had to make sure Gielle got her vials first.

Aefin helped her gather supplies from a few neighbors for the basket: bandages, dried herbs, ointment for wounds, and various assorted medicines that would help the vials of Earth Milk blend in. She had written the words "cough suppressant" on the vials in case anyone got curious. Even if the guards opened the vials, it was unlikely they would know what it was, or so she hoped. She doubted the mages were scanning for it; they'd be too busy running the spyballs.

Aefin wound her scarf around her neck and slung her bag over her shoulder as Cloti prepared to leave. She stopped, looking down with a pout, when Cloti shook her head.

"It's too risky." Cloti put a hand on Aefin's shoulder, and Aefin shrugged it off.

"I've hardly left the house in months! And besides, you've already let me in on your secret. If they scoop you up, they'll come looking for me anyway. Might as well save them some time."

Cloti studied Aefin's pout, which masked a more genuine sadness. She had a point; if Cloti was caught, Aefin and Ludo were doomed as well. And besides their daily walk around the neighborhood and the temple cycles, Aefin hadn't been out since the occupation had begun. The repeated lockdowns had taken their toll on everyone, but at least Cloti and Ludo got to go out into the city now.

"Okay, my love. But—" Aefin's kiss stopped her short, and it took her a moment to extract herself from her wife's tight embrace. "Just be prepared for some unpleasantness. The humans were suspicious enough before the latest attack. No matter what they say or do, don't fight it, and don't talk back."

Aefin's eyes blazed fiercely, but she nodded.

"I promise."

Cloti worried about Aefin's temper; she'd gotten into a bit of trouble with the neighborhood guards early on. If the humans were rough with her, she might not be able to hold her tongue. But it was that very spirit that had drawn Cloti to her in the first place. They couldn't afford to let the humans strip away what made them who they were.

Feddar's medallion got them through the various checkpoints without too much scrutiny. The basket was checked each time, but the human soldiers seemed to be looking for weapons or bombs, and they quickly waved them through. The wind picked up as they crossed through the park, and the rustling of leaves and the smell of impending rain filled the air. There were few Maer about, leading ox carts or pulling their loads themselves, all with human escorts. Aefin clung tightly to her arm as they approached the camp gate, where two soldiers advanced from either side, hands at the hilts of their swords, as another stepped forward with a clipboard. She didn't recognize any of them.

"Good morning. Please state your name and business."

Cloti handed him her medallion and gave their names. He recorded them, then stuck the pencil behind his ear and blinked expectantly.

"The reason for your visit?"

"We're delivering some medical supplies to a sector nurse named..." She made a show of checking the tag. "Fiola. Sector twenty-eight."

The soldier licked his finger, then flipped through the pages. He stopped, scanned with his eyes, then pressed his finger against the paper.

"Fiola, sector twenty-eight. Is she expecting you?"

"We were assigned her sector in the neighborhood charity pool. I don't know if she knows about that, but I was assured..." She pushed out a soupçon of sweetness, and he cracked a smile as he rummaged through the basket.

"You're fine to go on through. You have two hours to check out with us. After that, someone's going to come looking for you." His tone was concerned but with an undertone of menace. Her powers of persuasion could only get her so far with someone like him.

"Your concern is appreciated."

"Oh, and..." He pulled up his scarf over his nose. "We move active cases to the nursing camps, but there's always some out there."

Aefin's grip finally lightened as they crossed the open yard between the human compound and the endless grids of the camps. Maer moved quickly, sensing the approaching storm, and Cloti picked up her pace as she saw the dark clouds gathering.

"Slow down! I want to see." Aefin tried to drag her slower, and Cloti stopped for a moment, watching one Maer offer herbal tea to another, who was transcribing from a book to a sheet of bark paper in tiny, precise handwriting. A sharp-eyed dog with a pointy nose and ears watched them from in between two tents. The passersby sped up as the first fat drops of rain began to fall.

"Can we go now?" Cloti said, pulling her scarf over her head.

"Is it far?"

Cloti barked a small laugh. "Farther than you'd think, but only about a fifteen-minute walk."

It was raining steadily by the time they found the marker for sector twenty-eight. Cloti looked around, blocking the rain with her hand. She tried to decide which of the hunched passersby to flag down for help when a figure approached from between two tents.

"Cloti?" The Maer flashed a coin, and she smiled as she saw the eye and recognized it as one of hers.

"Can you take me to Fiola?"

"Follow me. We'll get you out of this rain. It should pass by halfternoon, I think."

The nursing tent was several times the size of the others, separated by curtains into four small rooms, each with a cot, plus a larger room with several chairs. Two of the cots appeared to be occupied, though the curtains prevented Cloti from seeing more detail than that. A Maer with a nurse's red bandana around her bicep and a scarf pulled up over her nose gestured them into the sitting area. Cloti rearranged her scarf to cover her nose and wiped her feet on a ratty mat, turning to thank whoever had brought them, but their escort had disappeared into the rain.

"Thank you, Cloti, and...who are you?" She bowed, glancing at Aefin, not unkindly, but the tone of her voice made it clear she was not used to asking twice.

"I'm Aefin, I'm..."

"She's my wife, and she helped me gather the supplies."

"She must be very dedicated or very brave. Not everyone who comes into the camps is allowed out, you know."

"We have a medallion from the Administrator. I think we're safe."

"No one is safe. Not even the Administrator," the nurse said in Ormaer, the same dialect of ancient Maer that Gielle had used. Aefin glanced at Cloti; Aefin hadn't studied Ormaer. Cloti touched her reassuringly on the shoulder, though Fiola's words had shaken her a bit. "Let's see what you've brought," Fiola said in Maer.

"Bandages, splints, cough suppressant, ointment..." Cloti stopped as Fiola took the basket and rifled through it, expertly sorting the contents into various drawers and shelves and pocketing the vials with subtle movements.

"We could use some fever bark tonic next time if you can find any and some tooth powder. I don't know what kind of access you have to supplies cliffside, but those would help."

"I'll see what I can do. We're not usually allowed to leave the neighborhood, and the carts they send around mostly have food but not much medicine."

"Sounds about like here, but I bet you get better food. Do you get darkroot tea?"

Cloti shook her head wistfully. "We've been out for a while. I heard there'll be a shipment coming at Midsummer, though. It might give us just the boost we need." A chill ran up her neck as she spoke. Was she playing the game right?

Fiola's blink showed she had understood. "Your lips to the gods' ears. Speaking of which, I know you have to check in at the gate before too long, but would you mind doing a short cycle with me? The stress of recent days has taken its toll." She gave Cloti a meaningful look, and Cloti nodded.

"Of course. Aefin, you'll join us?"

Aefin eyed Cloti nervously and lowered down to sit on the floor, which had been swept clean and was mostly dry, except for their footprints. Cloti joined her, and Fiola scooted a chair out of the way and sat two full arm's lengths away. A cough sounded from behind one of the curtains, and Cloti found herself holding her breath.

"You should be fine if you keep your faces covered, but if either of you should show the slightest symptoms in the coming days, make sure to isolate, and get some medicine if you can."

Cloti nodded, and Fiola's posture relaxed, her hands dropping to her sides, her eyes fixed expectantly on Cloti.

"Tell our friend to join the Thousand Worlds at dawn tomorrow. I will be there to guide her." Cloti said the words in Ormaer like an invocation, in case anyone was listening in. Fiola nodded and closed her eyes, and Cloti did the same.

As Cloti slowly raised her arms, she connected with Aefin right away, and Fiola joined them shortly thereafter. Like the other Shoza, she had a slightly rigid mental discipline, but their connection was solid. Cloti couldn't get close enough to pass words to Fiola, but they shared an understanding, and by the time their brief cycle was complete, Cloti was certain Fiola would deliver the vial and the instructions as intended.

"I will return by Fourthday next with more supplies. Fever tonic and tooth powder, plus whatever else I can bring."

"We could really use some clean menstrual pads too. It's one of the worst things about being here."

"I'll take up a collection," Aefin chimed in. "Most of our friends are in menopause anyway."

"That would be most appreciated. Thank you both for coming down. For the supplies and for the cycle." She pushed herself to standing on strong legs, then bowed. Cloti and Aefin bowed back, and Fiola's eyes brightened as a sharp ray of sun hit the edge of the tent, though the rain was still pattering across the canvas.

"Excellent timing!" Fiola said. "You can find your way back?"

"Yes, I think so. The main road is..." Cloti pointed toward one wall of the tent, and Fiola shook her head and pointed toward the one they'd come in.

"Just follow the path out and take a right. You'll run into the road soon enough, and it's all the way left."

The coughing started again behind one of the curtains, and Cloti checked her scarf, bowed once again to Fiola, and stepped out into a drizzling rain pierced by shafts of sunlight. Aefin tugged on her sleeve, and Cloti turned around to see a vibrant rainbow arcing over the valley.

"It's got to be a sign, right?" Aefin asked hopefully.

"It is if we take it that way." The rain picked up suddenly, and she clutched Aefin's hand in hers and splashed off toward the gate.

16

— · —

Cloti slipped out of the tangle of Aefin and Ludo's limbs early the next morning and set herself up in her study since the rain had persisted through most of the night and the garden was wet. A cascading jade plant in the window gave the illusion of being outside, and she lit a cone of incense to help set the mood. She took a careful drink of the Milk, which hit her more gradually than the pure ooze. She took another small sip, and soon she was spreading out across the Thousand Worlds, searching for Gielle's signal.

It was hard to miss. Gielle must have drunk a double dose at least; her signal blazed hot and bright. Cloti eased around it, framing it, adding her control, and soon she felt Gielle's consciousness, bewildered but determined.

Follow me, Cloti mind-whispered and tugged gently at the bubble surrounding Gielle. It stretched, then released from its moorings, and Gielle flowed with it. *You may not be able to talk at first but send a pulse if you can hear me.*

Gielle's pulse was strong and clear.

I'm taking you to the Shoza I've been in contact with. Pay attention, so you can find them on your own next time. Cloti sent a spark out into space, directing it to form a line between where Gielle had started and where the mountain Shoza was waiting, and she sensed Gielle's amazement.

I see it, Gielle said clumsily, as if drunk. *I can feel it. I can feel everything!*

Did you drink the whole vial?

Only about a quarter of it!

You only need a dram next time. Cloti was surprised Gielle hadn't passed out or begun hallucinating so wildly she would have been unreachable. It spoke to the strength of her training.

I can see that now. It's all so much...

Stay with me. Follow the spark's trail and feel for the signal.

I feel it! I feel it!

Good. Now ease up close, nice and slow. That's it. Cloti guided Gielle to the source of the signal and opened a space for the three of them.

I'm here! Gielle said giddily. *I can feel you. I think I recognize you. Who are you?*

You may leave us, Cloti, said the other Shoza. *We will keep in touch.*

Cloti sent a burst of warmth to them both, then left them to their conversation. She eyed the swirling blackness, the myriad points of light, and she flowed around and between them, feeling their moods. Some radiated bliss, others pain and death, some laughter, others sadness. There were a few that gave off no aura at all, and it was those that interested her the most. Were they points in time before there were Maer? Or were they from a future when the Maer were no more? Or perhaps another world, one with no intelligent life or with life so different it did not register to her mind?

She would begin visiting these other worlds again soon, but not today. Her mind was too full of the events of recent days, her nerves too frazzled at the actions she'd taken. If anyone caught wind of what she'd done, she would face the same fate as the twenty Maer locked in the tower, awaiting their day of public execution. She hadn't told Ludo or Feddar what she'd been doing, and it was eating her up inside. How could she build relationships if she lacked the basic trust to tell her partners the truth?

She told herself she was just trying to protect them, but the frittering fingers of her mind pulled apart this weak argument like a loose thread on a sweater. She hadn't told Ludo because he would have told her to stop, and she hadn't told Feddar because there was always a chance he'd be forced to do something about it. But what if the Shoza were planning something against him? He would certainly be a logical target for any reprisals. They'd targeted him before, and they surely would again unless she could somehow convince them not to.

The temple cycle went well, with a mix of returning and new acolytes. Gielle flashed Cloti a sheepish smile as she entered, looking a bit bleary-eyed. Cloti felt a bit light-headed herself, but she took a long drink from her Milk-laced water bottle, which set her mind right. Once the cycle started, it took a while for Cloti to find her way through Gielle's mental fog, but once she did, Gielle assured her everything was on track. Cloti noticed a few new Shoza she hadn't seen before, and she sent a welcoming pulse but did not seek further communication. She greeted them after the cycle, fixing their faces in her mind so she would recognize them if she saw them again.

As the acolytes departed, Feddar lingered by the door, motioning her over with his chin.

"Administrator," she said with a deferential bow since the guards outside were within earshot, though she doubted they spoke much Maer. Feddar pulled her to the side with a pained expression.

"You visited the camps without informing me?" he whispered.

"It was a charity mission. We were bringing medical supplies to one of the nurses." She spoke calmly, but her stomach churned at the half-truth.

"You were flagged by the overseer. He checks every record, and the nurse you met with has had several suspicious contacts with those believed to be Shoza."

Cloti covered her mouth, hoping her reaction would seem natural. "I'm sorry, I should have asked. I just—well, our neighborhood is starting a little charity for the camps, bringing what little we can. It feels wrong sitting up in our comfortable houses while they live in such conditions."

Feddar closed his eyes, and she could see his eyeballs twitching behind his lids.

"It's all right. I covered for you, but please, don't visit the camps again without checking with me first. If they flag you again, you might end up there yourself, and I—" He paused, his hands brushing against hers in the shadows of the temple. "I might not be able to help you."

Cloti nodded, linking her fingers with his, tiny sparks dancing in her chest.

"When can I see you again?"

He glanced at the doorway, angling his body to leave. "I can't come to your house, not so soon. But come tonight, at half dusk. Bring the book, the Delve chronicle. We can discuss what you read, and I'll have you escorted back after dinner."

"Just dinner?" She stepped closer, feeling his body heat radiating into her, caressing his palm with her fingers.

"I can't say no to you." He let go of her hand, bowed, and turned away without a word, though Cloti noticed him sharing a glance with Aefin.

"What was that about?" Aefin asked as they straightened the mats and sorted the bells and incense.

"Apparently, our visit was flagged. He said if we get flagged again, we might end up in the camps."

"Gods, they really want to control our every movement."

"We just have to lay low for a bit." Cloti dropped the last mat on the pile and wiped her hands.

"You're going to see him again, aren't you?"

"I am. Tonight."

Aefin's little pout squeezed Cloti's heart, and she took her in her arms, though Aefin turned away from her kiss.

"He can't come to our house again so soon. It would look suspicious."

"But it's not suspicious you going to visit him at his house?"

"The book. I'm going to tell him what I read about the Delve."

"I bet you delve into much more interesting topics while you're there." Aefin cracked a half-smile, and she accepted Cloti's kiss this time, sliding her hands down to cup Cloti's behind. "Promise you'll share with us after," she murmured. "We could use the Milk and share with Ludo too."

Cloti kissed her again with more heat as thoughts of sharing with Aefin and Ludo billowed through her mind.

"I'll see if I can't bring back something extra special."

Aefin spun Cloti around and pushed her against a column, pressing into her as she gazed deep into Cloti's eyes.

"Convince him he needs to come back to play."

Cloti gasped as Aefin lifted her buttocks and devoured her lips. Feddar's arrival in their lives had lit a fire in Aefin, and Cloti lost herself in the kiss, letting her wife plunder her mouth and grope her to within an inch of her life. If the guards outside happened to glance inside the temple, they were sure to have something to think about in their bunks in the dark of night.

Cloti gave herself a sponge bath and put on dabs of muskwood in all the important places. Aefin helped her pick out her dress, a simple but elegant brown silk number with dragons stitched in gold thread. Cloti adjusted the neckline in the mirror, smiling as she pulled it down just a hair.

"Good choice. The brown is understated, so it won't draw too much attention, but silk is always sexy." Aefin ran her hands over Cloti's hips, then rested her head on her shoulder, looking at her in the mirror. "You're beautiful, you know that?" She kissed Cloti's ear, then pulled back and straightened the dress.

Cloti turned around and kissed her gently.

"I love you too."

17

— • —

Feddar kept her waiting while he finished up a meeting, and the departing humans nodded rather too politely at her as she sat on a couch flipping through the Delve chronicle again. Once they had left, Feddar held his arms wide as if in apology, then gestured toward the garden. She followed him along the path to the table by the grill, where a bottle and two glasses were laid out. He turned, glancing toward the door, then his face relaxed, and he took Cloti's hand and brought it to his lips.

"Thank you for coming."

She took his chin and pulled him down for a kiss, pressing her other hand into his chest. His lips were soft, compliant to her every movement, and when he broke from the kiss too soon, she nipped at his chin, flashing him a little hurt look.

"Can we save that for after?" he asked with an apologetic smile.

"Whatever you want," she murmured.

He poured them drinks, and they sat at the gazebo to study the book. She summarized what she'd read and pointed out the drawings of him. They were exceptional likenesses, except for the wicked sneer the artist put into every picture save the last one, when he was being taken into the tower. His eyes had a softness Cloti recognized all too well as he glanced back at the Maer who had captured him.

"Who's she to you?" Cloti asked, pointing at the picture of the female Maer named Aene shedding a tear as Feddar was led away. It was such a small tear it could easily have been missed, but it had stood out to Cloti when she'd first seen it and doubly so now.

Feddar downed his drink, then refilled it and topped off hers, all the while studying the bottle rather carefully. When he finally set it back down, he raised his glass with a faraway look in his eye.

"Aene and I made love once." He looked tentatively into Cloti's eyes as if expecting to see jealousy or judgment.

"You had feelings for her."

"I did."

Cloti paused; the story of the Delve took on a different light now, and she almost wanted to reread it as a love story, though the end was not a very happy one for him.

"Do you know what happened to her?"

Feddar took a long drink and shook his head. "She said she was from Helscop, and I had the Administrator there comb the records, but he found no recent mention of her." He took another sip, swilling the wine in his mouth for a moment. "It probably wasn't his highest priority. And I don't know if she'd want to see me again anyway, after what's happened. Still, it would be nice to know. If she's alive."

"Well, at least you have these drawings of her. How accurate are they?"

Feddar's finger traced over the page, seeming to wipe Aene's tear. "Remarkable. This artist is a genuine talent. And did you see the waadrech?" He flipped back to the page showing the dragon rising up behind the human mage. "It gives me chills just looking at it."

"I suppose, as Administrator, you could keep the copy here in case you ever wanted to read it."

Feddar shook his head. "I still have nightmares about that place. The less I think of it, the better. But thank you for bringing the book and for doing my homework for me. I'll make sure it gets to the library once I've had another look." He tapped the book, then stood, gesturing with his wineglass toward the grill. "I've got some meatroot fresh from the market wagon. You said you're mostly vegetarian, right?"

"And he listens, too." Cloti stood and followed him to the grill, bringing the bottle with her. She refilled their drinks while he checked the fat red roots, which already had a nice char on the outside.

"They still need a few more minutes." He leaned against the table, his glass hanging idly from his hand. She could feel he was working up to say something, so she just watched as his face slowly composed itself to speak.

"How are Aefin and Ludo?"

A smile grew on Cloti's face. "They're fine. They asked after you too. They're very taken with you." She reached out and brushed her fingers across the back of his hand. "Aefin especially."

Feddar closed his eyes for a moment, smiling contentedly. "Aefin is amazing. And Ludo is..." He waved his glass around, searching for the word. "Ludo is a dream. And you..." He gazed down into her eyes with such sincerity she almost had to look away. "I don't have words in any language to name the way you make me feel." He looked down quickly, giving his head a little shake. "Sorry, it must be the wine. I've gone all sentimental."

"I love it when you express your feelings."

"You do?" Feddar let out a shaky breath. "I'm not so used to doing it, you know."

"I know." She moved closer, looking from his eyes to his mouth, daring him to stop her. Knowing he wouldn't. His breath caught as she captured his lips, nibbling them, plying them with soft strokes of her tongue. Her fingers ghosted across his chest, feeling his muscles through the thin layer of fabric, his chest rising beneath her touch, the slightest whine growing in his throat. She pulled back, and their lips stuck together for a moment before separating. He cradled her face in his hand, running his fingers through her beard, trailing them down her chest. She took a playful step back, adjusting her dress up a little.

"Later, you said."

Feddar closed his eyes and breathed out through his nose.

"Later."

He turned to poke at the bloodroots and declared them done. He heaped them on a platter and began slicing them lengthwise with a fine steel blade he pulled from his belt.

"Did you have that with you when..."

Feddar nodded, holding the knife up for inspection, then slicing the rest of the roots, whose flesh was dark red and soft, almost juicy looking.

"My father gave it to me when I left for the academy."

"To become...the human equivalent of a Shoza?"

"Something like that." He tossed some crushed herbs over the roots and drizzled them with oil from a vintage ceramic pitcher that had surely belonged to the mayor. "It feels like a lifetime ago. Now I..." He picked up his glass, waving it in the air before drinking. "I administer."

"Well, if it's any consolation, you administer better than anyone I've ever encountered."

"It's...good to hear you say that." He raised his glass. "I don't want to talk politics, but I worry about it every day. I hate it. I hate this fucking job even more than the one you read about in that damned book."

Cloti moved closer, letting her hand fall upon his arm. "I hate it too, so let's not give it any more space in our lives. Tell me about the herbs you put on these."

Feddar's face brightened, and he picked up the platter and held it just below her face.

"Mint, lickweed, and sorrel. I'd have used moster instead of lickweed, but you don't seem to grow it down here."

"Aefin planted a little in our garden. We'd be happy to share."

"No, I wouldn't want to impose."

"Well, if you're ever in the neighborhood, say, on Fifthday, in the afternoon, you could stop by to borrow some herbs. Maer custom would require you stay for dinner." She moved her hand onto his chest, watching him tense, feeling his pulse quicken. "And dessert, of course."

"You know, I am due to conduct an inspection of the Cliffside neighborhoods. I'll have to check my schedule, but I think we can make this work."

The bloodroots were delicious, succulent, and creamy, their sweet earthiness offset by the bright and bitter herbs. They talked cooking and gardening for a bit, tarrying in detailed discussions of their gardens and favorite recipes, though Feddar got stuck for vocabulary more than once. He told her the gardeners who'd worked for the mayor had continued working with him, and he rattled off the names of a handful of the plants in the garden.

"It's a perfect enclave from the world outside," Cloti said, admiring the lush greenery offset by splashes of color.

"I do love this garden rather a lot." He gestured with the wine bottle, filling her glass when she nodded. "And I love it even more when you're here."

Cloti hid her smile behind her wineglass as warmth spread through her chest.

"I love it when you say sweet things."

His soft gaze melted into her, and she leaned toward him, unable to reach him for a kiss, so she kissed him with her eyes. They talked for a while as they sipped their wine, but their gazes never faltered. A crackling tension built inside her, and she must have let a little bit slip because Feddar's eyes grew wide, and his breath caught.

"Yes," he whispered. "That...that thing you did." His eyes begged for it, winding her even tighter. "Do it again."

"You want this?" She released another pulse, and he braced both hands on the table, his mouth forming an O shape.

"I need it."

Cloti paused, looking away from Feddar's pleading eyes for a moment. She wanted to pour herself into him, show him everything she felt, how good he made her feel. But only if he understood what it meant. She rose from her chair and rounded the table to Feddar, who stood and turned toward her. She brushed a lock of hair away from his face, looking into his eyes, feeling his need bleed into her. Their connection had grown every bit as strong as what she had with Aefin; she could share with him fully if they were touching.

"I want to share everything with you. Every part of me. My body, my mind, my heart. And I want to share every part of you. I want to feel what you feel."

"I want all of that," he breathed.

"Even if it means you have to give up control for a time?"

"Especially if it means that. I trust you."

She put a hand on his chest and closed in for a kiss, keeping her eyes open to watch his face, so beautiful when it melted. The scars only served to make him look more vulnerable. More desperate. Perfectly imperfect.

Cloti undressed Feddar with her eyes as he stood before the large, neatly made bed in his sparse bedroom. He reached a hand up to undo the first button on his shirt, but she stopped him with a subtle shake of her head. She held his eyes as she unbuttoned her dress, seeing them falter when it slid to the floor, then brazenly stare when she shed her slip and stood naked before him.

"Do you like my body?" She stepped toward him, and his eyes lingered for a moment before snapping up to meet hers.

"I worship your body."

"I'm not too old for you?" She moved close enough to feel his heat and smell the wine on his breath.

"Cloti, I have no idea how old you are, and I—"

She stopped him with a kiss, losing herself in his soft, hot lips. She pulled back, gazed into his blazing green eyes, and drew him out with gentle nips, keeping his hungry lips from fully connecting as she raked her fingernails down the front of his shirt. His breath caught as her fingers continued down, finding him stiff beneath his muslin pants, straining against the fabric. She gripped him tight, and his lips froze, his eyes burning softer now. She released him and stepped back.

"You can get undressed now."

Feddar's face flushed as he unbuttoned his shirt and slid it off his shoulders, the bare expanse of his skin fanning the fire inside Cloti. She touched his face and shared her desire, and his neck flushed as well, his fingers trembling as they unbuttoned his pants and slid them down. He was fully erect, and Cloti kept her fingertips on his forehead, then wrapped her mind's fingers around his length, squeezing and caressing. She watched his face contort in disbelief as he bobbed and twitched under her control. She released with her mind, and he let out a groaning sigh, his eyes soft and pleading. She let her fingers trace across his chest, feeling his need radiate off him like a furnace.

"Do you want to share now?" she said as her fingers trailed downward, running softly along his length.

"I want to share everything," he murmured. "I want to feel what you feel."

"You need a word in case it gets to be too much. Something you won't forget."

Feddar opened his mouth as if to speak, gasping as she squeezed him tighter, then let him go.

"Honeydew," he whispered.

"Excellent choice." She moved her hands back up to his chest, feeling his heart throbbing beneath his skin, his blood coursing with desire. She looked into his soft green eyes, took a deep breath, and let herself flow into him and him into her.

The rush of his want was intoxicating. His eagerness to taste her. To lose himself in her pleasure. She gripped his pectorals and kissed him furiously, flooding him with her desire as her hands moved up to his neck, then the back of his head. She gripped his curly hair in her fingers and pulled him down, leaning into him with her breasts and stomach. She felt Feddar's pleasure soar as he nosed between her legs, and she shivered at the first gentle touch of his tongue. Her shiver rose to a thrum as he delved within her, feeling his ache at her sweet taste, the texture of her, and the way she pressed into him when he was doing something right. His tongue stuttered for a moment as the first low wave of pleasure rolled over her and into him, but he soon redoubled his efforts, lapping his way upward as he gripped her behind in both strong hands.

Use your fingers, she pushed out with her mind, and Feddar removed one hand from her behind, running his fingers across her thigh and in between her legs.

Like this.

She guided him into her, smiling at the whiffs of joy he gave off, the freedom he felt under her influence. She showed him exactly where to touch her and how, pouring her rising pleasure into him, feeling him grow close just from the act of pleasing her. She let go with her mind, and he paused for a moment, his eyes turning up to look into hers with a desire so pure it squeezed her heart like a lemon into a drink. His fingers quickly showed he'd learned his lesson, and he smothered her with his mouth as he massaged and coaxed her ever higher, locked in now on her sensations, anticipating her every need. She bucked into him as she came, her pleasure exploding as she felt him spill, shudder, then spill again. She kept him pressed tight against her as the tremors receded. She finally released him, gazing down into the shiny depths of his eyes. He sat back on his knees, staring up at her, his wet, shiny face stretching into a wide smile.

Did you enjoy yourself?

Feddar nodded, putting his hands on Cloti's thighs, moving his face in closer. She hesitated for a moment as a tingle of desire sparked within her, but she stopped him with a thought.

I want something else from you now.

"Anything!"

"I want you to take me like a frasti making a kill," she growled, backing toward the bed and falling down on it, spreading her legs.

"But I just—"

"You will get hard again for me," she murmured, pushing out a burst of heat, grinning at his gasp as he stood up, suddenly stiff as a stun baton.

Their connection was total now, even without touching. Even without the Earth Milk. Feddar's eyes darkened as she showed him what she wanted, and he stalked onto the bed, gripping her thighs and yanking her up against him. His eyes flickered as he paused, seeking reassurance, and she shared her desires with him again. His face was serious, focused, as his fingers found her, still wet, and began working a favorite spot she definitely hadn't told him about. He wound her up fast, then abruptly pulled his fingers out, shifted her position as if she weighed nothing, and eased himself inside her, one throbbing inch at a time.

He moved slowly at first, too slowly, holding her in place when she tried to push against him. His eyes stayed with hers as he moved, more forcefully now, but taking his time. He paused whenever her pleasure started to rise, then drove in harder, pushing her ever closer to the edge, then pulling back again.

Please, Feddar. Please!

He stopped suddenly, pulling out and letting her fall flat on the bed. He gripped her hips, and before she knew what was happening, he'd flipped her over. He pulled her halfway up, spreading her legs with his knees as he settled in behind her. He ran his strong fingers up and down her back, moved them around to cup her breasts, then back around to squeeze her behind.

"You're beautiful like this," he murmured as he pushed inside her once again. She sank back onto him, feeling his rush as their bodies smacked together. He moved slowly, his hands resting gently on her hips, wanting to make it last, in direct opposition to Cloti's growing need. She squeezed him with all her might and tried to push back against him, but he held her in check and kept up his torturously slow pace, hitting the spot she needed just often enough to make her squirm but not enough for release.

Finish me.

Feddar responded by slowing his pace further, sliding in and out with maddening patience.

Cloti swiveled her head around, locked eyes with him, and snarled:

"Finish me!"

She felt something snap inside Feddar, and he gripped her tightly and drove into her like an enraged beast. All the softness, the pleading, the desperation were gone, replaced by the singular drive to send her exploding over the edge. The strength of his arms, the sudden fury of his thrusts, and the dark flame of his desire carried Cloti away. She floated on each wave, her pleasure cresting ever higher as Feddar plied her with furious strokes. Her arms trembled, then collapsed as he changed his angle the tiniest bit, unleashing an ocean of pent-up ecstasy inside her that sent her face-planting onto the bed. His pleasure swelled to overflowing as she quivered against him, squeezing him like a wrung towel, and he collapsed atop her, the echoes of their cries still ringing in their ears.

***

Cloti kept her distance from the human guard who escorted her back to her house. He eyed her with open contempt when Feddar brought her out and asked him to escort her home. He knew, and Cloti doubted he would keep it to himself. She pushed out calming vibes as they walked, and his posture relaxed a little. She felt guilty using her practice in this way, but his hatred of her, purely because she was Maer, gave her little choice. If word got to the wrong people, Feddar's life could be in danger, and that was the last thing she was going to allow.

She tried to chat him up in the few words of Islish she knew, and he switched to Maer, speaking with surprising competence. She commented on the weather, and he agreed, adding his prediction, and they moved on to discuss the vegetables the growing heat would bring them. His father had grown up on a farm, and he used to visit around harvest time to help bring in the squash and tomatoes. By the time they reached Cloti's gate, they stopped and talked for several more minutes, and Cloti had long since stopped using her influence on him. All it had taken was a little push, and their commonalities overwhelmed their differences.

As she downed a glass of water in the empty kitchen, she wondered if there was a way to use that push on more than just the one guard. The Shoza's plan was too risky. There had to be a better way.

18

— • —

Cloti touched base with Gielle and the mystery Shoza during her morning cycle, partly to make sure Gielle had found her way back but also to warn them about Fiola being flagged. Gielle paused for a long moment before asking her to return to the camp two days hence with more Milk, and she'd find another nurse she could deliver to.

Cloti left them to their devices and drifted through the Thousand Worlds, wondering about the humans she'd seen in the sea cave in the Time to Come. Would they try to use the ooze to make their own Earth Milk? And if so, could she find them? As tempting as it was to look, she knew it was best to let the Time to Come play out without any further intrusion on her part, and she was drawn toward a world that radiated a kind of green energy. Her mind felt strong with the dab of ooze she had taken, and as she approached the green world, a copper tunnel appeared before her, and she flowed into it.

She emerged in a dense forest wet with rain, the air humid and rich with the smell of life and decay. Birds called in the canopy above, and other creatures too, though she saw nothing more than a line of ants running up a thick tree with leathery bark. The bird sounds stopped abruptly, and the underbrush parted to let a large feline pad through, more than half Cloti's size and covered in glossy brown fur. It paused, baring its fangs and staring at her with fear in its eyes. It slunk to the side, never looking away from her as it skirted into the forest and disappeared. Cloti's heart raced with the encounter; though no harm could come to her in the Thousand Worlds, it felt so real that it was hard to remember in the moment.

She wandered along a game trail, taking in the moss hanging from trees, the lush, colorful fungi, the small black quadrupeds with long tails hopping from branch to branch high in the canopy above, watching her with oversized eyes. She would set a mental marker to remember this place in case she ever needed to get away for a bit. The tug of her life broke the spell, and she took in one last humid breath, then closed her eyes and faded out of the rainy forest and back into the soft dawn light of her garden. The scent of tea hit her, and she turned to see Aefin sitting on a bench, sketching. Cloti smiled; Aefin hadn't sketched in the garden since before the occupation, and she hadn't been this happy in longer than that.

"You were in deep this morning," Aefin said, looking up from her sketchpad.

"I was...exploring." Cloti closed her eyes and saw the green shadows of the forest once again. "You want me to share?"

Aefin set down her sketchpad and pencil and turned toward Aene, crossing her legs. "Why not?"

Cloti sat on the bench next to her, crossing her legs so their knees were touching, and flowed into Aefin's open mind so quickly that Aefin let out a little gasp.

Sorry.

Aefin's warm response reassured Cloti, and she shared the vision of the rainy forest, the smell of it, and the glossy sheen of the big cat. Aefin experienced each sensation with the glee of a child, and Cloti realized how long it had been since they'd shared something like this. They'd tightened their romantic bonds during the occupation, but they'd lost something too. The chaos of the world outside had pressed them together so tightly that they forgot what it meant to have a little space to just relax with each other.

Thank you. Aefin's knee moved away from Cloti's for a moment, and their connection faded. Aefin leaned in with her shoulder, then sat back, picking up her cup.

"Can I get you some tea?"

"You sit. Draw." Cloti pressed her hand into Aefin's shoulder, and Aefin leaned over to kiss it.

Cloti found Ludo in the kitchen, hunched over a stack of papers with an untouched cup of tea next to him.

"Sorry, I know this is a non-work space, but I have to hurry down for an emergency meeting of some kind. They won't say what it's about, which has got me worried."

"It's okay." Cloti kissed the top of his head, pushing out a wave of calm, and she saw Ludo's shoulders relax a little.

"Thank you. I'm sorry I took the last of the tea. I'll—"

"Relax, love. I know how to make tea. And your meeting is going to be fine, I'm sure of it." He half-smiled at her, then took a sip, his eyes scanning one of the pages before him.

Cloti put water on to boil and put some clove tea in the strainer, just a little less than she would normally have used since they were running out and the last two market wagons hadn't had any. She heard a knock at the door, the official kind the humans used. She glanced at Ludo, whose eyes were weak with worry, and she smiled before turning away, wishing there was something she could do to assuage his anxiety. She took a deep breath, composed her face, and opened the door.

The human soldier was not much more than a boy, his hair dirty and disheveled, helmet under his arm.

"A package for the Ambassador." He held out a package the size of a thick book, though she could tell by the way he held it that it was not heavy.

"Thank you." Cloti bowed as she took the package, which was even lighter than she expected, soft but sort of crunchy, like dried leaves. She held it up to her nose, and the rich bouquet of darkroot washed over her. Tears rushed to her eyes, but she kept them in check.

"The Administrator sends his regards." The soldier bowed awkwardly, then turned and hurried away.

Cloti sniffed the bag once again, picturing Feddar smiling at her over a cup of steaming tea. Thinking of Ludo's face, and especially Aefin's, when they smelled it steeping. She returned to the kitchen quite casually, and Ludo looked up expectantly.

"Well?"

Cloti set down the bag, took his cup from his hand, and poured it into the sink.

"Cloti, wha—"

She stopped him with a kiss.

"Feddar sent us a big bag of darkroot."

Ludo's sudden shout took Cloti by surprise, as did the way he stood up and crushed her in a hug, then lay little kisses all over her face.

"I'll be late for the meeting, but I don't care—just brew me a cup. Oh, Skundir's balls! What a glorious day!"

They lingered over tea, all wide smiles and contented hums, until Ludo drained the last drops, smacked his lips, and pushed away from the table with a sign.

"I'll try to be back for lunch."

Cloti and Aefin shared a glance, knowing he wouldn't, but by the tone of his voice, he believed it.

They went out collecting supplies in the neighborhood, and several of the neighbors asked about the temple cycles. She put them off with a vague answer, but she wondered if Feddar would be able to get that approved, letting a certain number of residents from Cliffside and the other neighborhoods join the cycles. Those in the camps surely needed it more, but it would be nice to bring the whole city together. They got enough supplies to fill two baskets, though they weren't scheduled to go for another two days. They got back home just in time to hurry to the temple for the day's cycle. She sensed more Shoza among the acolytes this time, and she worried that some of them might not share her vision of a more peaceful future.

She pushed these thoughts to the side as she led the cycle, using the strength of the Milk she now mixed in with her water bottle regularly for the cycles. A vision came to her of a Maer standing by the time-worn battlements of a castle, extending her arm to release a pigeon off into the gray light of morning. She knew it was from the Time to Come; the Maer had survived and were rebuilding. Hope and pride swelled in her heart, and she shared her vision with everyone in the temple. She must have struck a chord; the bonds between everyone present grew denser and stronger than ever before, growing and spreading like ivy on a wall. She could have spoken to them without using her voice, and most would have understood, but she dared not risk it with Feddar present. He couldn't know what they were capable of if she harnessed their power. Not yet.

She tried to catch Feddar after the cycle to thank him for the tea, but he'd slipped out before she had a chance to make her way through the crowd to find him. She suddenly realized what a strain it must have been on his working day to come to the temple for every cycle, but he hadn't missed a single one. If he had, he would have had to send someone else in his place, as the agreement stipulated, and Cloti would have had a much harder time leading the cycle with an unknown human in the temple. When the last of the acolytes had filed out, Cloti found Aefin and slumped against her, suddenly weary and in need of rest. Aefin clasped Cloti's head to her shoulder, massaging the muscles on the back of her neck.

"Let's get you home and boil up a nice bucket of hot water for a sponge bath, and then you can take a nap."

"Mmm, sounds delightful. Will you carry me home?"

Aefin put her arms around Cloti's waist and heaved her up for a moment, then let her down with a giggle.

"I bet Feddar could carry you that far. Just sling you over his shoulder, and off he'd go, taking you up the stairs, laying you down gently on the bed, pushing your arms over your head..."

"He said he'd come on Fifthday. That's only three days!"

"It's so long," Aefin grumped. Cloti's first kiss fell on unresponsive lips, but her second was met with a more measured reaction, and by the third, Cloti smiled at the eagerness of her lips.

"I promised I'd share what happened last night. Maybe that would be enough to tide you over?"

"Gods, I need that so bad." Aefin squeezed Cloti's backside and kissed her again, her breath hot and fast.

"But first, you had said something about a sponge bath?"

Aefin washed Cloti with great thoroughness, her soapy fingers rubbing and massaging every inch of Cloti's body. She teased and lingered a bit, but she didn't push, and Cloti relaxed into her touch, which warmed her from head to toe. Cloti returned the favor, and once they were clean and dry, they snuggled on the bed, kissing softly. She could feel Aefin's restrained desire, and though she was exhausted, she slid her hands along Aefin's inner thighs to see if she wanted more. Aefin picked up Cloti's hand and pressed it to her chest, her eyes deep and earnest.

"I want you to share just a little for now, so I can dream about it as we nap, and then later, when Ludo gets home..."

Heat sparked in Cloti's belly at her words, and she was struck with the desire to pin Aefin to the bed and bring her quickly and roughly, but she pushed it all down with a deep breath. She kissed Aefin softly and pressed her hand into her chest, feeling Aefin's heartbeat as if it were her own, and their breath soon fell into a rhythm together.

"Share with me," Aefin whispered into her mouth. Cloti returned to the memory of the night before with Feddar, her body coursing with desire as she recalled all the things they'd done, the things she'd made him do. She wasn't sure what Aefin needed, and it was hard to pick one moment, but her heart leapt as she thought of the way he'd flipped her like she was a ragdoll, the strength of his hands as he held her in place. She gripped Aefin's hips as she pushed the feeling out through the tight bond between them, and Aefin's body arched into her, her lips devouring Cloti's as her body thrummed with arousal. Cloti dimmed the connection, and Aefin gasped a little whine, pulling Cloti's body tight to hers. Cloti pulled away from the kiss, though she couldn't break free of Aefin's grip on her.

"I want more. I want it all." Aefin's eyes were all-consuming, her hands like iron claws digging into Cloti's backside.

"I'm saving the rest for when Ludo comes home." She kissed Aefin again, straddling her and pressing down with all her weight. "You know it's always more fun if you have to wait."

Aefin pouted, and it took several more kisses to coax a smile from her. Cloti rolled off her, and Aefin shifted to the side to spoon her. It was nice being the little spoon for once, and after she had her fun wiggling against Aefin for a bit, she settled in with Aefin's arm draped over her and sank into a deep nap.

It was dusk when they awoke, and Ludo still wasn't home. They worked together to make a simple pasta dish with the last of the flour and some almost-too-old ox milk they salvaged into a sauce. At least the salad was garden fresh, but they had to water their wine. Their once-proud collection had shrunk to a single crate, most of which were bottles they hadn't drunk for good reason. Cloti and Aefin had used their alchemical equipment to make some dandelion wine, but the first batch had turned to vinegar, and they were still waiting for the second batch to ferment.

Ludo arrived, bleary-eyed and hunched, just as they were finishing their dinner. His face lit up when he saw the pasta, and he plowed through his bowl almost without breathing. When he had finished, he took a long sip of his wine, smiling at their inquisitive glances. They had managed not to ask him a single thing about work until he was finished, as was their tradition.

"The General is convinced there's a Shoza-led uprising brewing. They've brought several dozen Maer from the camps in for questioning and even a few from the Lower Cliffs. Apparently, they found a cache of circlets and even a channeling gauntlet in a house there."

Cloti and Aefin exchanged worried glances. If they were coming after Maer in the Lower Cliffs, Cliffside could be next.

"How in the world would they know who's a Shoza and who's not?" Aefin asked.

"How would anyone know? They did say something about surveillance data, which I assume means their spyballs." He glanced around and lowered his voice. "No one's seen any this high up, have they?"

Cloti shook her head. "If anyone had seen one, we'd all know about it."

He shook his head and downed his glass. "Well, thankfully, Feddar kept them from declaring full martial law, but they're calling it Code Brown, an unfortunate name that means they can enter any house without writ or warning and search it for..." he spread his arms wide. "Whatever they want." He glanced at the wine bottle, drumming his fingers on the table and looking up with embarrassed eyes.

"It's a strange way to go about de-occupation." Aefin's voice was little more than a whisper, but it left a thunderous silence in its wake. After a time, Ludo picked up the bottle and poured two careful fingers into each glass.

"Well, enough about work. How was the temple cycle?"

When Ludo tried to make his excuses and go to bed, Aefin stalked over to him and sat him back down as he was rising from his chair. She straddled him, clutching his face to her chest as she massaged the back of his head. Cloti watched, transfixed, as Aefin tormented Ludo in that chair, smothering him with kisses as her knees squeezed his thighs and her hands roamed inside his robe. Cloti felt Aefin's need viscerally, the physical drive to assuage the pain of the helplessness that she felt. That they all felt. Everything they'd ever known was going down the drain, and the only things they had left were the feelings and sensations in each moment. Aefin ground against Ludo, massaging his chest, and he clutched her gently, eyes locked on hers. Spellbound. Cloti pulled the vial of Earth Milk from her pocket, pulled the glasses together, and filled them halfway with water. Ludo's eyes turned away from Aefin's as Cloti held up the vial, questioning with her eyes. Ludo turned Aefin to get her attention, and a wide smile erupted on her face as she shifted toward Cloti.

"Yes," she said in a low voice laced with something darker.

"Yes," Ludo added, maybe a little nervously.

"Yes," Cloti murmured as she poured a dram into each glass.

They spoke no words as they raised their glasses and drank, but the shine in Aefin's and Ludo's eyes showed they had not forgotten her promise.

By the time they had drained their glasses, Cloti had already started to feel their minds creeping across the space between them. Her head grew light, and she opened herself to them, waiting in fuzzy peace as they adjusted to the Milk. It took Ludo the longest, as usual, but in time they shared a mental space like a greenhouse made of mirrors. Aefin projected an image of Feddar and Cloti, then sent out a blast of hot want that melted Cloti's loins.

Upstairs, she mindspoke, rising from her seat. They followed, Aefin gripping Ludo by the bicep like a soldier walking a prisoner to his cell. When they got to the bedroom, Aefin pulled Ludo toward the bed, then stepped back, fixing Cloti with soft, deep eyes.

I want you to show me. With Ludo. Show me what you did with Feddar. She crossed her arms, glancing at Ludo and back to Cloti again.

Cloti maintained eye contact with Aefin as she kissed Ludo and then guided his head slowly down her body and between her legs. She pushed out Feddar's hunger into them both, which sent Ludo into a frenzy that brought Cloti up to the edge far too quickly. She closed her eyes for a moment to settle herself as Ludo's fingers came into play, and she guided him as she had Feddar. She looked up, gasping as Ludo found his rhythm, and saw Aefin touching herself, licking her lips, and she felt her desire to jump in and take over. Aefin held back while Ludo plowed forward, bringing Cloti to a hard, early climax. She pushed the sensation out to Aefin, whose fingers froze, her face fixed in a soft oval of pleasure, her huffing groans rising above Cloti's and echoing off the walls.

Cloti pulled Ludo back by his hair, pushing out her desire as she crawled onto the bed. Aefin rushed to the bed and lay down beside her, eyes pleading.

I want this part.

Cloti rolled to the side, propping herself up on her elbow and gesturing Ludo forward with her eyes. He was still hard, and she urged him on, pushing out exactly what she wanted into him and into Aefin. Aefin wrapped herself in Cloti's wants and in the memory of those moments, and Cloti relived them anew as she watched Ludo play the part. He wasn't as strong as Feddar, but he knew how to make use of the strength he had, and he kept Aefin's lithe body mostly in check. He flipped her somewhat awkwardly, but Aefin guided him in and angled her body just right for her pleasure. Cloti opened herself to the rush of both of their desires as they hurtled toward climax, obliterating the boundaries between them and locking them together in a moment of tenderness, trust, and ecstasy.

As the pleasure ebbed out of them, their minds swirled and intermingled like their bodies in their usual aftermath tangle. Even in sleep, they were together. Tendrils of their thoughts and dreams seeped into Cloti's mind like a cat curled up on her pillow, purring into her ear.

19

Cloti visited Gielle and the mystery Shoza for a moment during her morning cycle and was given the name of another nurse, Loric, who would pass the vials along. She sensed a tension in them, but she did not pry. The less she knew, the better. Once she had left them, she flitted about through the Thousand Worlds and found herself drawn toward a familiar spot, one she had visited once before when she'd seen a moment of Uffrin's future. Eagle Lake. She generally tried to avoid the future or the past for fear of mucking something up, but she'd once made an exception in the case of her son. She'd needed to know he was okay, and she'd seen enough before to know that he'd made it. It had been years since they'd vacationed there, and whenever she thought of leaving Kuppham behind, she could think of nowhere else she'd want to go. To see Uffrin again, and Mara, and with a little luck, hold her grandchild in her hands, smell its baby breath, feel the soft fur on its cheek...The pull to seek them out in the Thousand Worlds was strong, to check on them once again. Or even farther in the future, to see if she'd be reunited with them. But the pain she'd feel if that future diminished into nothingness would be too great, and she'd never be able to survive the present.

She resisted the pull of Eagle Lake, returned to her own mind, and did a cycle, clearing out the thoughts of the Thousand Worlds and replacing them with visions of this one. The city in fall, effulgent with the colors of the trees' final blaze. Maer walking arm in arm, unhurried, gesturing casually as they spoke of pleasant things that made them smile and press closer together. Bees bumbling from flower to flower like drunks, knocking off pollen as they plundered the blossoms' liquid bounty, then moving, heavy with their load, to the next and the next.

Her vision sharpened, centering on the here and now. Her house, her neighborhood, tidy rows of small houses with lush gardens. The dusty-brown cliff they sat upon, the valley below, the river sparkling in the morning sun. She soared as if on falcon's wings, diving down into the valley and crossing over the vast stretches of the camps. It was impossible, but she felt she was seeing these things in real-time, as if she were truly there. On the opposite side of the valley was a smaller camp, with tents spaced further apart. The nursing camp, she knew. The one few ever returned from.

Cloti veered off toward the nursing camp, slowing as she cruised along, looking down. No one moved except for a Maer in nursing garb, who hurried from one tent to another, pulling their scarf down to breathe fresh air for a while before pulling it back up over their nose and entering the tent. Smoke poured from a rough pavilion of new wood, and a human soldier watched as several Maer stirred huge vats of something that looked like porridge. Cloti's mind began to shimmer, and she pulled back from the vision, slumping to her side and resting her elbow on the ground. She lay down all the way, relishing the cold stone on her face, the damp scents of the garden. She lay there for some time, watching the first bees of the morning arrive at the flowerbed, thinking of nothing. Nothing. Nothing.

Her brain felt fuzzy all morning long, but when she got to the temple and had a sip from her water bottle, everything came into focus. She silently greeted each acolyte as they entered, but she could tell by the surprised looks on their faces that they had heard her mindvoice. Gielle did not show, but Cloti got Shoza vibes from a half-dozen attendees. She let her warmth flow into them as to all the others, and their rigid shells relaxed a little as they greeted her back.

She nodded at Feddar from across the room, her heart fluttering at his sudden smile and the way he looked down as if embarrassed. She knew what he was thinking of. In two days, he would come to their house on some flimsy pretext, and they would ravish him, body and mind. Cloti hadn't allowed herself to dwell on it, but the thought kept crept into her mind that if things went as she hoped on Fifthday, their bond with Feddar might grow so strong they'd have no choice but to give him a larger place in their lives. She didn't know what was possible, given the situation, but she chose to believe not everything was impossible. They would find a way, no matter what the state of the world.

Aefin cleared her throat discreetly, snapping Cloti back to the present. Most of the acolytes were seated on their mats, and the candles and incense were lit. She drifted up to the dais, gazing out upon the assembled Maer. Her heart filled with joy to see their unity of purpose in a time of such uncertainty. She shared that joy with those assembled, and the room lit up with their smiles. She lowered to a cross-legged seat and let her arms sink to the floor.

"When we practice together, we return the pieces to the whole they came from."

She closed her eyes and began the cycle, and she had to raise her shields a little as everyone came rushing into her at once. It was too much. But little by little, she opened herself back up, and they were all drawn to her, into her. Their arms rose in unison, joining her slow, measured lead. She did not communicate with them individually as she sometimes did. She shared her vision of the bumblebees buzzing from flower to flower. She could smell the flowers now, lavender, their perfume released by the sun's touch. Feel the warmth of the sunshine, the lazy breeze, hear the burbling of a fountain, the low hum of the bees. They stayed with the bees for the whole cycle, and when at last their hands returned to the floor, Cloti basked in their radiant smiles.

"Please share this with your friends. You have this in you. All of you."

She bowed deeply, and the acolytes repeated her gesture as one. Even the Shoza among them. Even Feddar, who lingered as the acolytes filtered out, a sly grin on his face.

"Thank you for the tea, Administrator." Cloti pushed out a warmth that her words lacked, and Feddar stepped a little closer.

"I took it from the shipment meant for the officers."

"Well, aren't you the rebel?"

"I'm doing what I can." His green eyes burned dark in the shadows. "But that's going to be less and less, I'm afraid." He gestured to the soldier waiting outside the door to wait. "I've got your medicine delivery for tomorrow approved, at any rate. Just you, not Aefin." He shook his head at her questioning look. "I got them to make an exception for you, given your stature. Things are getting tight. Look, I have to go. See you at tomorrow's cycle."

"Don't forget about Fifthday."

Feddar's cheeks darkened, and his eyes grew glassy.

"Thinking of..." He shook his head. "It's the only thing that gets me through the day." His knuckle brushed against hers, and he looked down, then turned and left, taking her heart with him.

Ludo came back from work with a long, silent face. He absently accepted a kiss from Cloti and slumped down in his chair, flashing a feeble smile at her but making no move to pick up the glass of wine she set down in front of him. His eyes had a sad, faraway look, and she sat down next to him, not touching him, just watching.

"Something's wrong."

He nodded, picking up his glass and taking a small sip.

"They executed the twenty they rounded up after the attack on the barracks."

Cloti covered her mouth, tears welling up and spilling over before she could choke them down. An image flashed in her mind, all those bodies lying on the ground in the open space just inside the camp, blood soaking into the dirt, staining the grass. Scores of Maer watching, faces contorted in horror. Children gawking. Crying. This was not just her imagination. This was a vision of what had happened. The power of the Milk was opening her mind to the world in terrifying ways.

"They lined them up in the camp, hands tied behind their backs, and cut their throats one by one." Ludo covered his eyes with his hands. "In front of everyone."

Cloti put a hand on his knee, her mind reeling with the fading vision. He accepted the touch without moving. Aefin came down, hair still wet from washing, and stopped in the doorway, questioning with her eyes.

"They executed the Shoza—or the ones they thought were," Cloti spoke for Ludo, who showed no signs of opening his mouth. "From the attack."

Aefin's face twisted with sadness, and she sniffed, crossing the room on soft feet to touch them both on the shoulder.

"They won't stop there." Ludo held his wineglass, not drinking. "The General was on a tear. Feddar tried to talk him down but to no avail. If there's another attack, it will be much worse."

"When there's another attack," Aefin murmured. "The Shoza aren't going to stop as long as the humans are here."

"Then everything I've worked for is for naught. The humans will clamp down harder and harder, and we'll never be free again." Ludo's voice was thick, near tears.

Cloti opened her mouth to speak, then closed it again, her heart squeezed with dread and guilt. She'd made Aefin complicit in her dealings with the Shoza and Ludo, too, by association. As she looked into his sad eyes, she realized what she should have known all along. She had to tell him.

"What if I told you there's another way?"

Ludo's face sharpened at her words, and Aefin shot her a worried look. Cloti blinked at Aefin, whose face settled into a frown, but she nodded.

"What's this all about? How—" Ludo set his glass down and leaned toward Cloti, who closed her eyes and breathed out through her nose.

"I met someone in the Thousand Worlds," she said quietly. "A Shoza outside the city. They told me of a plan—"

"You've been in contact with the Shoza?" Ludo's voice rose, then lowered to a growl, trembling. She hadn't heard him speak like this in years, and it made every hair on her body stand up. "Cloti, you could get yourself killed! Get all of us killed!" He hissed the ending.

"And if we do nothing? What happens then?"

"If we don't cause any trouble, they'll leave once they feel we're no longer a threat. They can't spare this level of manpower forever!"

"They won't leave. Not until the city's in ruins." Cloti closed her eyes as a vision flashed through her mind: fire, running, explosions, blood, and more fire. Broken walls with crowds swarming through them. It was Kuppham, she was sure of it, in a state of chaos like she had never imagined. When she opened her eyes, Ludo was staring at her, an expression of pained disbelief on his face.

"Have you...seen something?"

Cloti shook her head. "Yes. Maybe. I don't know." She sighed, suddenly exhausted, putting one hand on his knee and the other on Aefin's hip, pulling her closer.

"What did you see?" Aefin's hand slid under Cloti's chin, pulling her head up gently.

"Fire and death." She swallowed the tears that rose up, but her heart tingled with a spark of hope. "But maybe something else, too. Walls falling, I don't know, I..." She closed her eyes and tried to grasp that spark, but it had fled. "There's still hope for us, I think." She turned back toward Ludo, who was watching her carefully, his expression inscrutable.

"There's no hope for us if they catch you working with the Shoza," he said in a low voice. Cloti's anger rose suddenly, and her voice exploded.

"Dammit, Ludo, can't you see? There's no hope for us if we let the humans do what they want! What part of fire and death was unclear?" Her heart raced, and her vision was blurred with tears. "I'm sorry I didn't tell you right away. I wasn't sure what it all meant, but I should have told you from the start. I made a promise when we wed, and I have not kept that promise."

Ludo's hand covered hers, warm and damp. She could not look into his eyes for fear of the expression she would see there.

"*We* have not kept that promise," Aefin said softly, leaning into Cloti's shoulder and lowering down to eye level. Cloti blinked her agreement. Aefin looked around the room, possibly searching for errant spyballs. "Cloti and I made a batch of the Earth Milk and delivered it to the Shoza in the camps."

Ludo gasped. "So that's why—" He stopped, looking down for a moment. "And you're going again tomorrow?"

"The Shoza have training in a practice very much like ours," Cloti said. "They can use the Earth Milk to communicate over distance, in the Thousand Worlds, where the spyballs cannot follow. You learned tonight what the mere suspicion of being a Shoza can cost. If we can give them this advantage, they may yet be able to resist whatever the humans are planning."

Ludo shook his head, his eyes bleary and weak. "The mere suspicion of being a Shoza, you said. Like visiting the camps on false pretenses to deliver the Earth Milk?"

"It's one more trip, Ludo. And I'm delivering to a different nurse, one who's not affiliated with the Shoza."

"Cloti, I can't risk losing you!" He gripped her hand tightly, his eyes wild and bright.

"It's the lowest risk we can get. And if we do nothing, the risk is surely higher. They've already declared that they can come into our homes anytime and look for whatever they want. Doesn't that feel like the prelude to something worse?"

Ludo fell back in his chair, eyes wet with tears. Cloti felt his sadness and despair seeping into her. She took his hand, which was limp and warm in hers, and she pushed out all the comfort she could muster. It wasn't much, given the way she felt. His hand tightened around hers, and he let out a shuddering sigh, looking from her to Aefin as he struggled to compose his face.

"I understand why you didn't tell me. You were protecting me, or you thought you were. I'm not going to pretend it doesn't hurt, but you two are the most brilliant, vibrant, incredible Maer I've ever known." His voice broke for a moment, then he cleared his throat and continued. "And you're probably right. I keep telling myself as I meet with the humans and negotiate the minutiae of their ever-tightening control over our lives that I'm helping, but all I'm doing is delaying the inevitable. Feddar is a good man, and as hard as he fights alongside me, the ink is on the parchment. I doubt if even he is immune to the General's wrath."

He dabbed his eyes with his handkerchief and blew his nose, then tucked it delicately into a pocket. He took in a deep breath, and a shaky smile returned to his face.

"I know I can't stop you from doing what you see as right, and I won't try. I won't tell you to be careful, either. If you were careful, you wouldn't be you. But I'm asking you, begging you, to be willing to step back, to pause whatever you're doing, if things start to go south. Because I don't know how I could continue without you at my side." He squeezed Cloti's hand, then put a hand on Aefin's hip. "Either of you. I love you both so much my heart wants to burst out of my chest."

They hugged him awkwardly, Aefin draped over one shoulder while Cloti leaned into his chest. Cloti felt a warm strength flowing into her from their shared connection, and she pushed it out to surround them like a blanket fort. Aefin lent her strength, and even Ludo, with his untrained mind, added his support. The bonds that linked them grew taut, humming with their collective energy. They stayed in this cocoon for some time until Ludo finally relaxed, and they pulled apart.

"I want to help," Ludo said, kneading Cloti's hand. "Tell me exactly what you need me to do."

20

— • —

On Fourthday morning, she took a dab of the ooze, though she wasn't sure if she'd need it, and joined the Shoza's signal in the Thousand Worlds. Gielle was nowhere to be found. She sensed worry from the mountain Shoza.

I am visiting the camps today. I will try to sense her.

Is there another you could put us in touch with?

Some have come to the temple sessions. I will try and find out.

Be careful. Gielle told me there is a Shoza faction called the Knife's Point that may be planning retribution against the humans for the twenty.

Cloti paused. How had they known about the executions, which had happened during the day?

Thank you. I will find you in the morning and let you know what I discover.

Cloti tried to explore the Thousand Worlds afterward, but her mind was buzzing with too many questions, and even the ooze could not help her settle in. She returned to her own mind, allowing her thoughts free reign. If the mountain Shoza knew about the executions, did they have another connection in the city? It was hard to imagine, but how else could they have known? Unless...She thought of her mind's trip across the city the morning before, her vision of the camps, and the vision she'd had of the executions. She wasn't sure how she had accomplished any of it, but it had felt real. Perhaps the Shoza had mastered such feats, and they had seen the executions as Cloti had. Maybe with a little effort, she could achieve the state again.

She moved through a cycle, trying to pierce her mind's clutter to summon the energy from the morning before. She pictured her house as seen from above, and she was suddenly swept away on invisible wings once again, soaring over the valley, gliding low along the river's cascades and pools. She passed the camps this time, drawn to the city center, past the library, and through the streets, empty except for the occasional pair of human soldiers or cart-driving Maer. She was drawn to the mayor's residence, which glowed with

Feddar's energy like a beacon. The guards at the entrance stood sleepy and unaware as she passed through the doors and up into Feddar's room. He lay half-asleep on his bed, arms splayed above his head, his tender skin adorned with tufts of scraggly hair.

She contemplated this man who had captured her heart. His people had plundered her city and put an end to life as she'd known it. She should have hated him or seduced him and plunged a knife into his heart, but she could not hold him accountable for the actions of others. His role in the Delve was no different from what their Shoza had done on innumerable occasions. He hadn't killed anyone, and he had tried to make amends at every turn. As Administrator, he had given them the temple back and helped keep the worst inclinations of the General at bay. He was a good person. She felt it in her bones. He had surrendered completely to her and her spouses, bringing a warm light into their otherwise bleak existence. But was it enough?

If the humans turned on him, if the General gave him an ultimatum, whose side would he take?

Cloti hovered above him, feeling the warmth of his body, the smell of him, the stuttering trill of his snore. She paused for a moment, unsure if what she was about to do was ethically right, but she had to know. She sank into him gently to give him time to adjust. He gasped and sat up, clutching at his chest.

"Cloti?" he whispered.

I'm here.

Feddar touched his hands to his head, looking around wildly.

I'm sorry to intrude; I just wanted to know if it would work.

"Please! Please intrude, and don't be afraid to linger."

Cloti smiled as heat rose within her.

Just relax.

Feddar lay back down, and Cloti flowed into him, her mind nestling alongside his.

"Is this comfortable for you?"

"Very," he answered aloud.

You can speak to me with your mind if you try. I'll help.

Oh—okay, he managed. *I...I think I get it. It's...weird. But it's so good to see you...sort of?*

Cloti shifted her focus to share her face. Feddar's eyes lit up, and his mouth burst open with sudden joy.

Gods, Cloti, it's really you! How are you able to do this?

Never mind that. I just wanted to be sure I could contact you if something goes wrong.

Nothing's going to go wrong. I promise.

You can't make that promise. But you can swear to be there for us when we need you.

Of course, I would do anything for you and for Aefin and Ludo. Anything.

I don't mean just for us.

A silence ensued, and Cloti's mind grew vague with the strain of the prolonged contact, but she refocused and waited until Feddar finally responded.

There's only so much I can do as Administrator, but you have my word. Always.

I don't mean as Administrator. I mean as you. Would you risk your life for me? She'd meant to say *us*, but it came out wrong.

The only risk to my life would be losing you.

Sweet man. She pushed out a pulse of heat, and he responded, body and mind. She channeled the heat through his lips and tongue, kissing him with her mind as he lay in his bed kissing the air, his arms reaching out for a body that wasn't there. She squeezed herself into focus, and his arms quickly found her back as their lips collided. She ground into his hardness, savoring the way his breath caught each time she pressed against him. His whines started low but grew more and more desperate, and she knew she could finish him like this if she kept it up.

She stopped suddenly, lifting off him, becoming insubstantial again, ghostlike. She could tell from the wonder and confusion in his eyes that he could see her.

Cloti, wait! Come back!

I'm afraid I can't stay to finish you now, but maybe this will give you a little something to think of when you pass by our neighborhood for inspection tomorrow.

Cloti, please. "Please!" He spoke the last word aloud, his normally deep voice pitched high with desperation.

I would really like it if you didn't spill before I see you again. Save yourself for me. For us.

She felt Feddar's sigh as a deep psychic gale.

I will do as you wish.

She hit him with one more pulse of heat, and he gasped as she pulled out and returned to her body in a great rush, like wind howling through a canyon. The flagstones rose to greet her, and she pressed her palms against their cool stability and rested her head on her hands. She kept her eyes closed but sounds soon filtered in. Someone walking in the kitchen. Aefin, making tea. Cloti's spirits lifted with the thought of the tea Feddar had sent them.

How could she doubt a man who so well understood the vital importance of proper darkroot tea?

There were several Shoza at the temple cycle, but Gielle was not among them. Cloti acknowledged them during the cycle, picking the one who'd come with Gielle the first time and pushing out an image of Gielle into their mind. They returned an air of resignation, struggling to form words. Cloti coiled tighter around them, lending her support.

Gielle was taken in the middle of the night, along with several others. Look for a child to lead you to her replacement.

Cloti's mind was troubled by the revelation, but she pushed out thanks and continued the cycle, and in time the collective energy of the assembled group lifted her spirits again. She could feel their anxiety, their sadness; they had witnessed a bloody execution, and the humans were tightening the noose, but she helped them rise above the flood of sorrow. She summoned and shared another vision of the Time to Come: Maer standing around a fire in the courtyard of what looked to be a ruined castle, dressed in rough clothes and skins but discoursing with passion and eloquence. One of them held a rod tipped with a burnished copper nugget, which was passed from Maer to Maer as they took turns speaking, just as in the High Council. There *was* a future for the Maer. She was sure of it, and as she shared her certainty, their spirits lifted higher, merging to form a temple within the temple, each of them a pillar supporting the weight of their united minds. She mindspoke to them all, sure that they would hear her words through the strength of their connection.

Whatever may come, remember this support and cling to each other. Though your bodies may be kept apart, your minds will always be as one. There are some things that cannot be taken from you.

She pushed out the excess from the Earth Milk, which she hardly needed anymore to bring them together in the cycles, and felt each of them take in a spark of her energy, even Feddar. His eyes remained closed, but his heart and mind were open like a sunflower, soaking in everything Cloti offered. When their hands reached the cool stone again, the bonds between them all lingered, even as they rose from their mats and milled about toward the door.

Cloti spent a moment after the cycle holding hands with Juiya, whose eyes shone with dedication and optimism. No matter the ugly reality of their current situation, no matter what the Shoza did, Maer like her would continue to spread the practice. The Time to Come was as much in Juiya's hands as it was in the steely determination and sharp knives of the Shoza.

Cloti shared a meaningful glance with Feddar, whose anticipation she could feel from across the temple. In a few short hours, he would visit her home, and the four of them would merge once again, tightening the bonds that sewed their hearts together. They did not speak, but she felt his heart lift and swell as their eyes locked. And then he was gone, along with the rest of the acolytes. Cloti stood in the empty temple, feeling a strange hollowness as the acrid smoke of the extinguished candles hit her. Aefin's arms wrapped around her, and she leaned into her wife's support, slipping her fingers to intertwine with Aefin's. Her eyes swelled with unexpected tears as a sense of finality descended like nightfall. Something permanent was about to happen. Everything was about to change. She felt it in her bones, just as she knew deep down there was no turning back, no choice that could stop the future from unfolding. Pain and heartbreak lay before them, as behind. But whatever happened would not be the end or the beginning. The present was but a ripple in the ocean, buried among endless waves that billowed up from the deep, crashing on the shore, only to return again to the depths and start the cycle again.

Cloti took a detour through the park on her way toward the camps. The dense canopy dulled the fierce heat of the sun, and though her basket was heavy, her feet were light. It was bizarre walking in the park with no one about except for a pair of human soldiers, who nodded when she flashed Feddar's medallion and left her to her solitude. Would these paths ever again be filled with lovers strolling arm in arm, children on class nature trips, old Maer taking their daily walks? Some of the trees were hundreds of years old. Generations of their forebears had welcomed Maer seeking solace from the lively chaos of the city, which was now a ghost of its former self. The city would thrive again; she felt it deep in her gut, but an equal certainty roiled inside her that it would only be reborn through blood and fire and long years of suffering.

Cloti sighed as she left the park and approached the camp gate, where she stopped to wait, medallion in hand, for the soldiers to come interrogate her. Their eyes were hard, but fear rolled off them in bitter, ashen waves she could almost taste. The officer who inspected her basket checked his clipboard several times and spent some time writing before finally waving her through.

"Sector thirty-one is about a half-mile down the main road and off to the left, on the river side. You have two hours to check back in."

She thanked him, pushing out a wave of warmth, despite his hard demeanor. She felt a moment of empathy; this was a man far from his home, family, friends, and all he knew, surrounded by Maer who wanted him dead. In that circumstance, how could he not harden his heart? The cold, suspicious look he flashed her as she passed through the gate almost erased her sympathy for his plight. Almost.

The sun burst through the clouds, bathing the trampled-down field between the humans' compound and the camps in blazing light. Two dozen little piles of stones stood in a circle around the center of a clearing, with an unruly heap of wildflowers in the middle, only just beginning to fade. Cloti walked to the edge of the circle on unsteady legs that threatened to buckle and leave her slumped on the ground. Sadness radiated from the circle like the heat from a campfire, sparks of grief popping out to sting her face. She counted the piles one by one, fury building within her as she approached the final count, which she knew long before she finished would be twenty. She closed her eyes, and the vision returned: bodies sprawled on the ground, their limbs twisted in lazy, impossible positions, blood soaking into the dirt from jagged ribbons of scarlet running across their throats. The twenty suspected of being Shoza that the humans had executed in full public view. Hands rising to cover gaping mouths. Tears falling unfettered. Eyes wet with tears and hard with fury. Children half-hiding behind their parents' robes, unable to look away from the spectacle of horror before them.

"Cloti?"

The small voice came from a girl no older than six who stood a few feet away, hands clasped in front of her, big eyes taking her in. Cloti crouched, and the girl approached.

"What's your name?" she managed in a shaky voice.

"Bilu," said the girl, stepping closer. "You're supposed to come with me." She held out her small, furry hand, and Cloti stood as she took it. The girl's warm, soft fingers intertwined with hers, and Cloti glanced back at the flowers, slowly wilting in the sun's heat, then followed as the girl led her across the field.

"Loric is in sector thirty-one. It's a long walk."

As they crossed the trampled-down path, Cloti's head snapped at a surprised cry from the human compound, followed by a rapidly stuttering hiss that iced her veins. She had heard the sound once before, at a military demonstration Ludo had made her attend. It was a scattershot flinging hundreds of tiny flechettes per second. Shrieks pierced the air, and Cloti pulled the girl tight against her body as wails and shouts echoed across the open space. Cloti tried to pull Bilu into a run, but her legs went soft as warmth spread throughout her back, and Bilu slumped to the ground. Cloti dropped her basket and fell beside her, staring into the girl's wide, fearful eyes.

"It's okay, I've got you," she murmured, clutching the child close. Her little body was trembling and warm, too warm, almost hot, and wet. Cloti gasped as she realized the girl was bleeding, and she rolled her onto her back. Bilu's body flopped, motionless, as blood squirted from a tear in her robe along her side. Cloti's back screamed in pain, but she tore apart the robe to reveal a thin laceration the length of a finger, pumping unimaginable streams of blood onto the ground. She pressed her hands against the wound, and something sliced into her hand like a finely honed knife. She pulled back her hand, which was bleeding too, and saw a bright golden shard jutting from the girl's ribs. Shouts rang out, the clash of metal, and screams so sharp they sent shuddering jolts throughout her bones. Movement all around. The girl's body convulsing. Footsteps pounding. Cries of rage.

Cloti slammed her eyes shut and walled up her mind to block out the sights and sounds. She brought all her focus to her fingers, which found the girl's wound, carefully sliding to the side of the metal shard. The world dissolved as icy heat coiled in her fingertips, flowing into the wound, freezing the blood in mid-spurt. Time seemed to stop along with it, and she saw the shard in her mind, not an irregular piece of metal but a tiny blade like a nail-sized knife, impossibly sharp, with jagged protrusions at the end like the feathers of a dart. Her jaw clenched as she willed the dart out, feeling it scrape across the bone, then drop onto the ground. The blood tried to flow again, but she stopped it, seeing the severed artery just behind the splintered rib. She watched in morbid fascination as the two ends of the artery stretched toward each other, fusing in an instant. Her mind trembled, and she was yanked out of the wound, crashing back into her body, which fell sideways onto the ground. A spike of hot pain radiated from her lower back, and she tried to reach around to feel it, but her arms were like rope.

The sunlight dimmed as shadows loomed over her, blocking out the bright sun. Voices sounded, and gentle hands found her back, pressing against her, holding her in place. The girl's hitching breath forced a smile from Cloti's tired face, and she relaxed as strong arms lifted her and carried her off into the dimming light, fading into darkness.

21

— • —

Sounds filtered in first: metal gently tapping against glass; the whisper of children; the distant shouts of soldiers. Pain followed, pulsing from a fissure in her lower back like a chemist's lamp being applied to her skin once a second. Her head throbbed in massive waves that distorted the sounds of the world outside, so the tiniest noise jarred her ears like clashing cymbals. Her mouth was so dry that her tongue was glued to the roof of her mouth. As she moved her jaws to try to unstick it, she felt a presence over her and heard a soft male voice.

"There you are. You had us worried for a minute. You lost a lot of blood."

"The girl," Cloti whispered.

"She's fine. More than fine, actually."

Cloti's eyes snapped open at the way the voice trailed off in disbelief. She slammed her eyes shut as light came flooding in, searing her mind like hotiron and turning her stomach inside out. She hadn't had migraines in years, but as the wave of nausea strengthened, she knew what was coming. She just got her head to the side of the bed before she vomited right into a waiting bowl.

"Want me to put a blindfold on you so that doesn't happen again?"

Cloti gave her head a little shake. "Water," she croaked.

"Yes, yes, just a few drops for starters." She felt metal touch her lips, and she took the water from a spoon, which cleared her foul, sticky mouth just a bit. A few spoons later, she was able to sit up enough to take a sip from a cup and then another. She reached for the hand holding the cup to bring it in for another sip, and a *tsk-tsk* sounded.

"Don't be greedy. Let me empty and rinse this bowl just in case, and you lie still and keep your eyes shut."

Cloti drifted between the pain of being awake and the horror of the visions when she slept. She saw blood pumping from the girl's wound, felt her life force slipping, then the bone-draining chill as Cloti poured her own energy into the girl, keeping her afloat and stitching her wounds back together. She'd used her mind before to help heal and speed recovery of less serious wounds, but she'd never known she was capable of something like this. She'd also never seen someone dying of a flechette wound right before her eyes. Her mind traveled backward from the point of impact, and she saw the beige canvas of the humans' tent sprayed red with blood and tattered with a hundred tiny holes. The sounds played in her mind again in gut-wrenching detail: the stuttering hiss of the scattershot, the dull *thwump* of the flechettes sinking into wood, earth, and flesh, the sudden, piercing screams.

The sounds echoed through her head when she woke, and visions lurked, waiting for a moment of distraction to flood her mind, this time with images from inside the tent. A half-dozen robed figures, human mages, she guessed, sprawled on the floor, some as still as toppled statues, others writhing in agony as they bled out. A Maer wielding the grisly machine rigged inside a food delivery cart. Pulling a knife from the cart and methodically slitting the throats of each of the humans on the ground, then turning to face a flood of soldiers who entered the tent. They paused for a moment as they surveyed the scene, and the Maer dashed for the nearest one, slicing up with the knife into his neck. The human dropped like an empty sack, and the others fell upon the Maer, cutting him down with their swords, sending jets of bright red onto the walls of the tent, where it joined the chaotic designs left by the scattershot attack.

Cloti's eyes flipped open as she awoke again, and she sat up just in time to grab the bowl from the table beside her cot. There wasn't much left in her, but she emptied what little she had at the vision of all that blood, and the sounds especially, steel hacking flesh, bodies dropping, lifeless, to the ground, the whimper and gurgle of the Maer's last breath.

"Steady now." A gentle hand supported her, and she took a few deep breaths and sat up, swinging her feet to the rough wooden floor of the tent. It must have been near dusk, as the light filtering in between the flaps was more of a whisper than a scream. She squinted up at the kindly face of a young Maer with a trim beard and hair pulled back in a ponytail. He wore a tattered red bandana around his bicep like the other nurses.

"I'm Loric, by the way. You were expected, Cloti, but in better circumstances."

"What happened?" she croaked.

"It seems someone attacked the mage tent with a scattershot." Loric moved to the other side of the cot and gently lifted the bottom of her shirt. She winced as the fabric brushed against the bandage, agitating the deep wound in her back. "Don't ask me how since the humans have been hard at work destroying every weapon and piece of tech they could get their hands on. In the case of the scattershots, I approve. Ghastly inventions." His fingers touched the area around the bandage, but he did not remove it. "Seven more Maer were injured, two of them fatally, all of them more than a hundred feet from the tent." Loric moved back around and offered her a cup of water, which she sipped, tentatively at first, then more avidly, though she willed herself to drink slowly.

"And the girl? Bilu?"

"She's resting in the other corner of the tent. She lost a lot of blood too, but she was awake and talking a little while ago." He took the cup from Cloti, his eyes darting to the curtain separating this little room from the rest of the tent. "You saved her."

Cloti closed her eyes, wishing she had the strength to read Loric, but her mind was too slow, each thought a pained struggle.

"I did." She realized it as she spoke the words. She could see the wound closing beneath her touch, feel the flesh stitching together, the bone re-sheathing itself.

"How?" he asked, using the Ormaer word. Loric was Shoza, or working with them.

"The...Earth Milk." She struggled to summon the word, and she was less sure of the truth of it, but what else could it be? "Do you have it?"

He eyed the basket on the floor next to him, switching back to Maer. "Someone grabbed your bag, too. It's over there."

Cloti leaned down slowly to retrieve her bag, feeling lightheaded at the searing pain in her back as she sat up again. She pulled out the water bottle and took a careful sip; it was tinny but still had the flowery funk from the Milk. Her mind eased a bit, and her thoughts came a little clearer. She took another sip, then closed the cap and slid it back into her bag, which she clutched to her chest. She felt almost normal again, and the pain in her back had subsided to a dull throb.

"Thank you. I was told you'd get the medicine to those in the best position to distribute it appropriately?"

"I will." The glint in Loric's eye said he understood her perfectly. "And the menstrual products will be most appreciated. But all of it stays here until the lockdown is lifted."

"The lockdown?" Her mind flashed with the image of the bloody, tattered tent. "Right. Of course. How long?"

He shook his head. "They've been checking every tent more than once. We've been checked twice. They won't say what they're looking for, and half of them don't speak Maer anyway."

Cloti looked around, then touched her forehead and gestured to his.

"Would you like to do a cycle with me? It might help settle my mind."

"Of course." Loric's eyes showed worry, but he scooted his chair to face her and leaned in to touch foreheads with her. With the Earth Milk back in her system, it took her only a moment to connect with him, and they stayed connected even when their foreheads peeled apart.

What happened to Gielle? she mindspoke.

She was taken in a raid two days ago. The humans think she's with the Knife's Point. They're the ones who did this, by the way. The scattershot attack. Took out half their mages at once, so no spyballs for the moment.

Taken where?

The Tower, we think.

And Gielle's vials?

Safe. She knew they might be coming for her, so she kept it with a grandmother who lives with her three grandchildren. They brought her doses each morning.

How many are trained to use it?

Only a few. He said something else, but Cloti's energy drained suddenly, and the connection evaporated. She slumped to the side, and Loric helped her lie down.

"We have much work to do," she managed as her eyelids grew heavy.

"You should rest. We'll talk more later."

She reached up and touched his cheek, studying his gentle eyes. He could be trusted.

As she drifted into a half-asleep state, she felt the throbbing in her back from the flechette wound, and she imagined her flesh stitching itself together, her shredded muscles filling back in, her skin regrowing. Heat flared around the wound, then a steady warmth flowed throughout her body, pulling strength from all over to put her back together. Even as she slipped into a deeper sleep, her body continued its work in steady silence.

Cloti awoke to the feeling of being watched. She slitted her lids and saw the wide eyes of a girl, Bilu, sitting in a chair and staring at her.

"You're alive," the girl stated.

"I might say the same about you." Cloti sat up, feeling almost no pain in her back as she did so. Her hand found the bandage and pressed gently on it, but it was not sensitive to her touch.

"They said you saved my life. Thank you."

"You are most welcome, though honestly, I'm not sure what I did."

"You fixed me with your mind." Bilu spoke as if she were reciting a well-agreed-upon fact. "How did you learn to do that?"

"I don't know, I..." Cloti paused, looking into the girl's wide, thoughtful eyes. "Do you know about our practice?"

"The cycles? Of course. Everyone does them now."

"Everyone?"

"Well, almost everyone. Sunup and sundown, and sometimes at midday." She closed her eyes, lowered her hands to her sides, and slowly began to raise them. She stopped, opening her eyes. "Like that, right?"

"Yes, exactly. How long have you been practicing?"

"I learned it from my teacher once they got the pod schools going. Around winter solstice, I guess." She looked Cloti up and down. "They say you invented it."

"Oh, it's been around for thousands of years in one form or another. I just reminded people about it."

"Well, thank you for saving my life. I still don't know why they shot us."

"People with weapons are going to use them sooner or later. It's why I never carry one."

"You should." Bilu pulled out a little bone knife hidden in her belt. "If a human ever tries to touch me, he'll wish he didn't."

Cloti pretended to scratch her nose to hide the sadness that threatened to overtake her. A child of six should not have to carry a weapon for self-defense.

"Let's just hope you never have to use it." She sniffed, then smiled to cover it.

Bilu sheathed the knife. "I'm still in training, but if I ever have to, at least I know what to do." She stood up, pressed her hands together at her chest, and gave an awkward little bow, which Cloti returned.

"Go in joy."

Bilu disappeared behind the curtain, and Cloti heard her lie down on her own cot in the other corner of the tent. There were two more curtained-off areas, one of them holding a Maer with an eye infection, the other a broken ankle. She'd heard Loric tending to each of them; there was very little privacy in such an enclosed space. Her fingers ran over her back again, and she peeled the bandage off. The skin beneath was scarred but whole. In the space of a little over a day, her wound had healed all by itself.

She took a sip of her water bottle, listening to the quiet moans of the Maer with the broken ankle. She wondered if she could heal him too. Her head was still a little fuzzy; she knew she needed rest before she tried anything else, but she realized with sudden certainty that she could do it. Her mind had already begun spinning visions of ankle bones, muscles, tendons, veins, everything she'd studied in anatomy class decades ago. She hadn't thought of any of it in years, but she could picture the pages in the book perfectly and the views the instructor had shared, showing the body's layers of skin, muscle, fat, and bone, how they all interconnected. Something had changed inside her, opening vast spaces in her mind she'd thought closed and lost forever. She was a tree, and she suddenly felt the vast network of roots beneath her, delving deep into the ground and spreading wide, hairy tendrils caressing the roots of other trees, just as her leaves above were part of a larger canopy.

It was like seeing the Thousand Worlds for the first time, but this was physical. It was *real*. She could reach out beyond the limitations of her body into the world around her. That was how she'd reached Feddar. Her heart lurched as she realized Fifthday had passed and she had not come home. Aefin and Ludo would be sick with worry, and Feddar too. Did any of them even know she was alive? Her heart skittered with panicked beats, and she took a long drink of her Milk-laced water. She lay down on her cot and closed her eyes, dampening the sounds of the world outside to rise from her body through the roof of the tent. The camp spread out past the edges of her vision, and she drifted along the tops of the tents, picking up speed as she rushed through the forest and up the sheer cliffs. Twin lights blazed like lamps in the fog, and she was drawn through the winding streets, through her house, and into the garden. Aefin and Ludo sat on the bench, holding hands, Aefin's head leaning against Ludo's shoulder.

She approached gently, surrounding them like mist. Aefin sat up straight, clutching Ludo's hand tightly. It took Ludo a moment longer to catch on, but he looked at Aefin with wide eyes, gasping as Cloti drew them both into a bubble of mental space.

I'm safe in the camps.

Cloti, gods, we've been so worried! Aefin's relief flooded the space, and Cloti squeezed with her mind to mimic a hug. *But how are you...here?*

It's a long story, and I don't know how much time I have, but I was injured in the scattershot attack. I'm fine now, and I'm in good hands. I'll let Feddar know I'm okay too.

Are you sure that's safe? Aefin's worry niggled at Cloti, and she shed it like water from a duck's feathers.

Feddar is on our side. Feddar loves us. He needs to know.

Aefin did not respond, but Cloti could feel her doubt, along with Ludo's attempt at communication, which took the form of a pulse of warmth. He lacked the training to communicate without the Milk.

Ludo will do everything he can to get you out, and I'm sure Feddar will try to help too, but after what's happened, I just don't know, Cloti.

It's okay. I'm needed here. She tried to overwhelm Aefin and Ludo with reassurance, pushing back the doubts that rose in her mind. *Midsummer is coming, and everyone needs to be ready.*

I love you. We love you. We need you back safe with us. Please, be careful.

I love you more than words can say. You need to prepare for what's coming, even though I don't know what it is. Ludo, gather what travel gear you can, whatever we'll need to strike off into the land. To Eagle Lake, with Uffrin and Mara. Kuppham won't be safe for anyone much longer. Aefin, I need you to make as much Earth Milk as possible. I'll visit you when I can, at dawn or dusk. We'll find a way out of this together.

The bubble wavered, and Cloti willed it to stay intact for another moment as she filled the space with her love. It intermingled with theirs until the bubble swelled, its surface quivering with the tension, then burst. Her heart raced as she crashed back into her body, but a wisp of their collective emotion stayed with her, and she wrapped herself in it like a cocoon and drifted off to unconsciousness.

22

— • —

The lockdown ended the next morning, but Cloti didn't leave the tent except to go to the latrines. She spent an hour working on the Maer's broken ankle, taking nips from her water bottle when she felt her energy flagging. It took more out of her than the flechette wound, as there were so many parts to manage, but the tincture helped her see everything with perfect clarity: where the bone had broken, what tendons had been damaged, which muscles torn. The Maer closed his eyes as she worked, gripping the edges of his cot in pain at first until she soothed him with a comforting thought. He watched her with glazed eyes and a faint smile as if he'd been given a dose of soma. When she had finished, she took a sip of her bottle to clear the headache, and the Maer put his foot tentatively on the floor. A smile broke out on his nervous face, and he held her arm as he stood, slowly putting weight on the injured leg.

"It's a miracle!" he whispered, bowing low to her with his hands pressed together at his forehead. She could tell from the gesture that he practiced too.

"It's no miracle. The power to heal lies within your mind. Keep up your practice, and in time you may be able to do the same." She didn't mention the Earth Milk since there wasn't enough of it to go around, and they would need as much as they could save for Midsummer. She extricated herself from his profusion of thanks and returned to her cot to lie down.

She didn't nap, but she closed her eyes and let her mind wander. At first, she was drawn toward the Shoza, whose presence she could feel scattered among the thousands of souls filling the camps, bright stars shining out of nebulous clusters of tiny dots. She could feel whenever one passed close to the tent, and she felt others too, not Shoza but regular acolytes who had developed their practice through long years of study. Their auras glowed with a warmer light, less bright but more inviting. She found Juiya this way and curled around her mind like a cat's tail, feeling Juiya's spark of joy at the sensation. She felt others too, some stronger than others, and soon it became too much. She rose above the tents and was drawn into the city, hurtling toward the white-hot blaze of Feddar's presence. She approached cautiously, as he was surrounded by humans, some of whom had training of their own. Mages perhaps. None of them seemed to notice her presence, and she slipped a tendril of warmth into Feddar's mind. He gasped, then sneezed, pushing her back out for a moment. She slipped back in again once he had settled.

Shhh. I am safe now. I will find you at dusk.

She felt the pulse of his bewildered energy, and she pooled around the corners of his mind, trying to soothe him. Voices penetrated their space, and she slipped away as Feddar stammered.

"I'm sorry, it...it must be the heat. I'm not feeling myself at the moment."

"We're moving ahead with the Lower Cliffside evictions." Cloti was surprised to find herself understanding their speech perfectly. "We need better quarters for the arriving officers. Your dissent has been noted." The human who spoke was tall, broad-shouldered, and wore a slew of medallions on his chest. He could only be the General.

"Let me at least see the list. There are some families who have proven helpful. Who've done everything we've asked. We can't just—"

"We can't trust any of them! At this point, I consider every Maer to be a Shoza!" The General's voice rose to a shout, and an older man sitting with a large open ledger in front of him raised a finger and spoke in a quiet voice.

"I will get you the list, Feddar, and you can put in your suggestions for the General's consideration."

"Thank you. That is all I ask."

"You ask for too much," the General snarled. "All these freedoms you seek for the Maer only encourage them to resist more. If you truly want less bloodshed, as you say, then keep the filthy beasts locked down altogether!"

Cloti drifted away, her heart too sick with rage to listen to another word.

She cured the Maer with the eye infection after her nap. It proved easy, as the Milk allowed her to see the concentration of infectious parthi as if she were using a microscope. She was able to shoo them into the corner formed by forking blood vessels, then draw them out onto a waiting tissue held just above the eyeball. Loric checked the patient and declared them free to go. The Maer with the broken ankle had already left, and they were alone in the large tent.

"How are you feeling?" Loric put his fingers on her wrist to check her pulse, but he seemed to be studying her eyes.

"I feel fine. Great, in fact. I'm learning fast. It seems so simple now. I can see on the smallest level what is wrong, and the solution comes clear to me as if I had studied medicine all my life."

"But you have no medical training?"

Cloti shook her head. "Nothing beyond anatomy and biology classes from school. I've always been a fast healer, and when I take care of someone, when I meditate with them, they get better faster. But never anything like this." She wasn't sure how much she should share, but she intrinsically trusted Loric.

Loric tapped his fingers against his lips.

"I've never seen anything like it either. And neither had Bilu, who told everyone she saw, who told everyone else. And I'm sure the other two will be spreading the word as well." He moved next to the tent flap and put one hand on it. "I don't know if you're up for this, but…" He opened the flap just a crack, and Cloti saw a line of Maer, some on crutches, others with slings or rough bandages, a few without any visible ailment.

"There must be thirty Maer lined up out there!"

"Closer to fifty. The humans have already dispersed them once."

"That's too many." Her head felt suddenly heavy. The day had taken its toll, and she wasn't sure if she had even one more in her. She needed to rest. "Can we tell them to come back tomorrow?"

"You could, but there will be more. How will you decide who to help?"

"You're the medical professional. Can you come up with something?"

Loric toyed with his beard, staring at the tent flap, then snapped his fingers.

"Yes. I've got an idea. Give me some time to think it through, and we'll see how to make this work."

"I'll need a few helpers. I'll make you a list."

"Anyone you need. I'm sure no one would refuse." He eyed the tent flap, then Cloti. "It might be best if you…"

She closed her eyes for a long moment, then shook her head. She couldn't face them, not now. She opened her eyes, pleading with Loric to take the initiative. He breathed out through his nose and nodded.

"Okay. You rest. I'll tell them to come back tomorrow." He slipped out through the flap, and Cloti heard a commotion of low voices, which fell silent as Loric began to speak.

"Cloti is resting from her injuries and from her efforts assisting me in the medical tent. I will take down your names and ailments in the order you are in line, so you won't lose your place, and I'll explain tomorrow at mid-morn how we'll proceed going forward…"

Cloti tuned him out, closing her eyes and summoning the leaf on the lake. Life had dealt her so many swift turns of late, and she needed the simplicity of this vision to ground her in the moment, lest she lose her way. She spread her arms off the sides of the cot, opened her mind to the sky, and became the leaf. She floated in perfect stillness, balanced and supported, with no pressure from any direction. She just was.

After a simple meal of bland porridge, which she thought might have been the same thing she'd seen in the nursing camp, she heard footsteps scuffing outside the tent, and Bilu slipped through the tent flap.

"Bilu, so nice to see you up and about. Are you healing well?"

"I'm fine." The girl lifted her shirt to show her side, where only a thin scab remained. "I'm supposed to ask you to come lead the dusk cycle down by the falls." She looked down as if in embarrassment, then back up, her eyes wide and oddly blank.

"Of course, let me just get my water bottle and visit the latrine." She picked up her bottle, which was empty, and eyed the basket. "Why don't you wait outside?"

Bilu slipped through the flap without a word. Cloti unsealed one of the Earth Milk vials marked "cough suppressant" and poured a dollop into her water bottle. She corked the vial carefully, replaced it, and filled her bottle with water from the barrel. She shook it and took a small sip, then summoned a slow-motion waterfall in her mind, flowing down it with such gentleness that it felt more like floating than falling. When her mind had settled, she joined Bilu outside the tent. Maer stopped talking, walking, working, whatever they were doing, as she passed hand-in-hand with Bilu. She acknowledged their bows with modest nods of her head, for there were too many to bow to individually.

She heard the rush of water as they approached the amphitheater overlooking the falls. It was nearly the only space remaining that looked like the park that had lined this river a year ago and for hundreds if not thousands of years before that. Her eyes clouded with tears as she saw the mist creeping over the brass rails she had gripped so many times as a child, looking down into the water cascading over the rocks. The crowd grew thick, the path narrow until they entered the little semicircle of the park, with its benches, flagstone paths, and carefully trimmed and weeded flowerbeds. The wide stone steps of the amphitheater were filled with hundreds of Maer, all seated cross-legged facing the stage, where a reed mat was laid between two burning sticks wrapped with herbs.

The crowd grew quiet as Bilu led her to the stage, only letting go when they stood next to the mat. Cloti thanked the girl with her eyes as she took a sip from her water bottle and lowered herself down. Bilu clambered up to the first stone step and squeezed in between several other acolytes, who made way with serene smiles. Cloti let her gaze drift across the crowd, taking in each face for an instant, fixing them in her mind. Some she knew: Juiya, Loric, a handful of Shoza who had been at the temple cycles, and a few others. There were many Shoza present, recognizable by their rigid mental discipline, and many others whose practice radiated strong, each with a slightly different flavor. Cloti smiled, feeling the variations among groups, like accents and dialects of a common tongue. The shape of the amphitheater helped focus their energies, which Cloti allowed to flow freely through her and back into the crowd. Their bonds were forming already, and they had not yet begun their cycle. They fell silent as she lowered her hands and opened her mouth to speak.

"The darkest day of winter shrinks the soul to a withered seed, which on the longest day of summer bears fruit to fill our need."

When her hands touched the stone, she felt hundreds of pairs of hands all connecting to the earth in time with hers. She kept her hands in place, feeling the cool weight of the stone beneath her, the warmth of the group's unity. When she lifted her arms, she could sense each pair of arms joining her, feel the strain in their muscles, their struggles to clear their minds. She pushed out ripples like a tiny stone dropped in a bucket and felt the worries of the acolytes wash away, leaving a smooth surface behind. She was the leaf, and they were the lake, still as glass, supporting her without effort.

They maintained this perfect stability as they moved upward through the cycle. When their hands came together, the mirrored surfaces of their minds formed a globe under Cloti's direction, seamless and unified. Their collective joy swelled as they saw each other, felt each other, all at once. Cloti's mind opened, releasing little bursts of energy from the Earth Milk like a thousand fireflies, each one finding and sinking into an individual mind. The globe shrank, more tightly bound, each detail and individual compressing and mixing with the others. The Shoza among the group seemed to resist at first, but they soon relaxed their outer shells and joined the greater whole.

I have given you all a seed. Water it. Tend it carefully. Give it room to grow. Share it with those you love. When the time is right, you will know what to do.

She gave it a moment to sink in, then separated her hands, feeling the group's consciousness stretch and distend as their arms made their way slowly toward the ground. She held her hands aloft, the hairs on her knuckles brushing the stone but not touching yet. She pushed out a single word, which echoed through their shared mindspace.

Midsummer.

Her hands touched the stone, and the group let out a collective sigh as the spell was broken.

She took one more sip as she lay back down on her cot. Loric hadn't specifically invited her to stay, but no one had provided her with anywhere else to sleep, so she decided to make her home in the nursing tent. It was fully dark now, and her body was exhausted from the day's events, but her mind was strangely energized. The power of the collective cycle had given her a boost, and her mind felt open to the universe, like she was laying on a blanket under the stars, which were so close she could reach out and touch them. She wanted to grab them all, collect them like seashells, stuff her pockets full, and run her fingers over their smooth edges.

Her mind drifted up away from the tent, and she thought of Ludo and Aefin, alone and worrying in their house, and Feddar, even more alone. At least Ludo and Aefin had each other. She would visit them in the morning, but she needed to know whatever Feddar knew about the General's plans, so she could spread the word. It seemed like things were about to get a lot worse very quickly. Midsummer was just over a week away, and she needed to know as much as possible before she could decide how best to help the Shoza. She wouldn't be part of any killings, but it felt like the humans were tightening the noose even further. With the General's attitude toward the Maer, a coordinated mass escape from the city might be the only option left.

She raced through the city toward Feddar's signal, which was dim and weary, but it flared into life as she approached. He was in his courtyard with only a single candle for light, though the brightstone lamps inside the house cast shadows throughout the garden in a hundred shades of green and gray.

"Cloti," he whispered.

I am here.

I still don't understand how... He gestured in the air, a confused expression on his face. He hadn't yet learned to mindspeak without using his hands.

Are we truly alone?

Feddar shook his head, looking around. *The garden walls have eyes and ears.*

Join me in your room.

She hovered around him as he went upstairs and closed the door behind him. He pulled the shades and sat down on the bed, looking around, his eyes full of hope and confusion. Cloti concentrated on the space until she could feel the floor and the bed, and she pulled gently on his mind, teasing out his memory of her face and body. His eyes opened wide as he stood, and his hands found her hips. She could feel their warmth, his tender grip, even his breath on her beard.

Cloti, gods, I've been worried sick about you!

It's okay. She closed the distance between them, running her hands down his chest, sweeping around to rest on his waist. *I'm okay.* She closed her eyes as she kissed him. His lips were soft and eager, and his hands slid around to her backside and held her gently. She kissed him slowly, savoring his growing desire, which radiated off him like steam. She gripped him tight and pulled him hard against her, and his breath grew rough and halting.

Cloti broke from the kiss and pulled back, staring hard into his eyes.

I'm going to take my time with you tonight. Make no mistake. But there are some things we need to talk about first.

Yes, of course. Cloti, you must be very careful. They're watching your every move. If they see any connection between you and the Shoza, they'll put you in the Tower, and there's nothing I'll be able to do to stop them.

Cloti paused, swept away by the feeling of loneliness and the bone-chilling winds whipping through the air slats in the Tower. Feddar had spent nine months there, no doubt undergoing the worst treatment the Maer could offer. Yet he was the only human she'd ever met who treated her as an equal person. She shook her head to clear it.

Tell me about the Lower Cliffside evictions, Feddar. They talked about housing the arriving officers. Why are more officers arriving? What happened to de-occupation?

Feddar's guilt poured over her as he spoke.

They're doing what they call a strategic evaluation. The officers are scheduled to arrive within the week.

That was just a few days before Midsummer.

I don't like the sound of that. And where will those evicted go?

To the camps, I'm afraid. They claim they're only evicting households that have harbored Shoza. We know there are some operating throughout the city, despite the General's best efforts to hunt them down. After this last attack…it's going to get bad. I've put in an administrative request to have you released through the proper channels. If they drag their feet, I'll take it up with the camp director myself. But I'm on thin ice here, too, Cloti. They know about us, and I'm one slip-up away from ending up in the Tower myself.

I would never let that happen to you. She took his cheek in her hand and pulled him in, holding him with her eyes as she nosed in for a kiss. *We will be together again once this is over. Until then, this will have to be enough.* His soft lips chased away her worries, and she lingered in their warmth. She savored his want, the way he held it back, how it bucked against his restraint.

I need you to take your clothes off now.

Cloti devoured his mouth, and Feddar's hands moved like frantic butterflies, unbuttoning and shedding his clothes in seconds. His hands moved more slowly as they found their way back to Cloti's body, lingering on every curve. She smiled as she felt him throbbing against her, and she toyed with him as they kissed. Feddar's breath grew short, and Cloti released him, breaking from the kiss for a moment.

Not yet.

Feddar's eyes remained with hers for a moment, then he lowered his gaze slowly down her body and back up again.

I will do anything you ask of me.

Cloti put her hands on his shoulders and pushed down.

I want you to sit on the floor, leaning against the bed.

Feddar slid quickly off the bed, looking up at her with wide, hopeful eyes. Cloti lifted one leg onto the bed, pressing herself against Feddar, whose hands gripped her backside as he pulled her tight to his face. The sensation of his lips and tongue was every bit as exquisite as when they were physically together. He moved at her command, ever attentive to her body's signals. She got carried away and let him bring her over the edge far too early, but Feddar stayed in close, breathing into her, holding her. It didn't take long before she felt a little tingle, and Feddar nosed in gently once again.

She gripped his hair and pulled him in slowly, guiding him with gentle touches. He took his time, and she let him play, her pleasure rising slowly with Feddar's languorous strokes. When he sped up, she pressed hard against him, pinning his head to the bed. He gripped her behind with strong hands as she rode him, hips creaking and knees popping and then explosions of chaotic ecstasy like a string of fireworks tossed into a crowd. She gasped as she pressed against him, pleasure flooding through her. But it was not just her own pleasure she felt; his joy echoed through her, his sense of complete fulfillment. She hadn't imagined such a deep connection from this distance, but with her and Feddar, it seemed nothing was impossible.

She slumped down on the floor next to him, wiping his face and kissing him, tasting herself on his lips. She looked down and saw he was still stiff as a lamppost. Her fingertips traced down his chest, fluttering over his nipples, which drew a sharp gasp. She let her fingers braid through the thickening hair down his stomach, then glide gently along his length.

Did you wait all this time for me?

Feddar nodded, his lip trembling as she toyed with him, barely touching with the pads of her fingers.

Do you think you're ready now?

"Yes," Feddar whispered out loud.

Cloti grinned and put her hands on his chest, pushing out her memory into him: the sweep of his silky tongue, the hard knob of his chin, the way he clung to her as she exploded above him. Feddar's eyes shot wide, and his breath came in trembling gasps as he twitched and spilled, over and over, without a single touch. He let out a groaning sigh, and as he looked up at her, she was struck with a blinding flash.

A vision. Flames. Explosions. Screams. Feet pounding into darkness. Feddar's eyes, weak and watery with pain but alive with hope.

The weight of Feddar's head on her shoulder brought her back; his sigh of contentment showed that her vision hadn't bled into him. She kissed his forehead, caressing the soft skin of his neck. She closed her eyes and wrapped her arms around him. Darkness fell like a soft blanket. They snuggled into it, into each other, and let sleep carry them off.

23

— • —

Cloti did a short pre-dawn cycle, zipping through the Thousand Worlds straight to the mountain Shoza's signal. They received her coolly.

We know what has happened, and in light of recent events, I'll ask you not to contact me again until Midsummer's Eve. It's not safe for any of us.

Surely the humans can't follow us here!

They can't, but they can detain you and make you talk. You know too much already, and you are not trained to resist.

Cloti coiled tightly around them, stirred with sudden anger. *"They may capture my body, but my mind is my own. They can never contain me!* She felt their energy flicker, and she loosened her grip, flushing with the unaccustomed loss of control. Their presence strengthened again, but their mindvoice was soft and steady.

They cannot contain any of us. Continue your work with the Shoza. Help make the people ready. Come to us at dawn on Midsummer's Eve.

Cloti left them, drifting among the stars as the last wisps of her anger bled out of her. This was not supposed to happen. She had always found peace in the Thousand Worlds, and now she was using it to prepare for war. Never mind that the humans had already done the same to the Maer, and much worse. Her practice was meant to bring stillness and joy, not foment rebellion. She had work to do to regain the steady hand she would need going forward. The Shoza would attack at Midsummer whether she helped them or not. The only question was how much blood would be spilled and what life would be like for the Maer in Kuppham in the aftermath.

She felt the Thousand Worlds slipping, and as she cast around for something to maintain her focus and chase away these intrusive thoughts, she was drawn to a bright light whose hue sent shivers of warmth through her mind. Aefin. She streaked across the worlds, swirling around Aefin's blazing beacon, and found her sitting in their garden, arms crossed in her lap, fingers looped in a new hand mood. Cloti settled like a feathery shawl around her shoulders, feeling Aefin almost purr at the sensation.

I knew you would come. Aefin's mindvoice rang crisp and clear. Cloti could tell her presence was boosted.

Did you make more Earth Milk already?

I had Ludo help since we're still under lockdown. Even the ambassadors are being kept at home.

How did you manage?

I used a taste of the ooze to inspire me, and I was able to remember everything perfectly. I passed word across the garden wall looking for bugbane. I got enough to make a double batch, and it came out just right. Aefin's pride bled through her words, and Cloti sent a wave of warmth to show how pleased she was.

I knew you would find a way, my love.

I still don't see how we're going to get it to you with this lockdown.

I will come to you.

But how?

Never mind that. Be on the lookout tomorrow night. Keep the door unlocked.

Cloti, that's impossible! They said any Maer found in the streets would be taken straight to the Tower, and their soldiers are everywhere!

No one can contain me. Cloti shushed Aefin's worries and her own as well, for in her heart, she knew it to be true. Regular use of the Milk had unlocked powers that continued to surprise even her. She would find a way. She pulled on Aefin's mind as she had done with Feddar, drawing out Aefin's image of her. Aefin gasped as Cloti appeared before her, seated cross-legged so their knees were touching. Cloti's hands found Aefin's, which unfolded from their looped mood and gripped her gently.

How...?

Cloti ran her hands up Aefin's arms, over her shoulder, and cupped her face. Aefin's wide eyes softened as Cloti leaned in for a gentle kiss.

"No one can keep me from you," she said aloud, pulling back and brushing her thumb down Aefin's lips. Aefin's sudden burst of desire swirled around her, and Cloti wanted to give in to it, but she could feel the pull of dawn and hear the scuff of Bilu's sandals outside her tent.

Be ready, she said, leaving a spark of heat in Aefin's mind as she pulled away.

Cloti led the morning cycle, and the collective energy was even greater than before. It felt like half the camp was present, and the other half was joining them in spirit. The strength of the group mind bolstered her concentration, and she was able to keep her thoughts of politics and Earth Milk and scheming at bay. She led them in a longer version of her usual cycle, focusing on hand moods at the beginning and end of the practice. It was a different way to access the core of stillness and something they could practice more discretely if the humans started cracking down on large-scale cycles. When the practice ended, Cloti felt their energy lingering in her mind, giving her strength to meet the day's tasks. Loric had triaged those needing healing, and only twenty waited in line, though she doubted she could work with nearly that many.

Juiya came to assist, and she brought another Maer whose face was somehow familiar, though Cloti couldn't place where she'd seen her before. They sat on chairs in the tent as Loric spoke with those in line. The new Maer was petite and quiet, with an intense gaze. Cloti took her hands and immediately felt her strong will and mental discipline, not exactly what she would expect from someone experienced with Cloti's practice. More like a Shoza or perhaps a mage of some kind.

"What is your name?"

"Aene."

Cloti suddenly recalled the name from the Delve chronicle and Feddar's story. This was his lover.

"You were on the Delve with Yglind Torl, weren't you?"

Aene nodded, her eyes darkening. "It was a long time ago, and I'd just as soon forget it."

"You are a mage, yes?"

Aene nodded again. "I am. Was. A channeler. But without the gauntlet, I've had to learn everything from scratch. I'm afraid I can't do much."

Cloti pushed out a wave of warmth through her hands, and Aene sat up a little straighter.

"You have strength in you. Did you channel healing spells?"

"I did, but without—"

"Never mind the gauntlet. Have you ever..." She paused, glancing at Juiya, then back to Aene. "Have either of you ever drunk of the Earth Milk?" Juiya nodded with a small smile, and Aene's face scrunched into a confused frown.

"It's a tincture, made from a rare element, that helps boost mental acuity and focus. We used it to access the Thousand Worlds, even without a cradle, before the humans came. Its use is forbidden by the humans, of course." Cloti pulled the open vial from the basket, uncorked it, and filled a dram spoon. "It may serve the same purpose as your gauntlet if you can remember the spell."

Aene eyed the spoon suspiciously. "The spell was stored in the gauntlet. I don't know if—"

"It might help you remember. If you feel like trying. It's fine if you don't."

Aene looked at the spoon, then at Juiya, who gave a slight nod, and Cloti had a sudden inkling that they might be lovers.

"What other effects will it have on me?"

"You may feel euphoria, even mild hallucinations at first, but they will pass. After that, your mind will open, and you should feel increased connections to others and to memories that have faded. With time and practice, it may help you regain some of the spells you've cast before."

Aene still looked unconvinced, and Juiya reached for the spoon.

"It's been a while, but I'll go first to show you it's nothing to worry about." Juiya took the spoon gingerly from Cloti and slurped down the Milk. She closed her eyes, and when she opened them again, they were glassy, her pupils large. She giggled, then her face grew serious, and Cloti felt her thoughts creeping into her mind.

Aene has more power than she lets on.

Cloti smiled, refilled the spoon, and held it out to Aene, who stared at Juiya for a moment before drinking it down. The spoon nearly slipped from her fingers, but she caught it and held it out to Cloti. Aene's confusion was palpable, and Cloti soothed and guided her, taking her hands again and opening her mind wide to let Aene in when she was ready. Aene's confusion soon turned to wonder, and Cloti felt her smile through their bond before she saw it on her face.

"This reminds me of the first time I put on a gauntlet."

You can speak without speaking if you like.

Aene's breath caught, then her mindvoice rang clear and true.

It's like wearing a circlet.

There are many ways to the same end. Try and see if you can remember one of your healing spells.

Aene nodded, and Cloti locked fingers with her, opening her well of energy so Aene could draw on it freely. Aene gasped, and Cloti saw golden symbols floating in the mindspace between them.

Yes, it's here! It's all here!

Are you ready to try it on someone whose injuries are minor?

Yes! Yes. Aene's face grew serious as she studied the symbols.

I can help soothe their pain while you work. Juiya's selflessness warmed Cloti's heart. She shared her pleasure with Juiya, who beamed with pride.

Let's take it slowly and see what we can do. Cloti nodded to Juiya, who opened the flap and spoke with Loric.

"Number eighteen," he called, and a Maer with a bandaged face hurried forward. Those in the front of the line watched her with whiffs of impatience, but they would get their turn. Cloti and Aene moved to the first treatment section, where a cot, two chairs, and a table of basic supplies waited for them. Juiya led the Maer to the cot, where she sat, looking up at Cloti in wonder.

"Thank you so much for taking the time to help me."

"Of course. Do you want to show me what's wrong?"

The woman peeled off her bandage, showing a large open sore from her nose to just below her eye. Cloti swallowed her discomfort; she had never been very good with blood and fluids. Juiya opened a window flap to let in light, and Aene stepped toward the Maer, pulling up her scarf as she leaned in close to examine the wound.

"It started as a scratch, but it got infected. I wouldn't bother you, but I'm worried it's going to get into my eye."

"You were right to come to us," Aene said as if she'd been doing this all her life. "I think I can help you. Just close your eyes and hold onto Juiya's hand. This may sting a bit."

The Maer looked worriedly at Aene, then forced a small laugh and took Juiya's hand. When she closed her eyes, Aene drew her fingertips together like a flower bud just about to open and held them in front of the wound. The pus bubbled and slowly evaporated, leaving only clean pink flesh behind. Cloti wanted to look away, but she was fascinated by what she saw. Faint tendrils of golden light poured from Aene's fingertips, and the flesh began to dry and firm up as the skin from either side slowly closed over the wound. Aene stopped when the skin was whole but still showed an irregular seam where the skin had stitched itself together. She took a deep breath and let her hand fall to her side.

"You can open your eyes now."

The Maer, who had been gripping Juiya's hand tightly, raised her fingers to her face, running them gingerly over the scar. She let out a joyful little laugh, her eyes wet and her face drawn with amazement.

"The hair should grow back in time."

"How did you..." She touched her face again, then took Aene's hand and brought it to her chest. "Thank you. I wish there was something I could do to..."

Cloti put a hand on her shoulder. "Go forth and spread peace and joy. We have too little in these difficult times."

"I will. I will! Thank you so much!" Juiya guided her gently toward the flap, and the Maer exited the tent. Juiya spoke to Loric, who called out:

"Number one!"

Cloti treated the next patient, a Maer with a badly broken and infected leg. Juiya helped put him at ease so Cloti could work. The Earth Milk showed her exactly what to do and how to do it, but it still took some time to clear the infection, reset the bones, and put all the tissues back in the right place. By the time she had finished, the man could walk with only a slight limp, but Cloti was exhausted. She took a sip from her water bottle, then as Aene worked on the next patient, she returned to her cubicle and took a dram from the vial. For work like this, she would need all the help she could get.

They took turns, refreshing their dose of the Milk several more times until all twenty of the day's patients had been treated and sent on their way. Cloti was dead on her feet, and Aene looked like she was going to pass out, but her gritty smile buoyed Cloti's spirits.

"I forget you've done this before," Juiya said, passing Aene a piece of the bread Loric had brought them.

"Healing is the first thing we learned in school, and gods know I had plenty of practice on that fucking Delve." She covered her mouth, smiling as she chewed. "Sorry, I forget where I am sometimes."

"You're in a tent in a prison encampment in your own city, which the fucking humans have stolen from you," Cloti said, touching Aene on the shoulder. "I think you've earned the right to curse." Though Cloti didn't often swear, it felt good to cut loose a little, and Aene rewarded her with a big smile. Juiya's eyes danced with amusement.

Once they had finished their meager lunch, Cloti's head felt heavy and thick.

"I'm going to take a long nap, maybe until dusk. I suggest you two do the same."

"Will we see you at the cycle?" Juiya asked hopefully.

Cloti smiled through half-closed eyes.

"If I don't sleep through it."

Cloti bid them goodbye and returned to her cubicle, where she took a small sip of her water bottle and was asleep before her head hit her pillow.

Cloti maintained the focus on joy as she led the dusk cycle in the amphitheater. It was so easy to get stuck in the cycle of worry, doom, and gloom, but it was even more important in such dark times to pursue the good with the same energy used to combat despair. She moved through several slow cycles, taking time to find and make contact with each and every mind present and not a few who were with them in spirit from a distance. She shared a spark of happiness with each of them, the curl of fingers together, a bee on a flower, a lizard sunning itself on a rock. They returned her joy many times over, and by the time the cycle was over, the amphitheater buzzed with positive vibes. Before she left, she shared a line from one of her old poems, which came to her suddenly, though she hadn't thought of it in years.

"Bring joy to each other. Bring joy to yourselves. Pollinate the world with your happiness, and it will blossom into whatever you need."

She hurried back to her tent after the most cursory of goodbyes, took a careful sip of her water bottle, and lay down on her cot. She found Aefin in seconds, her mind glowing with the Milk.

That was a beautiful session this evening.

Oh, I'm sorry I didn't reach you! There were so many present, and even more at a distance.

You've reached me now. Aefin's mindvoice was warm and inviting, but it grew concerned as she continued. *Ludo is worried about your visit. I still don't see how...*

I need to touch you. Kiss you. Both of you. I will come to you before long.

Cloti shared a fragment of her experience with Feddar the night before, the helpless look in his eyes as she put her hands on his chest and made him spill. Aefin gasped, heat rising suddenly through her mind, and Cloti cut the memory short.

Be ready, she said, then slipped back into her body.

She heard Loric lay down on his cot in the next cubicle over. She filled her water bottle and dosed it, then drank two drams straight from the vial, which was more than half empty at this point. The world came rushing in, and she into it. She closed Loric's eyes with a thought, pushing him gently down into sleep. She stood, scanning the paths outside the tent for active minds, but there were none. She slipped through the flaps into the night.

24

— • —

Cloti walked slowly through the little paths between the tents, her mind scoping ahead for anyone out. When she saw Maer walking or sitting in their tents with the flaps up, she sent little distractions to keep them occupied as she walked past. No one seemed to notice her, and after the first few times, she was able to do it almost without thinking, creating a tunnel of anonymity she could walk through calmly. She paused at the edge of the camps, taking stock of the human guards' positions, but they proved just as easily distractable, and she walked across the open space delineating the edge of the camp, past the signposts, and into the park. She took the long way around since the park was almost empty and only had to pass by one patrol before she got to the bottom of Cliffside Road.

She breezed past the checkpoint at the entrance to Lower Cliffside, bringing the guards' focus to a story one of them was telling so they took no notice of her passage. At each checkpoint, she created a small distraction, using whatever was foremost on their minds as she approached. It was as simple as tossing breadcrumbs to gutter sparrows, and her heart leapt when she saw a single candle burning in the window of her house. She breathed in the heady scents of the flowers in the garden, feeling Aefin's anticipation growing with each step. She did a final check to make sure there was no one within sight or earshot, then opened the door quietly and slipped inside.

Aefin's footsteps pattered across the stone floor, and Cloti smiled as Aefin rounded the corner and stopped, her eyes full and wet.

"You made it!" Aefin swept her up in a fierce hug, her body hot and strong as she clung to Cloti. Aefin pulled her face back for a moment, then fell upon Cloti's lips, inundating her with kisses as her arms gripped her waist tightly. Cloti broke from the kiss as Ludo's shadow fell over them.

"I hope you saved some for me."

Cloti held onto Aefin with one arm as she pulled Ludo in with the other, kissing him with soft heat. She pulled back just a bit, touching her forehead to Ludo's. Aefin joined in, and they stood, a circle of three bodies, three minds, three hearts fusing to form one. They remained together in their bond for some time, breathing together, until Cloti finally loosened her grip on them and took a half-step back. Ludo's smile was radiant as he turned toward the living room.

"Come, I found a bottle of ten-year-old honeycomb I seem to have overlooked in the cellar."

Aefin glared daggers at him, and he shrugged and put up his hands in self-defense as he backed away, then scurried off toward the kitchen.

They sat together on the couch with their wine, Cloti in the center with each of them leaning into her. She answered as many questions as she could, trying to reassure them that she was okay, that everything was going to be okay.

"But you're not staying," Aefin said in a defeated tone.

Cloti gave a little shake of her head. "I have to go back. To help them get ready. And you must be ready to run. I will come for you, but if something goes wrong, flee with the others at Midsummer. Meet me at Broken Horn Pass, and we'll wend our way up to Eagle Lake through the Middle Hills."

"You can't possibly mean this." Aefin's fingers gripped Cloti's arm. "Are things really happening so fast?"

"Have you heard about the Lower Cliffside evictions? They're going to trump up some charges of harboring Shoza and evict half the neighborhood to make way for a bunch of new human officers. And they took dozens more alleged Shoza to the Tower after the scattershot attack. They're planning another mass execution."

"They're not leaving." Ludo's eyes were soft with disappointment. He'd always chosen to believe that a better end was possible, one that didn't involve fire and explosions and screaming. Cloti had believed it too, but she couldn't unsee what she'd seen. Some of her visions were vague and hazy, but when she replayed this one in her mind, she could smell the smoke and taste her own blood in her mouth. It was a memory of something that hadn't happened yet, but she knew it was as real as yesterday.

"What will come will come. We must prepare, of course, but we can't let this be all we are." She raised Ludo's chin with a finger, turning his face toward hers. "We need to remind ourselves just what we have to live for."

Ludo's eyes softened as she drew him in, and a low hum vibrated up from his throat as she kissed him. Her hands roamed his eager body, and he rose beneath her touch. She kissed him roughly, lifting her robe and swinging one leg over to straddle him as she yanked down his pants just enough. He gasped as she gripped him tight, and his eyes melted as she sank down onto him and started moving. Her body was hungry, and she wound up quickly as she ground against him, kissing him sloppily as she moved faster and faster.

She caught a flash of movement out of the corner of her eye and saw Aefin with her robe open, pleasuring herself with both hands as she stared into Cloti's eyes. They maintained their gaze as Cloti bore down on Ludo, squeezing from within, her hands gripping his shoulders as she rode him toward a quickly building climax. The couch rocked with her thrusts, and Aefin's first cry of delight pushed Cloti over the edge. She clutched Ludo's face to her breast as she clenched around him, her whole body vibrating as he pulsed and spilled inside her, heaving for breath. She pulled his face toward hers and pressed her lips against his, breathing with him, feeling his satisfaction but also his eagerness to please her more.

She kissed him once more, then lifted herself off him, laughing at the mess they'd made on the couch and all over Ludo. Aefin lay panting, her legs askew and her arms draped over her thighs. Cloti slid off the couch and onto her knees, nuzzling Aefin's ankle, then up her calf. She gripped the back of Aefin's knee gently between her teeth, and Aefin's hand found her hair and threaded through it.

"I've missed you so much," Cloti said as she nipped her way up Aefin's thighs, her hands sliding up to wrap around her hips. She gripped her tight and yanked her toward the edge of the couch, and Aefin gave a little yelp, which quickly softened into a moan as Cloti nosed between her legs. It had been so long since she'd tasted her, felt her melt at the touch of her tongue. She worked Aefin up quickly, as she had Ludo. She did not tease or tarry. She hunted Aefin's pleasure without remorse, hammering away at her thin resolve until her thighs clenched around Cloti's head and her hips bucked. Cloti held her tight, finishing her with a merciless flurry until Aefin pushed her head away and collapsed onto the couch, curling into a wet, trembling ball.

Once they had finished the bottle and Cloti had reassured them for the dozenth time that she would be fine in the camps, Aefin stood up and padded toward the stairway, looking over her shoulder and beckoning them both with a glance that set Cloti's core tingling. Cloti followed, with Ludo on her heels, his hands resting on her hips as she walked up the stairs.

No sooner had she entered the bedroom than Aefin gripped her shoulders, shoved her against the wall with a thump, and crushed her lips against Cloti's. Aefin's fingers made short work of Cloti's robe, then raced across her body, grasping and pinching until at last they slid between her legs. Aefin massaged her inside and out, working her with deft, precise strokes as her other hand slid up to Cloti's neck, pinning her to the wall. Aefin held her securely but did not choke her or kiss her, instead staring into Cloti's eyes with deadly determination. Aefin's fingers moved with strength and purpose, working Cloti up so fast she struggled to catch a breath. Aefin smiled as Cloti cried out in ecstasy, and Aefin finished her with a few more hard thrusts, then released her.

Cloti leaned against the wall for support, gasping, but the devilish look in Aefin's eyes told her she was far from finished.

"Ludo, stroke yourself and be ready," Aefin said without turning around. Cloti watched Ludo undress, already hard again, his eyes glued to Cloti's.

"You don't get to leave until we've wrung every bit of pleasure out of your divine body." Aefin kissed Cloti tenderly, slipping her tongue in for just a moment. She wrapped herself around Cloti's body, rubbing circles on her back, working her way slowly downward. As her hands kneaded Cloti's behind, her lips began milking her ear, sending a new wave of tingles throughout her body. Aefin kissed her again, with more heat this time, then nuzzled her way down through her beard and neck. Cloti gasped as Aefin's lips found her nipple, sucking so hard it almost hurt, then moving to the other.

She kissed her way down Cloti's stomach, hands kneading her backside, humming into her fur. It was the hum that sparked Cloti's fire anew, and soon Aefin fell to her knees, spread Cloti with her fingers, and began a delicate dance with her lips and tongue. Aefin's desire swept over Cloti, the burning urge to send her pleasure spiraling to the Thousand Worlds and beyond. Cloti watched Ludo stroke himself slowly, his eyes filled with a lust so tender it made her already weak knees buckle.

Aefin's mouth knew Cloti's every fold and crevice, and her passion bled through as she worked her relentlessly up, then pulled back just before climax. Cloti tried to pull Aefin's head in closer and push against her, but she was no match for Aefin's steely determination.

Cloti whimpered as Aefin's tongue circled and swirled around her bud, brushing against it gently, leaving her just short of release. Ludo's hands had stopped moving, and he held himself firm, his eyes glassy with need. Aefin gripped Cloti's behind harder, lighting her core on fire with a few direct strokes, then she pulled back and stood up suddenly. Her eyes burned with a dark intensity Cloti had seldom seen, and Aefin took her hand and pulled her toward the bed. Cloti followed, her heart racing and her breath coming in short gasps as Aefin shoved her down onto the bed and lifted her behind in the air.

"Ludo, finish her."

Cloti propped herself up on her arms as she felt Ludo closing in behind her. He stroked her a few times with his thumb, sending shivers throughout her body, then he pushed inside her, filling her with stiff heat. His hands gripped her hips and pulled her body flush against his, and she gasped when he pulled all the way out. His fingers moved in to stroke her once more, then he was inside her again, pulling her hips back as his body smacked against hers. She was so close already, and she moved with him as he thrust, her body lowering with each stroke. Aefin lay down on the bed in front of her, staring lovingly into Cloti's eyes as Ludo increased the force of his thrusts, pounding her into the mattress and flooding her with ecstasy. Ludo let out a primal groan and collapsed onto her, throbbing and spilling inside her.

Aefin's hand slid across the sheets to cup Cloti's cheek. They shared a sideways glance in their awkward positions, and Cloti scooted closer as Ludo pulled out and rolled to the side. His arm flopped over Cloti's waist, and Aefin scooted over to rest her leg atop Ludo's shoulder. Aefin pushed a stray lock of hair out of Cloti's face, kissing her with her eyes. Cloti stretched one arm back atop Ludo's while the other slid around Aefin's neck.

"I love you, and I promise we will still be together when this is all over. Nothing will stop me from finding you, from protecting you. No harm will come to you while I am alive."

Tendrils of doubt leaked from Aefin's mind, drifting across the space between them. Cloti pushed back with a wave of hope, smiling as Aefin's eyes softened. They would get through this. They had to.

The way back was easy. She tested Aefin's Earth Milk and found it exceeded the one they'd made together. With a flick of her mind, she could shield herself from the attention of any number of people, passing beside them as if she were invisible. She made her way past the checkpoints, through the park, and past the clueless guards on the camp perimeter. No Maer were up at this late hour, and she slipped into her tent, pushing an extra hit of sleep onto Loric when he stirred. Her heart was racing, her mind spinning with images of her time with her spouses, the dark fire in Aefin's eyes, her increasing need to dominate. Aefin had always enjoyed control play, but the passion she brought to the endeavor was fueled by something else. Perhaps this was her response to feeling helpless and powerless in the world, her way of staking a claim to the fragments of agency left to her. Whatever it was, Cloti hoped to get a chance to see her again with Feddar because she would eat that man alive, and it would be an utter joy to watch.

25

— • —

Cloti spent the next few days leading the cycles and healing as many as she could, along with Aene, who'd proven every bit as effective as Cloti, if not more so, given her experience. Juiya was a rock for them both and for the patients, soothing them and dampening their pain while Aene and Cloti worked. During lunch, Aene paused with a thin sandwich held inches from her mouth, glancing sideways at Cloti.

"You haven't caught the cough."

Cloti shook her head. "I guess I've been lucky."

"Newcomers almost always get it right away. I guess it doesn't surprise me that you're different."

"I don't know how. I...I have to concentrate in order to heal. It's not like I'm immune to illness."

Juiya sat up, her finger raising shyly. Cloti blinked at her to speak.

"I think it's the Earth Milk," she said in Ormaer.

Cloti glanced down at her water bottle, wondering when the last time was she'd had a sip. She needed to wait, to space it out, but the healing was exhausting.

"I guess it could be." The Milk did allow her to access knowledge about healing she was never aware of being exposed to on her own. Maybe it somehow had knowledge woven into its parthi, the smallest elements of all life, which it was able to unravel as needed to access it. It was said that the sum of all knowledge in the Universe could be contained on the point of a needle if it was encrypted with the proper magics. Maybe each parthi from the ooze, each tiny drop of the Earth Milk, contained all that knowledge, and with the proper training and technique, one could pull from that knowledge as from one's own memory. Maybe this was what was happening to her.

"Cloti?" Juiya's voice was laced with concern.

"Sorry, I...was distracted. Say it again, please."

Juiya spoke in Ormaer. "We should begin inoculating the Shoza and training them with the Earth Milk tomorrow. We only have five days left."

Cloti nodded. "Make it so."

Juiya pressed her lips into a thin smile, glancing from Cloti to Aene and back.

"I'll go let Loric know. No healing tomorrow." She nodded and ducked out through the flap.

Aene flashed Cloti a smile, but something changed in the room when Juiya left. Aene burned with an unasked question. Cloti could see it in her posture and feel it in the air around her.

"Is there something on your mind, Aene?"

Aene glanced at her guiltily, and Cloti made a calming gesture with her hands.

"It's fine, whatever it is. You can tell me. Honesty is the cornerstone of my practice. I am an open book."

Aene looked down, chewing her lip for a moment. When she looked back up, her eyes were cool and soft.

"Is it true that you've been with Feddar?"

Cloti closed her eyes and nodded. "He and I are lovers and maybe more. I'm not sure yet. Things are complicated, as you know." She shot Aene a pointed glance, and Aene looked down again. "He told me about you. And I read the Delve chronicle."

Aene laughed, wiping her eyes. "Oh gods, I never bothered to look at that. The worst parts are hard enough to keep out of my brain as it is."

"What about the best parts? Your time with Feddar?"

Aene looked at her, eyes wet and searching. "I knew it was a mistake. It could have ruined everything."

"It couldn't have. Things were ruined already. We just didn't realize it yet."

"I guess." Aene sniffed, picking at her fingernails. "How is he?"

"Struggling between his duty and his heart. I know he gets painted as a villain, but he's trying to make things better."

"I know. I listen extra hard to the gossip about him. I can read between the lines. He helped you start up the temple practice again, right?"

Cloti nodded. "He's in a tough position. The General is a vicious bastard." She paused, anger welling up as she thought of the General's words: *Keep the filthy beasts locked down altogether.* "But in the end, I'm sure Feddar will do what he can to help us."

"He doesn't...he doesn't know, does he? About me?"

Cloti shook her head. "Not yet. But I trust him. When the time comes, I'll tell him what he needs to know."

Aene shook her head, her mouth tightening in a grimace. "I'm not so sure that's a good idea. Even if he means well, if they found out, they could make him say things. I'm not convinced the humans follow the continental ban."

Cloti pressed her eyes together, trying to keep images of Feddar being tortured out of her head.

"I'm not sure we have either. In any case, I'll wait until it's absolutely necessary."

Aene nodded. "Besides...all of that, how's he doing?" There was a tenderness in her voice, a slightly hopeful note.

"He's got a few scars, but he's doing well. He has a big heart." She paused, gauging Aene's expression. "I told you he and I are lovers, but that doesn't mean you and he couldn't be together. His heart is his own, and I wish him every happiness he can find."

Aene shook her head vigorously, her face hardening. "What we had was...I will always treasure it, but it was enough. I don't need to dredge up my past mistakes."

"It's never a mistake to bond with someone you care for. He has feelings for you. He told me so. He tried to find out what had happened to you but couldn't find any record of your presence. He thinks you're dead."

"It's probably better that way."

"If that's what you want, I'll keep your secret since you've managed to avoid getting your name in the records. But it would make him happy just to know you're alive."

Aene rubbed her face with both hands. "I don't know. I—"

Juiya returned, pausing awkwardly as she noticed the intensity of their conversation. Cloti waved her in.

"Sorry to interrupt. I've let Loric know, and he's adjusting the schedule. We've dealt with over half the most urgent cases already, and he thinks we can clear the rest before Midsummer. There are a half-dozen in need of terminations, which he'd scheduled for tomorrow, so we'll start with them the day after."

"No," Cloti said a little more loudly than she'd intended. "With all that's coming, anyone who's not ready to carry a baby to term in this situation needs to be helped right away. Do we not have any medicine for that?"

Juiya shook her head. "Contraception and termination tinctures ran out early in the occupation."

"Tell Loric to have the patients sent for right away." She took a long swig from her water bottle, her mind already swelling with the knowledge of how to accomplish the procedure without medicine. "Assuming you're both up for it?"

"Of course," Aene said. "But I don't know if it's in the Healing spell or not. The spell is mostly designed for combat injuries and toxins."

"I can share how to do it. Juiya, can you please check with the other nurses and round up some post-termination supplies?"

Juiya nodded and slipped out of the tent.

Aene flashed Cloti a weak smile. "I'm happy for you and Feddar. Really. Despite everything, he's a special person. I know not everyone sees it the way we do, but we all need comfort in times like these."

Cloti put a hand on Aene's knee. "Thank you. I agree, and I hope the Shoza don't try to kill Feddar again."

"That wasn't them."

"Excuse me?"

"The assassination attempt that you stopped. That wasn't the Shoza. They see him as, well, not an ally, but at least someone who's not trying to cause active harm. And they know anyone who replaced him would be much worse."

"Then who was it?"

Aene's eyes grew hard. "The Knife's Point."

A whistle sounded from outside, the one the Maer used when a spyball had been spotted. Cloti touched foreheads with Aene and opened a mindlink.

How many of them are there?

A few dozen, we think. We're in communication, but we disagree on a few key points. They will have a role to play at Midsummer, and we have urged them not to commit any further attacks since the humans keep taking their vengeance on us.

Now more than ever, we must be careful.

Aene nodded, turning toward the flap as footsteps approached. Juiya cleared her throat before entering. She carried a small bag of menstrual pads and other supplies.

"The first of the termination patients is here."

"Give us a few minutes." Cloti opened the vial and measured out a dram for Aene. "Take this, and I'll show you what you need to do."

The first termination patient was a Maer around thirty. She was thin and nervous looking, but there was strength in her eyes.

"It's hard enough taking care of two with..." she gestured around.

"Of course." Cloti smiled, pushing out a vibe of support. "How far along do you think you are?"

"I missed last month's cycle, then the morning sickness kicked in, and I knew for sure."

"We're going to take care of you. Juiya, the tea?"

Juiya handed the Maer a cup of cold fever bark tea. "It will help with the pain."

She drank it down, wincing at the bitter brew.

"Lie down, and let me help get you settled." Juiya's voice was soft and reassuring.

"Don't you need me to take my clothes off?" She gestured at her tattered robe.

"That won't be necessary," Cloti said. "Did you ever have magical healing before the occupation?"

She nodded. "Once for a broken arm, when I was a teenager. They used some kind of gauntlet, I think."

"What we do is very similar. Just lay back and relax. We're going to do some breathing exercises first to settle your mind."

She lay down, and Juiya put her fingers on her temples.

"Close your eyes and picture the lake in autumn, with the orange and yellow leaves reflecting off the water."

The Maer closed her eyes, and Cloti blinked at Juiya, whose eyes narrowed in concentration. The Maer's body relaxed, and her breathing steadied. Cloti led her through a simple verbal meditation, and soon she entered a calm, trance-like state. Cloti put her hands on the Maer's abdomen, gesturing for Aene to join her, so she could feel what was happening. Cloti closed her eyes, and the tincture took over, shutting off the blood flow to the embryo and rerouting the blood vessels around it. In a matter of minutes, it was done, and she removed her hands and opened her eyes. She blinked at Juiya, who began gently massaging the Maer's temples. Soon she opened her eyes, which were glassy and serene.

"We're all finished." Cloti took her hand, and the Maer squeezed it gently.

"Already? I didn't feel a thing."

"You wouldn't at this stage," Juiya said. "You may feel some discomfort later, maybe a little cramping, and there will be some blood, but not much more than a normal cycle." She took a few menstrual pads and a small sachet of fever bark from the basket as Cloti helped the Maer sit up.

"Try to rest for a few days and take fever bark tea for the pain. Do you have someone who can look after your kids while you recuperate?"

The Maer nodded, standing up tentatively. She looked down at her body, then back up into Cloti's eyes.

"Thank you so much. I..."

Cloti took her hands and smiled. "I'm glad we were able to help."

"If you have any issues, please come back and see us or send for us and we will come to you." Juiya put a hand on her shoulder, and the Maer glanced back at Cloti and Aene for a moment, then followed Juiya outside.

Cloti eyed Aene, who stood staring at the tent flap.

"Do you want to try the next one?" Cloti felt fine with the dose of Milk she had taken, but she didn't know if she could do all six by herself.

"I...I saw what you did, and it seems so simple, but I wouldn't want to mess anything up."

"It's no different from any other healing. I'll guide you through it, and if you feel up to it, you can take over."

Aene was able to complete the procedure on the next patient with a little guidance, and they alternated from there out. Juiya's gentleness with the patients showed she had some experience with maternal care, and they worked as a team, completing all six procedures in a couple of hours, with short breaks to rest. They re-upped their dose after the third termination, and by the end, they were all drained, but they shared a sense of warmth and accomplishment. The humans had taken so much from them, but they could still take care of their own.

After her nap, Cloti led the evening cycle, and she noticed several of the patients had joined them. The day had drained her, but she sent them little sparks of energy from the

Earth Milk, hoping they could use it to facilitate their healing. She led a slow, restful cycle, and the group responded to her energy with a collective sense of calm that warmed her heart. The days to come would be intense, and they would need this mindset to keep them grounded. As the cycle closed and she looked out at the faces surrounding her, she realized not all of them would make it through.

"This world is but one of many, this time but a moment in eternity. Nothing is lost that cannot be found again, though it may take another form."

26

— · —

During the morning cycle, Cloti found the three Shoza who were scheduled to meet with her for training. Their minds were among the most robust she had encountered; these were masters at their discipline, the ones who taught the others. Their minds opened seamlessly in unison, funneling together so Cloti could communicate with all of them simultaneously while the rest of the group's energy powered the cycle with little input from her. Once she had their attention, she pushed out her message.

The Earth Milk is precious. It is rare. It is powerful. It must be used at the absolute smallest dose appropriate for the individual. You know your members' capabilities. Once you have experienced it yourself, you can decide what dose is appropriate. But know this: our supply is finite. We may not be able to make more. Remember this first and foremost. The Milk is precious. Come to me at noon for your supply and further instructions.

They assembled around noon in Loric's tent, each arriving separately with the appearance of a different ailment. Loric let them in one by one, then gave Cloti a little salute and closed the flap.

None of the three even remotely resembled a Shoza. One looked like a grandmother, and she even put out a cozy maternal vibe to go with it. Another had a scholarly look, complete with ruffled hair and cracked spectacles. The third was quiet, withdrawn, and thin, almost fragile-looking, though their the piercing gray eyes and sharp movements left no doubt that their appearance belied the reality. Each of their auras matched their appearance, and she couldn't find a flaw in their masking techniques. They felt just like they looked.

When they tested the Milk and opened their minds, Cloti saw breathtaking mental architecture, strong and resilient, but with flexibility built in as well. They were not as rigid as they appeared at first. She showed them the communication pathways and explained how they worked as best she could. She'd never been very good with the technical side of magic.

Are there not other uses that can be made of this tincture? asked the grandmotherly figure.

Cloti paused, wondering about the wisdom of spreading this kind of power around. The Shoza's stock in trade was exploiting technology to further their murky, often violent agenda. There was no way this was ending without violence. The only question was whether, by sharing her secrets, she would limit the violence or increase it exponentially.

One could learn to do many things using the Earth Milk, but it takes extensive practice time and a supply we don't have. We have only four days left until Midsummer. It's barely time to teach the technique, let alone experiment.

After a pause, the scholar spoke. *Thank you for your willingness to work with us. I know you see us a certain way, and you're not entirely wrong. But you're not entirely right, either. Each one of us is an individual, and not all of us prefer the same means to our common end.*

I am most pleased to hear this. I know there will be violence. There will be death whether we act or not. I just want there to be as little as possible, except in self-defense.

We share that goal, though we may differ on the definition of self-defense. In any case, thank you.

The quiet one's mindvoice was little more than a whisper. *We need to talk about Midsummer.*

Cloti took a deep breath, feeling a shift in the atmosphere. This was the part she dreaded, but she listened to their plans. Her concentration lapsed a bit as they discussed strategy, but she caught the essentials. A group of Shoza would blow up the main gate, using hotiron explosives they'd somehow kept hidden from the humans. The Shoza outside would pour in, engaging with the soldiers and creating a distraction while the rest of them escorted the evacuees past the park and into an industrial area, which now stood empty and abandoned. The Shoza outside had dug a tunnel most of the way under the wall, and they would finish the job once they heard the explosion at the gate so it would be open by the time the evacuees started arriving.

She saw fire. Hair matted with blood. She heard screams. The sound of running. The clash of metal. Explosions. More screaming.

We have taken up too much of your time. The scholar's mindvoice brought Cloti back. *We will be in touch at dusk for our distance trial.*

Right after the cycle. Give me time to get back to my tent.

They sat in stillness, and Cloti felt their minds relax.

Speaking of cycles, would you mind leading us in one now? the grandmother said.

Cloti smiled, reaching out her hand into the space between them.

Touch my hand. Their four hands soon formed a pile, and Cloti used that connection to send them a view of a waterfall, with delicate puffs of mist rising from the bottom and birds hovering in the winds above. The sun rose behind a dense forest, sending soft golden light over the water, which flowed down endlessly into the mist.

Find the center. Feel the water flowing through you, but do not let it draw you below. Find that balance between gravity and hope. Stay in that space. Be with me there.

Their minds joined as their hands did, pressing together until it was hard to feel where one ended and another began. They hovered halfway down, and the water flowed through them, and they through it. They were the mist and the sky, the birds and the sunrise. They felt the pull of the rocks below, but they held each other up. Cloti felt a smile spread across her face as the realization hit her. She could trust them.

***

Cloti walked through the camp that afternoon, nodding serenely as Maer after Maer stopped and bowed to her. It was almost enough to make her want to use the Milk's powers to let her pass unseen, but she needed to preserve her energy and her supply. She heard the rushing water below as she approached Skundir's Bridge, which stretched in a graceful arc across the narrowest point in the valley. A half-dozen human soldiers guarded the wooden gate they had installed over the entrance to the bridge, helmets off, hair matted with sweat in the summer heat. One whose breastplate was adorned with colorful stars stepped forward, pulling up his scarf to cover his mouth.

"Access to the nursing camp is allowed only for Ulver's cough patients and medical professionals."

"Since I am a healer, I suppose that includes me."

He looked her up and down, and she could feel his confusion and hesitation. She narrowed her mind and sent out a wave of empathy, and his brows lifted for a moment.

"Where's your armband?"

"I am a healer, not a nurse or a doctor. I was never given one." He looked down at his clipboard, then off into the distance. "I only seek to help. I think you should let me through." She locked onto his mind, pushing down the feeling of guilt at using her powers on an unwilling subject, and boosted the suggestion.

He hesitated for a moment, then pulled out a pencil and readied his clipboard. Though he was masked, his eyes were smiling.

"I'll need your name and place and date of birth."

Cloti did not look down at the chasm below as she crossed, staying in the center of the bridge to avoid vertigo. As a child, she had been terrified of crossing, and her mother had had to hold her in her arms as Cloti clung to her and buried her face in her beard. Once across, she'd loved the Overlook restaurant district with its flowerpots, fountains, and smells of sweet and savory delights.

The drab camp that had been set up was a shock to her system, with beige canvas tents covering what were once bucolic patios. Whiffs of smoke and camphor drifted over from the camp as the guards on the other side checked her in and directed her toward the intake tent in what had once been a beer garden. She gave her name and birth details for the third time to a human nurse, who calmly recorded her information in a ledger. A Maer nurse sat beside him, watching her with recognition in his eyes.

"Are you sick?" the human asked.

"I am a healer. I've come to help."

He eyed her suspiciously as he wrote in his ledger. "Who sent you?"

"No one. As I said, I'm—"

"A healer, right. I'm not sure what the scientific basis for your *healing* is, but it's your life if you want to risk it. We can always use more help." His voice softened with the last sentence. "Gelann here can get you started."

Gelann rose, gesturing with his eyes for Cloti to follow him.

"Have you had the cough yet?" he asked once they were clear of the intake tent.

"No. Have you?"

He nodded. "I was one of the lucky ones. I had only mild symptoms, but apparently, I'm inoculated for now. Are you sure you want to be here? All the other nurses and doctors are ones who've already had it, and even then, there's some risk."

Cloti stopped, searching his eyes. He did not feel like a Shoza, but she could tell he practiced. At this point, she had no choice but to trust him.

"It seems some aspect of my practice has protected me." She looked around at the tent flaps lining both sides of the narrow street and lowered her voice. "I am here to help, but I'm also here for another reason. I'm hoping there's someone I can speak to about that."

He gestured with his chin, and they walked past the row of tents to the hanging gardens, which were a little overgrown and weedy but had seen at least some tending.

When they had made it far enough in that there was no one in earshot, he ducked between two of the massive planters overflowing with flowering goldblossom vines and fixed her with a serious look.

"Is it true about Midsummer?" he whispered.

She nodded. "I need to find a…" She made an S figure with her hands, the sign of the Shoza.

His eyes narrowed, then softened. "I will show you around the camp and let our friend know to come find you. We must use every precaution." He ducked to look between the vines. "Even here, the spyballs are watching. Come." He brushed past the vines, and his voice rose, presumably in case anyone was nearby and wondered what they were doing. "It's a good place to come when you need to breathe fresh air. Let's start with the recuperation tents. The patients there are the least likely to be contagious."

Gelann showed her around the camp, first the recuperation tents, then the intermediate tents, and finally the critical tents. She didn't get to look inside the critical tents, but he lifted the flaps of the others so she could see what was going on. The recuperation tents were next to the kitchen she'd seen during her mind travel experience, and they were full of Maer who looked well, busy reading, talking, or sewing masks. The patients in the intermediate tents were resting, but most of them were conscious, some of them talking or playing dice. A few of them were coughing, and she recognized the barking sound, which she'd heard in the camps on a few occasions. Little braziers poured steam into the air, and a whiff of camphor hit her nose. Gelann quickly closed the flap and led her away.

"Best not to stay too close unless you're sure you're inoculated. It's probably safe to work with the patients in the recuperation tents, though."

"How many are there?"

He looked out over the camps, tapping his fingers together as if counting in his mind.

"At last count, a little over five hundred, I think. The numbers fluctuate. About a hundred of them are critical."

"And how many of them will die?"

"Maybe half of the critical patients? There's no medicine to be had, so the best we can do is keep them comfortable and use camphor steam, though it doesn't help those who have stopped coughing altogether. But at least that's something we have a ready supply of."

Cloti's heart sank as she thought of the fifty who would die. She'd brought a vial of Earth Milk, and she was fairly sure if they were given a dose of it, most of them would recover, but she had no idea how much to give or how best to administer it. Given the already dwindling supply, she was reluctant to leave the whole vial here. Her fingers found the vial in her pocket, worrying the wax seal.

"Rumors say many never return from the nursing camp. What happens to those who die?"

"Of those who enter here, about ninety percent return, usually in a month or so. Sometimes longer. The humans cremate the dead, but..." He glanced around, steering her toward the empty plaza overlooking the valley, which echoed with the sound of the waterfall. "They won't allow us to return the ashes," he whispered. "They say it's for sanitary reasons, but that doesn't make any sense, medically." He looked out across the river to the camps and raised his voice to a normal pitch. "I chose to work here after I grew ill and recovered. I was surprised to find we were treated relatively well, all things considered. The human doctors and nurses seem to hold Maer life in higher regard than the soldiers do."

"Who is the head Maer doctor?"

"Dr. Jelefi. She was the head of the medical college before..."

"I know her family a bit. They're good Maer. I wonder if she'd consent to speak with me?" She paused, lowering her voice again. "I have a treatment that may be of use, but the humans can't know about it."

"I'm sure she'll be delighted. We never get any visitors except for patients. Why don't you have a look around the gardens while I go see if she's available."

Cloti took a sip of her water bottle, then wandered the gardens under the lazy eye of a human guard. She obviously didn't register as any kind of threat, and he left her alone with the plants. She couldn't resist weeding around the goldblossoms closest to the camp, even though it felt like trying to bail out a rowboat with a spoon. The overall effect of the garden was still pleasing despite the weeds. The vibrant yellows of the goldblossoms were offset by the deep reds and purples of the tinklebells, which made a nice contrast with the drab canvas of the nursing camp.

She recognized Dr. Jelefi walking with an unknown Maer. The guard nodded to them and stepped aside to let them pass. Cloti could sense that the other Maer was a Shoza as they approached.

"Cloti, it has been far too long. The younger Torl boy's wedding, I believe?"

"It was a lovely ceremony." They exchanged bows, and the doctor gestured toward her companion.

"This is Mishal, my assistant." Mishal bowed, and Cloti repeated his gesture. "He speaks Ormaer as well, and we were just discussing how nice it would be to have someone to practice with." She paused, her eyes sharpening. "There's no one else here who speaks it," she finished in Ormaer.

"Thank you for meeting with me. I have come to share a possible treatment for Ulver's cough."

"You have brought Earth Milk with you?" Dr. Jelefi raised her eyebrows. "They would throw you in the tower if they knew." Cloti wondered how she knew or if she had merely guessed.

"It's why I entrust this information to you alone. And your companion, of course."

"I was told you were training my colleagues to communicate using the Milk," Mishal said. "It would be useful to have someone on this side of the bridge in the loop."

Cloti sighed, fingering the vial in her pocket. Her stomach ached at the thought of giving it up. She took a deep breath, realizing what this meant. She'd been using it all day for several weeks now, and the thought of running out terrified her. Not because it meant she wouldn't have its abilities. Because her body, even her mind, had become dependent on it. It was going to get bad when she ran out.

"Of course. I will train you in the communication technique. It should only require a half-dram at a time."

"What about the critical patients? How would you apply it, and how much would you need?" The doctor spoke Ormaer better than almost anyone Cloti had ever met. She was said to know a dozen Free Maer languages, and she was the one other doctors came to when they were stumped for a diagnosis. Cloti could feel her intelligence, and though it didn't seem like she practiced, her mind bore some of the same signs of mental discipline as those who did.

"I'd start with just a drop in a cup of water."

"Many of them would struggle to drink an entire cup. Could we administer a drop directly into their mouths?"

"I don't see why not. But remember: every drop is precious. There are no more vials to be had, so use it sparingly." She turned her back to the guard and pulled out the vial. Dr. Jelefi palmed it and pocketed it in one smooth movement.

"We have much work to do. Can you train Mishal this evening after dinner?"

"Yes, but I have to get back for the dusk cycle. It shouldn't take very long."

"Lucky for you, I still have pull with the camp administrator. Otherwise, you'd be stuck here for a week, minimum, to guarantee you have no symptoms before you return. An early dinner, then. Shall we say half dusk?"

Cloti nodded.

"Well, thank you for the chance to practice our grandmother tongue," she said, switching back to Maer. "It has been far too long."

"You speak it like a native."

"It was my major before I found medicine." She touched Mishal on the shoulder, and he turned to go. "Gelann can help you with anything you need in the meantime. If you'll excuse us?"

Cloti nodded, her heart thumping and her hand sliding down to the cap of her water bottle, which was half empty. She resisted since she'd just had a sip before speaking with them, but she felt jittery and anxious. She needed to do a cycle or something to keep her mind off it. She found her way around the outside of the camp toward the overlook, nodding shyly to the guards. They didn't seem to know what to make of her, but they did not stop her. The rush of the water below drowned out her nagging worries, and she sat, lowered her arms to the ground, and began a slow cycle.

27

Over a humble dinner of lentil soup and dense, doughy bread, Cloti filled Mishal and Dr. Jelefi in on what she'd learned of the Shoza's plan, using Ormaer as before. Mishal seemed to know most of it already, but a few details were new to him.

"We only get information over here when there are new patients known to be trustworthy to carry a message. This tincture communication will help us a lot."

"How many of you are there over here?"

Mishal glanced at the doctor, who nodded. "Three at the moment. Four if you count the doctor. Not enough, that's for sure."

"Are you planning to try to give them all tincture and train them? I worry you won't have enough."

"Don't worry about your precious tincture. We'll use it like any supply: the minimum amount to get the job done. I'll make sure of that. And the patients come first, of course."

Cloti sighed, thinking of the drab tent with its smoke and camphor odor and the fifty patients inside, their hands on the knob of death's door.

"I wish I could stay. If the Milk doesn't work on the critical patients, please send for me right away. I've helped patients with milder cases. I might be able to do something for them."

"Let's hope it doesn't come to that." Dr. Jelefi glanced toward the setting sun. "I suppose you've got some training to do." She pushed slowly to standing. "And I have a mountain of paperwork to climb." She put her hands together at her chest and bowed to Cloti. "It has been an honor, and I look forward to seeing you again after Midsummer."

Tears welled in Cloti's eyes as she bowed to the doctor, thinking of Midsummer and what it might mean for the Maer. Their situation was terrible, but it could very easily be worse. If their efforts failed, if the humans stopped the evacuation, the retribution would make the public execution of the Shoza seem like a slap on the wrist. She absently raised her water bottle to her lips, then stopped and capped it. She needed to use the pure Earth

Milk to train Mishal. Her heart fluttered, and her cheeks flushed as she thought of how the Milk rolled up inside her like a gentle wave, lifting her above the trials of the moment. She could taste the Thousand Worlds like copper in her mouth. Her teeth ached for it, and she had to work to soften her jaw.

"Are you ready to begin? I assume you brought..."

Mishal pulled a vial out of a pocket, different than the one she'd given the doctor.

"We put a third of it in here, and the doctor has the rest." He retrieved a long double-sided spoon with different size bowls on either end. "One dram, one-half dram," he said, pointing to either end.

"Let's start with half a dram and see if it works. We can always up the dose as we go."

Her fingers clenched together as she watched him pour the tincture into the smaller end, and she finally let her breath out when he put it in his mouth without spilling a drop and re-corked the vial. He poured a splash of clear liquid from a flask into his hand and rinsed the spoon with it. He handed her the spoon and the vial, then drank the liquid from his palm, wincing and smacking his lips.

"Can't waste a bit of perfectly good alcohol."

Cloti's fingers trembled as she took the vial, imagining it dropping and smashing onto the floor, the Milk gone, wasted. She steadied her nerves and poured herself a half-dram, though she was used to taking a dram at a time. The bitterness made her tongue curl, and then it flooded her senses and into her mind. It felt like a lampshade had been removed, and she saw the dark corners of reality, the points between and behind the here and now. She basked in this nebulous sensation for a moment, then directed her mind to Mishal, who was staring at his hands.

"You may experience some mild hallucinations at first. Enjoy them, but they will pass."

"I can see...I can see... It's like a night sky, darkness filled with countless stars, each twinkling in its own way. Is this—"

"The Thousand Worlds. Hold on. I'll find you."

In a flash, she was at his mind's door.

"I feel you."

"Just relax and let me in."

The stiff exterior of his mind softened, and Cloti flowed through it.

Now you don't have to use your voice, she mindspoke.

"Wait, how?"

Turn off your mouth and direct your thoughts toward me.

Okay...Oh! I see! It's so weird, it's like...speaking underwater.

You will get used to it in time. His mind was disciplined, perhaps overly so for the kind of techniques she favored, but he had adapted quickly enough.

I imagine so. How long does it last?

An hour or two at full strength, then it begins to diminish. If you need to re-up your dose, do so as soon as you feel the lag. If you get too low, you'll have the adjustment period again.

I got it. Anything else?

We're doing a trial run right after the dusk cycle. This dose should just last you just long enough. At dusk, open your mind and be ready.

Cloti ran a short cycle in the amphitheater at dusk, conserving her energy for the trial afterward. She asked Juiya to sit outside the tent and turn away anyone who might try to enter. She sat cross-legged on her mat out of habit, though with the tincture, she could do this standing up or even walking around at this point. She took a careful sip of the bitter tincture, washing it down with a swallow from her water bottle. The tent vanished, replaced by the infinity of the Thousand Worlds, but she ignored their call. She sought and quickly found the four Shoza, the three she'd trained here and the one from the nursing camp.

You can communicate to the group with a thought, and if you narrow your focus on one Maer's energy, you can speak with them directly.

What is the maximum distance? one of them asked.

There is no limit, but the closer you are, the easier it is to make initial contact. Anything under a mile or two should be easy. Beyond that takes a little practice. Once linked, you can stay connected regardless of where you go until the dose wears off. Maybe four hours total, though the connection might weaken after two.

Anything else we need to know?

Not that I can think of. I recommend dawn and dusk meeting times, as it's easier to get everyone synchronized. Otherwise, you should be able to repeat this process at any time.

Thank you for your assistance. The grandmother mindspoke this time. *Now, if you don't mind, we have some confidential business to discuss. We will reconvene just after dusk tomorrow if that suits everyone. You're welcome to join, of course, Cloti.*

As you say. Until tomorrow, then. She let go of their signals and returned to the Thousand Worlds.

She thought of visiting Aefin to see if she and Ludo were taking solace in each other's arms. Or Feddar, alone in his courtyard, buried beneath a pile of papers. She could visit them if she wanted. All she had to do was stand up and walk out of the tent, shielding herself from prying eyes and minds. She could go anywhere she liked and take her pleasure with any or all of them. But she lay on her cot, staring up into the myriad worlds scattered across the darkness like diamonds spilled on black velvet. It had been a long, grueling day, and she needed to relax.

She summoned the image of the lush forest she'd visited before, the calls of the creatures in the trees, and the sinuous grace of the feline emerging between ferns. She needed something similar, something natural but more open and less dark. A tingle in her mind pulled her out of her torpor, and she found herself flying between worlds into the crenelated void. She followed its curved and twisting contours, drawn deeper into its folds until she emerged into another space, darkness of a different tone, glittering with thousands upon thousands of other worlds. She could see that each fold, each wrinkle of what appeared to be darkness, actually led to another hidden nexus, another Thousand Worlds.

One of those worlds called to her, and she drifted toward it, pausing as she felt its pull, then let herself sink into it. She emerged into dazzling sunlight glinting off endless waves. She drifted atop them, bobbing with their movement, but she was neither wet nor woozy from the motion. A salty breeze tickled her body hair and blew her beard up against her mouth. When she looked down, she could see the deep blue abyss of the sea and, above her, the sapphire sky. No fish or bird disturbed her vision, no sign of life. Only water, sky, and sun washing her worries away. She closed her eyes and floated, supported by the elements in perfect harmony. She was the glint of sunlight on the waves, their rise and swell, the sky above stretching out into the infinity of worlds.

28

— · —

Preparations for Midsummer began in earnest the next day. A wagon overloaded with cedar branches, bundles of herbs, and several casks of berry wine was brought in and left in the field next to the memorial for the executed Shoza. A note attached to one of the casks read "Happy Midsummer" in Maer, though the penmanship was clearly human. Cloti smiled when one of the Shoza brought her the note. She could feel Feddar's intentions, almost smell him on the paper. The cedar branches were ripe with tiny purple berries, which she crushed and used to stretch the Milk a bit. She gave three vials to the Shoza leaders, leaving only one vial and the remains of a second in her possession. She secreted the unopened vial among her belongings for use on Midsummer.

They healed a few patients that day, using up most of the partial vial. She'd instructed Loric to bring only the patients in immediate need, and she did all the healing herself since she could make the most efficient use of the Milk. Aene and Juiya helped keep the patients calm, and once the last patient exited the tent, she clasped hands with them and led them in a silent cycle.

We must pause our healing of bodies, but the work of healing minds and hearts will go on long past Midsummer.

She let their hands go, smiling at them through her fatigue as the last wave of the Milk ebbed.

"I must rest now. Go enjoy your time with each other. Celebrate the coming of Midsummer as you always have. Whatever happens in two days, no matter what comes after, we owe it to our past and our future to honor the present by living in it."

Aene and Juiya held hands as they bowed to her and left, and Cloti warmed at the joy flowing between them. She longed to visit with her spouses and Feddar, but the supply was so low she barely had enough to keep her water bottle stocked with a meager dose for each of the next two days. She lay down on her cot, forming circular moods with her fingers and crossing them over her chest, but her mind refused to clear. She dug deep for the well of quiet at the center of her being but found it empty. Thoughts of blood, fire, screams, and death echoed through her, and she could not keep them quiet on her own. Sweat broke out on her face, though it was cloudy and cool outside. She sat up with tears in her eyes and took a drink from her water bottle. Her thoughts quieted a bit, but it was not enough. She took another drink, lay back down, and finally found a few moments of peace.

She struggled to lead the evening cycle with only the tincture-laced water to power her. The energy flowing from the assembled crowd helped buoy her just enough, and she let them do most of the work. Though their joy lifted her spirits, melancholy pulled her down as soon as the cycle was over, and she returned to her tent without speaking to anyone. She poured a bit of her water bottle into the now-empty vial, swirling and shaking it to dissolve the last of the Earth Milk stuck to the sides. It gave her just enough energy to join the Shoza, whose conversation had already begun.

Cloti, we were just finalizing our plans. We have only enough tincture for one more dose for each of us, so we're going to save it for Midsummer night unless...

There is no more and no means to get more. Cloti felt her strength fading. *Once the bonfire is lit, I will reach out and try to help stabilize your connection.*

We will help clear the camps, but our presence Cliffside is blind since the lockdown. If there's any way you can send word to Ms. Torl, she can pass along our instructions.

And what are those?

Once the explosion sounds at the main gate, we think most of the soldiers guarding Cliffside will be sent down as reinforcements. Our forces should take out the remaining human soldiers and begin the evacuation immediately. The tunnel will open inside the Tube and Tile factory. The Shoza in Cliffside know of the escape plan, but we have not shared the exact location in case any of them were apprehended. If the humans get wind of this information—

They will not, and I will get the message through. Please, be careful. Our future is in your hands.

The connection dissolved, and Cloti's chest ached with its absence as her mind swirled with terrible and chaotic thoughts.

She mustered enough strength during the dawn cycle, with the help of the energy of the packed audience, to veer off in search of Aefin's signal. The Thousand Worlds were blurry, seeming to move and rearrange themselves as she ventured in, but she was drawn as if from beneath toward her first and greatest love. Aefin's relief washed over Cloti as they joined minds.

Gods, Cloti, we were so worried when we didn't hear from you last night. I worry all the time. I miss you every second.

I'm fine, and I love you too. Cloti felt tears soaking into the hair on her face, and she wondered if the participants in the cycle could sense her emotions bleeding through. *There's a lot going on, but things are on track. I need you to get a message to Ms. Torl: the Tile and Tube factory. Absolutely no one else can know this information. You must deliver it yourself.*

But we're still on lockdown!

You will find a way. You always do when it matters most.

I'll see it done, Aefin mindspoke with false bravery. *What else can we do?*

My Earth Milk supply is very low, but I think I've saved just enough. Do you have enough supplies to make another batch?

We used up everything we could get our hands on. I'm sorry.

Cloti's heart wrenched at the realization that even if she had enough to do whatever was necessary at Midsummer, what would she do the days and weeks after? She would need its strength to help during their travels, as there were sure to be many injured and frightened and in need of solace. Her stomach twinged at the mental gymnastics she was using. She'd become dependent on the Earth Milk, and she didn't know how she'd cope without it.

Could you find a hotsilver containment vessel? Maybe someone has one. We could transport the ooze like I did with the island, or we could—

They took everyone's equipment. Aefin's mindvoice grew agitated. *You were there when their mages searched our house! It's only through your manipulations that they didn't destroy what's in the greenhouse, too. You know there's nothing left.* Her tone softened a little at the end.

Cloti felt the connection slipping as her frustration shattered her focus. She slowed her breath and brought her mind back to the moment. Aefin came clear again, and Cloti saw her as if for the first time. The steely elegance of her mind. The freedom she embodied in her every word and gesture. The raw power of her emotions. Her wicked, knowing smile.

I'm sorry. It's been hard. The Earth Milk—

I know. Aefin's mindvoice was quiet, nervous. *I've almost run out, too.*

I really miss you. And Ludo, I miss him so much. She pictured his resilient smile, even at the worst news, the brave face he was surely wearing at this moment. *I hate that I never get to speak with him. Tell him how much, will you? He needs to know.*

You will tell him yourself after Midsummer. At Eagle Lake.

I will. Cloti realized the cycle was almost over. *I have to go, but there's one more thing I need from you.*

Anything.

I need you to pin Ludo to the bed and make him call my name.

I'll make him scream so loud you'll hear it echoing off the valley walls.

Cloti sent out a wave of warmth, and Aefin flooded her with a mental embrace that set her heart fluttering. She held onto that feeling, that connection, and shared it as her hands touched the ground, joined by hundreds upon hundreds of pairs of hands all connected to the same stone. She passed this flutter through the rock, this feeling of being wanted. Needed. She opened her eyes and spoke to the assembled crowd.

"This Midsummer's Eve, once the feast is done and the songs have been sung, you know your duty." Little peals of laughter echoed off the amphitheater walls, and Cloti smiled. "Make communion with those you love. It need not be of an amorous nature, though, as you know, that is a noble tradition for those who choose it. Open your hearts to each other in whatever way you can. Reach a new level of connection. In our darkest hour, the sun will shine on us the brightest. As the earth is renewed, so too must we be."

The audience seemed to glow in the morning sun. The semicircular shape of the amphitheater focused their energy on her in the center, and she felt charged by it, almost as if she'd drunk a dose of Earth Milk.

Almost.

She fingered the last vial, sealed in her pocket. The wax was starting to erode under her touch, so she stroked the glass gently, feeling the reassurance of its heft in her fingers. She withdrew her hand, pressed her palms together at her forehead, and sent back the energy they'd given her. They would need it for the days to come.

Cloti stayed in her tent most of the day as the sunlight had started to give her headaches, and the noises of the camp could be too much to bear. The children wove crowns of clover and played Search and Slay in and around the tents while the adults built their stick effigies of the General and Feddar to burn the following night. Sprigs of cedar were hung above the door to every tent, though the tradition of kissing beneath them was not widely followed, given the prevalence of Ulver's cough. The usual feast preparations were notably absent, as their entire diet consisted of barley, kuff, a bit of fish, and whatever scraps of vegetables the humans sent their way. It was grim eating, but no one was starving. Cloti had very little appetite, but Juiya forced her to eat some porridge, which had a few dried fish flakes mixed in. She choked it down, knowing she would need energy, but it left her already sour stomach on the verge of rebellion.

She saved her energy for the dusk cycle, and as she was taking her customary drink from her water bottle before heading to the amphitheater, she heard arguing and shouting outside. She peeked out the flap and saw a group of six human soldiers, fully armed and helmeted, being kept from her tent by a small crowd of unarmed Maer.

They were coming for her.

She could feel it in her bones, and if she didn't do something, there would be blood. She fingered the vial in her pocket, suddenly panicked at the thought of losing it. With the power of the Milk, she was sure she could find her way out of any situation, but she needed to save it until the right moment. She glanced around the tent, and her eyes fell on the sewing kit Loric used for stitches.

"Cloti Looris, by order of the General, we are here to take you into custody." The soldier spoke in clear but accented Maer. She poked her head out for a moment, blinking at the Maer to stand down.

"Give me a moment to get dressed, and I'll be right with you."

She didn't wait for an answer. She sat down, lifted her skirt, and pulled down her underwear halfway. She pressed the little vial into the hem in the back and closed it with six quick loops of the needle and thread. With any luck, they wouldn't search her closely enough to find it. The crowd outside grew agitated, and she adjusted her clothes, took a long drink of her water bottle, and stashed it in her bag. When she emerged from the tent, humans and Maer alike stopped what they were doing to watch her.

"There is no need to fight. I have done nothing wrong, and I go willingly to face whatever accusations may be laid against me." The crowd parted to let her through, each Maer putting their hands together at their chest. Cloti beamed a smile as she bowed to them, then approached the human soldiers, who stood nervously, clutching their swords. Their leader said something in Islish she didn't quite catch, and two of the soldiers approached, taking her by either bicep. A third slid the bag from her shoulder and tossed it to the leader. Cloti's heart lurched into her throat, knowing her water bottle was in the bag and she would likely never see it again. She calmed somewhat as she felt the vial press into her backside. The drink she'd taken from her water bottle was enough to get her through the next little while, and she'd manage one way or another.

The lead human looked her up and down, then gestured for the two soldiers holding her to move. They held her firmly but not roughly and guided her through the crowd, which split to let them pass. Palms pressed together all along the path back to the human compound until they passed into the open area and through the main gate. They turned south, following Two Bridge Road, and Cloti's heart sank when she saw the black spire of the Tower rising before her.

29

Inside the Tower, all was shadow. The only illumination came from thin slits near the ceiling, which let in the pale light from what must have been tiny brightstones set in the hallway outside. There was no change in the light, no evidence of the movement of the sun. The room was bigger than expected, almost ten feet square, and she wondered if it were designed to hold more than one Maer. The air was stale and stagnant, a mix of sweat, shit, urine, and mildew. Cloti's mind was no brighter or fresher. Hours passed, or it might have been minutes or days. Probably not more than two days because she had not heard an explosion, but time had no meaning, nor did space. She cradled the vial in her hand, but she did not open it, though she felt like her head and heart were being turned inside out. When her craving got too strong, she pictured the effigy of the General being burned at Midsummer, and that helped her hold on for a few breaths longer.

She tried to meditate, but the dark confines of the Tower stifled her thoughts just as they did her eyes. At one point, she heard a hissing voice echoing through the slit in her wall, but she could not make out the words. Shortly thereafter, heavy footsteps echoed down the hall, followed by the sound of a door opening, then heavy thuds and cries of pain. She knew that if she drank the Earth Milk, she could communicate with the others in the Tower, maybe even find her way through the heavy door, but it was too soon. The boom of the explosion from the gate would surely reach her even here. She just had to hold on for one more day, though every minute felt like a millennium.

She was fed cold porridge and stale water in greasy wooden bowls that were pushed through a slot in the bottom of the door. She drank the water and tried to eat the porridge, but her stomach rebelled at the first taste. There was a hole in the floor in a corner that served as a toilet of sorts, though without running water. She resisted using it for as long as possible, but in the end, there was no other option, and she was compelled to live with the smell of her own filth. A pile of straw on the floor was provided for sleeping, but sleep was as elusive as lucidity. She spent her hours in a dizzying whirlwind of broken thoughts and jumbled emotions. She lay on the straw, reliving the vision of chaos, fire, blood, and death over and over.

At one point, she saw Feddar's face through the chaos, streaked with sweat and blood, but he was smiling down at her, holding her head in his lap, saying words she couldn't hear. She clung to the image, using it to leverage her way up from the floor. Sweat broke out all over her body, and she brought the sealed vial to her lips. The glass was warm from where she'd been holding it, and she could feel its pull through the wax. It wanted to get through to her. A bitter taste filled her mouth, flooding her mind with a rainbow of streaking colors. She shivered, and the sensation dissipated, leaving her weak and trembling. She slipped the vial back into her pocket and leaned her forehead against the damp stone wall. It was not cool like she'd hoped, but it helped give her a point of stability, and she was too exhausted to move. She remained standing, hands and face pressed against the wall, for a dark, musty eternity.

It began with a drumbeat, tiny and frail as if played by ants in a bottle. Her ears perked up, and she opened her eyes, though she could see little in the cramped, gloomy chamber. Voices soon joined the drums, faint as a whisper, but she smiled as she recognized the tune. *Every End is a Beginning*, the song played to open the Midsummer festivities. Her lips moved as the words came to her, and she began to sing quietly to herself, the way she'd sung to Uffrin when he was a baby. Another voice trickled in through the slit, and another, and Cloti let her voice rise to join them. She'd always loved to sing, though she didn't have the greatest voice, and soon the room echoed with the sound of dozens of voices, singing together in passable harmony. Hands slapped doors, their rhythm driving the song, and she could almost see the Master of Ceremonies handing the torch to a toddler with serious eyes.

By tradition, the oldest Maer able to lead the ceremony passed the torch to the youngest child who could carry it. She pictured the child now, not in the time before the occupation, but in the camps, in the amphitheater where the effigy had been set atop the prepared bonfire. A thousand Maer or more were crammed into the space, and the child, no older than two, walked with tentative steps toward the heap of wood. They finished the last notes of the song, and silence descended as the child tossed the torch onto the pile.

Distant shouts filled the air, followed by roars echoing in from all around her as every Maer in the Tower filled the tower with hoarse, joyful cries. Footsteps pounded through the halls, and human voices shouted for them to be quiet, but they could hardly be heard above the din of shouts and thumps on the doors. The voices went silent as a distant boom sounded, vibrating the doors and sending a jolt through Cloti's mind. She tore the wax from the vial with trembling fingers as shouts erupted in the distance, and more explosions rang out. She raised the vial to her lips, already feeling the first effects of the tincture just from the smell, and tilted it back. Her mind flew open as the bitter drink burned down her throat, blazing through her body like hotiron.

She saw the Tower now as if she were viewing a matchstick model. Every room, corridor, and winding staircase glowed in golden relief, and she could see every Maer as fiery orange outlines amid the gold. The humans showed up in red, and her mind saw them all at once, a dozen of them on the bottom floor and another dozen roaming through the halls. She locked onto them, sending out golden tendrils toward each one, coiling around them like ethereal snakes. Once she had tapped into their energy, she flooded them with heavy darkness, and they collapsed as one. She heard a thud and a clatter in the hallway outside, where one had fallen and dropped his club. She walked to the door, seeing its locking mechanism as if it were a child's toy, and it unlocked and opened on her command. She put her hands to the wall and sent a pulse out through the stone and heard the doors unlocking and slamming open one by one.

She drifted into the hallway, reaching out with her mind to the Shoza, who stood in the open doorways, nervous wonder in their minds.

The doors are open, and the guards are asleep. Go now and help your people breathe free air again.

She followed their hurried footsteps down the stairs, letting her body guide itself while her mind was drawn toward the bonfire. The shouting and cheering masses began pouring out of the amphitheater, led by a group of Shoza. She could see their lines of communication spreading out through the city, and she flowed into their shared mindspace for a moment. It was chaotic, with so many minds speaking at once, so she sorted the threads by instinct, like a weaver sending a shuttle flying across a loom. One of them was sending panicked messages, and she followed them to the source and saw a Shoza shouting at those behind him to flee as a line of small glowing balls floated through the air toward them. The lead ball exploded, sending a dozen Maer flying and snuffing out the Shoza's signal in an instant.

Chaos ensued as a seemingly endless line of glowing purple balls filtered into the crowd, scattering them like deer before wolves. Another explosion followed, and then another, sending bodies careening into tents and starting a stampede in all directions. Cloti zoomed in on the advancing line of spyballs and began flicking them up into the sky one by one, where they exploded like fireworks. Her mind slowed the scene down, and she followed the stream back to its source, the mages' tent in the human compound. Six minds inside the tent were controlling the balls, taking turns directing them to their targets. Anger swelled inside her as she felt their wicked joy at the destruction they were causing. She corralled the balls with her mind and sent them back in a mass like a swarm of hornets. Panic radiated from the mages inside the tent as they struggled to regain control, but their magic was no match for the power of the Earth Milk. At the last moment, she sent a pulse to one of the balls, and they exploded in a chain reaction that lit up the sky and shook the very walls of the Tower.

She slumped against the wall of the staircase as she saw the burning and flattened remains of the human compound. She'd meant to knock them out, but she'd had no idea of the power of their devices. The mage tent, along with the others in the compound, floated in the air as cinders, then fell as ash. She had killed the mages, along with an untold number of guards and soldiers massed near the gate. The Earth Milk had never been meant to be used this way. This was what she'd feared the Shoza would do with it, and now she'd taken scores of lives in one rage-fueled moment. She crumpled to the floor, overwhelmed with sadness, furious with herself, with the world. She had become what she'd most sought to prevent, and the humans would make the Maer pay for what she'd done.

Shouts sounded outside the Tower, the clash of metal, screams of agony. She pushed out with her mind and saw a group of Shoza engaged with human soldiers. One fell to the humans' blades, then another. The Shoza were barely armed, and the humans wore steel from head to toe, slashing at the Shoza with wicked blades. Cloti pushed herself to standing, steeled her mind, and locked onto the humans en masse. She squeezed with her mind, and their bodies crumpled, crashing to the ground, swords clattering on the stone. She withdrew from the scene; she could not bear to see the Shoza finish the job, but she heard grunts and footsteps and the squelch of metal slicing through flesh. Her heart went numb as she climbed down the last spiral of the stairs and emerged into a hellscape of fire, smoke, and screams.

The city burned.

Cloti rose above Kuppham, viewing it from on high. Fires dotted the landscape from the hightops to Cliffside. Tents blazed in the camps, where very few Maer remained, sooty and dazed, clutching their meager belongings. Battle raged by the gate, in the park, and along the rear guard of the Shoza defending the evacuees against a small but determined group of human soldiers. She reached into her heart, seeking Aefin and Ludo's signals, and almost cried with relief when she found them near the back of the line of refugees moving into the industrial district. She searched for Feddar's signal and found him nearby, following the soldiers harassing the evacuees. He seemed to be keeping out of sight, dodging through the shadows between buildings when the humans were engaged with the Maer.

Something tugged at her mind, and she saw a group of five humans approaching quickly behind Feddar. Four were armored and carried crossbows and swords, while the fifth wore robes and a medallion around his neck. They stopped at a gesture from the mage, who twirled his hands in the air. Smoke spiraled from his fingertips, quickly forming a dense fog that spread across the wide street and engulfed the fleeing Maer. Cloti shot a message into Feddar's mind, feeling his shock at the unexpected intrusion.

Four soldiers and a mage right behind you.

She could no longer see Feddar in the fog, but she saw the mage lift a clear glass ball in the palm of his hand. He rolled it around, murmuring, then closed his hand. When it opened, the ball rose into the air, glowing faintly purple, and disappeared into the fog. Cloti clenched her hands into fists, flexing every muscle in her body to concentrate all her energy into her core, which surged with the Milk's power. She locked in on Feddar's signal, using it to anchor to the spot, and poured her mind into the funnel of space and time.

She nearly collapsed with the shock of landing, but she stabilized herself in a crouch. She stood immersed in a fog that reeked of vinegar and rot. Her mind pulled her into the fog, which lightened as she approached a floating purple orb the size of a shooting marble. The figures of the human soldiers pursuing the Maer loomed in the haze, and Cloti stopped the orb in mid-air and sent it flying back in the direction it had come from. She sensed the four soldiers and the mage and sent the orb directly toward them. If it had gone off in the crowd, it might have killed Aefin and Ludo and scores more. The time for compassion was over. This had to end now.

The mage pushed back, and Cloti had to strain her focus to keep the orb moving in his direction. The Milk's effect was waning, but she had just enough power to send it floating right at them. The soldiers broke formation as the ball grew close, and Cloti froze the mage in place with a thought, then sent the orb right at his heart.

A hooded figure surged out of the fog. A blade flashed, and the mage's scream was cut short as the sword cut halfway through his neck. His body dropped like a sack of coal, and two orbs like emeralds shone out at her from under the hood of his killer. Cloti sent the spyball straight up, and its explosion knocked Feddar and the human soldiers to the ground. She rushed to him, coughing at the slowly dispersing fog. Her heart leapt as he rolled onto his side to face her. His eyes were dim and confused, but they lit up when he saw her face.

"Cloti!" He reached up and grabbed her shoulder, then suddenly flung her out of the way and rolled to the side as a sword sparked on the stone where he had fallen. The human was on him in an instant, his sword flashing in the near darkness. Feddar spun the blade aside with his own, then swept the man's legs out from under him with his foot and stomped on his sword hand. The man screamed, releasing his sword. Feddar flipped his sword around and struck the man on the helmet with the hilt, and he stopped moving. Another soldier rushed him, and Cloti dropped him with a thought, stepping toward Feddar. He whirled around, rotating toward each of the three remaining soldiers who'd been guarding the mage.

Cloti heard footsteps and turned to see the humans who'd been following the crowd creeping toward them, crouched and leading with their swords. She felt her power slipping, but she gripped it tight and shot out her rage, and they crumpled to the ground, gripping their helmets and moaning. She felt suddenly drained, and an uncomfortable warmth grew in her stomach like she needed to throw up. She sat down, her vision fading in and out as she half-watched Feddar defending himself against the humans' attack. One of them struck him, she thought, but she could hardly see, and the pain in her stomach grew sharper. She put her hand on her belly and was stopped by a strange piece of wood that wasn't supposed to be there, long and smooth, with feathers on the end.

"She's been shot!" someone called out, echoing as if through the emptiness between the Thousand Worlds. She saw fire and smoke, heard screams and explosions, and inexplicably, the bleating of a sheep, then all went quiet. Strong arms held her, hands clutching her back and neck. Feddar's face was streaked with sweat and soot and blood, his eyes piercing with tender intensity. She smiled up at him, touching him gently on the chin.

"I told you I'd never let anything happen to you," she whispered.

"I wish I'd done the same for you." He glanced down at her stomach, and his eyes were weak when they met hers again.

"Come with us." She closed her eyes, conscious only of his stubbled chin beneath her fingertips, his warm hand on her neck, and his strong arms holding her up.

"I can't." His lips pressed into hers, the only thing connecting her to the world. She clung to them, breathing in his life, his strength. Her eyes popped open, and she looked into his, but he was already looking away. He lay her gently on the ground and stood up, looking down at her once more, the green of his eyes darkening with purpose.

"I will come to you next Midsummer," he whispered, then vanished into the shadows.

There were bodies around her, hands and arms and feet, and faces too, Aefin and Ludo. Cloti tried to reach out to them, but they were swallowed by the fog, which pressed her eyes and lips shut and wrapped her body tightly like a spider securing its prey. It was comforting in a way. The stillness. The freedom from any ability or desire to move. Like a cocoon. She buried herself deep inside its silky confines and sank into a deep peace.

30

— • —

"Set her down gently, Egg."

Cloti recognized Aene's voice. She opened her eyes and saw a kindly face covered in reddish-blond hair watching her with concerned eyes. Strong arms lowered her onto a bed of pine needles and moss. She blinked a thank you, as she was too weak to speak.

"We've got you," he said, slipping his enormous hand out from beneath her head.

"Thank you so much, Yglind." Cloti's ears perked up when she heard Aefin's voice, and tears formed in her eyes when her wife's face appeared above her. "You're going to be okay, baby."

"I don't feel okay," Cloti croaked. "I feel—" she gasped as a sharp pain stabbed her in the stomach, stealing her breath.

"Shh." Aefin's hands held hers. "Don't speak. Just rest. We're safe for the moment."

"Safe," Cloti whispered. "Ludo?"

"I'm right here, my love." Ludo's face appeared, and his lips pressed into her forehead. "We're all safe."

"Safe," Cloti repeated, then the world swirled around her, sucking her down into the darkness.

Cloti floated amongst the Thousand Worlds, but she was no longer in control. Worlds sucked her in as she passed, flooding her mind with images of fire and death. The cliffs on fire with rows of blazing houses. The gate in ruins, flames guttering out of the exposed beams. Bodies sprawled across the cobblestones, human and Maer, faces frozen in their final moments of agony. The sickening sound of blades sticking into flesh, making sure they were dead. The grim faces of humans standing in a plaza littered with bodies. Feddar sitting by the lake, staring at the reflection of flames all around, tears streaking down his blood-encrusted face.

Kuppham was in ruins, and her lover had stayed.

She passed in and out of these nightmares, waking briefly, feverish and dazed, to see Aefin or Ludo at her side, whispering sweet nonsense into her ears. Strong arms carried her, and she looked up from her haze to see Yglind's face, stern and strained. Another walked at his side, carrying her for brief periods while Yglind rested. She heard Yglind call him Ardo, and she smiled. She remembered them from the Delve chronicle. She was glad they'd made it through, but something wasn't right. Yglind was supposed to be in hibernation, leading the foolish expedition to the Time to Come. Maybe the war had come too soon. But she was glad for his strong arms and back, his steady eyes checking on her as he walked, the gentle way he set her down each night.

Her mind slowly cleared, but her body took longer to recover. It was a week before she could walk, and even then, it was only with Ludo and Aefin's help. Yglind still carried her while they traveled, but she could putter around whenever they set up camp. Aene had used the last of the power in a scavenged gauntlet to stop the infection, and Cloti's stomach had begun to heal, but it hurt when she talked, when she laughed, when she ate. Not that there was much to eat, but they always had something: nuts, berries, jerky, and even chewy bread sometimes. The Free Maer helped them wherever they passed, sharing a bit of food or medicine.

Yglind explained one night around the fire how the Shoza outside the city had made arrangements with the Free Maer to take in refugees from the cities. Ghulham had been evacuated as well, and Helscop, but the fate of the others was unknown. Each tribe had agreed to take in a certain number and help them get set up on the outskirts of their territory as best they could. Cloti's group was headed for the territory of the Crow Maer, who were said to already be hosting a small group of war refugees. Along the way, they met many groups of Free Maer, who warned them of the movements of humans scouring the hills for survivors and offered them what food and shelter they could.

Even the Skin Maer pitched in, letting them hide in a deep cave for a while when human raiding parties came hunting for them. The legends of the Skin Maer painted them as cruel cannibals who would take Maer to their underground lairs for dark rituals, and most of the group had as little to do with them as possible. Cloti did not; despite their freakish hairless appearance, they were timid and kind. Besides the fact that their women had beards, they looked almost the same as humans, though they were shorter on average. Cloti liked them best of all, perhaps because they reminded her of Feddar. As she sat in the cold, dank cave, listening to the drip drip drip of distant water, she heard them singing, slow and haunting, in minor keys, set to the rhythm of the water. She couldn't understand their language, but words bubbled up in her mind. Though she had nothing to write with, she engraved them in her memory as she went. She sang them to herself in a low voice as she sat alone while the others went out with the Skin Maer to collect food and other supplies by night when the humans wouldn't see them.

The soul shines like the setting sun;
Know its shape, and the door to all wisdom shall open.

"We're getting close now." Aefin crouched next to Cloti, offering a bit of jerky and a roasted root of some kind with the skin split open. She was thinner, her hair and beard unkempt, but her eyes still shone with fiery determination. Cloti scooped the mushy root out with her fingers, wincing at the bitter taste, but she licked her fingers clean and scraped every bit of fiber from the skin before tossing it.

"Glad to see you have your appetite back." Juiya sat down cross-legged, facing her, a soft look in her eyes. "Are you up to leading a short cycle?"

Cloti dug deep within her mind but felt only a tinkle of the focus she'd once had. She shook her head, tears welling in her eyes, and Juiya took her hands.

"That's okay. You've been through a lot. If I lead, do you want to join?"

Cloti nodded, wiping her eyes and lowering her hands to the ground. Even if she couldn't bring her mind to bear on the exercise, it felt good to spread her arms out once again.

Aefin and Ludo sat down next to her, and Juiya scooted back as Aene, Yglind, and Ardo joined in the circle. Cloti's heart lifted, and she felt the spark igniting within her as Juiya spoke in a low, steady voice.

"To find the Thousand Worlds, we must seek within, as without."

Cloti closed her eyes, feeling their collective energy welling up through the earth into her hands. As Juiya lifted them slowly toward the canopy of pine trees above them, she found a whisper of the strength that had been missing for a long, long time. The world she knew might have been gone, but the worlds of the Time Before and the Time to Come were all around her.

Cloti thought she recognized the terrain, but it wasn't until they saw the stone marker at the side of the path that she was sure. This was the path down to Eagle Lake. They'd come at it from the opposite direction than she'd taken on vacation so many times, but the smell in the air and the deep valley below left no doubt. A crow flapped off through the trees as they descended toward the lake, which she could see through the trees on occasion. There were twenty in their group, and they moved slowly down the rocky trail until Gielle held up her hand for them to stop at the top of the long set of stone stairs leading to the valley floor.

"I'll go ahead and let them know we're coming, so there will be no surprises."

Cloti clutched Ludo and Aefin's hands, recalling the vision she'd had of Uffrin and Mara, but there was a third figure in the vision now, a tiny face peeking out from the blanket it was swaddled in.

"We have a grandchild," she breathed.

Aefin and Ludo squeezed her hands from either side.

"Do you think it'll be a girl or a boy?" Ludo asked.

"Let's not be in such a rush to assign their gender, shall we?" Aefin replied, elbowing Ludo gently. "They've just been born."

Ludo chuckled; he'd always been a little old-fashioned about that sort of thing, but he took correction well.

"Well, either way, I call first dibs on holding them."

"Excuse me," Cloti said, "but I gave birth to Uffrin, so by rights, I get first cuddles. It's probably in one of the law codexes in the Archive." She paused, saddened as she thought of the thousands of cylinder scrolls now buried deep in the earth, beyond the reach of humans or Maer. The library in Kuppham had probably burned, and at any rate, the humans would have pillaged whatever was left. Any knowledge not contained in the minds of living Maer would be lost to history until their civilization was rebuilt in the Time to Come.

A crow alighted on a rock in front of them, cocking its head this way and that, seeming to study each of them. It turned and hopped onto a rock below, cocked its head at them again, then hopped down further.

"We're supposed to follow it," Aene said, leading the way down the stairs. "Careful, it's slippery."

Cloti knew all too well how treacherous the stone stairs could be, and she held onto Ludo's arm as she descended. When they reached the bottom and passed between the twin boulders, the lake stretched out before them, its waters smooth as glass in the evening's calm. The simple lean-tos they'd always used for camping had been transformed into huts with packed mud walls and porches adorned with flowers streaming out of clay pots. An elder Maer stood in front of a small crowd assembled behind him, and Cloti's heart leapt as she recognized Uffrin, Kaela, then Mara, with a fuzzy head peeking out from a baby carrier strapped to her chest.

The elder strode forward, leaning on a long staff, and bowed deeply when she neared them.

"We welcome you with open arms, provided you are willing to work together to make our community stronger and abide by our laws."

Cloti's group was silent, and to her surprise, she noticed everyone was looking at her. She cleared her throat as she stepped forward, bowing to the elder.

"We accept your terms, and we will strive to be worthy of your generous hospitality."

The elder nodded, then looked over her shoulder at the crowd, motioning them forward with her staff.

"I know a few Maer who will be most pleased to see you, Cloti."

Cloti wondered for an instant how the elder knew her name, but this and all other thoughts vanished as she saw Uffrin surge forward with the same awkward stride he'd always had. In moments, he was in her arms, kissing and hugging her, crying into her hair, and she into his beard.

"Gods, Maoti, I can't believe you made it! Maofin, Paodo, gods, you're all here! Is it really true? Is Kuppham—"

"That life belongs to the Time Before now. We'll tell you all the horrid details later, but first, I need to bury my face in this little belly!"

Cloti took the baby from Mara, hugging her with one arm as she cradled the child in the other.

"Cloti, meet Laeti."

Ludo and Aefin crowded around, and the jumble of voices, hands, and hugs faded away as Laeti grasped her beard, twirling one of her few remaining beads in her fingers. Cloti lifted the child, kissing her forehead and her chubby cheeks. She pressed her face into Laeti's soft, furry belly, inhaling that wholesome smell babies always seemed to have. She held her aloft for a moment, laughing as Laeti's mouth spread into a toothless smile, and her eyes lit up with glee. Laeti clung to a bead on her beard, pulling it free as Aefin swiped her away.

"Who's my precious little furball?" Aefin cooed, raising Laeti high in the air and bringing her in to snuggle against her chest. Ludo wrapped his arms around them both, and Cloti pulled Uffrin and Mara in for a hug, tears soaking the hair on her face. After all she'd been through, after everything they'd lost, in this moment, she knew that the Time to Come had never been in better hands.

As Midsummer approached, Cloti felt her awareness sharpening, her mind probing the valley for the slightest whisper of Feddar's energy. She didn't know how he would find her, but she knew with perfect certainty that he would. Aefin and Ludo had spent the weeks leading up to Midsummer beautifying their lean-to and expanding their bed, which was larger than the others but still not quite as big as they were used to. Aefin had cultivated several gorgeous mushroom logs thick with tall, thin yellow fungi that waved in the breeze like flowers and were delicious on salad.

They had worked extra hard to put away enough food for his arrival. There never seemed to be quite enough to go around, but they managed to set aside a few dried fish and some horsetail roots, which they kept in a bucket of water to keep them fresh. They'd made wine from berries Aefin had picked far afield, worrying Cloti and Ludo when she came back just after dark. Cloti had begged a few sticks of tarweed from a farmer friend of Mara and Uffrin. They had everything they needed except Feddar.

Aefin was anxious about Feddar's arrival, and she took it out on Ludo every night, riding him head to toe in every position imaginable—and a few Cloti had never thought of before. Ludo was in heaven. While he seemed happy enough to take charge once in a while, his passion shone when he was at the service of his spouses. Cloti joined in sometimes, but she let Aefin take the reins and wield them with wild abandon. Her heart filled as she watched Aefin bear down on one or the other of them, eyes ablaze with a depth of passion remarkable even for her. But it was different than before, coming more from a place of joyous anticipation than fear and desperation.

The thought of Feddar's arrival at Midsummer had filled them all with hope, not just for an amorous reunion but for a future made possible by living in the moment. They had lost much, but it was nice to awaken to the distant cawing of crows and watch the mist on the water as they drank their darkroot tea, which the Free Maer grew and drank in abundance. She missed her city, and she missed her books—gods, how she missed her books! But the stories shared over evening fires while harvesting horsetails, while weaving nets, formed a kind of living library. They passed their stories on, sometimes embellishing a little or straightening a crooked narrative turn, like the monks of old copying manuscripts by hand under the dim light of wax candles. The death of their city did not mean the death of their civilization, and it did not make their daily lives any more or less stressful. Only different.

After dark on Midsummer's Eve, as she was helping bind straw to the arms of the effigy of King Uimer, Cloti's fingers suddenly stopped moving. She dropped the twine on the ground as her heart flooded with a familiar warmth she'd ached to feel so many times. She walked out the door and looked to her left. A dark figure followed the shadowy path up from the lake, and an owl flitted by then flapped toward Mara's cabin. Cleo always had a sharp eye for anything unusual, but Mara knew to expect Feddar. Cloti lit a candle and put it on the deck post as agreed, so Mara would look out and know she need not worry.

As Feddar approached the main path, he stopped by a tree and watched in both directions for a moment, then crossed the road quickly, his green eyes flashing in the gloom as he bounded up the stairs and onto the porch. His smile shone out of the recesses of his hood, and he knelt before her, taking Cloti's hands and kissing them.

"You're early."

"The weather was fair, and my feet were light." He stood at the upward pressure from her hands. His eyes melted as she pulled him close with her fingertips, rising up on her toes. His breath was hot on her face, his body poised like a trap waiting to be sprung.

"I've missed you." She closed in so their noses were touching, then slipped her hands around his waist. She pressed into him with her body and felt him physically restraining himself as his hands slid gently down her back. She let her lips brush against his, feeling their heat as his hands reached her behind and gripped her with gentle strength. She kissed him softly, again and again, and he pulled back as she tried to deepen the kiss.

"I've a confession to make," he whispered before kissing her again.

"Tell me." She kissed him more deeply this time, and his hands gripped her behind and pulled her tighter to him. She could feel him hard as an olli against her belly, and she slid her hands in between his legs and ran her fingers along his canvas-sheathed length.

"I wasn't able—" He paused as she squeezed him tightly, then lightened the pressure, milking his lower lip. "It's just that, whenever I thought of you, I couldn't help but touch myself, and sometimes—" He gasped as she seized him in an iron grip.

"A year is a long time. I understand. Did you only think of me, or did you spare a thought for Ludo and Aefin as well?" She released him and ran her hands inside his shirt, up his stomach, and across his chest, kneading his muscles.

"Each of you. All of you." She kissed him, and he paused once more, bringing one hand up to cup her face. "Are they inside?"

Cloti nodded, biting her lip as she heard the floorboards creak just inside the door. Aefin and Ludo were listening in and probably watching through the cracks. She wrapped her arms around him and devoured his lips, pushing and pressing and squeezing until he was breathless and almost unable to kiss back, and then she stopped. She turned toward the door, glancing back at his glistening green eyes, his wet lips, and his broad shoulders. Aefin and Ludo shuffled back as she opened the door, peering over and around her at the figure on the deck. Feddar stood still for a moment, gazing at them through the doorway. A smile spread from shadow to shadow inside his hood, and he strode into the lean-to, pulling his hood back as he pushed the door closed behind him.

Aefin's eyes burned dark and hot as she saw Feddar, and Cloti moved out of the way to give her room. She would have her time, but Aefin's need was so intoxicating it was almost better to watch. Cloti sidled up to Ludo, slipping her arm around his waist as Aefin threw off her robe, rushed Feddar, and pinned him to the door with a furious kiss. His hands slipped around her waist, sliding under her tight behind and lifting gently. Aefin put her hands on his shoulders and leapt up, wrapping her legs around his body as he swung away from the door to make room. Cloti slid her hand inside Ludo's robe, massaging his chest and flicking her tongue in and out of his ear. Ludo moaned softly as she pinched his nipples and ground against his hip.

Aefin clung to Feddar, writhing against him as he backed toward the bed, supporting her with strong arms and firm hands. When his heels hit the bed, Aefin pulled back from the kiss, then flung herself against him, and he fell awkwardly onto the bed. Aefin shifted as she fell, landing on all fours atop him with the grace of a cat.

"Aefin, gods, I—"

She pressed a hand over his mouth, wriggling forward until her thighs were clamped around his neck.

"Shhh," she whispered, gripping his arms and flinging them above his head. "Don't talk." She rose up on her knees, then sank onto his face. Feddar's groan of pleasure was matched by Aene's hunched back, and only then did Cloti notice Ludo had dropped to his knees and was nosing between her legs. She shed her robe, watching Aene's lithe body arch and curl over Feddar, whose muffled groans were met with Aene's rising whines. She lost herself in the pleasure of Ludo's tongue, his hungry lips, his hot breath. She gripped Ludo's hair, and her pleasure rose with Aefin's, which bled into her for the first time since they'd left Kuppham.

Aefin's desire scorched through Cloti like wildfire as Feddar's hands gripped Aefin's behind. Ludo grabbed Cloti's buttocks at almost the same moment, kneading and lifting as he worked her with swift, precise strokes. She swam in a sea of ecstasy, feeling the deep pressure as Aefin rode Feddar's chin, the rapid flicks of his tongue meshing with Ludo's increasingly furious ministrations. When Aefin slowed, lifting off Feddar and making him crane up into her, Cloti pulled Ludo's hair back to slow his pace, keeping him just out of reach of her nub. His tongue frantically sought purchase anywhere and everywhere it could reach. When Aefin lowered back down, Cloti pulled Ludo hard against her, using the back of his head as leverage to grind into him. She felt her control slipping as her pleasure coiled and spiraled inside her, and soon she was flying with Aefin, whose back hunched and arched over and over, her buttocks clenching and quivering as she bore down on Feddar and held in place. Cloti bucked into Ludo as he clamped down and sent her off into the Thousand Worlds, and she only heard her own cries of ecstasy as she was coming down, holding onto his shoulders for support so she wouldn't crumple to the ground.

Aefin rolled off Feddar, who lay heaving with his arms spread apart, his thick erection straining the fabric of his pants. Cloti leaned against the wall as Ludo sat back on his heels, his face and beard matted slick. He smiled up at Cloti as he glanced over at the bed, where Aefin was now busy removing Feddar's clothes. Ludo stood up and shed his shirt and pants as well. Cloti draped herself against him, kissing and licking his ear as she stroked him. His breath grew uneven, but Cloti stopped when she saw the wicked glint in Aefin's eyes.

"Feddar, get up," Aefin said in a voice like a knife. He sat up quickly, his eyes wild and soft, looking from Aefin to Cloti to Ludo in joyous wonder. Aefin took his hand and pulled him to standing, then dragged him toward Ludo.

"Kneel before my husband," she commanded.

Feddar complied without hesitation, kneeling before Ludo and running his fingers delicately along his length. Ludo's mouth opened in surprise, then formed a pained O when Feddar began licking his tip like he was polishing a doorknob. Aefin approached, running her fingers across Ludo's chest and whispering in his ear. Cloti could not hear what she said, but Ludo's head snapped to Aefin, who kissed him, soft and slow.

Cloti watched the three of them, heat rising slowly as their sensations bloomed in her through their growing connection. She let it build without touching herself, opening her mind and heart to the feelings radiating out from them. Aefin was consumed with desire, less for her own pleasure than for Ludo's. She wanted him to be overwhelmed with sensation until he came undone and lost his usual calm, chipper demeanor. Ludo's aura showed Aefin's plan was working to perfection. He teetered on the edge, unable to catch his breath or slow himself between Feddar's mouth and Aefin's furious kisses and kneading fingers. Feddar sensed how close Ludo was and pulled off him, working him gently with his fingers. He flashed Cloti a delirious grin, sending a bolt of desire streaming through her body. His emerald eyes locked on hers, and she felt the full force of his need to please them in turn, over and over, until all four of them collapsed from exhaustion.

She knelt beside Feddar, palming the back of his head and pushing him forward. He winked at her before turning to engulf Ludo once again. Cloti ran her fingers through the thick curls on his head and moved her other hand to Ludo's thigh. She looked up and saw him gasping for breath, struggling to keep up with Aefin's kiss. Aefin took him by the beard and pulled his face closer to hers, and Cloti could feel the crackling intensity of her gaze even though Ludo was its target.

"Come for Feddar."

She smacked his behind, and he bucked as Feddar gripped his hips and took him in to the hilt. Ludo's hoarse cry rang in Cloti's ears, and she locked eyes with Aefin as Feddar finished him. A crow cawed, no doubt roused from its slumber by the noise. Cloti was sure the whole village had heard and was equally sure that she did not care. Feddar let Ludo go and stumbled back to flop onto the bed, still as hard as a lamppost. Ludo slumped against Aefin, who kissed him softly now, letting out a purring hum. She wrapped her arms around Ludo, then broke from the kiss for a moment, fixing Cloti with a searing look.

"Your turn."

Cloti walked across the room with slow steps, intoxicated with the sight of Feddar's bare skin, his tight muscles, and the soft green depths of his eyes. Her hunger grew as she approached, and Feddar nodded slowly as she crawled onto the bed. His desire burned so hot she almost couldn't look him in the eyes as she came to rest atop his thighs. He was stiff and hot beneath her fingers, and he emitted a low, vibrating hum as she toyed with him gently, like she was stroking a flower. She met his gaze again, and her heart melted to see the soft, earnest want floating in twin pools of liquid green. She slid forward, feeling him throb against her, sending tiny pulses through her core. Her fingers crept across his chest, tracing delicately over his scar and around his nipples. He let out a hissing breath as she gave them a gentle pinch, then slid her fingers up to his stubbled neck. He must not have shaved much during his travels to this faraway corner of the world.

"I know what you want," she murmured, massaging the thick muscles in his neck, sliding back and forth across his rigid length. Aefin and Ludo had crawled onto the bed on either side of Feddar and sat propped on their elbows, watching the scene unfold with love in their eyes.

"What's that?" He spoke in a desperate whisper.

"You want to stay with me, with us, in this moment, forever and ever."

Yes. His whisper floated across her mind in her mind, and the room grew dark as she lifted herself up and sank down onto him, one slow inch at a time. Stars glittered on the ceiling and covered their bodies as they merged, swimming in each other, bodies and minds. Hands covered them with caresses, and lips whispered sighs into their ears, urging them on to higher planes of ecstasy. When she could fly no higher, Cloti held in place, pressing back against him until she felt him teetering on the edge with her.

Wait for me.

From now until the Time to Come.

Cloti smiled as the words echoed in her mind. She pressed her hands against his chest, letting everything flow into him—her pleasure, her anticipation, her love. Feddar's thoughts became her own, and Aefin and Ludo's commingled with them as Aefin and Ludo scooted in closer, hooking their legs over Cloti's and running their hands over their bodies. She felt Aefin's kisses on Feddar's nipples as if they were her own, and she hung on the same delicate edge as Feddar, pressed against the fragile membrane between ecstasy and control. He throbbed with every heartbeat, sending ripples of euphoria cascading through her body and mind. She held him tight from within, growing closer with each breath. His pleasure coiled and swirled higher and higher, carrying her to unimagined heights as Aefin and Ludo's emotions flooded her heart.

Their bodies cleaved together, the four of them becoming more and more entangled as she and Feddar surged closer to the brink, dragging Aefin and Ludo with them. She felt a shift deep inside, and unbridled pleasure billowed through her like a raging Midsummer bonfire. Her nails dug into Feddar's chest as her orgasm flared out of control, spreading to immolate the four of them. Aefin and Ludo clung to her and Feddar as his body convulsed. His mouth opened in a silent scream, and he arched his back, lifting Cloti with him, then collapsed onto the bed with a long moan like a frasti howling at the moon.

The stars on their bodies glowed brighter and brighter until they eclipsed the darkness, bathing them all in an ethereal golden light. Cloti kissed Feddar, then Ludo, then Aefin before slumping off to the side next to her wife, who scooched back to let her nestle in. Their arms crossed over Feddar's broad chest, fingers intertwining. They breathed together as the heat between them slowly cooled, but it never went away entirely. One false move, one accidental touch, and they would be off to the races again. Cloti smiled.

This was how she'd always wanted to live her life. What did it matter if she lived it in a spacious Cliffside estate or a mud-covered lean-to in a Free Maer village? Their civilization was not gone. Only the buildings were. Everything that mattered was here in her arms on this oversized bed.

—·—

EPILOGUE

The village councilor squinted at Feddar, eyeing him with obvious distrust.

"A Skin Maer, you say? He looks like a human to me."

"That's actually a quite common mistake," Feddar said. Cloti hoped the councilor didn't know human accents. "We're nearly identical in physiology, and I'm tall for my kind."

The councilor grunted, then looked to Cloti, pointing at her.

"Do you vouch for him?"

"With all my heart."

The councilor nodded, her glare softening as she looked at Feddar one more time.

"He looks strong. I hope he's ready to put in work."

"Oh, he's as strong as an ox." Cloti clapped her hand against Feddar's bicep. "He's a very hard worker, too, and he takes direction well."

"Very good. He gets three days to settle in, then he reports for duty. Does that work for you, Feddar?"

"I live to serve."

Cloti giggled, leaning into Feddar's shoulder as the elder maneuvered down the stairs, leaning into her staff.

"I think she likes you."

"I like her too. Crusty, but fair."

Aefin drew up behind them, and Ludo soon joined, leaning into them and staring out across the lake. A family of ducks swam along the edge of a weedbed, and fish splashed in the shallows. A pair of crows cruised the shoreline, darting in and out of the forest and cawing at each other. Out of the corner of her eye, Cloti saw a familiar figure walking tentatively up the path toward them.

"Aene!" Cloti called, and she felt Feddar tense, but she calmed him with a hand on his shoulder. "Go ahead," she whispered to Feddar, who glanced back at her as he slipped from the group hug and went out to meet Aene.

"So, they were together?" Aefin whispered. "On that Delve?"

"They were."

"And you don't think—" Ludo stopped himself. They watched Aene and Feddar in silence, hearing only indistinct murmurs of their conversation. They were both tense at first, but they relaxed quickly. Cloti could feel Feddar's charm at work, breaking it to her gently, but Cloti could sense Aene didn't want him anymore. She just needed closure. After a few minutes, Feddar touched her on the arm, and she gave a little wave and disappeared.

"That went well, I think." He kissed Cloti, leaving Aefin and Ludo hanging for a moment before giving them both a quick peck on the lips. "She seems good! And she's with someone, I guess?"

"Juiya. One of my acolytes and the kindest soul I know."

"And Yglind and Ardo are here, though I'm not sure how keen they'd be to see me."

"Yglind carried me half the way here. Maybe he's changed."

"I suppose anything's possible."

Cloti cupped his cheek and turned his face toward her. She closed the distance between them and stood on tiptoes so their lips were almost touching, his chin nestled in her beard.

"Anything indeed," she whispered into his mouth before pressing into his soft lips, feeling the heat of his need rising with the kiss. Aefin and Ludo closed their arms around them, and they clung to each other as the surface of the lake darkened, and the owls replaced the crows in their winged vigilance. With no tech, no books, no bottles of fifteen-year-old mushroom wine, it was just like the Time Before. But as she felt the warmth of bodies and breath and hearts surrounding her, she did not mourn what was gone or worry about what was to come.

The tides of life and history flowed ever on. The only time left was now.

ACKNOWLEDGEMENTS

Writing a book may seem like a solitary endeavor, but it takes the support of a varied and stalwart crew to make it happen. In my case, that crew included, but was not limited to, the following:

My wife Sarah, who has supported me through some serious shit and without whom I would not be writing or publishing anything at all;

My generous beta reader Maxime Jaz, who helped give me the confidence to write full-blown smut featuring threesomes and foursomes, even if they like their men tougher and called Feddar "a wet towel of a man";

My editor and sensitivity reader Charlie Knight, a stone-cold professional with a sharp eye and a fabulous sense of humor. Wherever I may have erred either in prosecraft or in representation of identities outside my own, it is through my own fault, not theirs;

My cover artist, Virginia McClain, who set the world on fire with this cover;

My Siblings in Smut—*Cloti's Song* was a beast so intense to write that I almost didn't publish it, and it wouldn't have been possible without the help of my best and smuttiest writer friends and confidants (or smutfidants, as I like to call them), including but by no means limited to Krystle Matar, Fiona West, Connor Caplan, Angela Boord, Maxime Jazz, Em Strange, and so many others;

And as always, the unsung heroes of the online bookish community: The book bloggers who gave this ridiculously smutty book a shot, and who make it feel worth it to write; the fantastically supportive author community, especially my fantasy and romance peeps; and all the wonderful people I've met along the way who share my love of a good story.

— • —

Also By Dani Finn

The Maer Cycle, a classic fantasy trilogy with LGBTQ characters. It tells the story of the encounter between humans and the legendary hairy humanoids called the Maer and the struggle for the two peoples to reconcile their history and their future.

The Weirdwater Confluence duology (*The Living Waters* and *The Isle of a Thousand Worlds*) are a pair of romantic fantasy books with meditation magic. They are independent of the trilogy, but there are little connections. Both books are sword-free and death-free, in sharp contrast to the Maer Cycle. *Unpainted* is a standalone arranged marriage fantasy romance set in the same universe.

The Time Before trio: *The Delve, Wings so Soft,* and *Cloti's Song,* a group of linked romantic fantasy standalones set 2,000 years before the Maer Cycle. Meant to be read before or after the other books, they tell the story of the fall of the great Maer civilization of old.

Jagged Shard, a dungeon crawl romance set in the Time Before, is coming early 2024, and another Weirdwater romance is planned after that.

Stay tuned via my newsletter and find all my links and other info at https://linktr.ee/danifinn

Milton Keynes UK
Ingram Content Group UK Ltd.
UKHW022111190224
438095UK00017B/761